THE ORPHAN SHIP
Sterling R. Walker

For Dina —
Sterling R. Walker

The Orphan Ship
© 2012 Sterling R. Walker

Cover by Nathaniel Walker
and Michelle Ishihara

Printed in the United States of America

ISBN 13: 978-1484980361
ISBN 10: 1484980360

Science Fiction/Young Adult
Second Edition
1 2 3 4 5 6 7 8 9 10

PART I:
MARSBOUND

ONE
TRANSFER STUDENT

"I'm gonna be sick!"

"But it's a healthy liver this time!" Jake O'Brien shouted at the rapidly retreating back of his lab partner, Ricardo. "There's no cirrhosis like the one we found on Monday!" *When you threw up on my shoes,* he thought, ignoring the snickers of the students at the other stainless steel morgue tables. They were too busy removing the organs from their own cadavers to sympathize with Jake's plight. *I just want to finish an autopsy -- for once -- so I can get a decent grade.*

Jake adjusted the hygiene mask over the bridge of his nose, and thought about changing his blood-slicked gloves. He was frustrated with his lack of progress. The other premeds were already examining hearts, but Retching Ricardo couldn't look at a pituitary gland without getting queasy. Jake preferred to work alone, but logistically he couldn't; he needed someone to help position the uncooperative *rigor mortis* body, and to at least sponge up the blood so he could see what he was doing. He couldn't continue until Ricardo came back. *If he comes back at all.*

Jake kept his gloves on and glanced around the freezing autopsy room for his instructor. By habit, he breathed through his mouth, although he was getting used to the putrid smell of blood and decaying flesh. He decided to ask for assistance with his case – a 54-year old African man who had succumbed to pancreatic cancer. Jake was eager to get a look at the pancreas. He peered at the backs of the other students who were hunched over their own expired patients. From his vantage point, everyone's back looked the same, and it was hard to pick out Dr. Martinson. Jake listened with detachment to the hushed voices discussing the latest discoveries:

"Ew, better get a biopsy of that."

"Look, you can see tissue damage. This one lived close to the city."

"I've seen so many uteruses like that, I can't remember what a normal one looks like."

Jake finally spotted his professor straightening up from the table where he had been assisting an ashen-faced Asian student with a rib-spreader. Before Jake could get his attention, the elderly doctor wiped his hands on his blood-spattered lab coat and somberly announced: "This is probably not the best timing, but I must inform you all that this will be our last lab. The university is closed as of midnight tonight."

Jake lost the grip on his scalpel and it clattered to the tile floor. He quickly bent to retrieve it because he couldn't afford to replace it.

There were gasps of dismay from the other students around him as all eyes turned to Martinson. Jake had heard the rumors in his earlier class, so the announcement didn't come as a complete shock. Still, hearing it from his favorite professor made it a slap-in-the-face reality. *That's it, I'm 18 hours shy of a degree I'll never finish.*

"Isn't there any way we can finish the course?" asked one woman with a heart in her hand. "This course is all I need for my degree! I've worked so hard --." She turned away from the group and wept.

"I know. I'm sorry." Martinson shrugged helplessly. "But there's nothing we can do. The school is officially bankrupt."

$800,000 tuition down the toilet, Jake thought.

"Professor, where can we go? Are there any other universities still in operation?" another woman asked.

"Only Mars College, I think," Martinson said.

More gasps. This time one of them came from Jake.

"If any of you plan to continue your studies, you'll need to get copies of your records before you leave today. I will be happy to write anyone a letter of recommendation."

The woman who was crying sobbed louder.

Jake spoke up, "I'll be continuing to medical school."

"I wish you luck in locating one, Mr. O'Brien." Martinson gave him a sympathetic frown. He turned back to the hyperventilating Asian student and began pointing out the ventricles of the cadaver's heart. As if it mattered.

* * *

There were only a few crumbling buildings left on the campus. Jake walked over to the administrative office, his backpack loaded down with Advanced Physiology holographic-digitals, commonly known as HDs, that Martinson had given him, along with a hand-scribbled letter of recommendation on his datapad.

There was no one else at the desk. "I need my transcript," he told the secretary. He showed her his picture ID.

She rummaged through an ancient filing cabinet and handed him a compact HD, the size of a quarter. "Sign here." She offered him some kind of release statement on a datapad, but no stylus.

Jake dug his stylus out of his front jeans pocket -- the safest place he knew to keep it. *Jacob A. O'Brien, IV*, he scrawled.

"Thank you." She gaped at his signature, looking confused.

Probably wondering what the 'IV' means. He left the office thinking how anyone he met was astonished that he could be a surviving fourth generation. Jake's great-grandfather had actually been alive when he was born. The O'Briens were some lucky old Irish. Lucky to be alive.

But Jake knew there would never be a Jacob A. O'Brien, V. He might have been able to acquire 109 credit hours in five semesters, but there was a huge disadvantage in living near a battle site like New York City: toxins. Jake had no way of avoiding the chemical fallout in the air, water, and soil. He'd absorbed enough toxins to permanently alter his DNA.

Not that he was going to roll over and die from six forms of cancer before his next birthday, but Jake's cellular structure had mutated enough to produce a mentally retarded or deformed child if he ever wanted to be a father. *As long as I don't turn into a Mr. Hyde,* he thought, *I guess I can keep living like a monk.*

Jake faced the problem of getting home. His family wasn't expecting him for two months. It was the middle of planting season, and his father couldn't afford to take time off to come pick him up, even if Jake had a way to communicate with him.

Figuring out how to get to Mars seems impossible if I can't even get to Wilmington.

Jake walked to his tent on the Quad. Fang, his jet-black Rottweiler, was stretched out in front of the doorway. He jumped up and wagged his stump of a tail when Jake approached.

"Good boy." Jake unzipped the door and climbed inside, and Fang followed him. He dumped his backpack in a corner and started to pack: canned food, bedroll, a jug for water, datapad, clothes.

"No room for books, Fang." Jake stared at his collection of medical texts and journals, and his pile of HDs. "I can't leave all this behind."

Fang licked Jake's chin.

He patted the dog's ugly head and tried to figure out how he was going to get himself and his belongings home. *Of course, I could just hike and carry what I can, but then I'd have to leave most of it behind.*

Jake had an idea. "Stay, boy," he instructed Fang as he climbed out of the tent and made his way to the nearest pawn shop.

It took Jake almost an hour to negotiate a trade of his watch and St. Christopher's, both family heirlooms, for a beat-up bike with a tow cart. *I'm sorry, Grandpa*, he thought as he rode the bike back to his tent. *I'll try to get them back one day.*

But he knew in his heart it would never happen.

* * *

Jake navigated the bumpy dirt road for two miles before finally catching sight of the O'Brien homestead through the woods.

"We're home, boy," he told the dog panting alongside him. Fang started barking and ran ahead to announce their presence.

Jake wiped the sweat from his eyes on the shoulder of his filthy T-shirt. He had been on the road for 16 days and his leg muscles were stiff and sore. Not to mention the calluses on his butt. He pulled up in front of the gleaming solar panels, which were the only visible signs of the underground house from the road. Once stopped, he fell, rather than climbed, off the bike and limped after Fang.

Past the row of solar panels, the ground sloped sharply, and Jake took the stairs cut out of the hill down to a stone patio. This was the entrance to the O'Brien house. He pushed open the sliding-glass door and walked into a refreshingly cool family room that extended to dining and kitchen areas.

"I'm home!"

"We know, already." His older sister Deborah was in the kitchen, chopping vegetables from the greenhouse. "Put the dog out."

"Nice to see you, too." Jake collapsed on the couch.

"Oh, don't worry about her." His mom, Marilyn O'Brien, rushed into the room and planted a kiss on his face. "Ugh, you're ripe!"

"Sorry."

"Oh, never mind. We're so glad you're home!" His mother was a chatterbox and didn't give him time to answer. In the same breath she said, "Don't worry about Deborah; she's just upset because she had another miscarriage and the midwife told her she shouldn't try anymore."

"Mother!" Deborah protested.

Jake did some mental calculating. If she'd had another miscarriage, that would make a total of five. He felt bad for her. "I'm sorry, Deb."

Deborah just made a face and went on chopping vegetables.

Jake turned back to his mother, who was already getting him a glass of water and fussing over him. "I'm home because they closed the university."

"What a shame!" His mom made a sympathetic face, but Jake knew she was faking it. She would prefer to have her 'baby' home where she could keep an eye on him. "Your father will be so disappointed you can't finish school."

Sean Baker, Deb's husband, came into the house and greeted Jake with a handshake. "What's going on, professor? Giving up on higher education?"

"No. I was about to tell Mom that I want to transfer to another school."

Marilyn frowned. "Which school?"

"Mars College."

"Mars College? You don't mean the college on Mars Station?" Sean asked.

All three of his family members stared at him, mouths gaping, as Jake nodded.

"Son, there's no way we can send you to Mars," Marilyn finally managed after an awkward silence. "It's way too expensive."

"Yeah, professor, isn't there something closer?"

Jake shook his head. "All the other universities have shut down. Mars is the only place."

"I'm sure your father will say no, but let's not say anything more of this until I discuss it with him." His mother got up and marched into the kitchen. "It's good to have you home," she said, almost as an afterthought.

"Sure." Jake headed back outside to bring in his things.

"Take your clothes down to the sewing room," his mom called as he carried an armful of books down the stairs. "Let Beth see what can be salvaged."

"I'm going to need some jeans." Jake dropped his load onto his bed in the tiny room the family jokingly called the library. He noticed that his brother-in-law had thoughtfully put up two new shelves. He quickly put his books away and went back outside.

"I think we have enough denim for two pairs," Marilyn called after him, continuing their conversation.

"One pair should be fine."

After several trips, Jake took a much-needed shower, then gathered his clothes and went down the hall to the sewing room. He maneuvered around the bolts of fabric to the worktable, where Elizabeth Murphy was cutting out a pattern.

"Jake!"

"Hi, Aunt Beth!"

She drew him in for a crushing hug. "It's so good to see you!" She quickly took the armload of clothes from him and examined each one. "What do you do with these things? They all need mending." She wrinkled her nose. "And washing!"

"Sorry."

She laughed and flashed a toothy smile. "Ah, well! How long are you staying this time?"

"I don't know. Maybe forever if Dad won't let me go to Mars."

"Mars? You should go to Dublin, dear. That's where your grandfather went."

"I'd love to, but Mars Station has the only college still in operation."

Beth nodded, smoothing her jumper and graying red hair, which was pulled back into a bun. "Jake, your grandfather would be so proud of you. And I know my brother. Jacob might be stubborn, but he would gladly sell all the land if there was a chance you could become a doctor."

"You think so?"

"I know so! So don't you worry, dear." She shooed him out of the room. "Now go find Lorina. She's missed you so much."

Jake found his cousin Lorina in the root cellar, dating and shelving canned goods.

"Jake!" She also gave him a bear hug. "I've missed you!"

"I know." He took a step back and looked her over. Her wavy strawberry-blond hair now fell to the middle of her back, and she seemed a bit taller than he remembered. Her normally fair complexion was beginning to freckle, a sign that she had been out helping his dad and Sean with the spring planting.

Jake and Lorina were the same age and had grown up together, though Jake thought of her more as a best friend than a cousin. Lorina was easy to talk to, and she was smart. He wished she could attend college, too, but she hadn't been able to locate a business school that was, frankly, still in business. Jake had been fortunate to nab one of the few openings at Syracuse, and the O'Briens barely scraped together enough cash to send him. The plan had been to hold his spot for Lorina as soon as he graduated, but now it looked like Lorina had no chance of attending any college.

It's not fair, Jake thought. *She's been such a good sport about waiting.* He was afraid to tell her the bad news.

"Why are you home early?" Lorina asked.

Jake took a deep breath and told her the details. "Your mom thinks Dad will let me go to Mars."

Lorina was unfazed about the bankruptcy. "I knew it would happen sooner or later," she admitted. "Mars, huh? I don't know. You couldn't take Fang off-planet, and I don't think they'd let you go by yourself."

"I know." He sighed. "The shuttle fare alone would be unbelievable."

"And how would you live? Where would you live? You can't work and take ten classes at the same time, but you'd have to work just to eat."

"Dinner!" Deborah shouted down the stairs.

"We'll have to talk later. Mom said it's a closed subject until she discusses it with Dad."

Lorina nodded.

Jake greeted the rest of the family at the dinner table. His father and five-year-old niece Catherine were both glad to see him.

"Jake's home!" Catherine carefully felt her way to his seat at the table and climbed onto his lap.

"It's wonderful to see you." He sat still as she carefully traced his face with the fingertips of her right hand.

"It's wonderful to see you, too," she responded impishly after her inspection. "You need a shave!"

"Catherine!" Deborah scolded.

Jake gave the girl a squeeze. "It's okay. She's right. I haven't had a chance to scrape off the stubble."

"Let's eat now," Marilyn said.

"Okay." The dark-haired child let herself down from his lap and, feeling along the backs of the others' chairs with the stump of her left arm, found her seat at the table.

"Very good. You get around so well now!" Jake felt proud of her newfound independence.

"You should see me at the computer."

"Let's say grace now," Deborah said.

"Me, me, I want to say it!" Catherine clamored.

"Go ahead, dear." Marilyn nodded.

The O'Brien clan all held hands around the table and bowed their heads patiently while Catherine asked a blessing on everything she could think of, especially, "Jake, who has come home to stay with us forever, and will never go away again."

Jake squirmed uncomfortably and glanced at his mother out of the corner of his eye. She was frowning. *Somehow I've got to finish school. And if the college is on Mars, that's where I have to go, if I have to sell my soul to get there.*

Catherine was almost to the "amen" when he felt a light kick under the table. He glanced up at Lorina who was seated across from him.

'I know how,' she mouthed silently. 'I know how you can go to Mars.'

'How?' he mouthed back, his heart racing. 'Tell me.'

"Amen!" Heads came up and eyes opened. Grace was over.

'Later,' Lorina mouthed as she passed him the salad.

* * *

"It's really simple," Lorina explained in a hushed tone. She ran a comb through Jake's thick hair and skillfully cut off a length of curl over his left ear.

Jake glanced over at his parents on the couch, who were also talking in subdued tones. "Nothing is simple anymore."

"No, really, I've got it all figured out." She wet the comb under the kitchen tap and continued trimming his hair. "I'm going with you."

"*What?*" It came out much louder than he intended. His parents looked over. "Sorry," he called. To Lorina he whispered, "Are you *crazy*? You're not going with me."

Lorina none-too-gently pushed his chin down to his chest and snipped away at the hair on the back of his neck. "I've got a dangerous weapon in my hand, so you'd better hear me out."

Jake watched his dark hair collecting in piles on the linoleum. "I'm listening."

"You know they won't let you go off-planet by yourself. It's too dangerous."

"It's dangerous just going into town. You know they can't afford to send me, let alone two of us."

Lorina almost nicked his right ear. "Let me finish. I read an ad in the paper yesterday for a two-for-one seat special on the Mars shuttle next Saturday. If they let us both go, I can work waitressing or something to support us while you attend school."

"Who qualifies for the seat special?"

"Couples who are planning to immigrate."

"Couples?" Jake spun around in his chair and grabbed her scissors' hand to protect himself. "You mean *married* couples? You *are* crazy!"

"Shhh!" Lorina looked serious. She pulled her hand free of his grasp and glanced over at his parents. "Obviously, we'll just be *posing* as a married couple; we look different enough. I can forge a marriage license."

"They'll never agree to this insane idea." Jake frowned. Out of the corner of his eye, he could see his parents staring quietly at them. They were also frowning. "It doesn't look good."

"You want to finish college, I want to get out of here. I can't be stuck here forever, Jake, with no future. I'm not a farmer." Tears began to form in the corners of her hazel eyes. "We've got nothing to lose by going. If we're going to sell them on this insane idea, you've got to back me up. It can work. I know it can!"

"Jake, we'd like to talk now." Marilyn stood up, walked around the dining room table, and came into the kitchen.

"We're almost done here." Lorina quickly finished trimming Jake's bangs and combing the loose hairs off his mop-top.

Jacob O'Brien joined them in the kitchen. "Thank you, Lorina. Now please excuse us."

"If you don't mind, I'd like to stay." Lorina wiped hastily at her still-watering eyes.

Marilyn started to object but Jake said, "Please, Mom, I want Lorina to stay."

The senior O'Briens exchanged puzzled looks and shrugged their acquiescence. "Let's all sit down," Jacob said.

Seated around the dining room table, Jake felt his heart pounding. He waited breathlessly for his father to speak, afraid that the only word out of his mouth would be 'no.'

"We really want you to go to medical school, Jake. But for all practical reasons, we can't see how we can afford to send you to Mars Station." Jacob spread his large palms helplessly. "We think it's just beyond our grasp."

"But --" Jake felt as if all the air was being squeezed out of him. "But --"

"But we have a plan," Lorina spoke up.

Jake just nodded numbly and let her talk. Lorina had a real gift for persuading people to see things her way. She explained the two-for-one flight and even got the newspaper out of the kindling box to show them the ad.

"I don't like the idea of a deception," Marilyn said. "Forging a marriage license?"

"Remember, I forged Catherine's death certificate," Lorina said quietly.

Now it was Marilyn's turn to squirm. "Yes, so they wouldn't do those awful genetics tests on her."

"I think Beth needs to be in on this discussion," was Jacob's only comment.

"I'll go get her." Lorina headed for the stairs.

The three O'Briens sat in thoughtful silence while they waited. It was almost 15 minutes before Lorina returned with her mother. Both of them were smiling. Jake's hopes rose; if Beth were on their side, his parents would be persuaded.

"I think this is a wonderful idea!" was the first thing out of Beth's mouth. "A perfect opportunity to give our kids a promising future. Don't you think so, Jacob?"

"Do you realize how much it will cost just to send them to Mars?" her brother asked.

"Sure do." Beth reached into the pocket of her jumper and pulled out a blue velvet jeweler's box. "I think this will cover it nicely at two-for-one prices." She smiled at Jake. "With enough leftover, I imagine, for at least a year's tuition." She opened the box to reveal a large gold ring set with a diamond the size of a penny.

Jake jumped up and threw his arms around his aunt. "Thank you!"

"Your engagement ring?" Marilyn asked. "Are you sure?"

"It means nothing to me. When Lorina's father left, I wanted to throw this in the river, but I kept it because I thought it might come in handy some day." Beth beamed at her daughter and nephew. "And I think that day has come."

* * *

The ancient and twice-refurbished shuttle *Endeavor III* looked like it would never clear the ground, much less travel all the way to Mars Station. All Jake could do was stare out the hanger window at the old-fashioned craft, and try to will his stomach to relax.

"You put on a space-sickness patch, right?" Lorina whispered in an optimistic tone.

Jake tore his gaze from the black-streaked shuttle wings and looked again at his new 'wife.' Lorina was clutching his arm nervously, trying to appear affectionate and show off her wedding band -- her mother's -- at the same time. She was almost crushing her farewell corsage between them. Jake glanced at his own rosebud boutonniere and wedding band -- his father's -- and felt his stomach churn. "I hope we can pull this off," he whispered. "This whole married thing feels really weird."

"We'll be fine." She sounded confident, but her face was pale.

"I hope you're wearing a space-sickness patch, too, Mrs. O'Brien."

Lorina rolled her eyes at him. "It's Murphy. I'm keeping my maiden name."

"Whatever," Jake sighed.

The Baltimore-Washington Spaceport was crowded, as usual, so their families had said good-bye to them at the ticket terminal. There were lots of tears from his mother and Aunt Beth and Catherine, as Jake realized with a pang of regret that he might not see any of them again for years. Not until he finished college and was earning enough money for passage back to Earth. The return shuttle fares were often four or five times more expensive than the migrant fares to discourage people from going home.

They stood in line for almost an hour before reaching the security counter. A flesh-toned android scanned their carry-on bags, which was all they'd brought with them.

"Acceptable," the android chirped. It resembled a bald, unisex department store mannequin. "Move on to your gate."

The entire procedure had taken only 30 seconds. Jake couldn't understand why the line moved so slowly. *Computer efficiency*, he thought, glancing back at the android as they passed through the biological/defensive detectors. *I wonder why they can't make those things look or sound a little more human.*

He and Lorina walked the half-kilometer to their gate, occasionally feeling the floor vibrate from the force of lift-offs. Fortunately, the spaceport had excellent sound-insulation or they wouldn't have been able to hear themselves think. As it was, conversation was impossible. Jake wished he had brought some earplugs, but he didn't feel like paying $100 for a pair from the gift shop.

At the gate, their tickets, passports, and marriage license were scrutinized by a mean-looking stewardess. She sized up the two of them suspiciously and said, "Get on."

"Have a nice day," Lorina replied in such a sweetly sarcastic voice that Jake had to bite his lip to keep from laughing.

Finally they were taking the elevator up to the shuttle. Jake felt like his stomach was still on the ground. The higher they went, the more wretched he felt.

Lorina squeezed his arm and reminded him to breathe. The other six people in the elevator looked just as pale. "First space flight?" she asked a young woman who was also wearing a farewell corsage.

The woman just groaned and fanned her face with her datapad.

When the doors opened at the top, they could hear a man's angry voice just inside the airlock.

"This is outrageous! Two-for-one seats means *two seats*! How can anyone be expected to travel in these conditions? I want my money back! We're getting off!" A graying Latino man exited the airlock, pulling a frazzled-looking Asian woman after him. He brushed by Jake and got onto the elevator. "NASA is going to hear about this! Let's get out of here!" he snapped at the woman, who obediently joined him on the elevator. He punched the down button, barely giving the last people on the lift time to scurry out of the way of the closing doors.

Jake and Lorina exchanged looks of nervousness and concern, as did the others who had been on the elevator.

"Come on, people, let's move!" grumbled the steward at the airlock. "We lift-off in ten minutes!"

"We're staying," one man decided. He and his wife went back to wait for the elevator.

Some of the others seemed undecided.

"Come on." Lorina gave Jake a gentle push towards the airlock. "We have to go. It'll be fine."

Jake wished his stomach felt as confident as she sounded.

They stepped into the airlock and were directed to climb down to their seat. Jake held his duffel bag strap with his teeth as he reached out to grasp the ladder that was welded to the floor. He descended the aisle until he came to Row 13, Seat B.

There was a young couple in Seat A, next to the window. They eyed him without comment as he struggled into his chair. Now he was flat on his back, facing up.

Then Lorina climbed over and sat on his lap, her back against his chest, in imitation of their seatmates.

"What do we do with our bags?" Jake wondered aloud, pushing her hair away from his face.

"Just clip them on any hooks that are free," the young man said, pointing to the straps and clips along the metal wall and on the back of the seat in front of them. "Just be sure they're secure. I almost got knocked out on my last flight when someone's suitcase broke loose."

Lorina quickly secured their bags while Jake wrestled the seatbelt around both of their waists. When she finished with the bags, they struggled together with the shoulder harnesses.

"Wow, this is awkward," Lorina muttered.

"Tell me about it. I've got 50 kilos right on my chest," Jake said.

"I do not weigh that much!"

"She's gonna weigh a lot more than that on lift-off," said their dark-haired seatmate. "That's why I got myself a skinny wife." He had a friendly face and dark eyes that were hard to see behind thick glasses. He grinned broadly, revealing a gap-toothed smile that reminded Jake of some of the rednecks he'd attended high school with in Wilmington.

The bleached-blond young woman gave them a cool glance and said nothing.

"So you've traveled before?" Jake asked. "Where to?"

"Oh, to Venus Station once or twice, and a couple of times to the moon. Nowhere special."

"So, you've never been to Mars?" Lorina asked.

"Nope, but I've got a good job waiting for me, so I'm not worried."

"Great! Hey, I'm Jake O'Brien and this is my cous -- uh, wife, Lorina." He bit his tongue at the slip and hoped their seatmates didn't notice.

"Greg Tresser and this is Elaine." She glanced at them again without so much as a smile. "How long have you two been married?"

"We tied the knot yesterday." Jake wanted to get beyond the small talk and ask Greg if he knew anything about Mars College, but at that moment the steward climbed by and handed them oxygen/air sickness masks for lift-off.

"We'll be sitting beside these people for three days, so just relax," Lorina whispered over her shoulder before putting her mask on.

Jake knew she was right. He put on his own mask and started to breathe slowly, forcing himself to calm down for lift-off. He hoped the captain would mention that there were some empty seats, considering the couples who didn't board, but from what he could see, every chair was two-for-one filled. *They probably over-booked,* he thought, *typical spaceline.*

When the captain's voice did come over the speakers, she didn't have anything encouraging to say. "Flight attendants, prepare for lift-off! Sixty seconds . . . 59 . . . 58 . . . 57. . ."

Jake swallowed a few times, willing his stomach to settle down. When the captain got to 30, he heard a thunderous rumbling noise behind him and the shuttle began to shake. The rest of the countdown was lost in the roar of the engines.

When lift-off came, Jake didn't have to worry about his stomach anymore. Every organ in his body felt like it was being driven back into the recesses of the chair. Lorina's weight seemed to crush his chest, forcing all the air out of his shocked lungs. He wondered briefly about broken ribs while he fought desperately for a breath of air, which the oxygen mask didn't seem to be supplying.

Lift-off continued and Jake felt as if his eyeballs were being forced into the back of his skull, as if his spine was going to collapse from the weight. He still couldn't breathe. Seventy-five seconds into lift-off, he blacked out.

* * *

When Jake regained consciousness, he threw up.

"I'm glad I didn't take off your air-sickness mask!" said a familiar voice near him.

He opened his eyes slowly and was rewarded with a pounding migraine.

"Slowly. Take it easy." Lorina was floating just above him, hanging onto the handle of the seat in front of him, her long hair billowing around her head like an orange cloud.

"Are we already in free-fall? How long have I been out?" Jake's voice sounded shaky.

"Well, put it this way: you revived much quicker than some of these other guys." Lorina was trying to sound sympathetic, but she couldn't disguise the amusement in her eyes. "We'll have gravity back in about an hour when they kick in the Velocity engines."

Jake felt too horrible to be mad at her. He focused his eyes and looked over at their seatmates. Elaine was still sitting in Greg's lap, looking disgusted behind her clear mask. Greg was out cold, his breath coming in ragged gasps behind his own mask.

"Is he all right?" Jake asked.

"He'll be out for hours." She took off her mask and gathered up her cloud of almost-white hair, working it into a ponytail. "He hates space travel."

"Then why does he do it?" Lorina asked.

"Because he's a moron," Elaine fired back. Then she turned her head, looked at the retreating view of Earth out the window, and wouldn't say another word.

Then why did you marry him? Jake thought, his mind a jumble of confusion and pain.

Lorina shook her head at him and mouthed, 'They're not married. I'll bet no one here is really married. We should fit right in.'

Jake took a deep breath, grateful that none of his ribs seemed broken. He gripped the armrest with one hand as he released his shoulder harness with the other. Instantly, his body floated up from the seat until he was upside-down, hanging on with the one hand. It was a strange sensation and his stomach protested.

"Just be sure to always have a grip on something," Lorina said. "I'm going to the bathroom."

"How can you pee in weightlessness?" Jake asked, watching her reach for the next seat-handle.

"Didn't you read the passenger info card?"

"What, you mean before or after I passed out?"

"It's fairly simple, professor." Lorina couldn't hold back a chuckle. "The bathroom is equipped with a nice vacuum-cleaner-type hose that you put over your –"

"Okay, I get the idea! Thank you." He waved her off. "Have a nice time!"

Lorina laughed and ascended the aisle.

It's going to be a long three days, Jake thought.

TWO
COLD STORAGE

Danae Shepherd wiped at her uncooperative eyes and decided to take a break from taping. "Pause," she told her terminal and got up from the desk. She stepped out of her office and climbed the ladder to the galley.

There was no one in the small dining room; Danae had been the only occupant for the past six days. The eight square stainless steel tables, each with four matching stainless steel chairs bolted to the floor, were beginning to gather dust. She made a cup of chamomile tea in the crew's mess and sat at her favorite table near the kitchen. She warmed her hands around the navy-blue spill-proof mug and stared at the wording near the handle.

Ishmael. That was the name of her ship. Ishmael was her father's name, and she had renamed the ship when she inherited it from him eight years ago. Her father, Ishmael Thompson, had been a pioneer in the passenger-spaceline business, ferrying eager travelers between the eleven space stations along the Milky Way. His ship, -- Danae still thought of it as his --, could comfortably accommodate 100 passengers.

For the past year, Danae had been lucky to charter 30 passengers for any trip, making barely enough to break even. The economy had been in a downward spiral since the war on Earth, and even out here in the star lanes, everyone was feeling the pinch of poverty.

The captain drank her tea and resigned herself to finishing the transmissions she needed to send as soon as the ship broke Velocity. She climbed back down to her office and positioned herself in front of the terminal.

Danae hesitated as she stared at her reflection in the mirrored screen. *I look terrible.* The dark circles under her large blue eyes made her look ten years older. She noticed for the first time that her pale face seemed gaunt, her cheekbones more prominent. Her naturally curly brown hair, which she wore short for convenience, was starting to frizz around the edges of her face. It was also starting to show some strands of gray. She studied her mouth for a moment, noting the new frown lines.

Danae sighed and attempted to spruce up by tucking the frizz behind her ears. She reached up and fastened a silver button on the collar of her navy-blue jumpsuit. She was wearing her working uniform -- similar to a military fatigue and made of a breathable synthcotton fabric called Indestructa. The *Ishmael*'s uniforms had been designed by her seamstress mother, back when Danae attended public school on Mars Station, and her father was gone for months at a time with his fledgling business.

The long absences had been hard on the marriage, and Claire Thompson found solace in alcohol. Her mother sold the apartment and took a shuttle back to Earth when Danae was 17, and Danae went into space with her father, just as she'd always planned. She hadn't seen her mother in 20 years, and she didn't miss her. *She's got her bottle to keep her company.*

Danae roused herself from her self-pity mode and continued the recording: "Mr. and Mrs. Zimmerman, I can't tell you how sorry I am to send you this news. Your son was a valuable member of my crew. He was courageous and hard-working. He had a real gift for helping passengers feel at ease." Danae swallowed hard to keep her emotions in check. "He was a good friend to all of us aboard the *Ishmael*, and he will be missed.

"By the time you receive this transmission, the ship will be out of quarantine on Mars Station. Please let me know whether you wish to have his body returned to Earth or spaced. Either way, I will pay for the casket and shipping. It's the least I can do for Hugh. May God comfort you in your loss. Shepherd out."

Danae saved the recording and covered her face with trembling hands. Only one more message to record, and it would be the most difficult one she had ever composed. It would be a message for her husband's family.

* * *

Danae cycled the airlock and waited for the coroner to step through the first round doorway into the antechamber. Glancing at the camera monitor, she wasn't surprised to see that he was completely suited up. She cycled the second doorway and welcomed him aboard.

"Dr. Lawson." He offered her his gloved hand.

"Captain Shepherd." Danae shook his hand and tried to see his face behind the bowl-shaped reflective helmet. "Biohazard suits haven't changed much, have they?"

"No, they haven't. Where are the corpses?"

Danae felt offended at his casual use of the word. *They aren't corpses; they're my crew -- and my family.* "In cold storage."

"Isolated, I hope?" Lawson asked as Danae led him to the ladder.

"Yes." *Do you think I'm keeping them in the galley refrigerator?*

"Terrible thing, Zenithian Flu. It's so new, it passed all the bio-sensors undetected." Dr. Lawson descended the ladder after her. "You were lucky no passengers were on board, and it was a miracle half the crew survived."

You mean it was a tragedy half the crew died. Danae felt herself getting more and more irritated with the Mars Station coroner's flippant attitude. She bit her lip, forcing herself to keep a lid on her temper, and showed him down the long passageway on the lowest deck, which the crew referred to as the basement.

Danae checked the seal on the cold storage, which doubled as the ship's brig, although she couldn't remember it ever being used for that purpose. She pressed her thumb to the lock, and the door slid open slowly with a hiss of escaping frigid air. The lights came on automatically and she allowed the doctor to enter the room ahead of her while she zipped her coat, pulled on her own gloves, and mustered her courage to cross the threshold.

Dr. Lawson took out his palm-size medical scanner and stepped over to the first frost-covered body, shrouded in a thin purple blanket on the top bunk on the left side of the tiny compartment. He pressed the scanner's ID probe to the frozen gray thumb of the body's left hand.

"Natasha Martschenko, ship's med-tech," he identified her DNA from Earth's database. "Age 53." Lawson passed the scanner down the body, from head to foot, then checked the screen. "Cause of death: massive organ failure from Zenithian Flu." He hummed to himself for a moment as new information appeared on the scanner. "No sign of the virus left. She's clear for removal."

Danae bristled at the word 'removal,' but managed to keep her temper in check. The doctor had his back to her and was oblivious to her scowl. He bent over the body on the lower bunk, still dressed in a steward's uniform.

"Hugh Zimmerman, age –" here the doctor paused. "Age 22. What a shame," he muttered to himself as he continued his scan.

Danae folded her arms and watched Lawson scan the two bodies on the bunks on the right side of the room, verifying that they were her ship's engineer and navigator. He turned around to face her as he identified the navigator as, "Alexander Shepherd, age 41."

After an awkward pause, the doctor said, "I'll need to examine you and the rest of the crew to make certain no one is carrying the virus. Where are the others?"

Thanks for the words of comfort, Danae thought. "They're quarantined in their cabins, except for the helmsman, who's been quarantined on the bridge." She turned to the door. "I'll show you the way."

* * *

Danae studied the pale, drawn faces of her crew as they assembled in the galley for their first home-cooked meal in three weeks. She knew they were all still recovering from grief, from the boredom of being quarantined, and from the flu itself. They had all suffered from a mild case of Zenithian. Danae wondered for the thousandth time why her own fever, chills, and nausea hadn't developed into seizures, coma, and heart failure like it had in her husband and the others.

"So why did we survive?" Idalis Sanchez echoed Danae's thoughts. The 20-year old cook was the youngest member of *Ishmael*'s crew. She had managed *Ishmael*'s galley for the past eight months.

"You know, I've had lots of time to think about it," said Marco Ting, the helmsman who had been a crewmember since the day he graduated from Beijing Flight School ten years earlier. "The only thing I can figure is that none of us went to that restaurant on Ganymede Station because we were prepping the ship to lift." He ran a hand through his thinning black crew cut and turned to Danae. "Isn't that right, Captain?"

Danae sipped her tea and met the accusing glare in Marco's eyes. "Yes. The coroner told me everyone who went to The Black Hole restaurant that night is now dead, and the Central Intelligence Police are trying to contain the epidemic by determining who was the original carrier of the virus."

"Like that will ever happen!" Marco said. "The CIPs couldn't find a supernova if it was sitting in their backyard. I told Alex I had a bad feeling about The Black Hole. He should have listened to me!"

A retort was poised on Danae' lips but she held it back. Marco believed he was clairvoyant, and often made dire predictions about anything and everything. Generally the crew ignored their resident pessimist, but it sounded like this time he'd made an accurate prediction: *Ishmael*'s crew should have avoided The Black Hole. Whether it was a lucky hunch or genuine insight was anyone's guess.

But it doesn't matter now, Danae thought, *because it's too late.* She glanced over at the final member of the crew, who was sitting alone in the corner.

Heshima Oryang was staring at her untouched plate of pot roast and mashed potatoes. Danae could see that the Ugandan was still in shock. *And with good reason,* she thought, *since she and Hugh had been planning their wedding just before we docked at Ganymede.*

'Shima' was probably the most vital member of the crew. Officially, the willowy 23-year old was the ship's housekeeper. Unofficially, she was everyone's assistant; Danae was still discovering her many talents. When the medic had fallen ill, Shima had proven herself a capable nursemaid to everyone who was stricken. Shima had prepared the bodies for cold storage -- even Hugh's. And Shima had programmed the ship's coordinates for the jump to Mars Station, a task that normally fell to Alex.

Alex. No, don't think about him. Danae was still coping with her own grief, but she had settled into a surreal state of numbness. She felt like there was a giant empty place in her soul that would never heal, but she resolutely showed the crew a practiced calm exterior.

Danae moved over to sit beside Shima. Without a word, she rested the woman's neat cornrows against her shoulder and held her as she wept. The others were silent as Shima shook with sobs.

"What do we do now, Captain?" Idalis asked when Shima began to wind down.

"I guess we put it to a vote," Danae said quietly. "Do we hire new crew and carry on, or do we sell the ship and go home – wherever that may be?"

"Passage to Earth is now in the quadruple digits," Marco said. "Even if you got a good price for the *Ishmael,* it wouldn't be enough to cover our fares."

Danae frowned, but knew he was right. "Coffins are going to take every last bit of our reserves." She knew it would be nice for everyone to have a few days to think about it, but her gut feeling was that this decision couldn't wait. "Let's go ahead and vote."

The motion to hire new crew was unanimous. Danae was touched by their loyalty.

"Well, I guess I'll head down to the employment center and see if there are any interesting résumés on file. You should all go dirtside and get some recycled fresh air."

"Just stay away from any restaurants frequented by Ganymeders," Marco grumbled with his usual charm.

The *Ishmael* crew secured the airlock and took the lift down to the street-level of the spaceport/city known as Mars Station.

Danae had gone dirtside in some exotic locations, but her birth city was still the most colorful place she frequented. As the first successful independent space station constructed, it attracted people from every country and island on Earth. On Mars Station, the weather was always a comfortable 27° C. The pedestrian-friendly streets were lined with buildings 12 stories high. Penthouse apartment dwellers could touch the dome of the biosphere if they stood on tiptoes. At the street level were shops and restaurants representing every known Earth culture, with signs painted above the doors in many languages. Mars Station was now home to two million inhabitants; the population had doubled just after the war, and Danae suspected it would double again before Earth got back on its feet financially.

There was no rhyme or reason to the layout of the city; one wouldn't find a Chinatown or Little Italy on Mars Station. Here, diversity was mish-mashed together. It was normal to find a French café right next to an Ethiopian take-out or a boutique offering hand-made saris and henna tattoos. Mosques, synagogues, churches, and Buddhist temples could be found side-by-side on the same street. To call Mars Station "international" didn't come close to describing the place. It was exciting, vibrant, pungent –

And loud, Danae thought, wincing reflexively as they stepped out of the lift, right into a bustling Middle-Eastern street market. Vendors shouted at them in Arabic, Farsi, and broken English, shoving not-too-fresh fish and Mars-grown produce at them as they waded into the crowd. Music blared from an assortment of derelict boom boxes. The din of high-pitched wailing, which passed for popular tunes to these people, made Danae's temples throb.

"See here, buy this," insisted an elderly-sounding woman hidden under a bright blue burqa. She pressed a wheel of Wisconsin cheddar into Danae's hands.

"No, thank you." Danae pushed it back at her.

Undaunted, the feisty saleswoman tried to give the cheese to Marco, but he quickly sidestepped her and created a path for his shipmates by elbowing his way into the crowd. Danae kept close behind him until they made it through the marketplace and regrouped at the corner of the next street.

"I'm going to pick up some fresh produce, boss," Idalis said. "The prices are pretty good."

"You're going back into the fray?" Danae asked. Idalis usually found a cantina before she thought about work.

"I will go with her," Shima offered before Danae could begin her standard lecture that novice spacers should never venture anywhere alone.

"Okay, then. Be sure to get some peaches and –"

"Bananas," Idalis interrupted. She knew the list by heart.

"Mangos, limes, apples, and anything else that grows on a tree," Shima added.

Danae feigned a stern look. "No, I was about to say 'tomatoes;' you didn't buy enough last port. Please skip the durians this time; I don't care if they are a bargain."

"Aye, Captain," Idalis said with a teasing grin. The two young women turned around and waded back into the crowd.

Danae turned to Marco. He was looking across the street at a dubious establishment offering Thai massage.

"Um, Captain, I was thinking . . ." he began in an innocent tone.

Danae cut him off with an impatient gesture. "Go on. Just be more careful this time. I don't have enough credit for bail."

Marco looked offended. "It's just a *massage*, Captain."

Danae breathed out an exasperated sigh. "I just don't want to hear about it, is that understood?"

Marco flashed a roguish grin and headed across the boulevard.

Danae continued her walk into the city, navigating around the food vendors who lined the sidewalks, offering everything from apple turnovers to fried zucchini-and-tofu kabobs. She was glad she had eaten aboard the ship because much of the fare was tempting. *Mmm, chocolate-covered pretzels. Of course, I can't afford to buy any delicacies today, not if I'm going to hire replacement crew.*

She glanced at the street sign on the next corner and turned left, making her way towards a familiar establishment on Merchant Street, in the heart of the port district. A tram slid quietly past, gliding along its single electric track in the middle of the street, but Danae didn't want to waste money on a ride. *No matter,* she thought, *it feels good to stretch my legs.*

She slipped her hands into the hip pockets of her uniform and fingered the glossy surface of the credit flash which replaced the thumbnail of her left hand. With her right hand, she caressed the short barrel of her Glock. Danae tried to remember how much credit was left on the flash, and how many 9mm bullets were left in the clip of the small antique handgun, which had been her father's. She had more confidence in the gun.

Don't forget to figure in the docking fees, she thought. She resisted the urge to pull out her datapad, preferring to crunch the numbers in her head. *And hope the families want the bodies spaced – there's no way I can afford to ship them back to Earth.* She sighed to herself because Alex had always handled the finances. This was a burden she didn't want to shoulder, but she had no choice. *What am I forgetting? Hope the employment center didn't raise its fees since I hired Idalis.*

In a few minutes, Danae came to the Port District Employment Center. She walked in and glanced around; the spartan office was unoccupied. The place was fully automated, guarded by a single silent android tending the eight terminals.

Danae stepped over to the nearest terminal and pressed her right thumb to the ID lock. The screen immediately displayed her DNA record, verifying who she was and confirming that, as a ship's captain, she had a level-two clearance. In other words, she could take résumés home to peruse at her leisure.

"Employees sought?" inquired the terminal in a nasal Boston accent.

"Med-tech, engineer, navigator, and steward," Danae replied. Just saying the words brought a lump to her throat. She swallowed hard and tried to concentrate on the task at hand.

Her answers appeared on the screen. "Experience requirements?"

Danae frowned. She knew what the job market was like nowadays: abysmal. "I'm willing to consider entry-level, but would prefer at least 5,000 hours of shipboard experience."

Names began to fill the screen. "Please show me experience levels and criminal records for the engineers."

The screen complied. Danae easily narrowed the list to three candidates – none with criminal backgrounds. She was able to pare down the navigator list to five candidates. There were eleven potential stewards, but no medics. *That's odd.* She asked for the list of med-techs again, and the screen gave her just one name, with 'license revoked' next to it.

Wonderful, I can't even lift off without a medic on board. Bankruptcy was looking like a real possibility. "I want to take these résumés back to my ship," she told the terminal.

Now came the expensive part. An amount appeared on the screen. Because she was trying to hire four people, it was steep. "Please insert credit flash."

Danae felt like reaching for her gun and blasting the computer into a silent smoking crater, but she reluctantly drew her left hand out of her pocket. She slid the edge of her thumbnail/credit flash through the scanner groove, and picked up the compact HD that appeared in the slot next to the screen. "Nice doing business with you," she grumbled, turning to leave the office.

Outside, the artificial light was beginning to wane; it was dusk on Mars Station. Danae had one more errand to complete: she stopped by a newspaper kiosk and downloaded the Sunday *Martian Chronicles* onto her datapad. She quickly perused the index until she came to the advertisements and found the submission code.

Turning back to the kiosk, she typed in the code, scanned her credit flash, and downloaded the *Ishmael*'s standard advertisement from her datapad for the next issue. She pocketed the datapad and continued on her way.

Danae stopped by a vendor for some wonton soup and egg rolls. Chinese food, at least, was still a bargain. She headed back towards the ship with her take-out bag. The crowded streets were already beginning to wear on her nerves.

"Hey, mama, looking for a good time?" inquired a shabbily dressed homeless man who seemed to be trying out a new career as a male escort.

I'm old enough to be *your mama.* "No, thanks," Danae muttered, walking by.

"Then how about a bite to eat?" he called after her in a more subdued tone.

Danae stopped, turned around, and studied the expression on his haggard face. She handed him her take-out bag.

"Hey, thanks, lady!"

"You're welcome." Danae turned around and continued her trek back to the *Ishmael* to look over the résumés in the privacy and quiet of her office.

THREE
LIFE ON MARS

Lorina Murphy was feeling queasy from what she guessed was turbulence -- not that the aircraft turbulence she'd experienced could compare to the teeth-rattling, bone-jarring sensations of a space shuttle entering Mars' atmosphere.

"This is worse than lift-off," Jake complained in her ear.

Lorina craned her neck and tried to look out the window, but Elaine's greasy hair blocked her view.

"There's not much to see," Greg assured them when he turned away from the window and noticed the disappointed look on Lorina's face. "It looks like a big red dirtball."

Lorina shifted her weight on Jake's lap and tried to remember the holograms she'd viewed of Mars Station in *National Geographic*. The thirty-square-kilometers biosphere had been built over the south pole, directly over the planet's only source of water. Nearly seven square kilometers of the east corner of the station was cultivated farmland, though Mars' soil was nutrient poor and all the original topsoil had been imported at tremendous cost. Every scrap of garbage produced by the station dwellers was carefully composted into new topsoil. Likewise, every liter of water pumped up to the surface had to be carefully processed; water was a precious commodity for both crops and people.

There was a huge space dock on the western boundary of the station, which extended across four kilometers of the biosphere's dome. The dock was comprised of several levels of titanium airlock tubes extending outwards from the sphere, organized like docking slips at a marina. Each ship had to lock into a stationary orbit with Mars and choose an available airlock. It was simple in theory, yet complex in practice. A large shuttle like the *Endeavor III* could take several hours to dock.

Lorina wondered what life would be like on Mars Station. *Will Jake get into Mars College? Will I be able to find a job? Where will we live?* The questions were endless and Greg wasn't exactly a wealth of information since it turned out that his 'good job' was only a vague advertisement he'd received from a friend of a friend who worked at the Mars Hilton.

Greg had also confessed to them yesterday evening, when Elaine was in the bathroom, that she wasn't his wife, and that they only traveled together for convenience, pooling their limited funds to track down jobs off-planet.

"What does Elaine do?" Lorina asked.

Greg shook his head. "I'm not sure, but she's always ready to travel whenever I need a change of scenery."

To Lorina, it sounded like whatever Elaine did was possibly illegal, hence her eagerness to planet-hop. *Drugs,* she guessed, *or maybe she's a hired assassin.*

She shook her head as the shuttle hit a particularly rough patch of atmosphere. *Maybe I'm letting my imagination run away from me because I've been bored stupid for the past three days.*

"Flight attendants, prepare for landing," the captain announced over the com.

"Does that mean they'll hand out masks?" Jake asked hopefully.

"Don't even think about puking on me!"

Jake groaned.

Lorina could tell he wasn't kidding; his face was turning an interesting shade of gray. "Hang on, please," she advised over her shoulder. "Just think, in a few minutes we'll be on solid ground and can get something decent to eat."

Jake groaned louder; obviously food wasn't a welcome topic of conversation. But he managed to keep his nausea in check until the shuttle broke through the atmosphere a few minutes later. The ride became considerably smoother.

"I can see Mars Station!" Greg said.

Lorina leaned closer to the small window and caught a glimpse of the bright dome, though it was hard to see any details from five kilometers up. In a moment, it passed out of sight again as the shuttle banked, continuing its landing approach.

Two hours later, the *Endeavor III* docked at the spaceport. Lorina felt the pressure changing, her body growing heavier in the artificial gravity. Jake unhooked their shoulder harnesses and duffel bags. In a few minutes, they were standing on unsteady feet and stepping between the rungs of the ladder in the aisle, making their way to the airlock with the other passengers.

"So, I'll see you around," Greg said when they were in a lift, descending to street level.

Lorina spoke up. "Could we share a ride to the Hilton with you?" She had been toying with an idea for the past two days, and decided to go for it -- *nothing ventured, nothing gained.*

"I'm just going to take the tram," Greg explained as they stepped out onto a wide brick sidewalk. He watched Elaine move off into the crowd without so much as a 'goodbye.' He waved half-heartedly at her retreating back with a hurt expression on his face.

"Well, you could show us the way," Lorina persisted.

Greg pulled a map out of his oversized backpack. "I would, if I knew the way myself." He unfolded it and the three of them stood in the middle of the busy sidewalk, pouring over it.

"Do you have the address?" Lorina asked.

Greg nodded slowly, thinking. "Seven-hundred West Merchant Street."

Jake tapped a forefinger on his edge of the map. "That's not far from here. Merchant Street is only three blocks over and we could catch a tram there – if that's what this little green line means."

"Let's go," Greg agreed.

Lorina's hips, knees and lungs struggled with every step. She knew it would take a few days to get used to being in full gravity again, but she was too excited to complain about the discomfort. She looked around at everything, taking in the strange sights, sounds, and smells. It took all of her self-control not to gawk. She'd never seen such a colorful variety of people, dressed in every costume imaginable. Lorina noted many different languages and mannerisms. She caught snippets of Russian, Spanish, and Mandarin from passersby, but the African dialects were new to her ears.

"Is that a brothel?" she whispered to Jake. "No, don't look."

"Well, how can I answer the question if I don't look?" Jake argued with a mischievous grin, craning his neck to see.

Lorina jabbed him with an elbow. "*Don't look.*"

Jake started to turn around, but Lorina grabbed his arm and steered him down the sidewalk after Greg. "Never mind. A married man has no business leering at ladies of the night."

"Hey, we can drop the married act, can't we, now that we're here?" Jake asked.

"No, not until after I talk to the manager at the Hilton."

Jake raised his eyebrows at her. "What do you have up your sleeve?"

"You'll see." Lorina wouldn't say anything else as they caught up to Greg, who was waiting at the corner.

"You'll both need a credit flash to ride the tram," Greg said, cheerfully settling into his role as their unofficial tour guide.

Like the blind leading the blind, Lorina thought, recalling that Greg had never been to Mars either.

"Where can we get those?" Jake asked.

Greg pointed out the First Bank of Mars across the street and led the way.

"Is a credit flash safe?" Lorina asked as they walked past the armed guard at the front doors of the bank.

"Much safer than carrying cash," Greg replied. He held up his left hand to show them his shiny black thumbnail. "The credit flash is a part of you, a biologic implant, so no one else can use it, even if they cut off your thumb."

"Ugh," Lorina grimaced. "So why doesn't it work if your thumb is severed?"

"The credit scanners detect heart rate, blood flow. They can tell if you're being forced to use the flash against your will. It's foolproof."

Lorina had her doubts, but she forced a smile and asked the obvious question: "Does it hurt to get a credit flash?"

"Only for a second," Greg said. "It's like getting your ears pierced."

Lorina couldn't figure out how having your thumbnail ripped off would hurt 'only for a second,' but she made up her mind to be brave and get it over with.

When they reached the teller window, Jake and Lorina quickly discussed how much should go into each of their credit flashes.

"You have to keep most of it because you have to pay tuition," Lorina said.

"It was your mom's ring. We should split it 50-50."

Lorina shook her head. "She gave it to you."

"How much do you have?" Greg asked, standing behind them.

The cousins exchanged a cautious glance. "A lot," Jake admitted, "but it may have to last us a long time."

"Please extend your left thumb," the android interrupted, holding out what appeared to be the hose of an ancient vacuum cleaner. There was even a suctioning sound coming from the end of the device.

Lorina stifled a shudder of fear. She bit her lip as her thumb disappeared into the round tip of the hose. She felt a sharp pain in her thumb, like a bee sting, but the sensation was gone before she could even say "ow!"

The android turned to its left and tapped a computer keypad. "How much do you wish to deposit, Lorina Murphy of Wilmington, Delaware, USA, Earth?"

Lorina was dumbfounded. "How does it know who I am?"

"If you were born before the war, your DNA is in the database," Greg explained.

"But my DNA is messed up, right?" she asked Jake.

"I don't think the toxins affect your base DNA reading," Jake said with an 'I don't really know' shrug.

"I thought you were a medical student. Didn't they teach you this stuff?"

"How much do you wish to deposit?" repeated the android.

Lorina glanced at Jake, who was unclipping the money belt hidden beneath his shirt. She glanced at the exchange rate chart on the wall behind the android. "One credit is equal to one US dollar, so twenty should be enough."

"Twenty credits?" Greg scoffed. "That won't get you very far."

"No, 20,000 credits." Lorina ignored Greg's gasp of surprise as Jake unzipped the pouch and counted out the cash to the android.

"I thought you looked a bit chubby," Greg said to Jake. "Do you know how lucky you were not to get mugged between the port and the bank?"

"That seems like a good reason not to advertise how much cash you're carrying." Lorina noted the nod from the android and was able to extract her thumb from the tube. She stared at the smooth black sliver of technology right where her thumbnail used to be. There was no blood, which surprised her.

"Isn't there a bank fee for this service?" Jake asked Greg over his shoulder as he hesitantly offered his left thumb to the android.

"Yeah, five percent of every deposit."

"Ouch!" Jake yelped. Then he breathed a sigh of relief. "That wasn't too bad. Nice little racket they're running. Maybe we should keep some cash aside?"

"Can't," Greg said. "No one uses money here. It's an obsolete Earth custom."

When Jake had his new thumbnail with the remaining 100,000 credits on it, and Greg made a deposit to his Venus-issued credit flash, they walked over to Merchant Street and boarded a tram. It was a simple, android-driven no-frills type of transportation. Ten credits would take you anywhere you wanted to go in the biosphere. *Like a bus without a personality,* Lorina mused, watching the pedestrian-choked sidewalks pass by her window.

The Mars Hilton looked like a normal Earth hotel, except for the android bellhops. They crossed the fancy faux-marble lobby to the front desk.

"Checking in, sir?" A bored-looking desk clerk with a face full of piercing -- ears, nose, eyebrows, chin, and lip – sneered at them. She had unkempt bright purple hair and long black fingernails.

Very attractive, Lorina thought. *Vintage turn of the century – as ugly now as it was then.*

"Yes, we'd like to check in," Greg said. "Two rooms. And I'd also like to make an appointment to speak to the manager about a job opening."

The punk desk clerk gave him a confused look. "Job opening?"

"I need to make an appointment with the manager, too," Lorina said. "But tomorrow – definitely tomorrow. We're too dirty and exhausted to see him or her today."

The clerk appraised Lorina with narrowed eyes as she set two datapads on the counter in front of them. "First things first. How long will you be staying?"

"Two nights," Greg said.

Lorina watched him press his right thumb to the screen and then slide his credit flash/thumbnail through the slot provided. She read on the display that Gregory Tresser of Galax, Virginia, USA, Earth was confirmed for two nights at 1,000 credits per night.

Ouch. We won't survive long at these prices. "One night," she told the clerk, as Jake pressed his thumb to other screen, "and we'll need a room with two beds."

"A second bed will cost you extra," the clerk explained with a smirk.

Lorina and Jake exchanged a look of dismay as Jacob O'Brien, IV, of Wilmington, Delaware, USA, Earth was confirmed for one night at 1,500 credits.

"I could sleep on the floor," Jake whispered out of the corner of his mouth.

"I thought you two were married," Greg said.

"We are, but he has nightmares and thrashes around a lot in his sleep." Lorina could feel her cheeks turning pink as she faced the desk clerk again. "Two beds will be fine for one night. Now, what about those appointments with the manager?"

"The manager hires through the employment center," the clerk said. "No appointments will be taken in person."

Lorina felt her anger stirring. "Could we at least inquire if there are any openings? What's the manager's name?"

The desk clerk gave her a cold look. "Her name is McAllister, and she only hires through the employment center, *Mrs.* O'Brien. Rooms 410 and 412. Enjoy your stay."

Jake jabbed Lorina discreetly, and she got the message: don't go ballistic.

As they turned away from the desk, a com buzzed and they overheard the clerk answer it. "Front desk; this is McAllister."

Lorina felt her face turning scarlet as they waved off the bellhops and crossed the lobby to the elevators. "Don't say a word," she growled at Jake.

"Who, me? I was only going to say, 'welcome to Mars'."

"Are you two married?" Greg asked again. When neither Jake nor Lorina answered him, he added, "You argue like a married couple."

Lorina turned her head so Greg wouldn't hear her muffled giggle.

Jake pressed his thumb to the ID lock of Room 412, and he and Lorina said goodnight to Greg, even though it was 4:30 in the afternoon, Mars' time. Their room was clean, but looked like it had seen better days. The bedspreads and curtains were faded, the air conditioning didn't work, and the towels in the bathroom had frayed edges. Lorina was too tired to care; she'd only slept eight hours, on and off, out of the past 74. She kicked off her shoes and crawled into bed.

* * *

Lorina awoke to the sound of water running. She rolled out of bed and pounded on the bathroom door. "Move it, Jake! I've gotta go!"

She heard him laughing as he shut off the shower and emerged with a towel wrapped around his waist. "My, don't we look fresh this morning?"

Lorina elbowed him aside and slammed the door. She felt grimy and wanted to take a long shower, but a placard hanging next to the towel rack announced that penalty fees would apply after three minutes of water usage.

Is that three minutes per person or per room? she wondered, irked at Jake for getting up before her. She decided to chance the penalty fee, showered for three minutes with the plug in the tub, then sat down in the five centimeters of accumulated water, determined to scour herself thoroughly.

Jake rapped on the door. "When do we have to check out?"

"Ten, I think," Lorina shouted back, "What time is it?"

"6:30. I'm taking the tram to Mars College; I'll try to be back before 10:00."

"Okay, I'll try to have a job by then. Meet you back here."

Lorina dried and dressed in the only nice outfit she'd brought with her – a denim skirt and simple white blouse, both hand-sewn by her mother. She decided to get something to eat before paying another visit to McAllister. *Can't grovel on an empty stomach,* she sighed, glancing at her new black thumbnail.

Lorina stopped at the first food vendor kiosk just outside the hotel's front doors and paid 50 credits for a stale bagel and a paper cup full of something that was supposed to be orange juice but tasted like beets. She was too hungry to complain.

"You got any jelly to go with this?" she asked the turbaned vendor.

"Ten credits."

"Never mind." Lorina bit into the tasteless bagel. Once her stomach was placated, she screwed up her courage and went back to the hotel lobby. She asked the sleepy-looking desk clerk with an assortment of safety pins stuck through his earlobes and nostrils if she could speak to McAllister.

He laughed derisively. "Some guy with glasses asked to speak to her about ten minutes ago. She told him if he didn't stop bothering her, he'd be checking out today without a refund."

Poor Greg! "I don't suppose it's a crime to ask where the employment center is located."

"It's not a crime, but it will cost you 20 to look at the com directory." He slapped a datapad on the counter in front of her.

"No thanks." Lorina had had enough quality customer service for one day. She headed back out to the busy street.

After making a few inquiries of vendors and passersby, she determined that the closest employment center was only a kilometer away on Merchant Street. To save time, she took the tram.

Lorina met Greg coming out the front door of the employment center. He looked discouraged. "Did you find anything?"

He shook his head, not even feigning his usual optimism. "Not many openings posted, and there's thousands of résumés on file."

Lorina bit her lip. "I don't suppose you checked under the blue-collar section? You know, waiters, housekeepers, day care workers --?"

"Construction, road work, landscaping, sanitation workers, stock clerks, cashiers," Greg finished. "You name the position, I searched for it. No one is hiring, and if they are hiring, they're looking for a highly-specialized employee with several college degrees or decades of experience."

Lorina nodded, feeling her hopes plummet. She studied the sidewalk for a minute, thinking hard. "How much does it cost to post a résumé, Greg?"

"Five thousand -- more than I've got at the moment."

Lorina curbed her impulse to offer him a loan. *I need to think about this first. A prosperous city like Mars Station, but it costs money to find a job?* "What's the fee for locating an employee through the center?"

Greg raised his eyebrows at her. "I don't know how much exactly, but I'm sure it's expensive."

Lorina nodded, remembering their experience at the bank yesterday. "Nice little scam they're working, don't you think?"

"Yeah." He fidgeted with the knot of his ugly orange necktie. "I think you're right, but what's the alternative?"

Lorina decided to go with the plan she'd concocted aboard the space shuttle. "Did you happen to see any other hotels nearby?"

Greg gave her a puzzled look. "There's a Marriott a few blocks east of here."

"Let's check it out – what have we got to lose?"

Greg nodded and led the way.

Lorina was pleased to see that the Mars Station Marriott wasn't as opulent as the Hilton -- there were no android bellhops in the lobby. The attractive black front desk clerk smiled at them and said, "Good morning, may I help you?"

"I'd like to speak to the hotel manager, please."

The smile never faltered. "Certainly, ma'am. That would be me." She extended a hand in greeting. "Genevieve Peterson."

Lorina shook her hand and introduced herself and Greg. "Ms. Peterson, I'll get right to the point: do you have any job openings?"

Peterson's smile disappeared. "The employment center –" she began.

"Is a sham." Lorina launched into the speech she'd prepared: "I'm assuming that you have a difficult time keeping your fine hotel fully staffed – isn't that right?"

"Um," the manager shrugged, admitting nothing. She was neither smiling nor frowning, so Lorina took that as a good sign.

"High turnover among your staff? Every time you turn around, you've got to go back to the employment center. It's enough to make a modest business go broke."

Peterson's eyebrows raised slightly. "Your point, Ms. Murphy?"

"My point is that you should skip the center -- and hire me."

"And me, too," Greg spoke up.

"And why should I do that?" Peterson asked with a skeptical frown.

"Because I'll work for half pay in exchange for a room," Lorina explained.

Greg inhaled sharply, but echoed, "Me too," after a moment's hesitation.

The manager burst into laughter. "I'll have to give you credit for being creative, Ms. Murphy. So tell me what kind of experience you have."

Lorina smiled. *This crazy idea is working!* "To be honest, my background is in agriculture."

"We don't have many openings for farmers," Peterson said dryly.

"But what I really know how to do is work hard," Lorina continued. "I'm used to back-breaking 12-hour days. My domestic skills are excellent. I can cook, clean and sew like a professional."

"I have some experience as a bellhop," Greg said.

"I'm willing to start on a trial basis." Lorina kept her eyes fixed on Peterson's. "I'll work without pay for the first two weeks."

At this announcement, Greg emitted a squeak of surprise and made no comment.

"I'm a risk-free investment, Ms. Peterson. All I need is a place to live."

"But what would I do with you if the hotel was completely booked?" the manager asked.

Lorina stared at Peterson with an air of complete confidence.

"We haven't had a full house in years." Peterson lowered her gaze. Lorina could sense the grudging admiration in her tone.

"I'll take the ugliest room you have, so long as it has two beds."

Peterson glanced at Greg.

"No, not for him, for me and my husband Jake. He's a medical student at Mars College." She rested her left palm on the counter so Peterson could see the wedding ring.

"I'll need a separate room." Greg took a deep breath. "I'd be willing to take a cot in a storage room -- anything."

Peterson glanced back and forth between them for a moment. Then she said, "Wait here," and went into the back office. Lorina and Greg exchanged triumphant grins but waited in silence.

When the manager returned, she set two datapads on the counter in front of them. "You'll be a housekeeper assigned to the seventh floor," she explained to Lorina. "No pay for the first two weeks, half the hourly rate thereafter. One standard efficiency room with two beds, ready for immediate occupancy. Sign here."

Lorina pressed her thumb to the ID lock and waited as Peterson explained the terms of Greg's employment as a bellhop.

"You're in luck, Mr. Tresser; we actually have a small single-bed room in the basement, which is a designated sick room for the staff, but no one's used it in years. I'll bet it's dusty, but it's yours for the same terms."

"It sounds perfect," Greg said. "Thank you."

Peterson lowered her voice and spoke in a stern tone, scrutinizing their faces with her sharp brown eyes as she explained, "Since this is an unorthodox employment arrangement, I'm going to *insist* that you not disclose to anyone how you were hired by the Marriott. If you do, you will be terminated immediately." She waited a moment for that to sink in. "If at some future point you register with an employment center, you *will not* list this job on your résumé. Is that understood?"

"Why the secrecy?" Lorina whispered, nodding her agreement.

"This is Mars, Ms. Murphy. We do things differently here," Peterson explained, looking uncomfortable.

"Please call me Lorina."

"Welcome, Lorina and Greg." The manager cracked a smile. "Any chance you could both start work by noon?"

Lorina said, "I'll be ready at 11:00."

"Me, too," echoed Greg.

* * *

When Lorina returned to Room 412 at the Hilton, she found Jake stretched out on his bed with one arm draped across his eyes. *Oh, that's not a good sign.* "How did it go?"

"The premed program was phased out last semester." His voice was filled with bitterness.

"Any other majors?" Lorina tried to sound optimistic. She started to pack her duffel bag.

"Nothing. No nursing, pharmacy, dentistry, psychiatry, physical therapy – you name it, I asked about it. There are no longer medical degrees of any kind offered at Mars College -- and don't let the door hit you on the way out."

Lorina sat down heavily on the edge of his bed. *We've come all this way -- for nothing?* She resisted the urge to get caught up in Jake's despondency. "I'm really, really sorry. I know how much you want to be a doctor. Is there anything I can do?"

"You can't help me," Jake said, "no one can help me. I should've stayed home and milked the cows like Dad wanted."

Lorina snatched his arm away from his face. "I can help you stop feeling sorry for yourself. Get your butt out of bed, Jake. We've got a place to live, and I've got a job, so let's figure out what to do with you."

Jake sat up slowly and regarded her with a suspicious frown. "Don't I get a minute to mope before you start cooking up a new scheme?"

Lorina threw his duffel bag at him. "No. We have to check out, so get moving."

A few minutes later, they stopped by the front desk and learned that the bill for their room came to 1,800 credits. "Three hundred for using a few extra minutes of water?" Jake complained, swiping his thumbnail on the datapad again.

"Have a nice day," said the pin-cushioned desk clerk, giving them a nasty smirk.

Lorina dragged Jake away from the counter before he could tell the clerk what to do with his nice day. "Just ignore him." She escorted him out to the street. "Let's catch a tram and I'll tell you all about my new job."

They stood elbow to elbow on the crowded trolley, holding onto the overhead bar. Lorina quickly explained her success at the Marriott. "Greg was so excited when we left, he said, 'if you weren't married, I'd give you a big kiss'." She rolled her eyes. "I didn't think I'd be so grateful to be tied down."

Jake ignored her attempt at humor. "Two weeks without pay? Half the hourly rate?"

"At 1,800 a night, how long do you think we'll survive on 40 credits an hour? Did you flunk math? At least this way we have a place to live, and I'll make enough to keep us fed."

Jake shrugged and lowered his gaze in defeat, but Lorina began firing questions at him: "Have you considered asking around at the hospitals? Maybe a fire department could train you as an EMT. Or what about a local clinic? You don't need a license to stock the supply room or empty bedpans. You could work your way up to doctor with hands-on experience. Tell them you'll work for free."

"I have to be in medical school to do any of those things," Jake said.

"Why? Think about it: medical schools no longer exist, but hospitals will always need doctors. I'm talking about getting your foot in the door as an orderly. Isn't that what a residency entails? A hands-on apprenticeship?"

"A residency begins during the third year of medical school," Jake repeated, frowning.

"So you ask around until you find some overworked doctor who'll take you on as a resident. And if that doesn't work, all you need is a piece of paper that says you graduated --"

"Whoa!" Jake interrupted. "You're not forging a diploma for me. It's one thing to pretend we're married -- I mean, people do that all the time, -- but pretending to be a doctor is against the law."

Lorina laughed loudly, ignoring the vexed looks from the passengers around them. "At least you'll get free room and board in prison, Dr. O'Brien."

"Yeah, and you'll be in the cell next to mine, Mrs. O'Brien." Jake sighed as they climbed off the tram in front of the Marriott. "Okay, I'll try it your way. Let's get something to eat and I'll scout some hospitals this afternoon."

"Smart boy." Lorina grinned. "Let's eat fast; I start work at 11:00."

* * *

What have I gotten myself into? Lorina thought as she finished making the bed in the last room on her hall. *Thirty rooms by myself?* Which wasn't entirely true; an android assistant vacuumed and restocked her cart. Lorina bundled up the last of the towels and pulled the door shut to Room 730. She watched the stiff mechanical mannequin push the cart down the hallway towards the elevator.

"You take that down to the laundry, and I'll take out the trash," Lorina called after it half-heartedly. *And then it's quitting time. I've served my eight-hour sentence for today.* She pressed both hands against the small of her back and groaned. *Come on, don't be a wimp. You're not used to the gravity yet. This will get easier.*

Sure it will. You'll be promoted to the laundry room in no time. Lorina picked up the garbage bag and lugged it down the hall to the elevator. She wondered how Jake made out at the hospital. He'd decided to try the Mars Station Medical Center first, which was in the exact center of the biosphere, overlooking McConnell Park. She expected that he would be back at their room by now. *Please have some dinner waiting for me,* she thought, *before I drop dead from exhaustion.*

Lorina rode the lift down to the basement and carried the garbage down the long hallway, past the humid laundry room and Greg's new quarters with *Employee Health Room* engraved on a placard beside the door. She wondered how he was managing his first day on the job. *I hope he has enough money to live on for the next 13 days.* She felt a little guilty about roping him into the two-weeks-without-pay deal, but figured he'd manage. *At least I got him a job and a place to live; there were no guarantees with the so-called employment center.*

She pushed open the fire exit door to the alley, where two enormous composting dumpsters sat waiting for the latest offerings. It was getting dark, and Lorina felt a tremor of nervousness as she glanced up and down the narrow lane between the Marriott and a brick apartment building. Living on Earth in the aftermath of catastrophic war had conditioned her to be hyper vigilant. People who were careless usually didn't live long enough to learn from their mistakes.

Lorina held the heavy door open with her foot and leaned out as far as she could to pitch the bag in the direction of the nearest dumpster. She heard a quiet shuffling noise in the alley behind her, panicked, and bolted back inside without turning to see who, or what, it was.

Lorina yanked the door shut and stood panting in the hallway, listening to her heart hammering against her ribs. She couldn't hear anything moving outside, and felt safe for the moment since the titanium door only opened from the inside.

When her adrenaline rush subsided, Lorina realized she was still holding the garbage. She debated just leaving it by the door – *someone will come along eventually and remove it* -- but knew it would be a safety hazard. *This is a fire exit, genius. Don't be a baby, just take out the trash. There's nothing out there more dangerous than an alley cat.*

Lorina pressed her ear to the door and listened. She couldn't hear anything, so she screwed up her courage and pushed the door open, intending to pitch the bag and run.

She came face-to-face with the source of her panic.

A waif-like figure less than a meter high was standing in the shadow of the dumpster, peering into the opening. He or she squeaked in fright at Lorina's sudden appearance, and vanished around the far side of the dumpster. Lorina caught only a fleeting glimpse of a dark face with large eyes and a mop of matted, filthy hair. The soft shuffling sound she'd heard earlier was repeated as the tiny person fled into the gathering darkness of the alley.

Lorina tossed the bag into the dumpster, her hands shaking from the unexpected encounter with the child. She thought of Catherine as she went back inside the hotel. The little person she'd glimpsed had been about the same size as her five-year-old cousin. She felt a pang of homesickness as she closed the fire exit door again.

FOUR
INTERVIEWS

Danae hated the new interview program. She preferred to read a résumé first, so she could form an unbiased opinion of a potential employee, but the HD from the employment center contained only pre-recorded holo-vids – no reading required. *I need to know if someone can do the job, not how well they perform on camera.*

"Hey, my name is Robert Smith," drawled the nervous young man with an Oklahoman accent. "My friends call me Blaze 'cause I can fix things fast."

Blaze? Just what I need, another ego like Marco's. She was tempted to cut him off and move on to the next résumé, but she wrestled with her impatience. *All the other résumés are going to be just like this, so get over it.*

"I have a bachelor's degree in mechanical engineering from MIT, and my specialty is Velocity engines."

MIT closed a year ago, Danae recalled. *He looks like he hasn't been out of college very long.*

"I came to Mars Station in July, right after my dad passed away from leukemia," he added with a slight grimace.

Sorry, that's not a good enough reason to hire you. Danae tried not to think about her own losses. She studied Smith's dark crew cut, clean-shaven square jaw and pale brown eyes. He had high cheekbones and a wide, slightly crooked nose. *Probably some Native American ancestry,* she thought.

Smith smiled self-consciously as he continued:

"I have a part-time job at the port right now, doing basic repairs on solar cycles, but it's goin' nowhere. What I'd really like to do is work with the crew of a regular ship. I'd love to travel."

No experience in space, Danae thought, disappointed. She poised her thumb over the delete key, ready to move on.

"I'm hoping to join a tight-knit crew. I've got nobody left in my family, so I guess you could say I'm lookin' for a new family, you know?"

Danae hesitated, her attention riveted by the warmth of his expression, and the sincerity in the words, which undercut the awkwardness.

"I know I don't have a lot of experience, but I'm a fast learner and a hard worker. I think I'm easy to get along with, and I'd be an asset to any crew. Thank you for considerin' me. Smith out."

Danae hit the pause button. "Shima."

"I am in . . . gall-y, boss," came the static-laden reply.

"I know it's getting late, but I'd like you to take the lift down to the public com and call a Mr. Robert 'Blaze' Smith. Schedule an interview for tomorrow at 7:00 a.m. sharp. Tell him I'll meet him at the Number 16 lift, and I expect him to be on time."

"Com is break . . . up, Cap--in; I will come to . . . office so you . . . tell me again."

"Right. Shepherd out."

* * *

Smith was on time; in fact, he was early. Danae stepped out of the lift at 6:55 a.m. and found the tall, lanky engineer waiting by the doors in neatly-pressed green coveralls, which, she suspected, were the nicest clothes he owned.

"Captain Shepherd of the *Ishmael*." She offered her hand.

"Thank you for summonin' me, Captain."

Danae's hand disappeared in his large sweaty palm. She noted a strong grip and calluses, so his claim to be a hard-worker was genuine. "It's nice to meet you, Mr. Smith."

"Please, call me Blaze," he said.

Danae made an effort to disguise her amusement. "Okay, Blaze. Shall we go up to the ship?"

"Yes, ma'am – I mean, Captain," he stammered.

"It's okay, I don't bite."

Blaze nodded, looking slightly flustered. They rode the lift to Level 9 without speaking.

The *Ishmael*'s airlock was 10 meters directly opposite the lift. Built into the long, narrow concrete corridors for docking Levels 2 through 10 were hundreds of circular titanium airlocks, each separated by only 100 meters. The commercial corridors on Levels 11 through 14 had airlocks separated by half a kilometer. Smaller ships, like the *Ishmael*, didn't need as much room to dock. Danae would have preferred a lower docking level for passenger convenience, but 9 was the lowest she could afford this trip.

Danae and Blaze walked across the dimly-lit corridor to the airlock. She pressed her thumb to the ID lock and waited for the half-meter-thick door to cycle open before speaking. "We can start the interview here, Blaze. Are you familiar with airlock security systems?"

"Yes, Captain." Blaze took a deep breath and began: "This is a standard titanium airlock equipped with biological and defensive screening. A magnetic field strong enough to stun an elephant will create a barricade here --" he pointed across the antechamber to the second half-meter-thick door --," if I attempt to enter the ship with an unauthorized DNA signature. It'll also stop me if I try to walk inside carryin' a trace amount of any dangerous microbes in my system."

Danae snorted. "Yes, it works most of the time."

Blaze gave her a puzzled look. "What do you mean, Captain?"

"I mean the biosensors aren't updated often enough to suit me." Danae touched a code into the antechamber keypad just in front of the second door, which would allow Blaze to enter the ship. "Zenithian Flu took out half my crew two weeks ago. If you have a problem with that, we can conclude this interview right now." She studied his face carefully for a reaction.

"No, Captain." Blaze seemed more surprised than alarmed. "I'm sorry for your loss."

Danae nodded and they walked into the entryway of the ship. When the round door rolled shut behind them, she climbed the ladder down to the *Ishmael*'s basement. Blaze descended after her. She waited, not speaking, to see if he would take the initiative to demonstrate his skills.

"Well, this would be my area," Blaze began, sounding more confident. "The engine room should be right over here." He gestured to the correct door, which Danae unsealed with her thumb. He squinted, smiling, as the lights came on, and stood in the doorway for a moment, scanning the mechanical labyrinth that filled most of the 20 by 40 meter room. "I see you have Class IV McConnell Velocity engines with Boeing Solar back-up engines. Not as fast as the Class V which came out last year, but it'll get you there."

Danae folded her arms expectantly and trailed Blaze as he crossed to the main control board. He glanced at her for a nod of approval before touching the first keypad.

"Well, it looks like the *Ishmael* needs some basic maintenance, Captain. Your solar panels are depleted and need to be realigned with the next planetary rotation."

"Do you know how to do that?" Danae asked.

"Yes, ma'am – Captain, I mean." Blaze's large hands flew over the controls. "I can do that right now. I also see that your com system is on its last legs. It probably needs a complete overhaul. Yes, Captain," he nodded, before she could ask, "I know how to do that, too."

"So, tell me what you would do if the Velocity was damaged or malfunctioned during a jump."

"Turn down the fuel feed – slowly, by hand, and switch over to the solar engines – slowly, and at the same time." He grinned again. "It's sort of like lettin' out the clutch without givin' the engine too much gas. I learned that trick on my granddad's old Harley."

"And why is that trick important?" Danae asked. The answer would be obvious to any first-year engineering student, but she wanted to gauge his reaction.

"'Cause if you shut off the Velocity durin' a jump, the engines implode. I could show you the physics, but it's a lot of borin' math, and I'm sure you know it better than me." Blaze turned to face Danae, his expression serious. "I know how much a captain needs to trust her engineer. If you hire me, I swear I'll never let you down."

Danae nodded, revealing nothing in her expression. "I'd like to have you speak briefly to a member of the crew before we conclude the interview." She led him back to the ladder without waiting for his reply, and they climbed to the top deck.

Danae walked onto the small three-by-four meter bridge and spoke to Marco, who was studying the com control board with a look of consternation on his face. "Someone I'd like you to meet, Ting."

Marco looked up with a frown. "Why?"

"Ignore his sunny personality," Danae advised Blaze. "He's nursing a hangover this morning."

Blaze nodded and approached Marco with a hand extended. He towered over the helmsman. "Robert Smith; friends call me Blaze."

Marco shook his hand without smiling. "Marco Ting; I don't have any friends."

Danae stifled the urge to laugh. "Is he *okay*?" she asked Marco.

Blaze looked confused. He glanced back at Danae. "I don't understand, Captain."

"He's okay." Marco perceived what she was getting at. "No bad vibes from this cowboy."

Blaze shot Marco a frown and looked like he wanted to object to being labeled a cowboy, but Danae didn't give him a chance to speak. "You're hired, Blaze. You can move in today. We'll discuss your contract over dinner. I want the com system repaired before then. Do you have a problem with that?"

"No, Captain," Blaze stammered, flabbergasted. "Thank you, Captain."

Danae nodded. "Right. Marco, show Blaze to his cabin and clear his ID at the airlock and engine room."

"Okay." Marco sized up the newcomer with a cool glance. "Whatever you say."

"Now if you gentlemen will excuse me, I have to interview a navigator."

* * *

Danae walked into the galley and went straight to the hot water dispenser for some chamomile tea. Two disappointing interviews had taken up the rest of her morning. The first had been an unshaven, red-eyed Ukrainian who turned up late and reeked of vodka. She didn't bring him on board the ship. The second candidate, an older Australian woman, seemed promising, but her understanding of astrophysics was shaky, at best. When Danae asked her to calculate a jump, the numbers she came up with were glaringly incorrect. "I'll be in touch," Danae gave her the standard interview brush-off.

"Could I interest you in an enchilada, Captain?" Idalis poked her head out of the kitchen.

Danae noted Idalis's spiky new haircut, streaked with orange, silver and blue, but refrained from commenting. "With chicken?"

"You're joking. The price of meat has quadrupled since the last time we docked here. I hope you enjoyed last night's pot roast, because we're vegan till the next port."

"Okay. Extra cheese, please." Danae set down with her cup and tried not to think about how long it would take to find three more dependable crewmembers. Every day the ship remained docked at Mars Station was an added expense to her shrinking funds. In a week, she would be dipping into the red. Two weeks, and they'd all have to get jobs in the city just to pay the port fees. Then there was still the problem of what to do with the four bodies in cold storage. *I can't even afford a decent coffin for Alex.*

I've got to find a charter, she thought. Finding passengers had been Alex's responsibility. With his charisma and sharp business sense, they'd been able to stay in the black even during lean times. Danae blinked back tears, determined not to let Idalis see her lose her composure. *How can I do this without him?*

And then she had a new thought, one that sent a wave of despair washing over her: *What's the point? It's just a job. It's just a way to earn money. I'm just wasting time until I die, -- just like everyone else in the universe.*

"Captain?" Idalis interrupted her reverie. She set a plate in front of Danae and appraised her with a concerned frown. "Are you okay?"

Danae forced a smile and picked up her fork. She took a bite of enchilada and chewed with exaggerated appreciation. "I'm fine; I've just got a lot on my mind today. Thanks for lunch."

Idalis looked unconvinced, but didn't press Danae for an explanation. She adjusted her apron and headed back to the kitchen.

* * *

Four down, one to go, Danae thought dejectedly as she rode the lift down to the street. Her last navigation interviewee was waiting. She took one look at him and her hopes sank. *Another drunk.* She sighed. *Well, let's get this over with.*

"Hello, I'm Captain Shepherd of the *Ishmael.*" She offered her hand to the rail-thin Indian. He was dressed in dirty jeans and a slightly-less-dirty denim shirt with frayed cuffs. He had a touch of gray in his black hair, heavy stubble on his chin, and a nervous care-worn look in his large, dark eyes. "You must be Mr. Ganguli?"

He shook her hand hesitantly. "Yes, Vipul Ganguli." He had a strong British accent. He dropped his eyes and spoke with humility: "I'm grateful you asked me for an interview, Captain. I must apologize for my appearance, but I was evicted from my flat three days ago."

"Really?" Danae tried to keep the skepticism out of her tone. "That's too bad. How did you get my message?"

"My ex-roommate was kind enough to leave a note with my belongings when he chucked them out on the sidewalk this morning." Same downcast expression, same subdued tone.

Danae was tempted to ask the reason for his eviction. *Drunk and disorderly*, she assumed. *Get over it; you're here to question his work skills, not his personal life.* "Tell me again about your navigation experience."

Ganguli's chin bobbed once. "I attended Oxford on a full scholarship, but that was many years ago. I have worked as a navigator for eight ships since then. My last employment was aboard the freighter *Elmina.* I resigned my position four weeks ago, and have been unemployed ever since."

"I don't suppose there's a chance I could speak to your former captain?"

As expected, Ganguli shook his head.

"Why did you resign?" Danae didn't like to venture into this line of questioning, but she needed more background information.

"It's personal," Ganguli confessed, his eyes on his tattered shoes. "I'm sorry."

Danae thought hard for a minute, debating whether to bring the soft-spoken Ganguli on board. In a case like this, where she had so little to go on, she had to rely on her instincts.

Surprisingly, her instincts were urging her to give him a chance. *Oxford educated, thousands of hours of shipboard experience, and there's no one else left to interview.* "Please come aboard, Mr. Ganguli, and we'll test your navigation skills. I assume you also have some helm experience."

A glimmer of hope shone in his eyes. "Thank you, Captain. And yes, I have served as a relief helmsman on many ships. I renewed my flight license six months ago."

On the bridge, Danae found Blaze flat on his back on the floor, his head and shoulders hidden beneath the com control board. His large right hand searched the assortment of tools spread out on the floor next to him. He grasped what he was trying to locate – a small fusion laser – and his hand vanished beneath the panel. Danae tried not to disturb him as she stepped over his long legs and led Ganguli to the navigation control board, to the left of the helm.

"Please have a seat," Danae indicated the navigator's chair.

He sat and looked over the keypads and multiple screens with a nod of approval. Danae stood off to the side and tapped a few buttons near the far-left screen, bringing up the sample jump she'd used for the other interviews.

Without a word, Ganguli went to work. His hands flew over the keys with confidence, and streams of numbers filled the screens. In the center screen, a white HD grid on a black background emerged and began rotating, showing different views of the projected course. Ganguli continued entering numbers until the grid froze. The jump calculations were complete, the math perfect.

Danae kept a neutral expression as Ganguli looked up expectantly. "How's this, Captain?"

"I'll let you know in a moment, Mr. Ganguli." Turning her head in Blaze's direction, she barked: "Engineer, do you have the com repaired yet?"

There was a *clunk* of a power tool hitting the floor tiles, and then a startled, somewhat muffled reply: "Yes, Captain. Shipboard com is working. Ship to shore com still needs a few adjustments."

"Thank you, Blaze; shipboard is all I need at the moment." Without looking at Ganguli, she shouted: "Ting!"

"Yes, Captain," came the resentful reply over the speaker.

Danae frowned. She'd probably awakened him from a nap. She made a mental note to lecture Marco about his late night bingeing before he went dirtside again. "I need you on the bridge."

"Yes, Captain." When Marco appeared in the doorway a few minutes later, he took one look at Ganguli and said, "He's okay, Captain."

"Don't you need to shake his hand or something?" Danae asked.

"No, Captain. This one oozes warmth." Marco rolled his eyes. "I could sense the peace and tranquility all over the ship."

Ganguli's expression was more perplexed than Blaze's had been that morning. "What's he talking about?"

Blaze wriggled out from under the com station, sat up, and wiped dust and perspiration from his brow. He eyed the other three with a bemused grin.

Danae raised her eyebrows at the engineer. "Tell him what that means, Blaze."

Blaze nodded. "I think it means 'you're hired'."

Ganguli still looked confused.

Danae allowed herself a grin. "Can you move in before dinner, Mr. Ganguli?"

A smile crossed Ganguli's dark face for the first time. "Yes, I can. Thank you, Captain."

* * *

Danae helped herself to a bowl from the counter, nodded to Idalis and Shima seated at the corner table, and sat down with her new employees at the center table. Blaze and Ganguli started to rise from their seats as a show of courtesy, but Danae gestured for them to remain seated.

"How's the tofu chili?" She glanced at their empty bowls.

"Excellent." Blaze finished up his last bite of cornbread.

"The best meal I've had in weeks," agreed the navigator.

Danae nodded and blew on a spoonful of Idalis' specialty. "I still need to hire a medic and a steward," she began without preamble, "so we might be here for a few more days; hopefully no longer than a week. I trust that you two are clever enough to orient yourselves to the layout of the ship." She glanced up at Blaze. "If you're not sure about something, ask Mr. Ganguli."

"Please call me Vipul."

Danae took a bite of her chili and continued as soon as her mouth was empty. "Okay then, Vipul, Blaze, here are your contracts." She reached into the large cargo pocket on her right thigh and drew out two datapads. She placed them on the table. "You've heard the saying, 'you can't get blood from a stone'?"

Each nodded warily and began to read the screen in front of him.

Danae gave them a few minutes, then explained, "Right now, *Ishmael*'s having some serious financial woes, as you can see from your nonexistent salaries. About the only thing I can offer you is room and board until we start pulling in some capital. All crew members get the same benefits, regardless of seniority," she cast Vipul an apologetic glance. "When business is good, everyone gets paid; when it's bad –" she shrugged and took another bite of chili.

"Considering that I was homeless before you hired me, Captain," Vipul said, "I find these terms very reasonable." He pressed his thumb to the screen.

Danae took the datapad from him and verified that Vipul Ganguli of Harrogate, Yorkshire, England, Earth, was exactly who he claimed to be. "You don't look 48."

Vipul's expression showed a hint of mirth she hadn't seen before. "Do you mean I look more like 68?"

Danae grinned. "I was going to say you look much younger than you did a few hours ago."

"I feel younger," Vipul admitted. "It's amazing how invigorating it is to be employed." ∕

Blaze pressed a thumb to his screen. "For this kind of job experience and," he glanced towards the kitchen, "home cookin', it'd be an honor to work for free, Captain."

Danae took Blaze's datapad and verified his information. "Robert Smith of Tulsa, Oklahoma. Welcome aboard, gentlemen. How tall are you?" she asked Blaze.

"Just shy of two meters. Why?"

"I think my late husband's uniforms will fit you." She glanced at Vipul. "I can't afford to visit the tailor's, so I'm afraid you'll have to borrow a few of Marco's uniforms for now."

"Of course," Vipul's response was gracious. "I understand."

"Unfortunately, I think they'll be baggy on you."

Vipul shrugged. "I'm used to that."

Danae ate a few more bites of chili, then pushed away from the table. "Come with me, Blaze." She climbed the ladder down to the second level, followed by the lanky engineer. As they headed down the passageway, she pointed out some of the details of the ship.

"I'm sure you've been aboard other passenger ships, but the *Ishmael* is unique from the shuttles still used on Earth. It's shaped like a bird, with the bridge, galley, and infirmary at the top level, like an oval-shaped head. If you get to see the exterior, you'll notice it even has a beak."

"So the three main levels are the bird's body," Blaze said. "Two levels of cabins make up the wings, the entry/airlock level is the belly, and the engines extend out the back like a tail."

Danae nodded, pleased that he'd already studied the schematics. "That's right."

Blaze grinned. "I assume this fowl has feet."

"The tripods are only extended for surface landings."

"What about elevators?"

"Just one on the starboard, but it's only for freight and passengers."

"Good thinkin'," Blaze said. "Climbin' the ladder all day should keep me in shape."

Danae grinned. She led Blaze past several numbered cabin doors on either side of the passageway. "There's a lounge at the end of each wing for both passengers and crew. She stopped in front of a door without a number engraved on it and pressed her thumb to the ID lock. "Come on in. I'll get Alex's clothes, – they're in the closet."

Danae's spartan cabin was the same size as all the others – a cozy three by four meters, – but hers was the only one with a window. Blaze was immediately drawn to the view. He looked out at the dazzling assortment of starships docked near the *Ishmael.*

Danae stepped over to the narrow door to the left of the head. *Don't think,* she chided herself, trying not to notice familiar details, like the smell of Alex's aftershave. She tried to keep her focus on the task at hand, tried not to remember the man who recently wore these uniforms.

But the tears came unbidden as she touched the silver-threaded *Ishmael* monogram on the collar of the first jumpsuit.

Danae cleared her throat as she quickly took out four uniforms and draped them over her arm. "I think these will be a good fit." She spoke without turning around as she pretended to examine the closet for more items. "What size shoes," she wiped her eyes on the back of her free hand, "do you wear?"

"Your husband was one of the crewmembers who died." It was not a question.

Although Blaze spoke with quiet respect, Danae felt a surge of anger. *It's none of your concern!* "Yes," she managed, swallowing hard to hold back a sob. "I'd rather not discuss –"

"I'm sorry, Captain. I didn't mean to upset you."

"I'm not upset," Danae lied. She tried desperately to regain her composure, but it was like trying to stop a flood. Shaking, she cleared her throat again to get rid of the lump that was threatening to choke her. "Maybe I should give you these later."

"Yes, ma'am." She heard him move to the door.

Danae turned slightly, trying to keep her face averted, and studied Blaze out of the corner of her eye. He was watching her

55

from the doorway. He looked so young, yet the expression on his face seemed to belong on a much older man.

"If you ever need someone to talk to, Captain --," he offered in his awkward but sincere way. Then he stepped into the passageway, and the door slid shut after him.

Danae sank to her knees. She pressed Alex's uniforms to her face and sobbed until she didn't have any tears left. Then she cried until she was too exhausted to get up from the floor and climb into the bed she once shared with her husband of six years. She fell asleep in the pile of uniforms.

* * *

Danae snuggled in Alex's strong arms. They were admiring her prominent belly and discussing names for their baby.

"Anything but Ishmael," Alex laughed, his dark brown eyes crinkling at the corners. Danae hoped their child would inherit his warm chocolate-brown complexion, perfect teeth, and sly sense of humor.

"Let's name him after you."

"Alex Junior?" he scoffed, grinning more broadly. "Only if we call him A.J."

"A.J. it is," Danae agreed, tears of joy in her eyes.

Danae awoke with eyes so swollen she could barely open them. There was no Alex lying next to her, no bulging belly, and there would never be an A.J.

Although she and Alex wanted to be parents, the reality of life aboard a ship was that fetuses did not fare well under the extreme conditions of weightlessness or the multiple G-forces during liftoffs and landings. After her one and only pregnancy ended in miscarriage, Danae had accepted the reality of childlessness. She and Alex had each other, and that was enough; life was good.

Now the reality of being a widow was enough to crush her desire to go on living. Danae couldn't even muster the energy to untangle herself from the nest of Alex's uniforms.

"Captain?" Shima's voice over the com was filled with concern.

Danae felt annoyed, and her throbbing headache didn't help. *Blaze better keep his mouth shut if he knows what's good for him.* "Sorry, I overslept," she tried to sound coherent. "Something wrong?"

"Just wanted to remind you that you have an interview at 7:00 a.m."

"Please inform whoever it is that I'll be down in five." Danae didn't even look at the clock as she climbed unsteadily to her feet and stepped into the head. She peeled off her uniform and stuffed it into the laundry chute. Then she closed the door to the chamber, hooked up her breathing tube, and let the ultrasonic blasts of hot water revive her.

The shower cut off after the standard 60 seconds and Danae stood there for a moment, dripping, with one hand wavering over the repeat button. She sighed with disappointment, hit the dry button instead and was out of the head a minute later. She stepped into a clean uniform, slapped an analgesic patch behind her left ear, covered her bloodshot eyes with sunglasses, and hurried to the ladder. Danae ran her fingers through her damp curls, and tried to compose her scattered thoughts on the elevator ride down.

The steward interviewee was tapping his foot impatiently as he leaned against the tramstop sign. He was an athletically-built dark-haired young man with a thin mustache and intense brown eyes. He straightened up and smiled when Danae stepped out of the lift.

Danae stuck out a hand. "Sorry I'm late, Mr. . . . .?"

"Jackson," he replied in a thick Jersey accent as he gripped her hand firmly. "Wade Jackson. That's okay -- Captain's prerogative, right?"

"Captain Shepherd of the *Ishmael.*"

Jackson laughed. "I can't believe it. I'm interviewing on Hugh's ship. I thought 'no way can there be more than one *Ishmael* docked at Mars'."

"You're a friend of Hugh's?" Danae suddenly felt overwhelmed with a sense of dread. Would she have to break the news to him?

"Only his best friend, – we went to high school together. I haven't seen Hugh in four years, but I remembered your name from his last Christmas card-transmission. It's nice to meet you, Captain. I hope you don't mind if I have a quick visit with Hugh after the interview. It'll be great to see him." Jackson beamed. "And it'd be great to work on board the same ship, of course."

Danae took a deep breath and motioned for Jackson to sit down on the nearby tramstop bench. "There's something I need to tell you."

FIVE
DR. JAKE

Jake scanned the crowded ER waiting room at Mars Community Hospital. *Can't they find a way to make these places run more efficiently?* He approached the triage desk and spoke to a huge Asian man in blood-stained scrubs who looked more like a Sumo wrestler than a nurse.

"Could you direct me to the chief resident?"

The Sumo-nurse gave him a condescending glare. "You don't look sick or injured to me."

"I'm looking for a job." Jake tried to sound confident.

"Try the employment center, moron."

Jake turned away; he was getting nowhere with this line of inquiry. He'd visited all five of the biosphere's hospitals and 12 of its 15 fire stations over the past two days, and had been unable to locate a doctor, administrator, or paramedic trainer who would give him 10 seconds of their time. "Employment center," was the typical brusque response, and when he offered to work as a volunteer, they laughed at him.

Do I really want to be a doctor? He racked his brain for a new approach. He wished he had a tiny portion of Lorina's talent. *She would've landed a residency at the first hospital. That girl could coax a banana away from a starving chimp.*

As Jake walked slowly towards the exit, he noticed a handwritten sign tacked below the information terminal: *Outreach Clinic.* Beneath this was an arrow pointing left. He glanced back over his shoulder to make sure the Sumo nurse wasn't watching before heading across the waiting room in the direction indicated.

Around the corner from the ER was a curtained treatment area with another handwritten *Outreach Clinic* sign safety-pinned to the lime-green Indestructa fabric. Jake wondered if he would get tossed out by a security android, but decided, *what the heck,* and pulled back the curtain.

He found himself in a makeshift waiting room with six unoccupied folding chairs. Behind an old-fashioned steel desk to Jake's left sat a linebacker-sized man of indeterminate age with wavy blond hair so pale it was practically white. He wore a doctor's lab coat with a medical scanner in the breast pocket.

The doctor glanced up from a stack of datapads. "Can I help you?"

"I'm interested in learning about your clinic," Jake replied. He'd decided this was a better approach than, "I'm looking for a job."

The doctor smiled and stood up, offering his hand. "I'm Erik Sorensen, the doctor in charge of this pitiful organization."

Jake shook his huge hand. "Jake O'Brien, medical student."

"Really?" Sorensen grinned. "How did you manage that?"

Jake decided to be honest with the first genuinely friendly person he'd met since arriving on Mars Station. "I didn't. I'm two semesters short of that goal. Syracuse just went bankrupt, so here I am, scrounging for a way to get into med school."

Sorensen nodded and indicated for Jake to pull up a chair. "I know how you feel. I transferred from school to school, trying to stay ahead of the college closings. For grad school, I attended a different college every semester. My transcript is eight pages long."

Jake felt himself start to relax. "So is it always this quiet around here?"

Sorensen laughed and leaned back in his chair; the metal joints squeaked loudly in protest. "This is the calm before the storm. I see most cases after 5:00 p.m. This is the only clinic on the station that serves the homeless. Did you know that half the street population is under 13-years-old? I started the Outreach Clinic three years ago by convincing the administration that this was the best way to give the residents training in pediatrics."

"Don't the residents see children normally?" Jake asked, intrigued.

Sorensen raised his thick blond eyebrows at Jake. "Have you seen any children around Mars Station, Mr. O'Brien?"

Startled, Jake had to think about it for a moment. "A few. Is there a shortage?"

"This hospital delivers, at most, two babies a month. Yeah, you could say there's a shortage of children here."

Jake's jaw dropped. "I didn't realize the damage on Earth had such far-reaching effects."

"Believe it," Sorensen grimaced. "I worked in infertility for three years. The success rate for Earth-born couples is 0%." He picked up a datapad and pushed it across the desk to Jake. "Which brings us back to the subject of street kids."

Jake glanced at the datapad: *Fourteen-year-old healthy Mars-born female presented for counseling services. Three couples have approached her and offered up to two million credits if she would be a surrogate mother for them. She doesn't know what to do.* Jake realized his mouth was still hanging open; he shut it.

"Mars-born kids are hot commodities," Sorensen explained. "They're the last generation, and everyone here knows it. Street kids deal daily with a barrage of ruthless schemes designed to exploit them. This young woman's file is typical of the kids I see – when I can convince them to come in for treatment. The Outreach Clinic is a feeble attempt to keep these young people from becoming extinct."

Jake nodded. He studied the datapad, thinking hard. "Could I do anything to help?"

Sorensen nodded. "I would love some help. I've been flying solo for a long time. Occasionally, I can persuade a nurse to assist when I'm swamped, but the rest of the hospital staff won't give this place a second glance. I don't have anything in the budget." He waved his large hands, indicating their curtained surroundings. "This and the one exam room just behind me is the entire clinic. I have to beg, borrow, and steal from the ER for medications and supplies. I go out on my own time to talk to kids in McConnell Park and Mother Teresa's Juvenile Shelter. It's depressing, dangerous, thankless work. If you really want to help, it would have to be on a volunteer basis."

"I'm not qualified to treat patients," Jake said, "but I'm willing to help full-time, gratis." He smiled, thinking what Lorina would say. "Maybe we could help each other."

"I see where you're going." Sorensen nodded. "I don't suppose you have your transcript with you?"

Jake dug the compact HD out of his pocket and handed it across the desk. Sorensen fed it to a datapad and reviewed it for a minute. "Your grades are excellent. You'd be a top candidate for any medical school."

"If any were still in business."

Sorensen looked him in the eye. "I'd say you're more than qualified for a residency – wouldn't you, Dr. O'Brien?"

Jake stopped breathing. *Dr. O'Brien – I like the sound of that.* "I don't know how you'd get me approved by the administration. I didn't finish my premed, and I certainly don't have any medical school experience under my belt. And what about the malpractice insurance? I wouldn't want to jeopardize your organization, or your medical license, Dr. Sorensen."

"You can call me Erik -- since we're going to be working together. As you're a *volunteer*, I don't think we'll have a problem. I don't have to get volunteers approved by the uptight old farts who run this place. And you don't have to worry about the insurance because we don't need it. Homeless people never sue." He grinned. "Come to think of it, nobody ever sues because nobody can afford a lawyer."

Jake smiled. "Sounds like you've got all the angles covered. When do I start?"

"Now." Erik got to his feet. "Let's find some scrubs for you and see if we can borrow a scanner. It's the weekend, and I'm expecting a big crowd."

* * *

"Thanks for leaving a message with Genevieve last night. I was starting to worry." Lorina was in her long T-shirt nightgown, chopping carrots and potatoes and putting them into a slow cooker – her latest acquisition for their meager kitchen, which so far consisted of the hotel's tiny refrigerator, a cutting board, an electric skillet, and an assortment of canned foods and cooking utensils. The dresser top served as the food prep area.

Jake propped himself on an elbow and rubbed the sleep from his eyes. "I feel like a tram ran over me."

"How was your first evening as a resident?" Lorina glanced over her shoulder at him as she started to chop an onion.

"Rough. I've never seen so many pitiful-looking children in my life. Tiny children – with no one to take care of them. One little boy – he was six – brought in his three-year-old brother. No parents to speak of."

"What kind of treatments did they need?" Lorina asked.

"Mostly antibiotics for infections, but we also treated for lice, broken bones, viruses, and dehydration. It's no wonder their cuts get infected, – they're filthy. I thought nothing could smell worse than a cadaver. I was wrong."

"Water is scarce here," she reminded him. "I'm sure the street kids have a difficult time just finding enough water to drink."

Jake nodded. "I asked Erik if we could give each of them a bath, but he said even the patients with credit flashes don't have that luxury."

"What do you do with the more serious cases?"

"We sent one 11-year old Venus-born boy upstairs to oncology," Jake admitted. "Skin cancer. It's actually a common condition for kids born on Venus."

Lorina nodded and added the onions to the slow cooker.

"Erik told me he'll occasionally see a child who needs immediate surgery, and the hospital will take them so the surgical residents can have someone to practice on."

"That sounds barbaric."

"It's not. The residents don't see many children, so they're extra careful with the ones they treat. The ER sends us anyone who doesn't have an address. They don't want to deal with the homeless, even though they seem to be a large part of Mars' population. What are you making?"

"Vegetable soup. " She added cans of green beans and stewed tomatoes to the mixture.

"No meat?" Jake flopped back onto his pillow. "I'm dying for a steak."

"Beef bouillon cubes is the best I can do." Lorina set the lid on the pot. "This will be ready any time you want to eat. I need to get to work."

"Do you have to wear that?" Jake glanced at the frilly apron and bright pink dress on her bed.

Lorina frowned. "Well, at least it will save on laundry. What about you? What do you have to wear to work?"

"I can borrow scrubs from the ER staff supplies. There's only one thing I need to invest in: a medical scanner."

"How much?" Lorina frowned, gathering up her uniform and heading to the bathroom to change.

"48,000," Jake whispered.

Lorina gasped and turned slowly to stare at him. "You really have to buy one?"

Jake nodded. "Erik and I can see a lot more patients if we both have scanners." He studied the troubled expression on his cousin's face. "Too much money?"

Lorina shook her head. "Nah, it's about what I'd expect." She studied the ruffle on her apron.

"What is it?" Jake asked.

"I was just wondering if it would be possible for me to register at Mars College," she admitted. "But I guess it's out of the question now. Our funds will soon be gone."

Jake felt a surge of guilt. "Of course you should start school. I'll make do without a scanner."

Lorina shook her head. "No, let's be realistic. After I went one semester, then what?"

"Then we'd sell the wedding bands, and my datapad."

Lorina shook her head. "We're looking at two semesters, at most, before our funds are gone. It won't work, Jake."

"I could get a job, too."

"How long did you work at the clinic yesterday?" Lorina asked.

Jake could see he was losing this argument. "From about 4:00 in the afternoon until 4:30 – this morning."

"If you get a job, when are you planning to sleep?"

"On my days off."

"Which would be when?"

Jake pursed his lips. "The clinic is open seven days a week."

"Vacation time?"

"The homeless don't get vacations." Jake shrugged. "Erik told me that."

"He sounds like a saint."

"He is," Jake sighed. As Lorina retreated to the bathroom, he promised himself that as soon as he had his medical license, he would pay for every penny of her college education.

* * *

Jake wasn't sure how much he liked the sink-or-swim method of practicing medicine, but Erik seemed to have confidence in his fledgling skills. His mentor would show him a procedure – once –, and the next time he was on his own. Fortunately, Jake's patients had a limited list of complaints, so far. Re-attaching a severed toe had been his worst case.

He preferred to assist Erik with procedures, but most nights they were too busy to work together, so one would do triage in the waiting area while the other did treatments in the exam room. Jake quickly learned how to multitask. He became adept at jotting notes on a datapad with his right hand while using the new scanner with his left. Occasionally, he put down both tools to use his hands, though he still considered himself a novice at treating the living.

"Just give a holler if you need any help," Erik advised when it was time for Jake's shift as doctor. Jake was tempted to buy a rosary, so he could pray that he wouldn't kill anybody with his incompetence.

"You're hurting me," complained his latest patient, a tiny boy named Adi.

Jake relaxed his grip on the three-year-old's finger splint. "Sorry. We're almost ready to put it under the ray." He glanced over at Adi's caretaker, his seven-year old sister Tirza, who was monitoring his progress with a mistrustful scowl on her filthy face. "So who takes care of you?" Jake asked her.

"Nobody," Tirza snapped.

"Where are your parents?"

"Mom – I don't know. Dad's dead," the child replied, matter-of-factly.

Troubled, Jake turned his attention back to Adi's finger. "Okay, now we're going to put your hand under the blue light for about five minutes, and your finger will be as good as new." He hooked up the small subcutaneous fusion laser and held it over Adi's hand. "Hold still."

"Tickles." Adi watched the indigo light with great interest as he held surprisingly still for one so young.

When Jake switched off the device, he asked, "How's that? Can you wiggle your finger?"

"Yeah," Adi demonstrated, "but it still hurts a little." He squirmed to get down from the exam table.

"It hurts because you broke it in two places, and your nerve endings haven't figured out its fixed already." Jake knew the explanation was lost on Adi, but he always felt like talking after treating a homeless child. The habit seemed to be a subconscious attempt to keep them off the streets for a few more minutes. Helplessness was an emotion Jake had to battle several times a night.

Jake was reluctant to let Adi and Tirza go back to the streets, but his options were limited. Since there were no family or foster care services on Mars Station, homeless children were left on their own to survive. But there was one thing he could do.

"When was the last time you ate?"

"We don't need your help," Tirza said.

Adi turned his big sad eyes towards his sister. "I'm hungry, Tirza."

Jake was quick to head off a potential sibling spat by speaking to Tirza in a submissive tone. "I was just about to take a break and get a tofu dog from a vendor out front. How about just a tofu dog for your little brother since he's been so brave?"

He could see that Tirza was wavering, torn between her desire to keep up the tough act and her basic need to look after Adi and herself. Jake couldn't imagine the enormous pressure she must have felt to keep them both alive. *She's seven, going on 20.*

"Okay, just one tofu dog," Tirza declared magnanimously, like a queen granting a petition to a lowly commoner.

"Okay, come on." Jake led them outside the ER's front doors. He bought each child two tofu dogs, fully loaded, plus bottles of juice and apples to eat later.

"Be careful," he called as they scampered off down the dark street without looking back.

"You can't keep feeding them," Erik murmured as he escorted Jake's next patient into the treatment area and handed him a datapad.

"I have to do something." But Jake knew his mentor was right. He felt guilty averaging 500 credits a night on vendor food while Lorina was trying so hard to save what little money they had left. But he also knew she'd do the exact same thing if she were in his shoes.

Jake took out his scanner and examined his next patient: a nervous-looking toothpick-thin Jamaican girl named Sina.

"I'm sick," Sina said, fidgeting with the hem of her ragged dress.

"I can see why you'd feel that way." Jake frowned at the reading on his scanner. "You're pregnant."

Sina made a soft noise and her dark eyes filled with tears. "I guess that's why I can't keep nothin' down."

"How old are you?" Jake asked, hoping the information on the datapad was a mistake.

"Twelve." It was no mistake.

Jake felt a little sick himself. *Erik wasn't kidding when he said this was a depressing job.* "Well, Sina, I think we need to talk to you about your options. Could you stick around for a few minutes and talk to Dr. Sorensen?"

The girl was crying openly now. Jake helped her down from the exam table and seated her in a chair in the corner. He handed her a tissue and his brown-bag lunch. She shook her head no, refusing the food, but he insisted.

"Eat the sandwich slowly. You'll feel better if you keep something in your stomach." *At least, that was the advice Mom gave Deborah when she was pregnant with Catherine.* Jake sighed inwardly and made notes on the datapad. *I'm such a rookie! They don't teach you any of this stuff in college.*

Jake observed Sina out of the corner of his eye until she finally took a few hesitant bites of his peanut butter sandwich. Then he poked his head into the waiting area and told Erik, "I need some big-time help with this one."

The experienced medic glanced at the one adult and three children who were waiting in chairs. Jake knew Erik was mentally assessing their needs. Prioritizing patient care was Jake's least-favorite duty.

"Okay," Erik said. "You sit out here for 10 minutes and feed the mainframe."

Jake slumped into the desk chair, grateful for a break. He inserted a datapad into the notebook computer on the desk, instantly downloading the information. He withdrew the cleared datapad and was just about to insert the next one when the curtains flew open and someone started shouting:

"Help him! Help him! He's been shot!"

Two young men swarmed into the waiting area, supporting a third teenager between them who was bleeding heavily from a bullet wound to the abdomen. All three were dressed in torn jeans and matching black T-shirts with *Daggers* printed across the chest in white letters. The children in the waiting area began screaming at the sight of so much blood.

"We're not equipped for this! Take him to the ER!" Jake bolted out of his chair, fumbled for his scanner.

"We can't, – we're homeless," explained one of the ragged young men. They hauled the injured boy over to Jake and laid him out on the desk, scattering datapads onto the floor.

"Not here, not here," Erik was already next to him, taking charge, -- to Jake's relief. "Take him in there." He drew back the curtain and ushered the motley group into the exam room, where young Sina was cowering in the corner. "Get her out of here, Jake."

Jake's head was spinning as he grabbed Sina's arm and ushered her back to the waiting area. "Don't look," he advised, but it was too late; she saw the blood on the young man and the floor and started to retch.

Jake wrapped an arm around her skinny waist and half-carried her down the hall to the ladies' room. "Stay here, take your time. We'll talk to you after we deal with this emergency." He sprinted back to the exam room, hoping fervently that she'd wait to see Erik. All too often children disappeared before they could finish treatment or get counseling.

He wasn't surprised to see that the waiting room had been abandoned. Jake tugged on sterile gloves as he rushed to assist Erik. "We're not equipped to handle this, – are we?"

Dr. Sorensen was calmly spraying Hemorrhage Freeze over the wound. The young man on the exam table was already in the early stages of shock, shivering and nearly unconscious from blood loss. "Start an IV, Jake."

Jake's hands were shaking as he worked with Erik to stabilize the teen.

"We've got to get the bullet out," Erik muttered, peering into the wound.

Jake glanced over at the two gang members who had brought in their friend. They were standing to the side, watching intently with chalk-white faces. "Do you guys want to wait outside?"

"Is he going to die?" one asked. He looked very young, not even old enough to shave.

"I don't know," Jake answered honestly. He turned back to the patient.

Erik said, "Jake, go down to the ER and steal two liters of type O synthblood."

"Steal?" Jake gaped at him. "Aren't the synthblood supplies under DNA locks?"

Erik swore uncharacteristically and gestured for Jake to take over. "I'll be right back."

Jake felt a moment of pure panic, but fought to keep a straight face for his two observers. He watched the monitors and prayed that the young man wouldn't go into cardiac arrest while Erik was gone.

Erik was back in two minutes with the synthblood. Jake started the transfusion in the boy's free arm, grateful for the precision needle which ignored his shaking hands and found the vein for him.

Jake noticed that the two young men hadn't moved. "What's his name?"

"Lucky," answered the one with a big scar under his left eye.

"How did Lucky get shot?" Erik demanded, inserting a micro-size probe android into the wound.

"A CIP shot him," scar replied.

Jake thought he misheard. He watched the android's progress on the monitor. "Why would a CIP shoot a homeless kid?"

"I don't know. Maybe he thought we was tryin' to steal somethin'," scar said.

Erik shook his head and said, "Quiet, please." A few moments later, the probe latched onto the 7mm bullet and was easing it to the surface of Lucky's belly.

"I guess he really is *lucky*." Jake took a new scan. "The bullet missed his stomach, and the intestinal damage can be easily repaired. He'll live."

"Let's get him upstairs to surgery," Erik said. "Call Dr. Wharton, – he owes me a favor."

Jake stripped off his blood-slicked gloves and stepped into the waiting room to make the call. "Wharton, please. Surgery," he told the hospital's android operator.

"One moment, sir."

The com on the other end was ringing when a muscular CIP officer in a black military uniform stepped up to the desk. He crossed his arms over his broad chest and in a gruff voice said, "I'm looking for a young gang member with a gunshot wound."

"I'll be right with you, sir," Jake said, not looking up at the man's face.

"This is Wharton," said a deep voice in Jake's ear.

"I said," the CIP's tone grew colder, "where is the boy with the gunshot wound?" He leaned over and stabbed a large index finger down on the com, severing the connection.

"Hey!" Jake's chin snapped upwards. "I said, *sir*, I'll be right with you!" His adrenaline was still racing from the emergency. He felt like throwing out the arrogant officer with his bare hands.

"Do you know who I am?" the CIP asked, narrowing his eyes at Jake. He was very pale, with cold blue eyes and a brown crew cut streaked with silver.

Jake had to mentally count to 10 to bring his anger down enough to answer the officer. He unclenched his fists and stared him down. "The young man you want is in critical condition," he said, ignoring the question. "You can't see him now."

The CIP swore at him and slammed both fists down on the desk. He leaned close to Jake and shouted in his face: "I don't have time for this! Listen closely, doctor: I am the law in this town! You do not harbor a criminal from Hunter Acheron unless you want to share a cell with him! Now you tell me where that punk is right now!"

Jake didn't even blink. He had already weighed his choices and, opting to skip jail, decided a lie was in order. "He's worse than critical, he's dead."

A nasty sneer curled onto Acheron's lips. Jake felt a moment of panic, afraid he would ask to see the body, but the CIP's earcom distracted him. Acheron listened to a report in his left ear with a faraway scowl on his face.

"Take them both into custody. I'm on my way." He returned his focus to Jake. "What about the two punks who brought him in?"

"They didn't stick around long enough to see him die," Jake said, hoping the man wouldn't notice the fresh beads of perspiration on his forehead.

Acheron's posture relaxed. He nodded and uncurled his own fists. "What did you say your name was, doctor? You're new around here, aren't you?"

"O'Brien. Yeah, I'm new."

"You look awfully young to be a doctor."

Jake didn't care to comment.

"Where's Sorensen?"

"Sending the body down to the morgue."

Acheron moved away from the desk. As he turned to leave the waiting area, he looked over his shoulder at Jake. "You watch yourself, Dr. O'Brien. These street gangs are made up of dangerous criminals and should be turned over to me. Even if they come in here half-dead, you call the CIPs first. Understand?"

"Yes, sir," Jake lied with as straight a face as he could manage.

The officer was gone.

Jake's knees were shaking as he sank into the desk chair and picked up the com again. "Wharton, please. Surgery."

Erik stepped through the curtain and appraised Jake with a grim expression.

Jake just shook his head and made arrangements with Wharton to send Lucky upstairs. When he hung up, Erik said quietly, "I would have done the same thing, Jake, but you took a huge risk. I thought I was going to have to ask Lucky to play dead."

"I know, and I'm sorry. It was the first thing I could think of." Jake nodded to Lucky's friends as they filed out. "Something about that guy just seems so . . . *evil.* I had a feeling that if I turned Lucky over to him, he really would turn up dead."

"Acheron's probably the one who shot him," Erik said. "He's a law unto himself. Whatever you do, don't cross him or you'll end up in jail on trumped-up charges of obstructing justice."

"It sounds like you speak from experience."

"I do." Erik stripped off his gloves and tossed them into the trash. "Acheron has a real narrow view of homeless people. He thinks they're nuisances. I think he actually believes they *choose* to be homeless. His personal mission is to get them off the streets any way he can."

"I guess you have to be human to realize that the homeless are people, too." Jake sat upright, realizing he had forgotten about Sina in all the excitement. He dashed off to the ladies' room, leaving Erik to clean up Lucky's mess.

"Sina?" he knocked on the bathroom door.

There was no answer.

Jake tried the door and found it unlocked. The cubicle was empty. Sina had disappeared into the night.

* * *

It was almost 6:00 a.m. when Jake caught a tram back to the Marriott. He was physically and emotionally exhausted and just wanted to sleep. When he opened the door to Room 1115, he found the lights on.

"Lorina? Are you up already?"

No answer; the bathroom door was closed. He turned off some of the lamps and headed to bed.

And found someone lying in it, asleep.

"What the --?"

A pair of large brown eyes popped open and a small, dark-skinned child sat up and appraised him warily. As near as Jake could determine, the emaciated waif was Indian and female, probably no more than five years old. Her long black hair was a tangled mass of knots and she was wearing one of his T-shirts, which hung off her bony shoulders like a cape.

"Lorina!"

His cousin emerged from the bathroom in her nightgown. "Don't scare her. And don't worry, I gave her a bath."

"What's she doing here?" Jake leaned a little closer, peering suspiciously at the child's hair. "She's got lice. You're letting a kid with lice sleep in my bed?"

Lorina laughed and sat down next to the child who was starting to eye him nervously. "Her name's Niyati, I think. She speaks Hindi, Punjabi, Bengali, – I don't know, take your pick. Niyati," she pointed to her cousin, "this is Jake."

"Jek," Niyati tried to mimic Lorina. She grinned at him with a mouth full of decayed baby teeth.

"Close enough," Jake sighed.

"I'll change your sheets," Lorina said, "as soon as you go down to the drugstore and buy her a lice treatment kit and a toothbrush."

"It would be cheaper to shave her head and buy a hat," Jake said, still irked. "Why is she here? Where did she come from?"

"She's been living out of the dumpsters in the alley. I've been smuggling food to her for weeks, trying to gain her confidence. She was really timid, so I guess someone's hurt her before, but she finally decided to trust me. Last night I hid her in my housekeeper's cart and brought her up here."

Jake took out his medical scanner. "We can't keep her, Lorina. Taking in a child isn't like adopting a stray cat, you know. We can't just leave her a bowl of water and a litter box while we go off to work."

"Don't you think I know that?"

Jake paused, noting the edge to her tone. "I know you mean well, but we really can't keep her. There's a shelter for juveniles near my hospital. We should take her there." He frowned at the readings on the scanner. "She's dangerously malnourished, and she's got intestinal parasites, infected sores --"

"She's just a little girl, Jake. She needs someone to take care of her. Children shouldn't have to live like feral animals. What if she was Catherine? Would you leave your own niece on the streets?"

"Don't you think I know how you feel?" Jake argued. "I see 30 homeless kids at the clinic every night. Don't you think I want to do something besides patch them up and send them back to the streets? I know they need someone to take care of them, but Erik told me most people don't want to adopt street kids, -- they want babies, preferably newborns."

"That's just wrong, -- when there are so many in need."

"I know it is, and I'm sorry, -- but there's nothing we can do about it, given our small living space and limited budget."

Niyati had been observing their heated debate with concern. She looked to Lorina and burst into tears.

"Okay, it's okay, honey." Lorina gathered the sobbing child in her arms.

"Careful," Jake said, "you're going to catch her lice."

Lorina gave him a cold look.

Jake groaned and admitted defeat. "Okay, I'll go down and buy a lice kit, but we're taking her to the juvenile shelter as soon as I treat her at the clinic."

Lorina's dour expression changed into a triumphant grin. "Thank you, Jake."

Jake bought three lice kits in case he and Lorina inherited the pests. He winced as the android cashier deducted 750 from his credit flash. Back in the hotel, he took a cooperative Niyati into the bathroom and sat her on the sink counter. He wrapped her hair in the smelly purple plastic bag and hooked it up to the hair dryer. Five minutes later, the lice and nits were eradicated.

"You might want to cut her hair," he suggested to Lorina as he threw the treatment bag into the trash.

Lorina finished changing the sheets on his bed. She came into the bathroom and gave Niyati a big smile. "No problem. I'll cut it in here with the door shut so you can get some sleep."

Jake nodded and started to step out, but then his conscience nagged at him. "I should tell you I've been feeding some of the kids I see at the clinic. I've spent quite a bit."

Lorina nodded. "I've been spending most of my money on food, too. How much do you have left?"

"34,000. How about you?"

Lorina grimaced. "What have you been feeding them? I'm down to 7,500, and I just got my first paycheck yesterday."

Jake scratched the stubble on his chin. "We can't keep this up, you know, or we're going to become homeless ourselves."

"I know." Lorina looked as troubled as he felt.

"Let's see if we can get Niyati a space at Mother Teresa's. At least she'll get fed there."

Lorina nodded, looking unconvinced. She got out her scissors, and Jake went to bed.

He lay awake for a long time, his mind and emotions still in turmoil over Lucky and the CIP chief, Hunter Acheron.

SIX
IMPRESSIONS

Blaze Smith spent most of his time tinkering; he was thoroughly enjoying himself. During his first full day aboard the ship, he worked 14 hours straight. When he wasn't working on *Ishmael*'s engines, he was doing minor repairs on things the other crewmembers pointed out to him. Idalis, in particular, kept finding things that needed his attention in the galley.

8:00 a.m.: "Blaze, I don't think the refrigerator is set at the right temperature."

2:30 p.m.: "Blaze, the android isn't cleaning the silverware very well. I think it needs an adjustment."

4:14 p.m.: "Blaze, taste the spaghetti sauce and tell me if it needs more basil."

Okay, I don't have to be a rocket scientist – or even an engineer – to figure this out. Blaze was flattered that Idalis was interested in him, but he was too fond of his new job to respond to her not-so-subtle overtures. *Shipboard romances: bad idea.*

Blaze didn't consider himself much of a prize. *Too tall, too skinny, too awkward, big nose,* was his general assessment of himself, so he wasn't sure how to handle Idalis' attentions. He was courteous to her, and refused to let his eyes wander to the front of her uniform, which was unbuttoned conspicuously low. Nor did he let his gaze linger on her wild hair-do and heavy makeup. Blaze preferred women whose flirtations were subtle – not that he could remember the last time a woman had flirted with him. He decided there was nothing subtle about Idalis Sanchez. *How do you tactfully tell a girl, 'you're trying too hard'?*

9:00 p.m.: "Blaze, the android is acting up again."

"I'll stop by in the morning' if I can," Blaze replied. "I'm doin' an important diagnostic right now." He leaned against the port solar engine access panel and tightened a screw that didn't need to be tightened. *Well, I could be working on something important,* he thought, embarrassed to be making up excuses to avoid her.

"Okay, tomorrow then." He could picture the disappointed pout on her neon orange lips. "As soon as you have a minute."

"Blaze, could you take a look at the HD on my main screen?" Vipul's calm baritone broke in moments after Idalis signed off. "The shading seems to be distorted."

Blaze grinned, pleased to have some legitimate work to do. "I'm on it."

On the bridge, Blaze wriggled underneath the navigation console and examined the circuitry with a handlight. "Yeah, I see a loose connection." He blew some dust away from his face and made the adjustment. "How's that?"

"Much better, thanks," Vipul replied. "I thought, 'if this doesn't work, I'd better get my old eyes examined'."

Blaze squirmed out from under the tight space and wiped his forehead on the cuff of his borrowed uniform. "Would you like to go dirtside tomorrow evenin' and get some Indian food?"

Vipul's eyes were fixed on his main screen. "Trying to avoid our lovely cook?"

Blaze flushed. Even though the navigator was twice his age, the two newcomers had formed a bond. Vipul was quiet, but he was observant. *Maybe too observant,* Blaze thought wryly.

When Blaze didn't reply, Vipul glanced over at him. He did an admirable job of not gloating. "I know a good place, but it'll have to be your treat, mate; my credit flash is worthless."

"First payday, you owe me dinner," Blaze agreed, climbing to his feet.

"Shall we see if Marco wants to join us?" Vipul asked casually, studying the screen again.

Blaze was caught off-guard by the suggestion and floundered for a tactful reply. "Well, I guess, if you really want to invite him . . ." Then he caught Vipul's eye and realized the navigator was kidding. "Whew," he blew out an exaggerated sigh of relief, "for a minute, I thought you were serious!"

Vipul laughed. "See you tomorrow, Blaze."

"Goodnight."

Blaze descended the ladder to the third level. As he headed down the starboard passageway towards his cabin, he decided to stop by the lounge at the end of his wing. He wanted to take in the view from the huge picture windows before retiring to his windowless quarters.

Each of *Ishmael's* triangle-shaped lounges was equipped with lots of comfy seating, a large-screen holo-vid theater/entertainment system, and a snack bar. A row of window seats spanned one corner, forming an inviting V-shape beneath the long windows. Stored beneath the synthleather seat cushions were lots of old-fashioned board games, a vast collection of books in dozens of languages, and an assortment of toys suitable for toddlers to preteens. Space travel was purported to be boring, at least for the passengers; Blaze suspected that he would be too busy to be bored once the ship lifted.

The lights were off in the lounge and Blaze groped his way across the room to the tip of the V, which was a good spot for stargazing. He slumped into a window seat and admired the glistening dome of Mars Station just below the *Ishmael*. He did a double take when he realized Shima was sitting across from him, nearly invisible in the shadows.

"*Hu jambo.* Sorry, I didn't mean to intrude."

"You know Swahili?" Shima shifted her position on the window seat; Blaze could now see her face in profile, silhouetted against the dim glow of the station behind her.

"Just a few words," Blaze said. "My older brother served a two-year mission in Kenya, and I picked up some Swahili from him."

A half-smile tugged at Shima's full lips. "What else do you know besides 'hello'?"

"I think I remember that *heshima* means respect, and *rafiki* means friend." Blaze shrugged. "That's about the extent of my vocabulary."

"Not bad," Shima said. "Your Swahili is better than my Spanish."

Blaze started to get up. "You probably want to be alone –"

"No, you are welcome here. Please stay and tell me more about yourself. Did your brother serve a religious mission?"

Blaze settled back against the cushions. "It was a long time ago, before the war."

"Was he like one of the fellows I saw riding everywhere on bikes when I was a child? The ones with the white shirts and ties?"

"Yeah." Blaze felt a pang of sadness. "David was one of those guys. He was drafted right when he got home."

"Where is home for you?" Shima asked.

"Tulsa, Oklahoma – heard of it? What about you?"

"Kampala, Uganda – heard of it?" She had a soft, musical laugh. "Do you have family in Oklahoma, Blaze?"

"Not anymore."

"I am sorry," Shima murmured.

Though he wasn't much for long conversations, Blaze suddenly felt a real need to talk about his family. He took a deep breath and went on: "I had three older brothers. I was the surprise baby. My next oldest brother was nine – almost 10 – when I was born, so you can imagine what a shock it was to them when I came along."

"I was also the youngest," Shima said. "I had six older sisters."

Blaze whistled. "Six?"

"Yes, and we all shared the same room."

"That's hard for me to imagine. I was in third grade when my brothers were drafted. That was the last time I saw them."

"That must have been very difficult for you. Your poor parents."

Blaze felt a lump in his throat. "It was too much for my mom to handle. When all three were reported Missing and Presumed Dead after the Battle of London, she committed suicide."

"I am sorry," Shima whispered.

Blaze nodded, acknowledging her sympathy, and continued: "It was just my father and me for a long time. Then I went away to college, and he was alone. I didn't realize he was sick until right after I started grad school. I was home for Christmas break and noticed he was thin and vomitin' a lot. I quit school and came home to take care of him until he died of leukemia. I sold the house and caught the first shuttle to Mars. So that's the story of my life. Tell me yours."

Shima was quiet for a few minutes. Blaze finally broke the silence. "I'm sorry. You don't have to tell me, if it makes you uncomfortable."

"No. It is good to share our histories since we are going to be working together. I have not had anyone to talk to since . . ." her voice trailed off. She sighed and took a drink from the mug in her hand before continuing.

"My four oldest sisters were married. Their husbands fought in the war. When my sisters were widowed, they moved back home. My family banded together to conserve resources and take care of my sisters' children. I never had a room of my own," Shima explained. "I am not accustomed to so much privacy here on the *Ishmael*."

"How did you end up here?" Blaze asked.

"Well, that is a long story," Shima said. "I was content staying home to help care for my nieces and nephews. Our house was crowded, but there was so much love."

Blaze nodded attentively.

"But there was not so much food. As you know, Africa is not the most fertile nation on Earth. A century of civil wars, famine, and diseases have left the land completely barren."

"I'm sure the chemical weapons didn't help conditions," Blaze said. "How did you survive?"

Shima paused, her voice grew husky. "Near the end of the war, people were dying of starvation by the thousands in Kampala. My family decided to pool all their resources. 'We cannot just give up and die,' my mother said, 'we must send the children to Mars Station.' My father sold the house and everything of value on the black market. Then we had a family meeting, and my father put the names of the children into a bowl. He drew two names. Two tickets were all we could afford."

"He drew your name?" Blaze was stunned.

Shima nodded and wiped her eyes on the back of her hand. "Just me and my seven-year-old niece Zuri. I was 16 – barely old enough to be Zuri's guardian. We flew to Johannesburg and took a shuttle here, bringing nothing with us but the clothes on our backs.

"I took the last of the money to the employment center, and was fortunate to be hired right away. I got a job at a nursing home, cleaning rooms. The manager let me bring Zuri to work so I did not have to find someone to watch her. But we had no place to live. We slept in McConnell Park with the other homeless."

Shima snorted, suddenly angry. "It is ironic that the African people are always refugees, no matter which planet they live on."

"Where is Zuri now?" Blaze asked.

There was a long pause, then Shima began to sniffle quietly. "Zuri and I became ill one night. We both felt weak, and I remember I could not keep my eyes open. When I woke up late the next morning, she was gone."

"Gone? Where?"

"I do not know. There are many dangerous people on the streets who lure children away during the night. I was weak and not thinking clearly, or I would never have slept so long and let her out of my sight. Some of the other homeless people told me several of their children also disappeared that night.

"The Central Intelligence Police would not help me; to them I was just a crazy girl who did not even have a hologram of this child I claimed was missing. They would not let me file a missing person's report because I was not her legal guardian. I was desperate. I rode the trams all day long, searching everywhere. She was the last living member of my family, and I lost her! I would still be searching to this day if I had not met Captain Shepherd."

Blaze nodded, silently urging her to continue.

"She found me early one morning, just sitting on the sidewalk, crying. She took me aboard the *Ishmael*, listened to my story, and immediately ran an advertisement in the *Martian Chronicles,* offering a reward for information on Zuri's disappearance. She kept the ship at port for almost a month, waiting to hear if anyone had seen or knew what happened to her." Shima shook her head sadly, composed herself. "Now whenever we dock, the Captain posts a reward for Zuri's return.

"She is the kindest person I have ever known, next to my own family. In fact, she has been like an older sister to me for the past seven years. So, that is how I came to be a crewmember here."

"I can't imagine what you've been through. I feel like I'm a refugee, too." Blaze tried to think of something comforting to say, but found he was tongue-tied, as usual.

They sat in silence for a few minutes, staring out at the dome of the station. Shima lifted the cup to her lips and took a sip.

"What're you drinkin'?" Blaze asked, fishing for a lighter topic of conversation.

"Chamomile tea. The Captain swears by it. She says it helps her to relax."

Blaze nodded, thinking that Captain Shepherd had been avoiding him all day. "I'll have to try it sometime. It must work because she always seems so calm."

"I have never seen her shed a tear, not even on the day her husband died. She is a very proud, very strong woman. I cannot hold in my sorrow the way she can. I cannot think about Zuri or Hugh without weeping."

"Hugh?" Blaze asked.

Shima began to sob, burying her face in her hands.

Why do I have this effect on women? Blaze felt like a bull in a china shop, trampling fragile feelings under his big clumsy feet. He got up from his seat. "It's gettin' late," he stammered. "I really should turn in. If you ever need someone to talk to . . ." He left it hanging, embarrassed to say more.

Shima nodded. "I am sorry to be like this. Next time we talk, I will tell you about Hugh. It is too painful right now."

Blaze wanted to offer her a hug, but wondered if she would interpret it the wrong way. He settled for a feeble, "Thank you sharin' that with me. Goodnight, Shima."

"Goodnight, Blaze, *rafiki*." Shima drew her knees up to her chest and continued to cry as Blaze tried to make a graceful departure.

Halfway down the corridor to his cabin, Blare decided to try a cup of chamomile tea to take the edge off his now-somber mood. He climbed the ladder back to the top level and cautiously poked his head into the galley. Idalis was nowhere in sight, so he strode over to the hot water dispenser.

The crew's mess contained an entire wall of drawers with the contents clearly labeled, and it took him only a moment to find cups, spoons, and teas. He poked through the assortment of tea bags until he found one labeled chamomile. He seeped the bag for a few minutes and then tossed it into the trash.

Blaze took a sip, grimaced, stirred in two spoonfuls of sugar, and tried it again. *Ugh, I guess it's an acquired taste.* He found a lid for the cup and took it with him, heading back to the ladder down the short passageway that accessed the galley, bridge, and infirmary.

Blaze was almost to the ladder when he heard angry voices coming from the bridge. He froze in mid-step, debating whether he should backtrack to the galley, or nonchalantly continue on to his cabin, which would take him past the doorway to the bridge. He hadn't considered eavesdropping as a third option, but heard his name mentioned and forgot about the first two choices.

"But you asked me specifically about Blaze and Vipul," Marco's voice was grating and loud, "so why didn't you ask me to meet Jackson?"

"I think this fortune teller stuff has gone to your head," the Captain's voice was cold, low, and under control. "You're my employee, Ting. Your job is to pilot the ship, not give me advice - - especially when I don't ask for it."

"I thought you trusted my intuition!"

"Is that what you call it?"

"Just hear me out," Marco sputtered. "I have a feeling something's not right about Jackson. How could you hire a guy just because he claims to be a friend of Hugh's? Was it because you felt sorry for him? You know you have a soft spot for hard-luck cases."

"I hired him because he was qualified for the job. I'm not going to stand here and explain my decision to you. It's my ship, and you're out of line to question my authority. I think it's ridiculous that you've suddenly got a *feeling* about someone you've never even met."

"I didn't have to step foot in The Black Hole to know there was something wrong with the place!"

The Captain was silent for a long moment, but when she began to speak again, her tone was acid. "I don't care if you've been on this ship longer than any other crewmember, you answer to me, -- not the other way around. I planned to hire Blaze and Vipul *before* you met them, and I wasn't *asking* for your permission. I'm sorry if you took it as an invitation to appoint yourself my chief counsel, but you'll just have to get over it. There's nothing wrong with Wade. If he's half the steward Hugh was, we'll be in fine shape."

"He's not Hugh! He's probably nothing like Hugh, and you're making a big mistake by hiring him!"

"Everything is a big mistake in your opinion." The Captain's words were blunt. "I find your pessimism draining. If you weren't the best pilot in the star lanes, I would've fired you the day Dad turned up dead. Am I making myself clear?"

Marco seemed to have no response for this bombshell. It was quiet for a few moments, then Shepherd continued: "If you really want to help me, you'll use that sharp tongue of yours to ask around port about some potential passengers. We've had no response to our ads, and if we don't hire a medic and lift out of here in a few days, we'll all be out of a job. Is any of this getting through to you? Don't tell me how to run my ship, Ting. Wade moves in tomorrow, and I'll expect you to treat him like royalty."

Marco's voice was subdued, but frosty. "Yes, Captain."

"Now get off my bridge."

Blaze startled, gripping his cup in both hands; he was about to be discovered eavesdropping. He was too far from the galley to backtrack, so he started forward, mentally preparing to bluff his way through a potential confrontation. *Argument? What argument? I didn't hear anythin'. I was just comin' back from the galley.* He plastered an innocent expression on his face and picked up his pace.

Blaze reached the ladder just after Marco. The helmsman gave him a vicious look, and Blaze responded in turn with a confused expression. It must have been convincing because Marco descended without a word to the second level.

Blaze resisted the urge to glance through the doorway to the bridge; he didn't want the Captain to see him. He had a feeling she wouldn't be fooled by his bad acting. He descended again to the third level and walked quickly to his cabin. He had a lot to think about.

* * *

Blaze buttered a piece of toast in the crew's mess. It was early; he'd managed to avoid running into Idalis -- so far. He wanted to get down to the engine room before the rest of the crew showed up for breakfast. With any luck, he could avoid Idalis at least until lunchtime.

Blaze stuffed the toast into his mouth and pocketed an apple. He was just on his way to the ladder when he met Captain Shepherd and the newest crewmember as they exited the bridge. "Good mornin'." He managed to speak without spraying crumbs on them.

"Wade, this is Blaze Smith, the engineer." Blaze noticed that Shepherd still wouldn't look him in the eye. "Blaze, this is Wade Jackson, our new steward."

Blaze stuck out his hand. "Welcome aboard." The steward's smile seemed forced, his handshake clammy, but Blaze dismissed it as first-day-on-the-job nervousness.

"I was just showing Wade around the ship, but maybe you could take over for me?"

Blaze was surprised by the request, and his face must have shown it because the Captain quickly explained: "I know you're new, too, but I have a full day dirtside. I'm going to ask around at the hospitals to see if I can hire a medic."

"That's a good idea," Blaze said. "Sure, I don't mind. You go ahead, Captain."

The Captain's large blue eyes finally focused on his. "Thank you, Blaze." She gave him a fleeting grin, nodded to Wade, and stepped over to the ladder.

"Are you hungry?" Blaze asked, glancing at Wade's broad shoulders as the steward stared after the Captain. He noted that the newcomer was focusing intently on her backside.

"No," Wade finally answered his question when the Captain was out of sight. He turned to Blaze with a mischievous grin. "Nice figure for an old gal, huh?"

"I wouldn't know," Blaze answered cautiously. "I make it a point not to ogle my employers."

Wade snorted with laughter. "Right. Hey, no offense, but I'd rather ask one of the ladies to show me around."

Blaze wasn't sure what to make of this request. He decided to humor the new recruit and get to the basement before Idalis turned up. "Okay, the galley is that way. The cook's name is Idalis. The housekeeper's name is Shima. I'm sure either of them will be along shortly, so help yourself to coffee or somethin'."

"Shima," Wade repeated thoughtfully, not looking at Blaze. He had a restless manner Blaze found disconcerting. "Is she the girl who was engaged to Hugh?"

Engaged? Blaze frowned. *No wonder she didn't want to talk about him.* He was tempted to ask Wade why he was interested, but shrugged instead. "I don't know; I'm new here myself."

"That's right. Sorry, I was just curious. Hugh was a good friend of mine." Wade kept glancing up and down the hallway as he spoke. "There was some kind of virus on board a few weeks ago –"

Now Blaze understood. "Was he was one of the crewmembers who died?"

Wade nodded slowly, but Blaze noted no grief in his expression. *He's either immature or has ADHD,* he decided. "I'm sorry about your friend."

"Thanks." Wade started towards the galley, telling Blaze over his shoulder, "You can go on; I'll just wait for Shima. I really want to talk to her, you know, about Hugh."

"Okay, I'll see you around." Blaze puzzled over Captain Shepherd's newest acquisition as he climbed down to the basement. *So many different personalities in one small crew,* he thought, pressing his thumb to the engine room lock. *I guess it wasn't realistic to hope for one big happy family.*

Soon he was too preoccupied with engines to dwell on it.

* * *

Blaze and Vipul were at the airlock antechamber, heading out for the evening, when they met Captain Shepherd coming in.

"Going dirtside?" she asked. Blaze thought she looked tired and discouraged, but was trying hard to hide it.

"Just dinner, Captain," Vipul said. "I've been craving chapathi."

"Well, since you're in uniform, I'll expect exemplary behavior from both of you. *Ishmael* has a reputation to uphold, especially if we want any charters."

"Is there a curfew, ma'am?" Blaze asked.

"What?" A smile tugged at the corners of her mouth. "A curfew? Do I look like your mother, Blaze?"

"No, Captain." Blaze could feel the color creeping onto his cheeks.

"That's right, I'm not your mother." Shepherd narrowed her eyes. "But I'd advise you not do anything that might embarrass your real mothers, -- or get you fired. Is that clear, gentlemen?"

"Yes, Captain."

Blaze thought he heard laughter as the airlock finished cycling shut behind him and Vipul. "Do you think she's havin' second thoughts about hirin' me?"

The older man shrugged and led the way over to the lift. "Nah, why would she sack you? You're free entertainment."

"Thanks." Blaze made a face. "Just tattoo 'rookie' on my forehead."

A few minutes later, they boarded a red line tram that took them near the center of the station. Blaze didn't recognize the street where they disembarked. He followed Vipul into a pungent little restaurant called Surya's, overlooking McConnell Park.

"What *is* that smell?" he whispered to his friend as they waited for a sari-clad waitress to seat them. He noted that the place was packed – a sign that they were in for a good meal.

Vipul sniffed the air with approval. "Garlic, curry, spices. I guess you've never eaten real Indian food?"

Blaze shook his head. The waitress led them over to a table near the bar. Blaze watched as Vipul gracefully took a seat on the floor and propped his triangular silk pillow behind his back.

Blaze sank down to the floor, trying his best to imitate his shipmate, but found that his long legs didn't want to fit under the low table. He attempted to fold them pretzel-style, but managed instead to knock some cutlery off the table with his knees.

He could tell Vipul was trying hard to keep a straight face. "They have regular tables with chairs," the navigator suggested, rescuing a teacup before it slid off onto the floor.

"No, I've got it." Blaze scooted back from the table, stuck his legs straight out in front of him, and then scooted back into position.

The waitress, who was giggling, adjusted the pillow at his back.

"Um, thanks." Blaze focused on the menu so he wouldn't have to look her in the eye. To Vipul he said, "Why don't you order for both of us, -- since I have no idea what any of this stuff is."

Vipul smiled mischievously. "Let's start with two Cobras," he told the waitress.

"Is that an appetizer?" Blaze asked, not too thrilled with the idea of consuming snake.

"No, it's beer," Vipul explained. "Very popular in India and the UK."

"Make that one Cobra," Blaze told the young woman. "I don't drink," he explained to Vipul.

Vipul's thick black eyebrows almost disappeared beneath his heavy bangs. "Okay, he'll have a Coke."

Blaze politely shook his head no.

"Water, then." Vipul shrugged. "Are you a health fanatic, Blaze?"

"Somethin' like that." Blaze felt too awkward explaining his beliefs to the older man, so he just smiled and encouraged him to order. "I'm starved."

A short while later, Blaze was sipping his water and watching Vipul demonstrate the fine art of dining Indian-style.

"Just use your hands," Vipul said. "Tear off a piece of chapathi – dip it into the potato curry – or this vegetable curry – add some chilies here if you're brave – and eat it, like so."

Blaze followed his example, stuffing a piece of chapathi into his mouth. "This is good." A sudden heat began to sear his tonsils and he gulped his water. "And spicy! Okay, I'll skip the chilies."

Vipul laughed and ordered another Cobra as they tucked in. While they ate, they discussed their new jobs, and speculated where the *Ishmael* would be traveling. Blaze was interested to hear about the many places Vipul had visited during his long

85

career. He asked the navigator to describe things in detail, and he seemed happy to oblige.

"Titan sounds interestin'. I can't wait to see it. What do you do when you're not navigatin'?" Blaze asked.

"When I'm not taking a shift at the helm, I like to make things out of junk. It's sort of a hobby I picked up to pass the long hours in space."

Blaze raised his eyebrows in newfound respect for his friend. "You're an inventor?"

"Nah, I'm just an overgrown kid who likes to take things apart and try to put them back together."

"What are some examples of your work?"

Vipul laughed and opened another beer. "I've gone through different phases of experimentation. I almost blew up my flat in Harrogate when I was interested in explosives. Nearly drove my poor wife crazy, wondering if I was going to burn the place down. I once made a vodka still for the crew of the *Celina*. It was the worst stuff you ever tasted!" He shook his head, remembering. "For a time I tinkered with broken androids, trying to make improvements, but I'm no mechanic."

"I've tinkered with androids, too," Blaze said, "but they're poorly designed. The best improvement would be to start over from scratch with better materials."

"You know, I 'aven't 'ad another 'uman being to talk to since I left my last job weeks ago," Vipul's proper English began to slur into a thick Cockney accent as he finished his fourth Cobra and opened a fifth.

Blaze nodded. "I know what you mean." He thoughtfully savored his last bite of rice. "You mentioned a wife. Are you still married?"

"I thought we were talkin' 'bout my bad inventions." Vipul gave Blaze a serious look. "I's married once, a long time ago."

"Any kids?" Blaze knew he was repeating his bull-in-the-china-store routine, but he really wanted to know more about Vipul's background.

Vipul looked down at his plate. "My wife wanted children, but we lived too close to London. I tried explainin' to 'er about our damaged DNA, but she refused to listen to reason. She was determined to 'ave a baby. She 'ad four miscarriages and I thought, 'that's enough, she's gonna keep tryin' till she kills 'erself,' so I went out and got m'self fixed – you know, snip-snip." He mimed a pair of scissors with an index and middle finger. "And that was the end of my marriage. So, why're you askin' me this? Are you thinkin' of gettin' married?"

"No!" Blaze said, flushing. "I was just wonderin' if people do that anymore."

"I'd say yes -- definitely. Marriage is great. You should try it sometime," Vipul's stern expression transformed into a mischievous smirk, "with Idalis, maybe?"

Blaze shook his head and laughed. "I don't want to get married that badly." He leaned back against his cushion and suddenly realized he was exhausted. "I think we should call it a night."

"Check, please." Vipul waved over their waitress.

Blaze slid his credit flash through the slot of the proffered datapad and added a generous tip. The waitress graced him with a big smile of thanks.

"The women from my country are very beautiful," Vipul confided in a loud whisper.

Blaze shushed him as the waitress moved off, giggling. He managed to get up from the floor without knocking the table over, then went around to help Vipul to his feet. "I think you've had enough."

Vipul just grinned and leaned heavily on his shipmate's arm as they headed back to the *Ishmael*.

"I thought the English could hold their ale?" Blaze asked as he cycled the airlocks.

"We can," Vipul insisted, laughing, "but I usually don' drink more'n two."

"You had five," Blaze said, trying not to sound like a nag. *I should know; each one cost as much as an entrée.* He kept an eye out for the Captain as he gave his staggering shipmate a boost up the ladder. Fortunately, they didn't run into any of the other crewmembers. Blaze had the feeling this type of behavior would definitely qualify as 'embarrassing your mother' in Shepherd's view.

"I'n make it from 'ere," Vipul assured Blaze when they reached the third level. The navigator's cabin was on the opposite wing from his.

"Are you sure?" Blaze asked. "You're not gonna be sick?"

"Why would I wanna waste a pe'fectly good meal?" Vipul laughed at his own joke. He turned towards his cabin and pressed one hand against the wall, using it to steady himself as he made his way down the hallway. "Goodnight. Thanks."

"Goodnight." Blaze watched until Vipul made it into his cabin, then turned around and headed for the lounge.

He stopped just outside the doorway to the dark room as two voices reached his ears: Shima's and Wade Jackson's. *Eavesdropping again? You're going to get yourself fired before the ship lifts.* But he listened, nonetheless.

"I can see why Hugh cared about you." Wade Jackson's voice was tender, nothing like the distracted brat he'd been that morning.

"He was the caring one," Shima replied, her voice husky. "I miss him so much, but I hope we can be friends, you and I."

"I'd like that," Wade said.

Their voices dropped to whispers, and Blaze heard Shima laugh softly. He turned away, feeling like an intruder. He walked back to his cabin and thumbed the lock.

As he got ready for bed, Blaze was overcome with a feeling of foreboding. He tried to dismiss it with a shake of his head. *Marco's pessimism is rubbing off on me.* He said a short prayer and burrowed under the covers, but sleep eluded him.

When was the last time I had a nagging feeling like this? Memories began to flood his mind. *That day Mom didn't come out of the bathroom. I finally had to pick the lock.* Blaze shuddered, trying to mentally blot out the awful scene. He felt the sharp pangs of guilt renewed as he remembered how long it had taken him to respond to the impression that something was wrong with his mother; that she'd been in the bathroom too long.

I could have stopped her. I could have saved her if I'd done something, told someone. Blaze felt a lump in his throat. He reminded himself, *I was just a child. I didn't know the war could push people to the brink of madness.*

The impression persisted. *I'm not a child anymore, so what's my excuse now?* Blaze sat up, frustrated and nervous, wondering what it meant. He swung his feet over the side of the bed and pulled on sweatpants.

Blaze stepped out into the hallway. He wasn't sure what he was going to do, but decided to have a look around the ship just to assure himself that nothing was amiss. He started to turn left, thinking he'd walk by Vipul's cabin first, but found himself, inexplicably, turning right. His bare feet tread silently on the cold deck plates as he slowly approached the lounge.

Why do I feel the need to eavesdrop again? He paused near the doorway, but heard nothing inside the dark room. *Have they already returned to their cabins?*

Then the silence was broken by a muffled gasp.

"Just shut up and I won't have to hurt you!" Jackson's voice was low and threatening.

"No!" Shima's plea was abruptly silenced.

Blaze was across the lounge in three strides, calling for the lights as he ran. "Let her go!"

In the sudden illumination he saw the steward glance up in surprise. He was lying across the window seat with Shima pinned beneath him, struggling desperately to push him away. Jackson had one hand clamped tightly over her mouth as the other struggled to imprison both her wrists. He didn't have a chance to focus his vision before Blaze seized his collar and dragged him off of Shima.

"Blaze!" Shima sobbed with relief.

Blaze wanted to see if she was hurt, but he had his hands full with the enraged steward.

The first blow came so fast it caught him by surprise; it felt like a boulder slammed into his stomach. Gasping for breath, Blaze doubled over. Jackson shoved him to the floor, straddling his chest and pinning his shoulders to the carpet. It was all Blaze could do to defend himself; he was no match for the other man's brute strength.

"Captain!" Shima cried. "The third starboard lounge, come quickly!"

Blaze felt something like a sledgehammer rattle his teeth. He tasted blood. He seized Wade's wrists and tried to flip the steward off of him.

Jackson drove his sharp elbows into Blaze's shoulders, breaking his grip. Hands free, the steward punched him again in the face. Blaze was momentarily disoriented, his left cheekbone throbbing with pain.

Jackson got to his feet, but Blaze grabbed one of his legs and twisted, bringing him down again with a *thud.*

"What's going on here?" Captain Shepherd was racing across the room towards them.

The steward rolled away from Blaze and kicked out hard, catching him just under his left armpit. Blaze heard something crack, and then he couldn't breathe.

89

Jackson was up again, seizing one of Shima's arms and yanking her to her feet. Shima screamed. Blaze could only watch the scene unfold as the searing pain in his side made it impossible for him to move.

Jackson pulled Shima close, looping one arm around her tiny waist and pinning her arms to her side. He gripped her neck with his free hand. Using the housekeeper as a shield, he told the Captain, "Stay back, or I'll break her neck."

Blaze watched, dizzy with pain, as Jackson glanced around frantically for an escape route. Blaze was sprawled on the floor in front of him, and the Captain stood between him and the door.

"You have to let me out of here," Jackson tightened his grip on Shima's neck, "or she dies."

From the floor, Blaze glanced at Shima's terrified expression and then looked at the Captain, expecting to see the fear reflected in her face.

He was wrong; Danae Shepherd was completely calm. Blaze thought her demeanor was a tribute to years of experience as a ship's captain, -- but then he noticed she was holding a small gun in her right hand.

"Let her go or, so help me, I'll put a bullet right through you."

Wade Jackson laughed nervously, trying unsuccessfully to hide his bulk behind Shima's slender body. "That antique of yours hasn't seen any action."

"How much do you want to bet?" Shepherd took a step closer.

The hand on Shima's neck moved upwards; Jackson gripped her jaw firmly. "Just one little twist, and she won't feel a thing. I swear, I'll kill her if you don't let me go!"

Shepherd released the pistol's safety with an audible *click*.

"You can't shoot me," Jackson said, "you'll miss and hit her, or hit the window and then we'll all be dead."

"A rocket launcher couldn't break that window. And I'll let you in on a little secret: I never miss. I'll give you 10 seconds to decide whether you'd like to live or die."

"I'll only need one second to finish her!"

Blaze glanced back and forth between the coldly determined faces of Shepherd and Jackson. He witnessed Jackson's incredulous expression when the shot rang out.

Blood streamed from a ragged hole in the steward's right thigh; the Captain had aimed low. Jackson moaned and slumped to the floor, still trying to hold Shima. The housekeeper squirmed free of his weakened grip and ran to the Captain.

"Well, sue me; he still had five seconds left." Shepherd gathered a hysterical Shima into her arms. "I decided to let you live, Jackson, because there's no more room for bodies in cold storage."

"A little help?" Blaze wheezed. He hoped Jackson was in a lot more pain than he was.

Captain Shepherd bent over Blaze and gently touched his left side. He gasped at the fresh, stabbing pains and she quickly withdrew her hand with an apologetic murmur. "Probably a broken rib. What a time to be without a medic!"

"What about him?" Shima asked, casting a disgusted look in Jackson's direction. Blaze noticed her bleeding lip for the first time as she wiped at the blood on her chin. Her long brown fingers were shaking.

"Let him bleed?" Blaze suggested, ignoring the blood trickling down his own swollen lip.

Shepherd sighed angrily. "Ting!"

"I'm right here, Captain," announced a cool voice from the doorway.

"Well, why don't you give us a hand?" she asked, rounding on him. "Call an ambulance and the CIPs."

"Yes, Captain." Ting smiled grimly as he came forward into Blaze's view.

"I guess I'll be interviewing a few more stewards tomorrow," Shepherd said under her breath.

"Yes, Captain," Ting repeated. "Good idea."

The Captain held Marco's gaze for a long moment, then she nodded and turned away. Blaze decided that was as close to an apology as the helmsman would get from Shepherd.

* * *

"I'll be fine. I don't need to go to the hospital."

"You do not like hospitals?" Shima sat beside Blaze's gurney in the ambulance, dabbing her puffy lip with a chunk of ice wrapped in a napkin.

Blaze touched his tongue to his own split lip and winced. "No, I just don't think this is serious enough to justify a hospital visit."

"No? So it is not serious that you are having difficulty breathing?" She caught his eye, gave him a warm smile filled with gratitude.

"Doctors," Blaze whispered, embarrassed.

"Excuse me?" Shima leaned closer to hear.

"I don't like doctors." The pain in his side flared when the vehicle turned a corner; even the slightest movement was agony. "How much longer?"

"Mars Community Hospital is only five kilometers from the port." Shima reminded him. "We will arrive in just a moment. Why do you not like doctors?"

Blaze shut his eyes, trying not to remember his last visit to an emergency room. "Because doctors only make an appearance when someone is dead, or dyin'. At least, that's been my experience."

"Dr. Martschenko, *Ishmael*'s medical-technician, was the only doctor I knew." Shima's voice grew husky. "She was very kind and gentle. She reminded me of my grandmother."

"I don't think you'll find many Dr. Martschenkos in an emergency room." Blaze frowned. "I brought my dad in seven or eight times, but we always seemed to get the Dr. Jekylls – or worse, the Dr. Frankensteins."

Shima gave him a puzzled look. "Who?"

"Um, never mind." The ambulance came to a halt and the cargo doors opened. Blaze winced in apprehension as two medic androids lifted his gurney down from the back of the vehicle.

A third android helped Shima down to the pavement. Despite her protests, she was seated in a wheelchair. Blaze gave her a smile of encouragement as he was wheeled, facing backwards, through the ER entrance.

A dark-haired young man in oversized blue scrubs stood back from the automatic doors and watched Blaze go by. He was carrying a small, wide-eyed black boy, probably no more than three years old, on his shoulders.

Blaze had an impression that he should speak to the young man. "Are you a doctor?"

"Sorry, I can't help you. I work at the homeless clinic down the hall." He smiled self-consciously, adjusting his grip on the tattered pant-legs of his giggling passenger.

"Well, could you tell me which doctor here falls into the 'kind and gentle' category?"

"Sure, just ask for Dr. Kamara." The clinic doctor waited for Shima to be wheeled past, then waved to Blaze before heading outside. "Good luck."

"Much obliged," Blaze called after him, feeling strangely at peace as he faced the ER with this advice from a stranger.

SEVEN
MOTHER TERESA'S

Lorina stopped off at a discount department store called Martian Mart on her way to the Outreach Clinic. She didn't think about the expense as she filled her cart with a pink backpack, underwear, several sets of clothes, a nightgown, tennis shoes, toiletries, and a small cloth doll. These items, along with a washcloth, towel, and samples of shampoo and soap from the Marriott were all for Niyati.

Lorina paid for everything – nearly 3,000 credits – and caught a tram to Mars Community Hospital. She didn't want to admit to herself that she was getting attached to Niyati, but she was uncomfortable with the idea of leaving her at a shelter. Obviously, someone had abandoned the little girl to the streets. *But children shouldn't have to suffer for someone else's stupidity,* she reasoned.

We can't keep her, she argued with herself. *We can barely afford to feed ourselves.* Lorina blinked back tears of frustration as the tram passed a pair of black children sitting under a streetlight begging food from passersby.

She turned her head to keep them in sight as the tram moved on. No one gave the children a second glance, not even a woman who walked past with her arms loaded down with bags of groceries.

Lorina got off the tram and walked into the ER entrance. Following Jake's directions, she found the Outreach Clinic. In the empty waiting area, she discovered Jake at the desk bouncing a happy Niyati on his knee while he tried to work on datapads. The imp was still barefoot and dressed in his T-shirt because Lorina had thrown her disgusting, lice-ridden clothes in the garbage.

Niyati looked up, shouted, "Lorina!" and dashed over to hug her left thigh.

"I've got something for you." Lorina crouched down and opened the Martian Mart bag.

"As soon as you left this morning, she took the room apart," Jake said. "She ate everything in the 'fridge and emptied all the drawers. So much for 'get some sleep while she watches a holo-vid' – brilliant idea! We need to take her to the shelter, Lorina."

Lorina ignored Jake's barrage, assuming he was cranky because he was tired. She was too busy basking in Niyati's excitement to acknowledge his half-hearted wrath. In short order, she had the child completely dressed; even the shoes were a decent fit.

"I think she cleaned up nicely." Lorina turned Niyati to face Jake. With the chin-length bobbed haircut Lorina had given her and the new clothes, she looked a normal child – skinny, but normal.

Jake looked up from the datapad and forced a smile. "I cleared up all her parasites and infections. Erik said I could leave for a few minutes so we can walk her over to Mother Teresa's."

Lorina presented Niyati with the doll and winced at the child's delighted shriek too close to her ear. She started packing everything else into the pink backpack. "What's she going to think? She doesn't even know what we're saying. What's she going to think when we walk away?"

"We can't keep her, Lorina. I'm sorry."

Erik stepped in from the exam room and Lorina stood to greet him. "You must be the Dr. Compassionate I've heard so much about?"

Erik shook her hand. "And you must be the so-called wife who's really Jake's tender-hearted cousin?"

"Tender heart, hard head," Jake said, earning himself a swat from Lorina.

"It's easy to tell you two are cut from the same cloth," Erik said.

Lorina glanced around the room. "I thought this place was usually packed?"

"We get a lull every now and then." Erik smiled. "So I guess now would be a good time to take Niyati to Mother Teresa's? She's been a lot of fun to have around this evening."

Jake snorted. "She almost broke my scanner, and she unrolled all the toilet paper in the ladies' room! She's acts just like –"

"A preschooler?" Erik raised his eyebrows at Jake.

"A little girl who's been starved for attention?" Lorina added.

Jake got up from the desk and came over to take Niyati's hand. She wouldn't part with the doll, so he gently gripped her bony wrist. "We'd better get going."

"Say hello to Kirsten for me," Erik said.

"I will."

Lorina shouldered the pink backpack, took Niyati's other hand and the three headed out of the ER. "Who's Kirsten?"

"Erik's sister; she runs the shelter."

Lorina nodded. "Cut from the same cloth."

"All I know is they really love what they do." Jake escorted them down Farmer Street, past the front of the hospital.

Niyati skipped along happily between the cousins, talking a stream of gibberish they couldn't understand. When they passed a fruit vendor, she said, "*Ami may-ch-er ko-lay*," and pointed at the bananas.

"I think she wants a banana," Jake said.

"I'm almost broke."

Jake bought her two bananas at 10 credits apiece. "She just ate my lunch – and Erik's – so she shouldn't be hungry."

She wasn't. Niyati carried her bananas until they came upon a pair of street children begging in a doorway. She gave each a banana, then paused to show them her new shoes. "*Ju-to*," she explained, striking a model's pose.

The children just stared at her as they devoured her offerings.

Niyati waved goodbye, grabbing Jake and Lorina's hands as they moved on.

Lorina bit her lip. She glanced at Jake out of the corner of her eye and saw that he looked as guilty as she felt.

Two blocks later, they arrived at Mother Teresa's Juvenile Shelter, a double-wide row house on the ground floor of the Church of Jesus Christ office building. They skirted around a wino sleeping in the recessed doorway. Jake reached up, pressed his thumb to the ID lock on the stained-glass transom, and the door opened.

"My, aren't we important?" Lorina asked. "You have DNA access?"

"Erik and I are cleared for emergency house calls." Jake shut the door firmly behind them.

They were standing in a dimly-lit foyer, similar to one in a traditional Colonial-style home, although it looked like the place had seen some hard use. Several boys of different nationalities came bursting through a swinging door down the front hall and ran straight at them. They swerved at the last moment and stampeded up the wooden staircase, whooping and hollering.

Niyati laughed and gripped Lorina's hand tighter.

Moments later a tall, heavy-set woman in a long purple nightgown poked her bushy white-blond head out of the same swinging door and hollered up the stairwell: "Lights out, I said! Mohammed, get back in bed!"

"Excuse us," Lorina said.

The woman caught sight of them and quickly came forward, the door swinging shut behind her. "Jake! Nice to see you." She shook his hand firmly, looking completely unembarrassed to be caught in her nightgown.

"Kirsten, I'd like you to meet my cousin, Lorina Murphy."

"Wonderful to meet you." Kirsten pumped Lorina's hand and immediately squatted down in front of Niyati with a friendly smile. "And who do we have here?"

"Niyati," Jake supplied.

"Hello, Niyati."

Niyati smiled shyly at the big woman and showed her the doll.

"How pretty!" Lorina could see that Kirsten was great with kids. "I suppose you're looking for a place for her to stay," she added, speaking to Jake, though she never diverted her smiling face from Niyati's.

"Do you have any beds open this late?" Lorina asked, hoping the answer would be no.

"There's always room for one more." Kirsten nodded. "I take it she doesn't speak English?"

"Not much," Jake said. "We do charades to communicate."

Kirsten straightened up and offered Niyati her hand. The child let go of Jake's hand to take it, but never relaxed her grip on Lorina's. The two women exchanged a look of mutual understanding as Kirsten led the group through the door she'd just exited.

Lorina glanced around the bright yellow kitchen with its two mismatched refrigerators, a cracked and faded vinyl floor, and a massive square table which took up most of the room. She counted 24 folding chairs around the perimeter of the table. Kirsten indicated for them to take seats at the corner closest to the blackened antique eight-burner Viking stove.

"Give me the facts." Kirsten reached for a datapad in a crooked overhead cabinet and set a box of graham crackers in front of Niyati's chair.

"She lived in a dumpster for who-knows how long," Jake said. "Lorina took her in yesterday, hence the new clothes and haircut. I treated her for lice, parasites – all that fun stuff. And here she is."

Lorina put Niyati's book-bag on the table. "Here are some things for her."

Kirsten gave Lorina a sympathetic look. "That's very generous of you, but I'll have to keep her belongings in my room, or else the older girls will steal them."

Lorina was crestfallen. "Why?" She shook her head before the matron could respond. "Never mind, I understand. But what about her doll?"

"That," Kirsten said, "will be the first thing to get snatched. I'm sorry."

Lorina slipped the doll into the book-bag and had to wipe her eyes before Niyati, who was busy gobbling graham crackers, noticed the tears. "I wish we didn't have to leave her."

"It's hard not to get attached." Kirsten patted Lorina's arm. "My heart breaks every time one of my regulars goes missing."

"Missing?" Lorina asked.

"She means 'back to the streets'," Jake said.

Lorina glanced at Kirsten's furrowed brow and had the impression that 'back to the streets' wasn't what she meant. But before she probe further, Jake said, "Come on, we'd better go. I need to get back to the clinic." He got up from his chair, and Lorina did the same.

Niyati stopped eating and looked up in alarm. "Lorina?"

Lorina smiled and pointed to Kirsten. "Niyati stay here. Okay?"

Niyati shook her head and started to cry.

Jake sighed loudly. "I'll wait for you by the door." He headed out to the front hall.

Lorina thought fast. "Would it be okay if I spent the night here with her?"

Kirsten frowned. "It's not a good idea. Besides, I don't have the room. I was going to make up a bed for her on the floor."

"I don't mind sleeping on the floor."

"It's better to say goodbye and get it over with." Kirsten's expression was filled with sympathy.

"But she won't understand." Lorina blinked back tears again. "She trusts me."

"You can visit her anytime you want, for as long as she'll stay. I've had kids come back every night for years. They don't want to sleep on the streets any more than we do."

"But —"

"You're not her mother, Lorina. You've done the best you can for this child. I could always use you as a volunteer if you can spare the time."

Lorina nodded, knowing she was right. She wiped Niyati's tear-stained face and gave her a hug. "Goodbye, Niyati."

"*Lorina!*" Niyati sobbed. Kirsten had to restrain her as Lorina walked quickly to the front door.

Jake held the door open without a word and they stepped over the wino, out onto the dark sidewalk. Lorina could still hear Niyati shrieking her name after the door closed behind them. Jake put a comforting arm around her shoulders and steered her in the direction of the hospital.

"I know it's hard, but we can't save them all," Jake said softly.

Lorina nodded, wiping her eyes on her sleeve. She felt like a failure. *No, we can't save them all.* On that point, she had to agree. *But if I'm stuck here on the station in this dead-end job for who knows how long, I* can *do something for this child.*

* * *

Lorina arose at 6:00 a.m. and returned to Mother Teresa's, falling into a daily routine she would adhere to for months:

As soon as she arrived at the shelter, she helped Kirsten with breakfast preparations. Most mornings, it was just cold cereal, fruit, and soymilk for 18 to 50 children, depending on how many had spent the night. But on Sundays, Lorina's day off at the Marriott, they had time to cook several types of hot cereal: congee for the Asian kids, porridge for the Europeans, mazamorro for the Latin kids, and oatmeal for everyone else.

There was so much that needed to be done to keep the shelter running. The children were all given chores to help out, but there were several toddlers in diapers who needed to be changed and fed, and mountains of laundry, especially bedding. Lorina took over this chore on her own initiative.

The boys slept upstairs in four rooms filled with as many bunk beds as could be accommodated in the space. Lorina inspected every pillowcase for lice and nits, and stripped any bed that showed signs of the persistent pests. Then she went downstairs and did the same in the two large rooms off the kitchen where the girls slept. She was surprised to learn that there were more homeless boys than girls.

"Something about boys," Kirsten explained. "I guess people consider them too rambunctious or aggressive. Boys are abandoned with alarming frequency."

Next, Lorina tackled the bathrooms. There were two on each floor, and the boys' bathrooms were always disgusting. She soon bribed two of the older boys, Mohammed and Vladimir, to be in charge of cleaning up the puddles around the toilets. If they did a good job during the week, she paid them with cookies on Sunday.

As soon as the bathtubs were clean, Lorina filled them with water and selected the dirtiest and smelliest children for baths. There were always plenty to choose from. With Genevieve Peterson's approval, Lorina kept the shelter stocked with soap, shampoo, and old linens and towels.

Niyati shadowed her as she worked, chattering in her Indian dialect and practicing her fledgling English. "Lorina bring treat?"

Lorina laughed and scooped up the child in her arms for a twirl around the room. "Not today. Treat on Sunday. What's today, Niyati?"

Niyati shrieked with laughter and guessed, "Wesday?" She knew the days of the week, but always guessed wrong to get some extra tickles; it was her favorite game. Then Lorina would set her down and get back to work, but it wouldn't be long before Niyati asked, "Lorina bring treat?" again.

Mother Teresa's had a few other volunteers: older ladies who came once a week and cleaned for a few hours. They seemed to enjoy spending time with the children. One of them, a 'Miss Jane,' always took several bags of laundry home and brought them back clean the next day.

"My husband died two years ago," Miss Jane confessed, "but I never told the water department. I use his water ration to do the extra laundry." Lorina was impressed by her courage.

Five grocery stores donated packaged and canned food on a regular basis, but Lorina supplemented the children's diets with fruit. When she finished work at the Marriott at 7:00 p.m., she went out and circulated among the local street vendors before they packed up for the night. This way, she could get a bargain on the fruit they would normally throw away.

Lorina also used her gift of persuasion to convince a local dentist to spend a few hours each week at the shelter, cleaning teeth. She likewise appealed to two local churches to donate children's clothes.

"You're a godsend," Kirsten told her on a regular basis. But Lorina felt that Mother Teresa's was her godsend; it was the only thing that gave her life purpose. Her work at the Marriott was mind-numbingly dull, and she desperately missed her family, but the smiles she received from the children gave her the motivation she needed to face each day.

Monday through Saturday, 10:30 a.m. always came too soon, but by the time Lorina was heading out the door to go back to the Marriott, the children who frequented the shelter had already departed. About half of them had parents who were homeless, but the others, like Niyati, were abandoned. Five toddlers and three preschoolers, including Niyati, stayed at Mother Teresa's all day. The small living room served as a playroom with a holo-vid that continuously played old Walt Disney movies and an assortment of donated toys. Niyati seemed to have no inclination to leave this little paradise after living in such deplorable conditions in the alley.

"See you tomorrow, Niyati!" Lorina called.

Niyati scampered after her and hugged her legs. "Tomowow Sunday?" the girl asked. On Sundays, Lorina took Niyati with her to Mass, then treated her to lunch at a diner. The child seemed to be doing well under Kirsten's care, but Lorina tried to spend time alone with her whenever possible because the shelter was such a busy, crowded, noisy place. She was fond of some of the regular children, but Niyati felt more like a little sister. *Or even a daughter,* Lorina thought, surprised at the depth of her feelings.

"Tomorrow Sunday," Lorina assured Niyati with a big grin. She laughed as the tiny girl jumped up and down with delight. "See you tomorrow."

* * *

"Lorina?"

"Jake, what are you doing here?" Lorina looked up from slicing a banana into a tiny Latino child's bowl. It was breakfast time at Mother Teresa's, and she and Kirsten had their hands full supervising 30 hungry children.

"Did you come to help?" Kirsten was walking down one side of the table, pouring soymilk into cereal bowls. "Luz, don't use your hands. Vida, slow down; you'll choke."

101

"Is something wrong?" Lorina wiped her hands on the ruffled apron of her Marriott uniform. She came over and took Jake's arm, ushering him into the relative quiet of the front hall.

"I don't know how much longer we can live like this." Jake's words came out in a rush.

"What do you mean?" Lorina frowned.

Jake shook his head. "I don't know. Nothing . . . everything."

"You look tired." Lorina hadn't seen her cousin awake at 7:00 a.m. since the day before she began volunteering at the shelter. "Did you come here straight from the clinic to talk, or do you just need to vent?"

Jake seemed at a loss for words, even though it was the first time they'd had a conversation in two months. "Maybe I just want to go home."

"It's too late for that now," Lorina replied bitterly. "We're stranded. But at least we're needed here."

"We're needed? All we're doing is putting a bandage on a wound that needs a tourniquet."

"Nice analogy, doctor. I don't have time to debate this with you right now. Why don't you tell Erik you need a day off?"

"I did that already."

"Then go back to the room and sleep for the next 24 hours. Maybe you'll see things differently when you wake up." Lorina turned on her heel and started back to the kitchen, but stopped in her tracks when they heard pounding on the front door.

"Open up! Police!"

Jake and Lorina exchanged a stunned look.

Kirsten stuck her head out of the kitchen. Her pale blue eyes were wide with fear. "Try to convince them to leave," she asked Jake.

Jake nodded and went slowly to the door. Lorina was a few steps behind him.

"Police! Open the door!"

"I'm going out to talk to them," Jake muttered over his shoulder.

"I'm right behind you," Lorina said.

Jake didn't argue. He opened the door and they both moved quickly out onto the stoop, barring the officer's way in. Lorina hastily pulled the door shut behind her.

"Can we help you?" Lorina noted the strain in Jake's voice. They stood face-to-face with a CIP he seemed to recognize.

"Well, if it isn't Dr. O'Brien." The officer was a big man, pale, with streaks of gray in his dark crew cut. He had the coldest eyes Lorina had ever seen. He barely glanced at Lorina, focusing his intimidating glare on Jake. The CIP was armed, his pistol in plain view, in the holster under his left arm.

Lorina eyed the two armed CIPs standing on the steps behind the leader. She remembered Jake's caution about the CIPs' view of homeless people. *But why are they here now, and armed?*

"I'm looking for a member of a street gang," the officer said to Jake. "He assaulted a lady down on Architect Street last night, nearly killed her. A witness told me he might be hiding out here."

"I didn't see any gang members inside, Chief Acheron." Jake's tone was cool and composed. "No kids over the age of 10, in fact."

"We'd like to determine that for ourselves." Acheron's tone was colder.

"Not unless you have a warrant."

"You've been watching too many old holo-vids." Acheron laughed without smiling. "I don't need a warrant to search for a felon – not in my town. Now if you're not going to let us in, you need to stand aside, Dr. O'Brien." A nasty smile tugged at the corners of his mouth. "If you really *are* a doctor, that is."

Lorina felt her stomach knot with fear, but tried not to show it. "I think Miss Sorensen would like to talk to you before you go barging in and scaring the kids. Why don't you wait here, and I'll get her?" She tried to sound as confident as Jake.

Acheron's eyes focused on her face. "And you are?" His glanced down at her chest, seeing the answer for himself.

Lorina flushed, wishing she'd had the foresight to remove the nametag from her uniform. It clearly said, *Lorina M.* and *Marriott Housekeeping.* "I volunteer here at the shelter. I know the kids, and I can assure you there aren't any gang members inside."

Acheron shook his head. "Nice try, but I recognize a stall tactic when I see one. You're trying to give Sorensen time to hide him." He took a threatening step forward, crowding Jake and Lorina against the door. "She's done it before. Harboring criminals, claiming they're 'just children', but not today. Now stand aside."

Jake stood firm, but Acheron merely nodded to his flunkies. In a moment, Jake and Lorina were manhandled off the doorstep. They watched in fury as Acheron kicked open the door to Mother Teresa's, splitting the doorframe hard enough to shatter the stained glass transom above it.

Lorina expected to hear lots of children's screams, but the search was surprisingly quiet. She and Jake hurried back inside on the heels of the CIPs and found the shelter kids still at breakfast. Obviously, Kirsten had charged them to stay still and quiet. A few whimpered as the CIPs tore through the house, searching, but none of them moved from their seats.

Lorina gathered up a trembling Niyati in her arms and retreated to a corner of the living room until the CIPs had finished opening every door and peering under every bed. As the three men regrouped in the front hall, Acheron gave Lorina a look that sent a chill down her spine.

Then she realized he wasn't looking at her; he was leering at Niyati.

Kirsten held the door open, ushering the CIPs outside without a word. Lorina could see that her face was ashen.

"Thank you for your cooperation," Acheron said to Kirsten. "Next time, open the door."

Then they were gone and Kirsten slammed the door behind them, dislodging the last shards of glass still clinging to the transom.

"I'll help you clean this up." Jake moved off to find a broom.

Lorina set Niyati on the couch and went to Kirsten's side, broken glass crunching under her shoes. She could see that the matron was shaking like a leaf, and put an arm around her shoulders. "It's okay; they're gone."

"No, it's not okay," Kirsten's voice cracked. She looked like she was going to be sick. "They weren't searching for anyone, Lorina. They were taking an *inventory* of the children."

EIGHT
VIPUL'S SECRET

Danae rarely touched alcohol, but she decided to make an exception after her second discouraging day dirtside. However, once she'd plunked herself down on a barstool at Thanatos' Greek Taverna, she had a vivid flashback of her mother passed out on the living room couch in the middle of the afternoon. She ordered a lime soda instead.

The fake-Greek bartender put the glass in front of her with a cheerful "*Opa!*" but Danae only glared at him.

"That'll be 80 credits." He returned her grim look and offered her a datapad to scan her credit flash.

Danae sipped slowly and played with the little straw, pondering her bleak future. *No med-techs in this city willing to give up a lucrative career for adventures in space without pay. No passengers to charter. Three families who want the bodies shipped back to Earth. One hospital bill for a broken rib and two busted lips. One court date a month away to testify against that slime Jackson, who I still haven't replaced. No way to pay the port fees for a lengthy stay.* She shook her head in disgust. *It would have been so much simpler if I'd killed him.*

If I don't kill myself first, she thought, fighting a wave of despair.

"Happy star trails," a bass voice sang out in her direction.

Danae glanced up to see a ruggedly handsome middle-aged man in a dark green spacer's uniform approaching her with a confident swagger. He was solidly built with jet-black hair, dark eyes, and an olive complexion. "What's your cargo?" He slid onto the stool next to Danae's.

Danae glanced at the logo on his crisp uniform: *Elmina. Where have I heard that name before?* "My cargo's passengers."

"Passengers," he laughed. "I used to do that, but I found there's more money in livestock. My name's Thanatos."

The man gave her the creeps, but Danae hoped a few words of polite conversation would jog her memory about the *Elmina.* "Thanatos? Is this is your restaurant?"

"Why, yes it is." He flashed a proud smile. "What do you think of it?"

Danae made a pretense of looking around at the décor. "It's very – um, Grecian."

Thanatos laughed. "You're too kind. I didn't get your name."

"It was nice to meet you, Mr. Thanatos." Danae turned back to her drink.

"Are you here alone, Miss No-Name?" He leaned closer. "Because if you are, we could always get a room."

"I'm *married.*" Danae put as much ice into her tone as she could manage.

"So?"

Danae was too appalled to come up with a snappy retort. She stood abruptly and moved down to the far end of the bar, Thanatos' laughter ringing in her ears.

Danae settled down again and sipped her drink. She tried to gather her thoughts, but the lewd proposition had rattled her. She watched Thanatos out of the corner of her eye as he approached another woman at the bar, was rebuffed by her boyfriend – who was sitting with her – and cheerfully hailed someone coming in the door.

Danae continued to observe, trying to be discreet.

Thanatos shook hands with the uniformed CIP officer and they sat down together at a table within her view. Thanatos had his back to her and was speaking animatedly to his guest, who was built like an ox. Danae squinted at the CIP's face; he seemed familiar.

When the bartender came to see if she wanted a refill, Danae asked him about the CIP on the pretense of wanting to buy him a drink.

He glanced over at the table and quickly turned back to Danae with an uncomfortable expression. "That's Acheron, the station police chief," he whispered. "You don't want to buy him a drink, ma'am."

"Why not?"

"Trust me; you don't want him to notice you at all." The bartender moved away to wait on someone else.

Danae was intrigued. She observed them cautiously, quickly dropping her gaze to her empty glass whenever Acheron's eyes strayed a millimeter from Thanatos' face. The two men spoke at length, then Acheron took out a datapad and showed it to Thanatos.

Danae's curiosity got the better of her. She decided to risk a glance at the datapad. Heart pounding, she got up from her seat and headed to the door. She kept her eyes focused straight ahead as she walked slowly, ready to take a fleeting glance as she passed their table.

Unfortunately, Acheron saw her coming and tossed his napkin over the screen. He eyed her suspiciously as she passed, but Danae didn't break stride. Before she was out of range, she overheard Thanatos say, "The harvest is on schedule." She didn't look back as she stepped out onto the dark sidewalk.

A moment later, someone seized her left arm from behind.

Danae's spacer's reflexes took over. She snapped her right elbow back, delivering a solid blow to her assailant's chin. Driven backwards, he released her arm. She was facing him with her gun leveled at his forehead before he could make another move.

"I assume you have a license for that?" Acheron rubbed his jaw. He stepped towards her again, his stance threatening.

"Yes." Danae didn't flinch. "What do you want, officer?" Slowly, she put her gun away. She didn't step back because she knew that was exactly what he wanted; he wanted her to feel afraid. She stood her ground.

"I want to know who you are, and why you were spying on me." The CIP's face was about a decimeter from hers. His breath was foul.

Ruthless and paranoid, she thought, *a very bad combination.* Danae feigned a sultry pout and batted her eyelashes at him. "I wasn't spying on you; I was trying to get your attention. I was thinking about buying you a drink." Remembering the bartender's advice, she sidestepped the name question again. "If this is the way you treat an admirer, I'm glad I changed my mind." The false flattery made her sick to her stomach, but Danae knew she'd be in deep trouble if he suspected the truth.

"Interesting statement coming from someone who turned down my friend Thanatos."

Danae successfully maintained her poker face. "Oh, him? He's not my type."

"You told him you were married."

"It's kinder than saying 'get lost'," Danae explained with a coy smile.

"I see." Acheron's pale blue eyes traveled down her body and returned to her face with a lecherous sneer that made her skin crawl. "So what is your type?"

Danae had a retort ready, but Acheron's flirtatious manner abruptly vanished. He seized her left hand in a paralyzing grip. "Keep the other hand where I can see it." He forced her imprisoned hand up to his view for inspection.

"No wedding ring." He didn't take his eyes off Danae's. "Who are you?"

Danae returned his glare. It took every bit of her self-restraint not to hurl her right fist into his nose. "I'm a Mars citizen who doesn't think much of CIPs who abuse their power."

Acheron's malicious grin became a threatening scowl as he eyed the *Ishmael* monogram on her uniform. "Don't tout your 'natural rights' speech at me. I asked you a question: who are you?"

When Danae remained silent, Acheron said, "It's easy enough to find out."

With his free hand, he withdrew a datapad from the cargo pocket on his thigh. He nearly dislocated Danae's thumb, forcing it against the ID lock. Then he released her hand with a satisfied smirk and watched the CIP database records quickly fill the screen.

"I remember seeing your name," he said slowly, his cold eyes flickering back to her face. "Danae Thompson Shepherd, captain of the *Ishmael*. You're the one who keeps filing a missing person's report every time your ship docks. Still trying to find some kid who doesn't exist?"

Danae flushed, her temper escalating as she massaged her aching hand. "Zuri Oketta *does* exist, and I know she disappeared from this station."

Acheron snorted. "People disappear all the time, Captain. The CIP force doesn't have time to search for every low-life street rat who turns up missing."

"Did I *say* she lived on the streets?" Danae was immediately suspicious.

Acheron smiled. "Lucky guess. I suggest you abandon your search, Captain. If you don't stop harassing my headquarters with your useless petition, I may have to use my own brand of persuasion to get you to back off." He narrowed his eyes as he glanced again at the datapad.

"Well, you actually have a license for that antique weapon, but I see you've recently filed charges against someone for assault." There wasn't a trace of humor in his arrogant laugh. "Stop wasting my officers' time. I'll see that he's released tomorrow morning."

Danae was waging a losing battle with her temper. "You're not a judge. You *can't* do that."

"The judges do whatever *I* tell them, Captain. And I'll tell them Mr. Jackson should be a free man. Let's see what else I can do to *help* you. This may be useful," Acheron continued to scan the data eagerly. "I see here you have a crewmember who's been in and out of my jail a few times for drunk and disorderly. No convictions – yet. Marco Ting? I think I remember him."

The police chief smirked at her, clearly enjoying himself. "Short Asian guy? Small eyes, big mouth? I'm sure I can find a reason to bring him in for a nice long stay." He glanced again at the information. "It says here he's your helmsman. Too bad. I know they're nearly impossible to replace."

"You've got nothing on him. You *can't* do that." Danae's voice went up an octave. *Stay in control! Don't get yourself arrested for assaulting a police officer.*

"I think we both know I *can*, Captain." Acheron's eyes lit up one more time as he finished reading the screen. "Well, it says here the *Ishmael* was in quarantine last week. You never know about those alien viruses. Sometimes they can never be completely eradicated. It would be a shame to impound and destroy such a beautiful ship. Maybe I'll look into that."

Danae felt a stab of fear. He wasn't bluffing. *He really is corrupt enough to arrest Ting and impound the* Ishmael. She glared at him for a full minute before she managed to say, "If you've finished harassing me, I have to get back to my ship."

"I think we understand each other, Captain." Acheron tucked his datapad back into his pocket. He grinned and blew her a kiss. "Maybe the next time we meet, I'll let you buy me that drink."

"Next time we meet, I'll conveniently forget you're a cop – and break both your kneecaps," Danae promised.

Acheron laughed. "Goodnight, Captain." He watched for a moment as she turned away, then he went back into the bar.

I haven't seen the last of him, Danae thought, boarding the first tram that came by to put some distance between herself and Acheron.

As soon as she returned to the *Ishmael,* Danae paged Vipul to her office. "Please sit down. We need to talk."

The navigator perched warily on the chair beside her desk. "It must be important if you needed to speak to me this late," he said in a respectful tone.

Danae glanced at the clock – 23:48 – and apologized for waking him. "Vipul, I met your former captain tonight."

Vipul's dark eyes grew wide. "Thanatos? He's back on Mars? Where did you meet him?"

"He tried to pick me up in a bar."

"What did he tell you? Did he ask you about me?"

"Should he have mentioned you, Vipul?" Danae asked, studying his expression carefully.

"No, Captain." Vipul lowered his gaze to the floor.

"I think you need to tell me about the *Elmina.*"

"I – I can't, Captain."

"Why not?"

"Because –" he closed his eyes, searching for the words. "Because it might jeopardize my position here. And because Thanatos said he would kill me if I ever divulged his business secrets."

Danae folded her arms and perched on the side of her desk facing him. "Vipul, I've only known you for four days, but I've been pleased with your work. But if there's something you're not telling me because you're afraid of Thanatos, then you don't know *me* very well."

"Captain?" Vipul looked up at her, baffled.

"The only thing that would jeopardize your position on my ship is a lie. If you were involved with something aboard the *Elmina,* I need to know about it."

"No, Captain," Vipul shook his head, "I didn't do anything wrong."

"Then you don't have anything to fear from me. And I'll protect you from Thanatos. That's a promise. And while you're spilling your guts, you can tell me what you know about the station police chief, Acheron."

"Acheron? He came aboard the ship a few times to speak to Thanatos. Why?"

"They seem to be old friends, and tonight I observed them planning something together. Since they're both corrupt, amoral predators, I'd wager that whatever they're working on is illegal."

"It is," Vipul said, nodding slowly.

Danae returned the nod. "I'm listening."

Vipul ran a tongue over his dry lips. "Captain, *Elmina* is a slave ship."

Danae hadn't been expecting this confession. She gripped the desk with her nails to steady herself. "Go on."

"When I first began working for Thanatos, I didn't know about his cargo. I spent most of my time on the bridge and was never allowed to go down to the hold because he kept armed guards at the ladders. He always assured me the ship was carrying livestock."

"Livestock is what he told me, too." Danae grimaced.

Vipul nodded. "I began to realize livestock doesn't need to be kept under lock and key, Captain. Livestock is usually fed grain, not packaged cereal and peanut butter. Cases and cases of the stuff arrived after each landing."

"That's what tipped you off?" Danae asked. "Didn't anyone else on the crew know?"

"Yes, but they were loyal to Thanatos and refused to tell me. I began to suspect that the cargo holds were full of people, but it took me awhile to realize that those people -- were children."

Danae drew in a sharp breath. "What children?"

"Homeless children." Vipul buried his face in his hands. "No one notices them. No one misses them. I didn't know how he was doing it, and I was afraid to stand up to him after he threatened me. I jumped ship as soon as we docked here. I didn't realize Thanatos had inside help, not until the moment you mentioned Acheron."

"Zuri," Danae whispered with a jolt of realization.

"What?"

"Shima's niece. Long story," Danae brushed the question aside as she stared intently at the navigator, her mind reeling from the overload of information. "Vipul, I need to know everything. It's important if we're going to find a way to stop them."

Vipul's head jerked up, his eyes wide with amazement. "You want to take on Thanatos and Acheron? How?"

"I don't know. But we have to." She dismissed his astonished expression with an angry gesture. "Don't you see?

This isn't about us! It's about hundreds, maybe thousands, of innocent children. Vipul, I have some questions for you and I need you to answer them as best you can."

"I'll try, Captain." Vipul sat up straighter, took a deep breath.

"How long do you think Thanatos has been shipping children as slaves?"

"The helmsman told me he'd been shipping livestock for 10 years."

That long, Danae grimaced. "How does he abduct them?"

"Since you mentioned Acheron, it all makes sense to me now. The CIPs must do the dirty work. The code word for a round-up is 'harvest' – I heard the word used often right before a lift."

Danae rocked backwards, stunned. "I overheard Thanatos say the harvest was on schedule! There must be something we can do to stop it! Are all the CIPs on the station involved?"

"I'm not sure," Vipul confessed. "But if the station chief's involved, I'm sure the corruption runs deep."

"Where does he sell them?"

"Earth, Captain. There's a great demand for workers in Asian factories. The Middle East and Baltic States don't think twice about where the labor comes from. The *Elmina* always returns to Earth after a harvest, no matter which station she lifted from."

"How did you learn all this?"

"I just put the facts together, bit by bit. I was in denial for a long time before I got off the *Elmina*." He smiled grimly. "You don't know what a terrible risk I took in posting a résumé, but I had to have work to survive."

"We all do," Danae murmured. "But --." She was having a difficult time grasping the horrible reality of the situation. "But children, especially street children, are resilient – they're survivors. Do any escape?"

"I once accepted a shipment for a large case of sedatives when the *Elmina* was docked at Titan Station."

"He drugs them?"

Vipul nodded. "I think Thanatos pumps them with so many tranquilizers, they don't have the strength to resist."

Danae thought hard. "We can't just stand by and do nothing, it would be criminal. We need to have a crew meeting."

"Now, Captain?"

Glancing at the clock, Danae realized his caution was justified; she felt too drained to make any tough decisions right then. "First thing in the morning." She nodded at him. "Try to get some sleep." *I know I won't be getting any.*

* * *

Danae paged her crew at 6:45 a.m. "I want everyone in the galley at 7:00 sharp. Attendance is mandatory."

Everyone took the dire announcement seriously. A bleary-eyed Marco showed up in his pajamas, but Danae sent him back to his cabin to change.

As the small group assembled at three tables, Danae stood and recounted the entire history of the *Elmina,* as Vipul had described it to her.

"Zuri!" Shima shrieked. "She is a slave! But where? Where?" She broke down into hysterical sobs until Danae asked her to step out of the room and pull herself together.

"Begging your pardon, Captain," said Marco, "but what can we do about this if the CIPs are directly involved?"

"We can do a lot more than you think, Ting. We're going to stop this harvest."

"We are?" Marco scoffed. "What, with all our money and political influence?"

"Shut your mouth, Ting!" Idalis rounded on him. "You obviously don't know anyone who's had a child go missing!"

"This is crazy, and I don't want to get involved." Marco returned Idalis' glare.

"That's your right," Danae agreed, cutting off Idalis' next retort with a stern look. "But I'm ordering you to set aside your nasty attitude for a few minutes and brainstorm with us." She looked over the other faces in the galley.

Shima and Blaze I can count on to take risks. Vipul and Idalis will help, but they probably won't do anything dangerous. Marco, Danae sighed mentally, *Marco's made his position clear. I may have to keep him on board so he doesn't ruin things. Plus, he'll be safer here; I don't want to give Acheron the opportunity to arrest him.*

"I want to hear your ideas, people. Sing out."

"We need to find out exactly how Acheron intends to round-up the children or lure them aboard the *Elmina,*" Blaze said. "And we need to know the exact day and time of the harvest."

"We need to warn the children." Shima sounded composed as she walked back into the galley and resumed her seat at Blaze's table.

"But they're scattered all over the station," Marco said.

"No, they are not." Normally quiet Shima spoke to the group with fierce determination: "Most of them live in McConnell Park. Mother Teresa's Juvenile Shelter also houses many young children." She nodded to Danae. "Zuri and I spent a few nights there."

"So we can spread the word at those two places," Blaze said.

"And then what?" Marco asked.

"And then we give the kids an alternative to slavery." This suggestion came from Danae herself. She'd spent all night going over the details in her mind, and now she was ready to announce her daring plan: "We'll bring them aboard the *Ishmael* before the harvest, and lift out of here."

A chorus of "what!" resounded in her ears.

"Are you insane?" Marco slapped a palm to his forehead. "We're broke and we can't legally lift without a med-tech."

"Where would we take them?" Idalis asked, a horrified expression on her face. "How can we afford to make a jump without a paid charter? We'll need food and supplies –"

"Not to mention *fuel*." Marco slapped his forehead again.

Danae turned away from the helmsman and searched the faces of the other crewmembers. "This can be done. I have a plan. But before I can explain it, we have two major hurdles to consider. First problem: capital?"

Blaze held out his left thumb. "I've got 43,000 left from the sale of my parents' house. Take it, it's yours, Captain."

Danae was touched. "Thank you, Blaze."

"It's not enough," Marco said.

Danae took out her pistol and set it on the table. "This should be worth 50 grand."

"Still not enough – ouch!" Marco rubbed his arm where Idalis pinched him.

"There must be some way to earn money," Shima said. "We could get jobs dirtside."

"Not enough time," Idalis said. "We need a lot of money, and we need it now."

Blaze snapped his fingers. "The books!"

"What books?" Danae asked.

"The rare books you have stashed around the ship, Captain. Your paperback copies of *Tao Te Ching* and *Catcher in the Rye* are worth at least 30,000 each. Your complete set of hardcover *Harry Potter*'s could fetch 10 times that."

"How do you know this?" Danae asked, astonished.

Blaze shrugged. "I like to read. Datapads aren't much fun to read because there's no pages to turn, and I'm not the only one who feels this way. Have you looked at the ads in the *Chronicles*? Books are so hard to find that people are willin' to pay outrageous sums of money to own them."

"Who would've thought my father's packrat problem could be a godsend?" Danae looked around at the hopeful, worried, determined, and cynical expressions on her crew. "Okay, we'll sell the books. Second problem: med-tech."

"Um, I think I can help you there, as well, Captain." Blaze cleared his throat. "On the way into the ER for my broken rib, I spoke briefly to a young doctor who works at a homeless clinic."

"Name?" Idalis asked.

"I didn't get his name, but he shouldn't be difficult to track down. He mentioned that the clinic was just down the hall from the ER. Shima, you saw him, didn't you?" He turned to face the housekeeper.

Shima nodded. "I would recognize him if I saw him again."

"So we don't know his name or if he's interested in a new career. That's not much to go on." Marco rolled his eyes towards the ceiling.

"That's *plenty* to go on!" Danae added, "Shut up, Ting!" before he could make another protest. She picked up her datapad and began to make some notes. "Let me outline the details. Those of you who are with me will have a lot of work to do."

"I'm in!" Blaze raised his hand.

"Me, too!" Shima cried.

Vipul and Idalis had their hands in the air a moment later. Marco scowled and looked down at the table.

"Marco, we'll need you to mind the ship when the rest of us go dirtside. In fact," Danae's tone hardened, "you're ordered to stay on board until we lift." When Marco started to protest, she spoke over him. "We can't risk your big mouth getting us all arrested – or killed."

"Captain," Marco responded with feigned humility, "I have a feeling this mission of yours is going to be very dangerous."

115

"Yes, it will be dangerous." Danae smiled, determination coursing through her veins. It was good to feel alive again.

NINE
HARVEST

Jake was used to working under pressure, but Kirsten's warning of the coming 'harvest' had ratcheted the tension up to an unbelievable level. He was worried, and he didn't know how to help Lorina, who was near hysteria. She'd called in sick to the Marriott for the past two days, refusing to leave the shelter. He hoped she wouldn't get fired, but he also knew that the potential loss of her income, and their room, was insignificant compared to the crisis at hand.

"What did Kirsten mean by 'the harvest'?" he asked Erik during a down time at the clinic.

Erik frowned. "About twice a year, a number of kids disappear – permanently. We're not sure *how* or *why*, but we figured out *who*: Acheron. This is the first time we've had some advanced warning, but we still don't know how to stop it from happening."

"What does he do with them? Does he kill them?" Jake asked.

Erik shook his head. "Acheron's scum, but I don't think he's blood-thirsty. I'd say he's moving them off the station somehow, so he must have outside help."

"What would someone want with a bunch of homeless kids?" Jake forced a smile as a pair of Asian children stepped into the empty waiting area.

"Warn them as best you can," Erik whispered as he gestured for Jake to take the two Japanese brothers back into the exam area.

Jake nodded and closed the curtain. "So, which one of you is sick?" He took out his scanner and waited as the youngsters spoke rapidly to each other in their native tongue.

The younger of the two finally pointed to his own chest and climbed up onto the exam table.

"What's your name?" Jake asked.

"Hiroshima."

"I suppose your name is Nagasaki?" he asked the older brother.

"How you know that, doc?"

"Lucky guess." Jake frowned at his scanner. "How old are you boys?"

"I'm eight," Nagasaki replied. "Hiro six."

"Do you feel weak?" Jake asked Hiro.

The child nodded.

"He want to sleep all the time," Nagasaki supplied. "I sleepy today, too. Maybe we sick?"

Jake passed the scanner over Nagasaki. "Have you boys eaten something strange recently? You both seem to be carrying a trace amount of the same drug." He studied the older brother's expression to see if this was registering. "Did a stranger give you something to eat or drink?"

Nagasaki nodded. "A CIP give us juice last night. He give juice to all the kids in the park."

"He said he bring muffins tonight," Hiro piped up.

Jake forced himself to remain calm. "Boys, it's really important that you don't take the muffins from the CIP. Do you have any of the juice left?"

Nagasaki nodded and withdrew a plastic bottle from his ragged backpack. There were only a few milliliters left, but Jake knew it would be enough to analyze. He took the bottle from the boy and forced a smile. "You're not sick, but you need to rest for a few days to feel better. I think it would be a good idea if you stayed at Mother Teresa's tonight. Do you know where that is?"

Nagasaki nodded. "We stay there before," he assured Jake. "Miss Kirsten nice to us."

"Promise me you'll go there right now."

Nagasaki nodded and helped Hiroshima down from the table. "I promise."

* * *

"It's Valeridum." Erik waved the datapad with the lab report in Jake's face. "It's a time-release tranquilizer, very powerful. Small kids are going to feel the effects more dramatically than older children, who weigh more. I'd say that by the time the kids get a second dose in the muffins, they won't be putting up much resistance."

Jake was on his feet. "We've got to do something!"

"I agree, but what? How can two people protect hundreds of kids from a CIP round-up?"

Jake bit his lip, trying to think. "We should go to the park, collect as many as we can, and take them to Mother Teresa's."

"That might buy them a few hours, but you can bet Acheron will be kicking the door down again by morning."

"We'll think of something," Jake said. "Let's get to the park, and see if we can stop the muffin feast."

"Yeah, you're right; let's go."

* * *

"Let's split up," Erik said as the tram approached the west entrance to McConnell Park. "We'll cover more ground that way."

"I'll get off here; you change trams and get off at the east entrance." Jake was perspiring from nervousness, still not certain how this was going to work. *What if one of us runs into Acheron?*

As bad luck would have it, Hunter Acheron was the first person Jake met when he walked through the gate.

"Good evening, Dr. O'Brien." The CIP chief was holding a large box of bakery muffins. He had an incredibly evil smirk on his pale face. "Isn't it late to be out for a walk?"

Jake's mouth went dry. "Just following up on a baby I delivered yesterday." He hoped the lie sounded convincing. "The young mother lives here."

Acheron handed him a blueberry muffin. "Why don't you give her this? Compliments of the Central Intelligence Police."

Jake took it without a word, resisting the urge to smash it in Acheron's face. "Thank you." He moved on with a purposeful stride, trying to put some distance between himself and the CIP.

"Where's your medical bag?" Acheron called after him, his tone challenging.

Jake patted his pockets without turning around, hoping the CIP would be convinced that he carried supplies on his person. He was spared from pursuit by a group of children rushing past him, converging on Acheron for free muffins.

Exactly what I didn't want to happen, Jake lamented, glancing back over his shoulder to make certain Acheron wasn't watching before he stepped off the path and walked into the trees. He tossed the muffin into a trashcan, hoping a child wouldn't unearth it later.

Then he got to work. He approached the first make-shift home he saw. An elderly lady was sitting beneath a cardboard lean-to, reading a tattered Dr. Seuss book to a collection of motley preschoolers. He recognized her from the clinic.

"Miss Carlotta?"

She raised the handlight to his face. "Is that you, Dr. Jake? I thought you might be one of those CIPs handing out more food."

Jake grimaced. "Have they already been here?"

In answer, several of the children held up empty muffin wrappers.

Jake made a quick assessment of the group: the youngest was around three and already asleep. The others ranged from four to six; they all stared back at him in a quiet stupor. He decided he would have to act quickly before they all fell asleep on him.

How to get them onto a tram without a CIP noticing? The logistics of the task were daunting, but Jake realized that time was his enemy. He had to take this group to the shelter and come back for more, moving as many youngsters as he could before daylight.

"How would you guys like to go to Mother Teresa's with me tonight?" he asked, plastering a smile on his face. "Miss Kirsten has prepared a special meal in honor of –" he tried to remember what day it was, "Halloween."

"Halloween's next week," one boy spoke up in a drowsy voice.

"So we're celebrating a little early this year. What's your name?"

"Abdul."

"Nice to meet you, Abdul. How about it? Would you like to go to a Halloween feast?"

There were a few mumbled assents, so Jake came forward and helped several children to their feet. He reached out to Miss Carlotta for the sleeping girl who was using her leg as a pillow. "Here, I can carry her."

The elderly lady gave him a shrewd look. "Something's up, Dr. Jake?"

"Yeah, you could say that. If you wouldn't mind spreading the word that the muffins are d-r-u-g-g-e-d?" He spelled it out so the children wouldn't become alarmed.

"Go with Dr. Jake, right now!" She ushered the rest of the listless youngsters to their feet. "Hurry up, now! He's going to take you on the tram."

Jake moved across the dark grassy area with six kids in tow and the sleeping one slung over his shoulder. The east gate was the closest exit, but Acheron was still hovering near it. *Standing guard, no doubt,* Jake thought with exasperation. He led the slow-moving children towards the north gate, which was a much longer walk, but it couldn't be helped.

"I'm tired of walking," Abdul announced.

"Almost there," Jake said. "Think of all the yummy food you're going to have." He was about to step back onto the main path when he spotted a CIP loitering next to the north gate with a tell-tale box of muffins tucked under his arm.

Jake thought of the all the curses in all the languages he knew. He made a quick decision. "Come on, guys, we're going to tell the nice policeman we're going to the hospital."

"I thought we were going to Mother Teresa's." Abdul seemed to be the only child in the group who was still coherent.

"Yes, but we're going to *tell* him we're going to the hospital. It's a secret game I like to play with the CIPs. It's called 'Confuse a Cop.' They think it's fun." This explanation sounded ridiculous even to Jake's ears, but the boy made no further protest.

The CIP put up a hand to stop him as the little group converged on the gate. "Where do you think you're going?"

"To the hospital," announced Abdul.

Jake did his best imitation of his golden-tongued cousin, as he let loose the most plausible explanation he could concoct: "I work at the Outreach Clinic. All of these children are showing symptoms of Zenithian Flu, which you probably know is fatal. This epidemic could take out the whole station if I don't get these kids into quarantine before *I* drop dead."

The CIP took several nervous steps back. "Get them out of here."

Jake ushered the kids through the gate. "You might want to get yourself quarantined as well," he called back over his shoulder. "There's always a chance you might survive." The CIP looked panic-stricken.

Jake allowed himself a grin of triumph as he escorted his charges around the corner to a tramstop. Thirty minutes later, he was herding them in the door at Mother Teresa's.

"The harvest is beginning," he whispered to an astonished Kirsten, who met him in the front hall. He handed over the sleeping little girl. "Prepare for as many children as you can safely accommodate."

"Acheron will come here first," Kirsten protested.

"Maybe not." Lorina descended the stairs to join them. "I have an idea."

TEN

ALLIES

Blaze had only walked through McConnell Park once before, when he lived on Mars Station. The woodsy square kilometer was predominantly a homeless village, with blankets, tents, and cardboard lean-tos occupying any spare patch of drought-resistant grass. There were eight self-flushing toilets hidden among the shrubbery. The city council recognized the need to assist the burgeoning homeless population in this small way, or else risk fouling the entire park with their waste. Since it was never cold or rainy, people could sleep outdoors in relative comfort. The park had a number of water fountains, and the small lake was a popular place to bathe.

If I were homeless, I guess this would be a good place to live, Blaze thought, trying to keep pace with Idalis' purposeful strides as they entered the park through the west gate. He took a second look at the famous park, named for the inventor of the Velocity engine. *What would the richest man in the universe think of all this poverty? We can reach the stars now, but we aren't any better off than when we lived on Earth.*

"We should post a flyer on each fountain and toilet," Idalis decided. She was holding a stack of hand-printed paper signs. Blaze couldn't remember the last time he'd used a pen and paper, but the Captain had produced the supplies from some hidden stash and put them to work immediately after the crew meeting.

Blaze took a page from Idalis and glanced at the large bold letters:

Warning!

The CIPs are planning a raid to abduct children!

Please do everything possible to ensure their safety!

Do not let them out of your sight!

Beneath this was the same warning, hand-written in Swahili, Spanish, and Chinese. Tacked on to the bottom of the page were a few other computer-assisted translations, including Russian, Hindi, and Arabic.

Blaze took a roll of super-tape out of his pocket and followed Idalis to the first fountain. He scouted the faces around them, noting that most of the park's occupants were children. The youngsters watched him and Idalis with curious detachment. Blaze wished he'd brought some food to hand out, although no one had approached them for anything. He remembered being swarmed for handouts the first time he'd walked through the park. *Are the CIPs cracking down on panhandling?*

"What if they can't read?" Blaze asked, tearing off pieces of tape for Idalis.

Idalis attached a sign to the cement base of the drinking fountain. "I don't know." She wouldn't look at him, muttering to herself as they worked. Blaze did his best to ignore her nervous whispers of "crazy Captain" and "What is she trying to do? Get us all arrested, or deported?" He was relieved when she lapsed into Spanish monologues, though he still got the gist of her complaints.

The mission had certainly put a damper on Idalis' interest in Blaze – for which he was grateful. But he was beginning to realize he actually preferred her flirtatious approach to her nervous grumbling.

Idalis strode quickly to the next drinking fountain and barked at him to hurry up with the tape. The toilets were harder to locate, being hidden among the shrubbery, and it took them until noon to finish posting flyers.

"We should save a few for the shelter, and see if we can track down that doctor at the homeless clinic." Blaze took the last four flyers from Idalis.

"The Captain already went to the shelter. She told us to go straight back to the ship when we finish here to help Shima sell books. She's sending you and Shima to the hospital later this afternoon to locate the doctor. This is what we all agreed to."

"We still don't know how or when the harvest is going to take place," Blaze said. "Maybe we should talk to a CIP."

"Are you *loco*?" Idalis headed back towards the perimeter of the park at a crisp pace. "No CIP is going to tell us anything."

Blaze's gaze lingered over the children's faces as he trailed the feisty cook. He wasn't sure what he was looking for; he just had this nagging feeling that he needed to be observant.

They sure are – quiet. Blaze frowned, slowed his pace. He focused on a group of black siblings stretched out on a nest of old blankets and towels beneath a cottonwood tree. The little girl was fast asleep, but her two older brothers just lay there with a glazed look in their eyes.

Blaze left the sidewalk and approached them. "Hello?"

Neither boy answered him.

"Could I buy ya'all somethin' to eat?" Blaze asked.

The youngsters just stared at him lethargically. *An offer for a free meal doesn't even register? What's wrong with this picture?*

"Blaze!" Idalis turned around and shouted to him.

Blaze beckoned for her to join him, but she put her hands on her hips in the universal gesture of feminine impatience. Blaze ignored her. He went over and sat down on the grass next to the boys.

"Can you understand me?"

One of the brothers gave a barely perceptible nod, though his detached expression remained.

"Are you sick?"

"Feel . . . strange," whispered the other boy. "Can't . . . move."

An alarm went off in Blaze's mind as he remembered Shima's account of the night Zuri disappeared. *She said they felt weak and couldn't stay awake – just like these kids.*

He moved quickly to the little girl's side. She didn't respond to his touch, even when he shook her shoulder and shouted, "Wake up!"

"She sleep . . . all morning," the first brother whispered.

"Blaze!"

Blaze looked up to see Idalis racing towards him. She looked scared. He quickly got to his feet.

"A group of CIPs is coming this way!" She grasped his arm as she reached him, urging him to move. "They're armed! Let's go! If they realize we posted the flyers, we could be arrested!"

Blaze wanted to stay and protect the children, but he saw the wisdom in her suggestion. They ran, avoiding the main path and staying under cover of the trees as they headed for the nearest gate.

"We've got to find the Captain," Blaze panted as they finally reached the sidewalk outside the east gate. "She's right about the harvest, but she doesn't realize it's happening right now! The CIPs are going to collect the children tonight!"

It was three kilometers from McConnell Park to Mother Teresa's Juvenile Shelter on Farmer Street. Blaze and Idalis boarded a tram and didn't say a word to each other the entire ride. Idalis looked pale and scared; Blaze didn't want to alarm her further, so he stayed quiet and tried to think.

They disembarked at the closest tramstop, in front of an English pub, and walk-jogged towards Mother Teresa's. They were half a block away when Blaze saw the large orange sign posted on the lopsided front door with a boarded-up transom:

Warning -- Quarantine

Idalis stopped dead in her tracks and refused to go any closer. Blaze tugged on her sleeve. "Come on, I just want to read the sign."

Idalis shook his hand off. "No! Captain Shepherd's not here. Let's go."

Blaze left her standing on the sidewalk and approached the front door of Mother Teresa's. The sign was an official Board of Health document, explaining that the occupants had contracted Zenithian Flu. He felt a tremor of fear, recalling the devastation that the *Ishmael* suffered so recently from the disease.

Naturally, the quarantine would be a strong deterrent – for the CIPs. Blaze folded his arms across his chest, the answer suddenly clear in his mind: *It's a ruse.*

Acheron will know it's a diversion, but the quarantine looks genuine. Maybe it'll buy them some time, but it's only a temporary solution. And what about the kids in the park?

Blaze walked back to where Idalis was waiting. "Go back to the *Ishmael* and help Shima sell books. The ship needs to be stocked and fueled today. If you see the Captain, tell her the kids in the park are going to be slaves unless she can get them aboard by tonight."

Idalis studied his face with a nervous scowl. "Tonight? And what are you going to do?"

"I'm gonna keep watch here for awhile, try to gather more information."

"You're not going inside?" There was a touch of hysteria in Idalis' voice. "If you need more information, why don't you call Mother Teresa's from the ship?"

125

Blaze shook his head. "I have a feelin' I should stay here and watch for CIPs."

Idalis shrugged and turned back towards the tramstop. "Don't be long; Captain Shepherd will need your help."

"I know." Blaze watched her hurry away.

So this is what it's like to go on a stake out, Blaze thought, crossing the street in front of the shelter and walking into a Mediterranean café that was almost deserted after the lunch-hour rush. He sat down at a grimy table next to a grimier window and kept an eye on Mother Teresa's. He ordered a plate of hummus with pita and stuffed grape leaves, which he paid for as soon as it arrived at his table. Blaze took his datapad out of his pocket and pretended to read the *Martian Chronicles* as he nibbled his greasy lunch.

He didn't have to wait long. He saw the curtains move at a front window. A minute later, the door opened. A woman stepped outside, glanced quickly up and down the street, and shut the door behind her. She hurried up the block in the direction Idalis had departed.

Blaze exited the café and followed as quickly as he could without breaking into a run. Even though there were a number of pedestrians separating him from his quarry, he had no trouble keeping her in sight; her bright pink dress and auburn ponytail were hard to miss. Blaze tried to rehearse in his mind what he would say to her, but it was useless. *Anything I say will sound suspicious, or insane.*

Blaze was still half a block away when she stopped at the tramstop sign in front of Shield's pub. A tram was quickly approaching. He gave up discretion and broke into a run.

"Excuse me, -- miss! Lady in the pink dress, please wait!"

She didn't turn around. Blaze thought she must have heard him, but chose to ignore his shouts. The tram glided to a stop and she was about to board.

Blaze pushed through the knot of people at the tramstop and grasped her arm before she could get on. "Please wait! I need to talk to you!"

He expected her to be surprised, maybe even alarmed, but he was completely unprepared for a thrashing.

Without turning around, she grabbed his wrist with her free hand and yanked him forward, throwing him off balance. She turned to the side, slammed an elbow into his stomach and, when he doubled over, grasped the shoulders of his uniform and continued his forward momentum, shoving him into the open doorway of the tram.

Blaze managed to bring up his arms in time to break his fall, but struck a glancing blow on the metal step with his nose. A white-hot pain seemed to slice through the center of his face.

"Green line tram to Merchant Street, ten credits," the android driver announced in a monotone without looking down at Blaze.

"Excuse me, I need to get on!" said someone behind Blaze.

Blaze's lower body was sprawled on the road; he withdrew his upper body from the tram doorway and struggled to a standing position. He stepped back to make room for the impatient passengers. No one offered him a word of sympathy.

He felt something damp on his chin and realized his nose was bleeding heavily. He hadn't noticed because he was in so much pain.

Blaze scanned the street for a pink dress and auburn hair. She was nowhere in sight. He couldn't blame her for being cautious.

He put a hand over his streaming nose and made his way to the tramstop bench. He sat down with care, keenly aware of several new bruises. With his free hand, he searched his pockets for something to staunch the flow, and tried to gather his scattered thoughts.

"You don't look like a CIP. Are you undercover?" asked a cool contralto behind him.

"I'm not a CIP." Finding nothing of use in his pockets, Blaze touched his nose to his sleeve and recoiled from the fresh shock wave of pain. The front of his uniform was damp with blood.

"Here, try this." She came around the bench, holding out a white cloth with ruffles around the edges.

Without looking up, Blaze took the proffered fabric and held it cautiously to his nose. He thought about thanking her, but didn't -- since she was the one who gave him the bloody nose. He decided to introduce himself instead.

"My name's Robert Smith. I work on a passenger ship called *Ishmael.* I'm an engineer, not a cop."

"Why were you following me?"

Blaze raised his chin to look at her face, and every thought in his head vanished like a puff of smoke.

She was gorgeous; one of the most beautiful women he'd ever set eyes on. He stared at her for a full minute before recalling that he was a bloody mess. He felt embarrassed, and a little annoyed.

"Why were you following me?" she repeated, her long-lashed hazel eyes crinkling at the corners as she gave him a suspicious frown.

"I need to talk to you. Can I do that now, or are you gonna give me a black eye first?"

"That depends." She ignored his feeble attempt at humor as she cast a nervous glance up and down the street. "What do you want?"

Blaze decided to cut to the chase. "I want to help you save the children from the harvest."

She let out a little gasp. "How do you know about that?" She moved to sit down on the bench beside him. "Did Acheron send you?"

"No." Blaze took a deep breath. "Look, it's a long story, but my captain has a plan to rescue these kids from slavery. But we have to move fast or the kids in the park are gonna to be picked up by Acheron tonight."

"*Slavery?*" She looked horrified. "Is that what he's doing with them?"

Blaze took the cloth away from his face, but his nose continued to bleed. "Look, I don't know who you are, but I saw you leave Mother Teresa's, so I know you don't have Zenithian Flu. The deception might buy some time for the kids at the shelter, but the kids in the park have been drugged. Acheron will have no trouble roundin' them up tonight."

"Don't say anymore." She reached over and gently placed the cloth back over his nose. "I'm Lorina Murphy; I volunteer at the shelter. If there's something you can do to help, I need to take you to see Jake at the Outreach Clinic."

Blaze's hopes soared at her mention of the clinic. "Does this Jake happen to be a doctor?"

Lorina hesitated. "How do you know --?" She shook her head. "Never mind, you can tell both of us when we get to the clinic. Let's hurry." She slipped her arm through Blaze's and helped him to his feet.

"I didn't realize you were so tall." Lorina smiled up at him, and Blaze stopped breathing for a moment. "Maybe Jake can do something about your nose," she murmured apologetically. "It might be broken."

"It won't be the first time." Blaze felt something like an electrical charge course through him when Lorina touched his arm. He was disappointed when she let go.

"Come on," she led him down the sidewalk, "it's only another block. Hopefully, he's still there." Lorina glanced around nervously and urged him to walk fast.

Lorina led him through the familiar ER entrance of Mars Community Hospital, then down a hallway and around a corner to a curtained wall bearing a paper sign: *Outreach Clinic.* She pulled aside the green curtain and drew Blaze into the makeshift waiting room.

"Jake!"

Blaze grinned, recognizing the slack-jawed young man sound asleep in a chair, his head on an old steel desk.

Jake startled at Lorina's shout but didn't open his eyes. "You can't leave the shelter. Acheron will see you."

"Wake up. There's someone you need to meet."

"Not another orphan. We can't squeeze any more into the shelter," Jake said, still not moving.

"Wake up!" Lorina grasped a handful of Jake's unruly hair and lifted his head from the desk.

"Ow, let go!" Jake's eyes were open now. He shook free of her hand and took a long look at Blaze. "Back so soon? Didn't you come in by ambulance a few days ago?"

"That was me."

"I barely recognized you through all the blood." Jake gave Lorina an appraising glance. "Did she do that to you?"

"Yeah." Blaze felt his face getting warm. "But it's my fault; I surprised her."

Jake got to his feet and ushered Blaze and Lorina through a curtain behind the desk, into an untidy examination room. "Lie down and let me take a look at your nose."

Blaze did as instructed, though his legs hung down awkwardly from the end of the short table.

Jake got to work: he covered Blaze's eyes with some kind of cloth mask, said, "Hold your breath," and sprayed a shockingly cold blast of Hemorrhage Freeze over his face. Blaze's nose immediately stopped bleeding. Next, Jake swabbed some type of topical painkiller over his nose, around his nostrils, and even up into his sinuses. In moments, the middle of Blaze's face felt completely numb, like nothing existed between his eyes and mouth.

While Jake was working, Lorina began her interrogation: "Jake O'Brien, Robert Smith. Tell him what you told me, Robert."

"I actually go by my nickname, Blaze."

"*Blaze*?" Lorina chortled. "I once had a horse named Blaze."

"Me, too. That's how I broke my nose the first time – Blaze reared and threw me into a fence post."

"Hold still," was the only thing Jake said. "You two can swap equestrian stories later."

Blaze sensed that Jake was manipulating the cartilage of his nose, but it was hard to tell exactly what he was doing.

"Tell us your captain's plan for rescuing the street kids," Lorina said.

"Yeah," Jake said, "please fill me in."

"Well, my crewmate Vipul used to work aboard a ship called the *Elmina*. He thought it was a freighter, haulin' livestock. Turns out it's a slave ship."

"Slaves?" Jake interrupted. Blaze could tell from his tone that he'd touched a nerve. "Is that what Acheron's doing with the kids? That evil son of a –"

"Yeah," Blaze spoke over him, "he sells them to the *Elmina*. Now my captain, Danae Shepherd, ran into Acheron and his partner in crime, Thanatos, last night –"

"Who's Thanatos?" Lorina asked.

"The captain of the *Elmina*." Blaze tried to keep his thoughts on track with all the interruptions. "Anyway, Captain Shepherd starts puttin' two and two together and got Vipul to tell her the whole story. Then she shocks us all by sayin' this is unacceptable, and we're gonna do somethin' to stop it."

"She sounds just like you," Jake said. Blaze assumed this remark was intended for Lorina.

"Look who's talking. How many kids did you round up last night?"

"Not enough. What does your captain have in mind, Blaze?"

"I was gettin' to that, if y'all'd give me a chance to finish."

"Sorry." Lorina rested her hand on his shoulder. Blaze felt his heart rate speed up.

"And I'm sorry, but you're going to have to be quiet for five minutes while I finish with the fusion laser," Jake said.

Blaze shut his mouth in consternation. He heard a low-pitched humming and had a vague sense of something warm penetrating his sinuses. It was the same odd sensation he'd felt in his chest when the ER doctor healed his rib.

"Hopefully, this will also repair the original break," Jake explained, "although I have to tell you I've never fixed a nose before."

Blaze resisted the urge to grimace. He lay still and listened to Jake and Lorina's banter:

"Blaze saw me leave the shelter. He tried to catch me at the tram. That's when I decked him." Lorina gave Blaze's shoulder a squeeze, which he took to mean, 'I'm sorry.'

"I told you not to leave. If Acheron has anyone watching the shelter, they're going to know the quarantine's a forgery."

"I left to buy food. We don't have enough on hand to feed 108 kids."

"You could have called Erik to bring something over. He could wear a biohazard suit. That would look convincing."

"Kirsten's tried to reach him all morning, ever since he brought in the last kids at 8:00. Have you seen him?"

"No, I was waiting for him to come back to the clinic."

"Do you think he's been arrested?" Lorina sounded nervous.

"Let's not jump to conclusions. He's probably at home, sleeping so soundly he can't hear the com."

"I think he would have checked in with you or Kirsten before he went home."

Jake made a frustrated noise and switched off the laser.

"I have an idea where he might be." Blaze took the mask off his eyes and sat up. "Captain Shepherd and Vipul went to the shelter this mornin'. It's possible they ran into him."

"If it's possible, where would they have gone?" Jake asked.

"My best guess is they took him to the *Ishmael*. If there's any way we can get the kids on board today, we can lift out of here, take them somewhere safer."

"That's your plan?" Jake frowned. "It's got some major holes in it."

"I know," said Blaze, "but at the moment, it's more secure than your quarantine ruse."

"He's right, Jake," Lorina said. "Let's check Erik's apartment first, then head to the *Ishmael*. I have a feeling we've got a lot of work to do if we're going to pull this off."

Jake nodded. "I'd better call Kirsten and give her a heads-up." He stepped through the curtains back into the waiting area.

Blaze started to get up from the exam table, but Lorina gestured for him to remain seated. She dampened a hand towel at the sink and began washing the dried blood off his face. "We don't want you to attract too much attention. Maybe Jake can find some scrubs for you to change into."

Blaze shut his eyes and tried not to look like he was enjoying himself. "I can change when we get back to the ship. I certainly attracted a lot of attention at the tramstop."

"I'm so sorry," Lorina murmured. "How does your nose feel?"

"I can't feel anythin', but I can breathe through it, at least. We'll see what it looks like when all the bruisin' goes away."

"Speaking of bruises –" Lorina studied his left cheek. "This looks recent; did I give you that?"

"No, someone else punched me a few days ago. See, one of my shipmates was bein' assaulted and I jumped in to defend her, not realizin', of course, that the guy was gonna pulverize me. He managed to break my rib, -- this one –" Blaze reached across with his right hand and pointed out the spot to her under his left arm. "That's how I met Jake coming into the ER when he was on his way out."

Blaze opened his eyes in time to see a flash of emotion in Lorina's expression, but then it was gone. *Maybe it's just sympathy, since I'm sure I look like something the cat dragged in.* But he couldn't help hoping there was something more than sympathy in her glance.

Then Jake rushed in and Blaze had to focus on reality. He didn't have time to daydream.

"Let's get moving." Jake slipped his medical scanner into his pocket. "It'll be dark in five hours."

* * *

There was no answer at Erik's apartment, which was in the building next door to the hospital. When they boarded a tram for the port, Blaze tried to bring Jake and Lorina up to speed on the hurdles they still faced.

"If my shipmate Shima managed to sell a lot of books this mornin', we just might have enough cash to get fueled, stocked, and ready to lift. If the rest of the crew managed to take care of the preparations, all we have to do is find a way to get the kids onto the ship. There's only one problem."

"Only one?" Jake scowled. "You just mentioned several."

Blaze focused on Jake's cynical expression. "*Ishmael* can't lift without a med-tech on board."

He watched Jake and Lorina exchange a worried glance.

"In that case, you'd better pray that we find Erik Sorensen," Jake said.

"I don't understand."

"I'm not licensed to practice medicine."

"But you fixed my nose –"

"Yes, I can mend broken bones, and I can do simple things like cure infections and treat dehydration, but a ship's med-tech needs to be qualified to handle anything from alien diseases to open-heart surgery. I'm just a medical student. I can't help you."

Disappointed, Blaze shut his mouth and glanced at Lorina's worried expression. He had an urge to wrap his arms around her and tell her everything would be all right. *Maybe later,* he hoped, *when all this is behind us.* He marveled at his own audacity: he was already assuming Lorina would lift with the *Ishmael.*

The three disembarked at Lift 16, and Blaze took them up to the ship. As the elevator doors opened in front of the *Ishmael,* he was dismayed to see an armed CIP standing guard outside the airlock.

"Now what?" Jake whispered.

Blaze took a deep breath and gestured for them to follow his lead. He walked up to the officer. "Excuse me, I need to report to Captain Shepherd."

"Are you part of *Ishmael*'s crew?" The young Latino regarded them with a suspicious frown.

"Yeah, I'm the engineer. Is there a problem?"

"Only crewmembers are allowed to enter the ship, on Chief Acheron's orders." He glanced at Blaze's blood-stained uniform. "Did you lose a fight?"

Blaze ignored the CIP's sarcasm and reached around him with his long arm, pressing his thumb to the ID lock. "Excuse me."

The officer glanced at Jake and Lorina. "What about you two? Are you crew?"

133

"Dr. O'Brien and Miss Murphy have just been hired as the ship's med-tech and steward," Blaze said smugly, impressed at his own resourcefulness. "The Captain's expectin' them." He stepped past the CIP into the airlock's antechamber, then glanced back at Jake and Lorina, hoping they would follow his lead.

The CIP looked like he was going to bar their way, but Jake brushed past him with the confidence of a man who belonged on the ship. Lorina was right on his heels, but her expression wasn't convincing; she looked terrified.

"Wait, let me check your IDs." The CIP reached for his weapon.

Blaze held his breath as all three turned around to face the officer. Lorina was standing just inside the first doorway; one foot on the threshold. *Step back,* Blaze thought, *just take one step back.*

The CIP made a move towards Lorina.

Blaze moved faster. He grabbed the back of her dress, yanked her into the antechamber and punched the 'emergency close' button on the keypad.

The airlock door cycled shut in the blink of an eye, leaving the enraged CIP outside.

"We are now officially in trouble." Blaze punched the visitor code into the keypad as Jake and Lorina eyed him with a mixture of shock and admiration. "Let's hope your Dr. Erik is here."

They could hear the CIP attempting, unsuccessfully, to penetrate the first airlock door with something metallic, like the butt of his gun. The second door cycled shut behind them, sealing off the noise.

"Welcome aboard the *Ishmael.*" Blaze started up the ladder. "Captain Shepherd?"

"Blaze, where've you been?" Vipul's voice greeted them. He sounded tense. "The Captain wants to lift at 20:00."

"Tonight?" Jake gasped.

"Who's that?" Vipul asked.

"Jake O'Brien, the clinic doctor I told you about." Blaze reached the top level and waited to assist Jake and Lorina from the ladder – especially Lorina.

"Only I'm not a doctor," Jake said as Blaze ushered them onto the bridge.

"Oh, great!" Marco turned around in his seat at the helm. "Why don't we all just turn ourselves in and save Acheron the trouble of arresting us?"

"Where's Captain Shepherd?" Blaze shot Marco a withering glance as he led Jake and Lorina over to the navigation console.

Vipul rose to his feet and solemnly shook hands with Jake and Lorina. "The Captain and a Dr. Sorensen are dirtside arranging for a private tram to get the children here. She took an earcom, but left me in charge."

There was a muttered complaint from Marco, something about seniority. Blaze's back was to him. He widened his stance, deliberately excluding the helmsman from their huddle.

"Good, Erik's with the Captain," Lorina said. She and Jake exchanged a look of relief.

"What orders did she leave?" Blaze asked.

Vipul shook his head, looking discouraged. "*Ishmael*'s fueled and watered. We managed to get a shipment of produce on board before Acheron posted a guard, but the Captain's arranged for at least 20 more deliveries. I'm not sure how to get them past the guard."

"Not to mention the minor problem of how we're going to get a tram-load of children past the guard," Lorina said.

Blaze grimaced. "After the stunt I just pulled at the airlock, Acheron's probably gonna post a garrison."

Lorina shook her head. "No, Blaze, you did the right thing. Jake and I could have been arrested."

"Not you, just me," Jake said. "As soon as they check my background, I'm going to jail."

"We're *all* going to jail," Marco interjected, "any minute now."

"Ignore his sunny personality." Blaze didn't bother to turn around and glare at the helmsman.

"I'm the voice of reason in the midst of this insanity, and you know it!"

"What should we do now?" Blaze asked Vipul.

"Isn't there another way to get on or off the ship besides the airlock?" Jake asked.

"Oh sure, but you'll need a pressure suit." Marco turned his back to them as he faced the helm again.

Blaze and Vipul exchanged a thoughtful glance. "That's an idea," Vipul muttered.

"What?" Jake asked. "*Is* there another way?"

"There's a hatch in the basement," Blaze explained, "it's used for surface loading and unloading."

"Yeah, and there's a ship docked just below us on Level 8," Marco interrupted again. "So if you think you can get out through another station airlock, you're crazy."

"I've been accused of being crazy a few times in my life." Vipul rubbed his chin, thinking.

"Zip line?" Blaze asked.

"Just show me the spare parts workshop, and I can put together a suspension harness." Vipul grinned. "I've done it before."

"A zip line would take care of the deliveries," Blaze said, "but we still need to bring the children in through the main airlock."

"Why don't we just take out the guard?" Lorina's suggestion drew surprised looks from the men. "I don't mean kill him, -- I mean just hit him in the head or something."

"You'd be perfect for that." Blaze smiled at her.

Lorina shot him a bemused grin. "Seriously, all we need is something to distract the guard long enough to get the kids on board."

Blaze noticed a sudden gleam in Vipul's dark eyes and lowered his voice so Marco wouldn't overhear. "You have an idea?"

Vipul nodded slowly. "Maybe." He turned to Jake. "Take a look around the medical lab; see if there are any glass bottles or test tubes."

Jake raised his eyebrows at the navigator. "Glass isn't used much anymore, but I'll look."

"You'll also need some alcohol, the higher the proof, the better." Vipul drew a datapad from his pants pocket and jotted down some instructions for Jake. "Blaze and I will get to work on the zip line. We don't have much time."

"What about him?" Lorina murmured, nodding towards Marco.

"Feel free to hit him in the head," Blaze whispered.

* * *

Blaze was flat on his belly at the basement hatch, checking the seals on the smaller airlock.

Vipul knelt down next to him, pressure suit helmet in his gloved hand. "Do you think the cable is going to be long enough?"

"I calculated 75 meters to the nearest open airlock." Blaze pointed with his thumb, indicating the direction his shipmate would need to traverse in open space. "Are you sure you don't want me to attempt this?"

Vipul snorted. "We've been over this, Blaze. Stop treating me like an old man. You're too tall for the suit. It feels like it was designed for the Captain, so only another woman or a skinny bloke like me can wear it. Besides, I've actually been inside a suit before, – you haven't. Now shut up, and let's get moving."

Blaze nodded and helped Vipul attach the titanium cable to his rappelling harness. "Try not to get this tangled with your life line."

Vipul nodded and put on his helmet.

Blaze could hear the pressure suit filling with oxygen. He double-checked the monitors, assuring himself that Vipul's suit was functioning properly. "One more thing, before you head out?"

"What is it?" Vipul's voice sounded strangely mechanical inside the helmet.

"What do you think of Lorina?" Blaze grinned.

Vipul paused, and Blaze half-expected the older man to berate him for bringing this up when there was work to be done, but here was nothing but kindness in Vipul's answer.

"Did you happen to look at her hands, Blaze?"

"Her hands?" Blaze shook his head.

"She's wearing a wedding ring, mate. And since Jake's wearing one too, I assume they're married. Sorry."

Blaze felt like all the air was being forced out of his lungs. "No, I didn't notice her hands." He turned to the airlock controls, grateful for the opportunity to avert his face. "Are you ready?"

ELEVEN
MOTIVES

Danae and Erik settled in for a long ride to the tram roundhouse, on the south corner of the station.

"You have a loyal crew," Erik said. "I'm impressed by their dedication."

"Now that you've spoken to Shima, I guess you understand why I'm determined to stop the harvest," Danae replied.

Although the doctor's attitude had softened since their initial confrontation outside the shelter, they still regarded each other as uneasy allies. Not that Danae blamed him for being skeptical; they still didn't have any idea how they were going to get the children aboard the *Ishmael*.

"How are we going to move them right under Acheron's nose?" Erik asked, voicing her concerns aloud.

Danae shook her head. "I just hope we can afford a private transport."

Erik frowned and stared out the window. Danae studied his profile, recalling their uncomfortable first meeting on the front steps of Mother Teresa's.

She and Vipul had been reading the quarantine sign on the door when Erik brushed right past them on the sidewalk. He had been carrying two small children, one on each hip, with three more trailing behind him, trying to keep up with his long-legged strides. Ignoring the quarantine notice, he'd pressed his thumb to the ID lock and ushered the children quickly inside. Then he pulled the door shut and turned around to face Danae and Vipul, noticing them for the first time.

"Can I help you?" He looked extremely nervous. Danae noted his blood-shot eyes and unshaven cleft chin.

"We'd actually like to help you," Vipul replied.

"Who sent you?" Erik eyed them suspiciously.

"No one sent us." Danae felt her own defenses rising. "We came to help rescue the children."

Erik gave her a startled look, but said nothing.

"We know about Acheron's plan," Vipul explained. "We want to help." He extended a tentative hand. "I'm Vipul Ganguli, and this is Captain Danae Shepherd of the passenger ship *Ishmael*."

"Erik Sorensen." He shook their hands warily. "I don't know how much you know, but unless you have some influence over the CIPs in this town, I don't see how you can help."

"I'm willing to risk my ship to get the kids to safety," Danae said.

"You want to take them on your ship? Where?"

"I don't know, but any place I take them is better than what Acheron has in store for them."

"Which would be *what*?" Erik demanded.

"Slavery," Vipul whispered.

Erik's eyes widened. "How do you know this?"

"I used to work for Acheron's right-hand man, Thanatos. Ever hear of a ship called *Elmina*?" Vipul asked.

"No." Erik folded his arms across his barrel-like chest. He did nothing to disguise the skepticism in his tone. "You said you *used* to work for Thanatos? Are you still loyal to him?"

Danae lost her temper. "Why would we be here, sharing this information with you, if he was loyal to Thanatos?" She felt like the entire plan was in jeopardy because of this one stubborn man. "You need help, and we're offering it to you! Your fake quarantine won't work for long!"

"You think it's a fake? Why don't you go inside and find out?" The doctor's fair complexion began to take on a crimson hue.

"Of course it's a fake! Why else would you send some healthy children inside? If Acheron has this place under surveillance, your quarantine won't be worth the paper it's written on!"

Danae tried to lower her voice as several passersby stopped to stare at them. She nudged Vipul with her elbow, lowered her voice. "Come on. Let's see if we can find that young doctor from the homeless clinic."

"How do you know about Jake?" Erik asked.

"Jake, is it?" Danae studied Erik's expression carefully. "One of my crewmembers met him outside the ER three nights ago. If you won't help us, maybe he will. Clearly, *he* has a vested interest in helping homeless children."

Erik appeared to let his guard down a fraction. He looked exhausted. "Jake's my assistant. I run the Outreach Clinic. You seemed determined to get involved, so why don't we calm down and take a minute to listen to each other?"

"That's what I was *trying* to do," Danae said.

Erik offered her a sheepish smile of truce and took a deep breath. "Tell me about your plan."

"I have a better idea. We'll show you the plan. Come back to the ship with us," Danae said. "You can see for yourself the preparations we're making. *Ishmael* is a passenger ship, not a slave ship."

"Why are you doing this?" Erik asked, reluctantly nodding his agreement.

Danae felt her anger smoldering anew as she thought of Acheron's threats to arrest Marco and impound her ship. "Just because . . . it's the right thing to do."

We're on the same side, she thought, studying Erik's drooping eyelids as he leaned his platinum blond head against the tram window. *We have to trust each other.* She ran her tongue over her dry lips, trying to gather the nerve to pop the question.

"Erik, even if we can pull this off, the portmaster won't give me clearance to lift without a med-tech on board. Would you go with us?"

The doctor's eyes opened halfway; he focused on her face with a surprised expression. His answer was frank, but gentle: "Danae, my sister and I are the only advocates these children have. Yes, we might be able to rescue a group of kids from Acheron's clutches, but what about the next group, and the next? As long as there are homeless children on the station, I'm needed here."

Danae was startled to feel how personal the rejection felt. She bit her lip. "Then all this work is for nothing, Dr. Sorensen. I won't be able to lift out of here, and we'll all probably end up in jail."

"What about Jake?"

"He's not a doctor."

"He might be all you need for a single jump. Earth is only three days from here. You could hire a licensed medic dirtside when you land."

"If that's where we're going. I haven't decided yet." Danae resented feeling pressured to make so many decisions without adequate time to think them through. *Or someone to talk them over with, like Alex.*

"Earth was just a suggestion," Erik conceded. "Food is scarce, but there's a lot more places to land; more places to *hide,* if you catch my meaning."

"Acheron should be the one hiding! That amoral low-life – he's supposed to be *protecting* the public, not selling out innocent children to slavers!"

Erik whistled softly. "Does everyone get to see this side of you, Danae?"

Danae pursed her lips. "I'm not normally like this. I'm running on too little sleep and too many confrontations with my helmsman."

Erik nodded. "Ting does have a talent for rubbing people the wrong way. What did he mean by 'you're going to kill someone'?"

Danae shrugged. She didn't want to think about Marco's latest – and most absurd -- prediction. She massaged her temples, feeling fatigue down to her bones. "How many more stops?"

Erik pondered the map on the wall near their seats. "Twenty."

Danae closed her eyes for just a moment, but when she opened them, the tram was pulling into the roundhouse. She was embarrassed to realize she'd fallen asleep with her head against Erik's broad shoulder.

"Sorry." She sat upright and winced, noting the beginning of a sleep-deprivation headache.

"Don't worry about it, I nodded off too." Erik yawned and rubbed his eyes.

They were the only passengers still on the tram. They disembarked and looked around. It was noisy in the roundhouse, with dozens of trams being re-routed onto a labyrinth of tracks. They navigated between the slow-moving vehicles to reach the dispatcher's office.

An elderly man with *stationmaster* stitched across the brim of his traditional train engineer's cap looked up from a bare desk where he was reclining backwards in his chair, feet up, sipping coffee, and reading the *Chronicles* on his datapad. He seemed surprised to see another human in the roundhouse. "You folks lost? Miss your stop?"

"No, we meant to come here," Danae said. "We're interested in hiring a tram for tonight."

The stationmaster put his feet on the floor and studied their faces for a moment with a bemused grin. "Been workin' here 20 years, and this is the first time I've had two trams hired on the same day."

Danae felt a stab of fear. "Someone else hired a tram today?"

"Yeah," the man replied, "CIP chief Acheron hired one for 9:00; said he wanted to surprise a special lady with a romantic ride around the city."

Erik cleared his throat. "Isn't that something? My wife and I had the same thought – it's our tenth anniversary."

Danae was startled to feel Erik's arm around her shoulders. She forced a smile, trying to play along.

"Happy anniversary!" The stationmaster came over to shake their hands. "You two make a handsome couple. Any kids?"

"No," Erik replied, at the exact same moment Danae said, "Yes."

The stationmaster's smile morphed into a suspicious frown.

Danae slapped her hands over her belly. "We're expecting our first one in June!" She turned to give Erik a sheepish grin. "I wanted to surprise you, honey."

"I'm certainly surprised!" The doctor looked like he wanted to crawl under the desk. "That's wonderful!" He gave her an awkward hug. "I'm going to be a father!"

Danae struggled to contain a giggle.

"Well, double congratulations!" said the stationmaster. "Let's see if we can arrange a private tram for you." He stepped over to a control board/terminal next to his desk.

"We'll need the biggest one you've got," Erik said.

The stationmaster shot him another suspicious look.

"We want to invite our extended family to celebrate this special day with us," Danae said. "And the miracle of this baby."

"Miracle is right," Erik said, deadpan.

Danae had to pinch herself to keep from laughing.

The old man seemed to accept the reason with good humor. He focused on the display screen. "What time do you want the tram, and for how long?"

"7:00 p.m., and we'll only need it for an hour," Danae said.

"Mighty short ride," said the stationmaster, pursing his lips.

"Let's go for 6:30," said Erik, "and we'll take it for two hours."

Danae nudged him with her elbow. "You're too generous, *honey.*"

"I can rent you the largest tram, which will hold 100 passengers, with android, for 20,000 an hour." The stationmaster began tapping numbers into a keypad.

Danae was grateful his back was to them because she couldn't help grimacing. She shot Erik a nervous look.

The doctor extended his left thumb. "This should cover it."

Danae was amazed Erik would use his own money. She gave him a grateful look, which he acknowledged with a grin. The uneasy alliance was now a solidly forged friendship. Danae returned the grin.

The stationmaster turned back to them. "Where should the tram pick you up?"

Ten minutes later, Danae and Erik boarded a regular tram to head back to the city. As soon as they sat down, they looked at each other and burst into laughter.

"Let's rehearse our story next time, *dear,*" Erik said.

Danae was about to offer a retort when her earcom chimed. "Shepherd here."

"Captain, I hope you don't mind, but I've hired a medic and a steward." Vipul sounded pleased. "They're already on board."

Danae nodded. "Erik appraised me on their unique talents. Do you think Lorina could create a fake medical license for Jake? It has to look good enough to impress the portmaster."

"I'll tell her as soon as I'm back on the ship."

Danae frowned. "How did you get past the guard, and where are you now?"

"Airlock 15 on Level 8. Blaze and I are loading the *Ishmael* with a zip line to the basement hatch. Shima's already called the vendors to reroute the deliveries. Acheron doesn't have a clue."

Danae's jaw dropped. "Remind me to give you a raise, Mr. Ganguli."

Vipul laughed. "Don't thank me till we lift, Captain."

"Did you happen to come up with any clever ideas to get the kids past the guard?"

Vipul hesitated. "We have an idea, Captain. It involves a few homemade explosives."

Danae didn't like the sound of this, but she tried to keep an open mind. "Is anyone going to get hurt?"

"No, Captain. You have my word on that," Vipul replied. "Jake and I are working on a diversion. I'd give you full details, but I have a feeling you probably don't want to know."

"Really?" Danae was impressed by his audacity. *This is coming from my timid, soft-spoken navigator?* "So you just want me to trust you?"

"Yes, Captain, that's all I'm asking."

"You don't ask for much." Danae blew out a long breath. "Try not to blow up anything on my ship, Vipul."

"Yes, ma'am."

"Oh, and Vipul?"

"Yes, Captain?"

"Calculate the jump to Earth when you have a free moment." She gave Erik a half-smile. "Shepherd out."

* * *

Danae went over the list of deliveries with Shima. "Will that be enough rice?" She glanced around the spartan waiting room of the Outreach Clinic and tried to concentrate on the younger woman's soft voice.

Danae was waging a losing battle with fatigue. She yawned and tried to focus through the haze masquerading as her brain. "Did the fruit arrive? Good. What about the diapers?"

She adjusted the com on her earlobe, not sure if she'd heard correctly. "Clothes? You know we don't have enough money, Shima. One change of clothes for each child would cost more than the fuel and water combined."

Danae laughed at the housekeeper's response. "You want a box of safety pins to make *togas* for them? Using what?"

"The *sheets*? I must be exhausted, because right now that sounds like a perfectly reasonable idea." Danae leaned back in the swivel chair and nearly lost her balance, laughing.

Erik poked his head out of the exam room where he had been tidying up, securing the medical supplies. He raised his eyebrows at Danae, but she just shook her head and mouthed 'tell you later.' She knew he was anxious about closing the clinic for the evening, and marveled that he'd never taken a day off in three-plus years. *And I thought* I *was a workaholic.*

"I'll put safety pins on my list. Shepherd out." Danae glanced at the time: 3:30 p.m. "I still need to contact the portmaster, and pick up a few supplies." She turned around in the chair to see if Erik was listening.

He was. He studied her face with an intensity that made her feel self-conscious. "Plenty of time. Do you want to return to the ship?"

"No, I don't want to raise the guard's suspicions when we leave again to meet the tram. I think our time would be better spent at the park."

Erik nodded and drew the curtain closed to the exam room behind him. "Yeah, I'd like to get an idea of how many children are still in danger."

"And where they are," Danae said. "It's a big park."

"A lot of the kids will already be unconscious from the sedatives." Erik raised his eyebrows at her. "So, how much weight can you lift?"

"I'll carry the *little* ones." Danae got up from the chair. "We'd better get moving."

To her surprise, Erik pulled out his scanner and passed it in front of her. He studied the results with a disapproving frown. "You're not going to be able to stay on your feet much longer, Danae. You need some food and some sleep."

Danae laughed. "The food part I won't argue with, but caffeine will have to substitute for the sleep, doctor." She appraised the stubble on his chin, the shadows under his eyes. "Test that thing on yourself, and you'll come up with the same prognosis."

He gave her a sheepish grin. "Chinese okay?"

"My favorite."

"I know a good place near the park."

"Lead the way."

Thirty minutes later they were sitting at a tiny café table, sharing lo mein, spinach dumplings, and a Sichuan vegetable dish that was so spicy it brought tears to his eyes. Danae had chugged an iced cappuccino before the food arrived. Now she gulped a Coke between bites. The haze in her mind began to dissipate.

"Try plain rice if your mouth's burning." She tried not to laugh as Erik gulped his own Coke. "Those little red things aren't bell peppers."

"Thanks for the tip."

"I thought you liked Chinese."

"I'm an egg roll and wonton kind of guy." He grinned and slid the Sichuan serving bowl closer to her plate.

As her hunger and headache receded, Danae decided to indulge her curiosity. "What motivates a nice, obviously well-educated person to run an under-funded clinic for the homeless? It can't be the rewarding pay, the great work environment, or the convenient hours."

Erik chewed thoughtfully, swallowed. "Most of my pay goes right back into the clinic. And I stopped keeping track of the hours a long time ago. As for the environment, well, I try to focus on the big picture. I feel like I'm doing something to improve the quality of life for these kids."

"But why? Why do you feel so driven to help homeless children?" Danae studied his expression as she heaped more lo mein onto her plate.

"Because 30 years ago, I was one of them."

Danae put down her chopsticks.

Erik lowered his eyes to his plate and continued: "Kirsten and I lived on the streets of Stockholm with a mother who was always high on something – anything she could get her hands on. I spent half my time worrying she'd OD, and the other half worrying my little sister and I would freeze to death. I was eight years old when the city finally took custody of us, and we were adopted by a childless couple. It was a relief to grow up in a secure and loving family, but I never forgot how horrible it was to be on the streets." He took a long drink of his Coke.

"Danae, I never forget how lucky I am to be on the other side; educated, sheltered, well-fed." He patted his stomach, attempting to lighten the mood. "Maybe a little too well-fed."

"We have something in common." Danae's throat was too dry to swallow her dumpling. She washed it down with Coke. "My mother's substance of choice was alcohol. I wasn't homeless, but I was still trapped -- taking care of her, trying to avoid her when she was in an abusive mood -- until I finished high school." She studied the blond lashes and brows framing his glacier-blue eyes. "Does the responsibility ever feel like too much of a burden?"

"I never felt Kirsten was a burden because I honestly didn't *know* it wasn't my job to take care of her, not until we had a responsible mother -- and father." He paused, thinking. "But, if what you're asking is: do I feel overwhelmed with the responsibility of looking after all the homeless kids on the station? Do I feel like I sacrifice too much for the clinic, like a normal job with good pay and decent hours," he looked into her eyes, "and coming home to a family every night?"

Danae felt a flutter of fear at his implication. She looked down at her plate. "Yes, I guess that's what I meant."

"To be honest, I'm too busy to think about what's missing in my life. I just know how much I'm needed here. I wish there'd been someone like me around when I was on the streets. What about you?"

"What do you mean?"

"You've lived on a ship most of your life. Don't you feel lonely sometimes, isolated? Did you have to sacrifice a lot for your career?"

Danae poked at a cube of tofu with her chopsticks until it fell apart, her appetite suddenly gone.

"Sorry," Erik said softly. "I didn't mean to pry."

"It's okay; I pried first." Danae lifted her chin, looked him in the eye. "My sacrifices haven't been voluntary, like yours. The nightmare of the last jump has forced me to question every decision I've ever made." Her brow furrowed as she tried to put her feelings into words.

"I mean, why am I in this business? Is it just for the money? Can my ambition ever justify my father's unexplained death or my husband's fatal illness? And there have been other lives lost, as well. Lives I was responsible for. Unlike you, I shoulder the burdens with great reluctance. I no longer feel any motivation to stay on this career path.

"If I had a child, I think he would have become a casualty as well." Danae felt a shock of pain welling up inside, a memory she'd been trying to suppress for too long. "I guess he was, indirectly."

Erik waited, focusing on her every word.

"The only responsibility I've ever really wanted to claim was motherhood, but I had to sacrifice that for my career." Danae felt tears stinging the corners of her eyes and blinked hard to force them back. "I never admitted to anyone how devastated I was after the miscarriage, not even my husband. I had the medic put me on an antidepressant patch so I could keep pretending I was okay." She studied her empty Coke bottle. "I overhear my crew sometimes, talking about how well I cope with loss, how calm and composed I look all the time. They've never seen me cry."

She took a deep breath. "Do I feel lonely? I can't even begin to describe the sense of isolation. I mean, what's the point of living when everyone you love is gone? When I learned about the harvest last night, I felt like I'd been given another chance to do something with my life."

Danae paused, ashamed at the magnitude of the lie. "No. It sounds noble, but that's not really why I'm doing this, Erik. The truth is I'm committed to this because Acheron threatened me.

He'll arrest Ting and impound my ship if I interfere. He knows I'm on to him, but he doesn't know how determined I am to stop him. I'm not looking for sainthood, just revenge. He's not going to abduct any more children like Zuri, not while I'm still breathing."

Erik gave her an understanding smile. "You're not the only one who'd like to get even with Acheron. Revenge or rescue, it doesn't matter what motivates you. Either one takes a lot of courage. The result will be the same, and you'll get to be a mother – at least, for a few days -- when you take responsibility for the children who need you."

Danae felt a chill when Erik mentioned the word 'mother.' *Is that why I'm doing this?* She was mortified she'd revealed so much to him. She started to get up from her seat, fighting to hold back the tears. "I need to go to the ladies' room."

Erik caught her hand before she could escape the table. "It's okay. You can tell me. You don't have to keep everything bottled up inside."

Danae laughed bitterly, her face red with embarrassment. "I guess people feel like its okay to unload their burdens on a doctor. Are you my therapist now, Erik?"

"I'm your friend, Danae." He released her hand with a disappointed look.

Danae fled to the restroom. She cried for a few minutes, then splashed some water on her face, pulled herself together.

She was wearing her practiced calm expression when she returned to the table. "We should get to the park. We've got a lot of work to do if we're going to stay a step ahead of Acheron."

Erik nodded without looking at her. By unspoken agreement, the 'bearing of souls' conversation had been shelved. "Let's go."

TWELVE
SEARCH

"Is it working?" Lorina poked her head in the doorway and watched as Blaze cycled the airlock in the floor. Once it was open, he reached into the antechamber and lifted out five large stacking pallets of bread, one at a time.

"Workin' fine," he said, not even glancing her way. He closed the airlock and stood up. He turned his back to her, watching the progress of the zip line suspension harness on the monitor. The makeshift contraption wheeled swiftly back to Vipul's airlock for another load of supplies.

"I'll help you carry these up." Lorina moved over to the pallets.

"No, I can manage. They're not heavy." Blaze bent his knees and picked up three. "Why don't you see if Idalis and Shima need a hand?"

Lorina detected the coolness in his tone, but dismissed it as nerves. They were all jittery, working as quickly as possible to prepare the ship to lift in four hours.

"Shima and Idalis are trying to kid-proof the *Ishmael*." Lorina picked up the other two pallets and hurried to keep up with his long-legged strides as he moved down the corridor to the starboard lift. "They hid all the mature holo-vids in Idalis' room, and right now they're going from room to room, setting the override controls on the showers and locking up the mini-bars. I think it's going to be chaotic no matter what they do; the *Ishmael* will seem like a theme park after Mother Teresa's."

"Uh huh," Blaze muttered, studying the elevator control panel.

Lorina took the hint and curbed the chatter. At the top level, they carried the pallets to the galley and set them on the floor. "I'll put this stuff away."

Blaze said, "okay," and was gone.

Lorina made up her mind not to feel slighted. She understood that people behaved differently during a crisis. *And if this isn't a crisis, I don't know what is.* Despite all the things that could go wrong, Lorina felt a thrill of excitement. *We're getting off this rock. -- We're going home!*

She opened the door to the huge pantry and arranged the pallets of bread on a bottom shelf labeled *pan*. Idalis' galley was immaculate, and Lorina didn't want to put anything away in the wrong place.

Blaze soon reappeared with six plastic boxes of supplies, this time stacked on the anti-grav unit. He left the boxes next to the pantry door and departed again without a word. Lorina glanced briefly at his retreating back, then resigned herself to figuring out the Spanish phrase for 'peanut butter.'

Time flew as Blaze brought in more boxes, and Lorina methodically unpacked them. She took a break to get a drink of water and discovered the kitchen android stored under the gigantic sink. She flipped the switch on the back of its neck to turn it on. "Come with me."

The stiff, faceless mechanical followed her back to the pantry. Lorina instructed it to open the crates and hand items to her. After that, the work progressed more quickly. She wondered how Jake was coming along with the diversion project, which she still didn't quite understand.

Something to do with explosives? Well, Jake was always good at chemistry.

"Lorina?" It was Shima's voice over the com.

"I'm in the galley."

"Com for you on the private line. It's Kirsten Sorensen."

Lorina glanced around the galley and spotted a receiver on the long counter which separated the kitchen and dining areas. She snatched it up. "Kirsten?"

"Lorina, I hope everything's going well on your end." The matron's tone seemed oddly formal.

"Yes, we're ready to lift on schedule. Have you explained to the kids what's happening?"

"Yes. I've been checking my records all afternoon, trying to make sure the ones with parents here don't accidentally end up on the ship. I wish you were here to help me, this place is a madhouse." The jest seemed forced, awkward.

"I can only imagine how you're coping with wall-to-wall kids."

"You'll be lifting with the *Ishmael*, of course?"

Is that what this is about? Lorina wondered. "Yes, and Jake, too. He's going to be the temporary med-tech. I've already forged a medical license for him."

"Good. Your quarantine has kept the CIPs away so far. You've been a lifesaver, literally. Did you leave anything here?"

Lorina sighed, glancing down at her ugly pink housekeeper's uniform. "Nothing I can't live without. I already called my manager to tell her I won't be back to clean out my room. So, I guess this is goodbye? Sorry it's not in person."

"Well, under the circumstances . . ." Kirsten's voice trailed off.

"You did call to say goodbye?" Lorina asked.

"Yes, but there's something I need to tell you first."

Lorina felt a stirring of fear. She ran her tongue over her dry lips. "I'm listening."

"It's Niyati. She's missing."

Lorina gripped the receiver tightly. "*What*?"

"Niyati's missing. Vladimir saw her slip out the front door shortly after you left. I think she was trying to follow you. I waited this long to tell you because I was hoping she'd come back. I don't know where she is."

Lorina felt like she couldn't breathe. "I've got to find her."

"Lorina," Kirsten's tone was sharp, "in two hours, we're going to move over 100 children to the *Ishmael*. You don't have time to search the station for one child. You need to stay right where you are. We're depending on you to take charge of this exodus; the children know you, they'll follow your directions."

"I'm not leaving without her!" Lorina put the com down. Her hands were shaking.

Blaze came in carrying two more boxes of food. "This is the last load." He set them on the counter and was about to turn away.

"Blaze?"

He glanced over at her and immediately came into the kitchen. "What's wrong?"

"A little girl . . ." Lorina had a difficult time getting the words out, "Niyati. She's very . . . important to me. She's missing from the shelter." She looked up at his concerned expression. "I have to find her. I won't leave without her."

A full minute passed as he scrutinized her expression. Lorina was grateful Blaze's first reaction wasn't to try to talk her out of it. Perhaps he already realized that arguing with her was wasted breath. *Jake still hasn't figured that out, -- and he's known me for 21 years.*

Although Lorina had known Blaze for only a few hours, she felt her heart racing whenever he was near her. It wasn't because of his looks – he definitely wouldn't pass as handsome. But Lorina had decided years ago that attractiveness wasn't a good indicator of character.

It was his gentle unassuming nature that she found irresistible. In Blaze she recognized the rare qualities of compassion, courage, and resourcefulness. She could tell he was the type of man her mom would classify as 'a good catch' because he genuinely cared about people and put others' needs ahead of his own.

"I'll come with you –" Blaze began, but then shook his head. "No, that wouldn't be appropriate."

"*Appropriate*?" Lorina couldn't believe her ears. "What are you talking about?" But before he could answer, she found herself getting angry. "Never mind, I don't need your help!" She started for the dining room.

Blaze caught her arm before she could slip past him at the counter, but then hastily let her go. "Wait, Lorina. You can't go dirtside alone. It's too dangerous."

"Well, it looks like I don't have a choice!"

"But Jake –" Blaze began.

"*Jake*? What about Jake? He's kind of busy right now, if you haven't noticed! Vipul has him searching the ship, looking for parts to make *explosives*!" Lorina felt tears of frustration stinging the corners of her eyes. "I don't have time for this! I've got to find Niyati!" She turned on her heel and headed for the door.

"It'd be safer if your husband went with you," Blaze called after her.

Lorina felt like a bucket of ice water had been dumped on her head. She was speechless as she turned to face him again. Blaze looked miserable, the purple bruises under his eyes standing out against the bright pink flush on his cheeks. Suddenly everything made sense. *This is why he's been acting so distant.*

Lorina took off the wedding ring. "Jake's not my husband. We're not married."

Blaze looked more uncomfortable at this announcement. "I don't understand why you'd deny --"

"We've been posing as a married couple for a lot of reasons, but we're not husband and wife. Jake's my cousin; his father and my mother are siblings."

"But you share a room –"

"We have separate beds, –" she felt her temper boiling over at his skeptical expression. "It's not what you think! Yes, we're close, but you have to understand we grew up in the same house, – like siblings! We're cousins, Blaze, and *we're not married*!" Lorina held the ring up and shook it at him. "This is my mother's wedding band. Look at it. Look at the inscription on the inside: *E.O. to S.M.* -- Elizabeth O'Brien to Silas Murphy."

Blaze wouldn't look at it. He backed against the counter, his features clouded with confusion.

"Look at the date!" Lorina pressed the ring into his hand. "That's 23 years ago! I'm telling you the truth." She stopped herself, realized she was beginning to sounding desperate. She forced herself to lower her voice and take a step back.

Blaze still wouldn't look at the ring. He set it on the counter and turned away from her.

"I need you to believe me." Lorina stared at his back. "I've got to find Niyati, but I'm afraid to go out there alone."

Blaze's response was calm, but his tone was odd. "So, let's see: basically, everythin' you told me was a lie. Jake's not a doctor –"

"I never said he was."

Blaze paused, thinking. "That's true."

"And I never said he was my husband. The rings . . ." she felt a catch in her throat as she tried to explain this, tried to make sense of the whole misunderstanding, "I forgot I was wearing the ring. We only put on this stupid charade so we could get a two-for-one ticket on the Mars shuttle."

Lorina tried to blink back the tears, but this time they wouldn't stop. "That was such a long time ago. I feel like I've been trapped on this miserable station my whole life. I just want to find Niyati. I'd never forgive myself if anything happened to her."

There was no response from Blaze.

Lorina felt her frustration giving way again to anger. She dried her eyes on the back of her hand. "I've got an hour and 45 minutes to find her. Tell the Captain to lift without me if I don't get back in time." She squared her shoulders and ran out of the galley.

Blaze grabbed her elbow as she reached the ladder. "I'm goin' with you."

"I thought you would've learned not to sneak up behind me." Lorina tried to smile but couldn't. She felt overwhelmed with conflicting emotions.

Blaze's hand on her elbow moved down her forearm until it reached her hand. Their fingers intertwined. The physical contact helped Lorina feel grounded. This time she was able to muster an appreciative smile.

Blaze said simply, "Let's find Niyati."

Lorina reluctantly released his hand and took the ladder as fast as she could.

"Vipul," Blaze called, descending after her.

"What's up?" the navigator replied.

"Lorina and I are goin' dirtside."

"*What!*"

"Just keep workin'," Blaze spoke over his protests, "we've gotta find someone."

"Captain Shepherd will be furious," Vipul warned. "We can't lift without an engineer."

"I know," Blaze said, "but we'll be back in time – I promise."

Don't make a promise you can't keep, Lorina thought, her stomach in knots.

"Take an earcom," Vipul said.

"We don't have time to go back –"

"I don't care about the time! I'm ordering you not to leave this ship without a com!"

Lorina blinked. *Still waters run deep,* she thought, impressed at Vipul's sudden display of leadership. She looked up the ladder at Blaze, who was looking down at her, a frustrated expression on his face.

"Wait by the airlock," he said, "I'll be right back." He rapidly began ascending, and Lorina finished her downward climb to the entryway.

Two minutes later, she heard Blaze descending the ladder again. "Okay, I've got an earcom. Happy?"

"Just be careful and don't take any chances," was Vipul's more subdued reply.

"I will." Blaze stepped off the ladder next to Lorina. "Let's go."

Lorina stared at the monitor, which displayed a quartet of CIPs standing guard outside the airlock. "How do we get past them?"

"Gettin' out's not the problem." Blaze touched the keypad. "It's gettin' back on board; that'll be the real problem."

Lorina swallowed hard as the first door cycled open. In a minute, she and Blaze were standing outside the second doorway, facing the enemy.

"Where do you think you're going?" One of the CIPs pointed his rifle at Blaze.

Lorina wanted to scream and run back inside, but Blaze calmly closed the airlock behind them. "We're goin' down to the station."

"You're not going anywhere without Chief Acheron's authorization," said the officer.

"Acheron said no one except crew could board the ship." Blaze smiled wearily. "He didn't say anythin' about who could leave."

The CIP seemed stumped for a moment. He touched his earlobe and spoke quietly to someone -- Lorina assumed it was Acheron. Blaze took advantage of the distraction and escorted her past the CIPs, moving straight ahead to the lift. She noticed that his large palm was damp with sweat.

"You will not be allowed to re-board," the CIP called after them, lowering his rifle.

Blaze didn't say anything. He stabbed at the elevator control panel and gave the CIPs a belligerent look until the doors closed. He gripped Lorina's hand, his face pale as the lift sank to the street level.

"Where to?" he asked as the doors parted.

"The dumpster behind the Marriott." Lorina pointed to the green line tramstop at the corner. "Hurry."

"This little girl," Blaze asked as they found a seat on the crowded trolley, "how could she get all the way from the shelter to the Marriott?"

Lorina grimaced. "I took her to the bank for a credit flash awhile back. It was just 50, but I wanted her to have something in case she got hungry or –"

"Wandered off?" Blaze nodded.

"Stupid, huh?"

"Not at all. Niyati's lucky to have someone like you in her life." He turned to look out the window. "I should be so lucky," he murmured under his breath.

Lorina heard him and blushed. She tried to concentrate her thoughts on where they should search.

* * *

There was no sign of Niyati in the Marriott alleyway. They took another minute to question head bellhop Greg Tresser in the main lobby, but he hadn't seen her either.

"Thanks anyway. Goodbye, Greg."

"Goodbye, Lorina, and good luck." Greg shot Blaze a half-envious, half-suspicious look as they turned away and hurried out the front lobby doors.

Lorina wanted to grab some belongings from her room, but they didn't have five minutes to spare. *It's just stuff, it can be replaced. – Niyati can't.* "Let's catch a red line tram at the corner."

"Now where?" Blaze asked, breathing hard as they sprinted to get on the tram which was already at the stop.

"The park."

"It's almost 7:00." Blaze stood next to her on the packed trolley, gripping the overhead bar which came to his shoulder. "Lorina," his voice dropped to a whisper, "what if she's not in the park?"

Lorina lowered her gaze, shook her head. "I don't want to think about that. She's got to be there."

Blaze didn't answer. When she looked up at him, she realized he was listening to his earcom. He pressed an index finger to his left earlobe. "We can help you load the kids on the tram because we'll be there in 15 minutes, Captain. East gate?"

He paused to listen again. "Jake's on his way? Yes, Captain, I understand. But we need to find someone –"

Blaze bit his lip and wouldn't look at her as he listened to a long monologue. Lorina assumed the Captain was bawling him out for leaving the ship. She felt a pang of guilt, but her determination to find Niyati never wavered.

"Let me speak to her." Lorina reached up to his ear.

Blaze caught her hand and shook his head no, his warm brown eyes reflecting a resolve, an inner strength, she hadn't noticed before. "Trust me."

Lorina wasn't certain whether he was speaking to her or to the Captain. This time his eyes never left hers as he continued to listen. Finally he frowned and said, "Yes, Captain. Smith out."

"Bad news?" Lorina was suddenly conscious of how close they were standing, and how many pairs of curious eyes were fixed on them.

Blaze whispered, "Captain Shepherd wants us to help gather children onto the tram. She said they've had to pick them up and carry them, but several homeless people are helping out. Jake's on his way."

"What about Niyati?"

Blaze looked away. "Let's pray she's with the group of kids on the tram. I don't think we'll have time to search for her."

Lorina bristled. "You mean, *you* don't have time. I'm not leaving the station without her."

Blaze leaned down, his mouth brushing her ear as he whispered, "And I'm not leavin' without *you*."

Lorina turned her head away, blinking back tears of frustration, but Blaze slipped his free arm around her shoulders, drawing her closer. She was too emotionally drained to resist. She encircled his waist with her arms, leaned her head against his chest. The silver buttons on his uniform felt cool against her cheek. She drew strength from listening to the steady beat of his heart.

As the tram approached the east gate of McConnell Park, Blaze peered out the window, over the heads of the other passengers, and went rigid.

"What is it?" Lorina asked, craning her neck to see.

Blaze parted the crowd as they pressed forward to get to the door. "Trouble."

They disembarked and hurried into the park, where they found Erik and a slender dark-haired woman in an *Ishmael* uniform just inside the gate.

Lorina glanced at the stern expression on her new employer's face and immediately felt guilty for putting the mission in jeopardy by persuading Blaze to leave the ship. She tore her gaze from Captain Shepherd's and noticed the crowd of homeless people standing behind Erik.

Each person was carrying an unconscious child -- or two, in Erik's case. Each was staring off into the distance with a look of fear on his or her face. It took Lorina only a moment to realize why the group had come to a standstill: Acheron.

The CIP chief was approaching swiftly from the direction of the lake, aboard a solar cycle. Lorina determined that he'd already shouted a warning because he had a gun out and trained on Erik.

"Captain, he's alone," Blaze said.

"Careful, he's up to something," Erik spoke through clenched teeth.

Lorina quickly realized what the doctor meant. As the solar cycle pulled up to within five meters of the group, she noticed a tiny figure draped over the seat behind him.

"*Niyati!*"

Lorina was in motion before Blaze could put out an arm to stop her. "Wait, Lorina!" But she had already reached Niyati and was attempting to pick her up as soon as the CIP chief dismounted.

"Leave her," Acheron ordered.

Lorina gave him a venomous look and gathered Niyati into her arms. The child was like a limp rag; breathing, but unresponsive.

Acheron took a step towards Lorina. "I said *leave her*."

Lorina's blind concern for Niyati hadn't allowed a moment for fear, until now. She glanced over at Blaze and was surprised to see the Captain next to him with firm hand on his sleeve, holding him back.

Lorina faced Acheron. She would have to handle this alone. *I can handle this.* "You have *no right* to take *any* child off the station."

Acheron's pistol was now leveled at her. "I have an order from the city council to remove the homeless children from the park. They've been declared a public nuisance." Acheron was the picture of calm. He seemed to be thoroughly enjoying the confrontation.

Lorina retreated a few steps, keeping some space between herself and the CIP chief. "You're a liar! The only nuisance here is *you*. This little girl – none of these children – have done anything to deserve a future as slaves. Only a *monster* like you would exploit the weak and defenseless."

Acheron's smile broadened. If he was surprised she knew about the slavery, he gave no indication. "So, you're Lorina Murphy." He was practically gloating. "Your manager at the Marriott was *persuaded* to report your background to me. Of course, she'll lose her job for illegally hiring you."

Lorina felt a tremor in her knees; she had no response. She adjusted Niyati's weight in her arms and continued to back slowly away from Acheron until she was just a few steps from Erik, Blaze, and Captain Shepherd.

"I don't know what the laws are in Delaware, but here on Mars we convict people for forging official documents." The CIP took a pair of handcuffs off his belt.

Lorina didn't realize Jake had joined the crowd until she suddenly found herself staring at his back. He placed himself between her and Acheron, like a human shield. "*I* created the quarantine notice! Arrest me instead!"

Acheron gave a short, bark-like laugh. "Excellent idea, *Mister* O'Brien. You're just the man I was hoping to see."

"What?" Lorina felt a chill. *It's really Jake he was after?*

"You are Jacob O'Brien, IV, formerly of Wilmington, Delaware?"

Jake had no response. Lorina could see he was breathing hard, the armpits of his scrubs dark with sweat stains. He was wearing a small backpack with *Ishmael* and a Red Cross symbol embroidered on it.

"I have a friend on Earth, Mr. O'Brien. He managed to look up your information for me. It seems you never graduated from medical school, which would make you –" Acheron's paused, smiling broadly, "a felon. You're under arrest."

Lorina felt frozen, scarcely aware of Blaze's hand on her shoulder, drawing her into the relative safety of the homeless group.

"Down on the ground, hands behind your head, –"Acheron began.

"Run!" Blaze hissed the warning to Jake.

"Run where?" Acheron laughed. In a flash, he clamped one hand over Jake's wrist and twisted his arm behind him, forcing him face down onto the grass.

Lorina screamed, "No!" just as a shot ring out.

Acheron crumpled to the ground, his mouth forming a silent 'O' of surprise as his right shoulder transformed itself into a fountain of bright red blood.

The next few minutes were a blur for Lorina. Blaze yanked Jake to his feet and everyone ran. There was a firm hand between Lorina's shoulder blades, urging her through the gate. A few steps later, she was boarding a tram with an 'out of service' sign in the driver's window. There were at least 25 homeless kids already on board. Some of them were asleep on the benches, but the ones who were awake had their heads down so they couldn't be seen from outside the tram.

"Dr. Jake!"

Lorina spotted a girl who was cradling a little boy's head on her lap. "It's okay, Tirza, just stay down." Jake took his own advice, found an empty seat, and crouched down.

Lorina sank onto an empty bench with Niyati on her lap. Blaze squeezed in beside her a moment later, his face pale. The homeless adults placed their burdens on the seats and floor and quickly scurried off the tram with a hasty "thank you" directed at Erik.

"415 West Farmer Street," Captain Shepherd barked, the last one aboard. The tram started to move. She grasped an overhead bar behind the android driver's seat. "I hope you have a better plan for getting the shelter kids onto the tram, Jake. Taking on Acheron by yourself didn't seem to work well."

"I do have a plan, Captain." Jake grimaced. "Trust me."

Shepherd returned the grimace.

"When word of this gets out –" Erik's face was paler than usual as he propped up his two unconscious youngsters on an open seat.

The Captain didn't take her eyes off Jake. "Tell Kirsten to have the kids ready. I'll give her 90 seconds to have them on the tram as soon as we're at the door."

"They won't let you off the station, Danae!" Erik checked another child sprawled on a bench, but kept glancing over at the Captain, his expression wavering between shock and admiration.

Lorina's jaw dropped as she finally noticed the pistol in Danae Shepherd's hand.

"We still have a few minutes before Acheron's discovered. We're lifting out of here, Erik." Captain Shepherd's expression was composed, calm.

Lorina found her voice. "You shot Acheron?"

"Yes, but he'll live." The Captain tucked the gun into her pocket. "I knew I was going to shoot him the moment I saw the little girl on his cycle, but Ting was wrong about me killing him."

She turned to Lorina. "You handled him beautifully. Telling him off while he was waving a gun in your face took a lot of courage."

Lorina could only nod, still numb with shock.

Captain Shepherd continued, speaking to the entire group: "The fact that Acheron confronted us alone convinces me a lot of CIPs on the station may not know about his illegal activities. But we still have to get past the guards at the airlock."

"Vipul has it all planned out. He'll be ready for us," Jake said.

"I wish I had a portion of your faith, Jake." Shepherd frowned. "But right now I guess I don't have a choice except to trust both of you."

She touched her right earlobe and began rattling off orders to Shima: "Tell Ting to run pre-flight. I want you, Vipul, and Idalis at the airlock, ready to move in 30. Do you have a problem with that?" She listened for a moment, worry and exhaustion showing through her emotional armor. "Shepherd out."

The Captain scanned the faces on the tram. "Everyone will need to carry a child, or two, onto the ship. The older kids at the shelter will have to help carry this group. We won't have much time to get everyone aboard."

"I'll explain it to them." Lorina nodded.

"Welcome to the crew of the *Ishmael,* Miss Murphy."

"Please, call me Lorina."

THIRTEEN
STANDOFF

Blaze fidgeted, nerves taunt, as the tram made quick progress across town. His offer to hold Niyati had been politely refused; Lorina seemed to need something, or someone, to hold onto, so the tiny girl remained cradled in her arms. He was still in awe of the way she faced down Acheron without even breaking a sweat. *Love is a powerful motivator,* he decided, casting an envious glance at Niyati, who continued to sleep through all the commotion.

"Won't Acheron come after you, Erik?" Lorina asked.

Sorensen shrugged. "The hospital administrators will vouch for me; bail me out, if necessary. They've done it before."

Blaze turned his attention to Jake, who was seated across the aisle. He had begun removing items from his backpack. "Is *that* what I think it is?"

Jake had unrolled a small towel, revealing a glass test tube filled with clear liquid. The neck of the beaker was sealed with a wine cork and a short strip of cloth. "Yeah, it's a Molotov cocktail." He unrolled a second towel and placed both beakers in the shirt pocket of his scrubs. "I only found enough grain alcohol for two."

"What do you plan to do with them?" Blaze asked.

Jake lowered his voice so only Blaze could hear: "I'm still working on that part."

Blaze frowned. "You might want to work *faster*."

"We're coming up on the shelter." Shepherd turned away from the front window of the tram and glanced sharply at Jake.

"Stop at the pub." The Captain relayed Jake's request to the driver.

Sorensen peered out the grimy front window as the tram drew to a halt in front of the Shield's stop. "Looks like we have company."

'Company' turned out to be a group of armed CIPs standing outside the front door of Mother Teresa's.

"What's the plan, Jake?" Lorina's voice was shrill.

"Let me off here." Jake moved to the door of the tram. "Get as close as you can to the shelter and wait for my signal."

"What are you going to do?" Lorina called after him, but Jake was already on the sidewalk, vanishing into the crowd of pedestrians.

"Pull up to the next corner," the Captain instructed the driver. The android mentioned that it was not a regular stop, but she responded with a sharp, "It's an emergency!"

'Emergency' seemed to be the key word; the android continued driving as instructed.

Blaze tried to spot Jake as the tram rolled up to the corner, 20 meters from the juvenile shelter, but the apprentice medic was nowhere in sight. The six CIPs turned to face the trolley with suspicious expressions.

"Here they come," Shepherd warned, stepping to the door. She reached into her right-hand pocket, but didn't draw her weapon.

"Jake said to wait –" Blaze's words were cut off by a huge explosion that seemed to rock the vehicle. Tirza and a few of the other children screamed in fright.

Blaze looked out the driver's side window at the fireball on the sidewalk in front of the Mediterranean restaurant. Pieces of smoking garbage can rained down on the street, sending bystanders scurrying for cover. "That should distract them."

"Not for long." Lorina set Niyati on the seat and moved over to stand beside him. They watched two CIPs race across the street to investigate the disturbance, but the flames were already shrinking to campfire size.

Shepherd's attention remained riveted on the juvenile shelter. "We still have four CIPs heading our way."

"Jake had two bombs –" Blaze's words were again drowned out by an explosion, followed by more screams. "Never mind."

This time all the CIPs raced across the street to the opposite corner, where a row of parked solar cycles burned out of control. Clouds of black smoke billowed up from the smoldering wreckage.

Lorina grinned. "Somebody's not going to be happy."

"Now's our chance. Let's move!" The Captain hit the sidewalk running.

"Blaze, Lorina, stay here; watch over the kids." Erik Sorensen disembarked a few steps behind Shepherd.

Blaze was secretly relieved to have an excuse to avoid the armed guards. He gave Lorina's shoulder a reassuring squeeze and moved to the doorway, where he split his attention between the juvenile shelter and the crowd gathered around the flaming CIP cycles across the street.

The big doctor raced up to the front door of Mother Teresa's and pressed his thumb to the ID lock on the transom. "Let's go!" he shouted through the open doorway.

A flood of children burst from the house and ran towards the tram. Blaze's jaw dropped when he saw how many there were. He quickly disembarked and stood beside the tram door, ready to assist with the mass boarding.

The swarm of wide-eyed youngsters moved quickly but with care, leading smaller children by the hand so none would be trampled in the rush. It could be compared to the most orderly fire drill Blaze had ever witnessed.

Erik Sorensen took a squirming, sobbing child from a heavy blond woman at the doorway of the shelter. Captain Shepherd also accepted a toddler and datapad hand-off from the woman. The two followed the crowd of children back to the tram.

Blaze was back on the packed trolley behind the last child. Dr. Sorensen and the Captain squeezed on moments later.

"That's all of them," Shepherd announced.

"Where's Jake!" Lorina was frantically scanning the crowded sidewalks.

Blaze glanced over at the still-burning rubble of solar cycles. The officers were just now beginning to realize that something was going on at the shelter. They were turning away from the commotion, drawing their weapons, moving towards the tram. "We're out of time, Captain."

"Let's move!" Shepherd shouted at the android. "Spaceport Drive, Lift 16!"

"No!" Lorina shrilled. "You can't leave Jake!"

"I can't risk everyone's life to wait for him!" Shepherd fired back.

Lorina screamed "No!" again as the tram began to move.

Blaze was torn between supporting the Captain's decision and taking up Lorina's protest that they wait for Jake. Before he could decide what to do, he caught a glimpse of blue just outside the tram door.

Jake was running alongside the slow-moving shuttle. "There he is!" Lorina shouted. "Open the door!"

The android said, "The door must remain closed while the vehicle is in motion."

The tram was picking up speed, coming closer to the CIPs who had already crossed back over to the shelter side of the street. Blaze realized they would reach Jake before he could get aboard.

Blaze reached over several children's heads and punched the door controls, over the driver's monotone protests. He descended the step to the open doorway and leaned out as far as he dared.

Jake was running flat out now, one hand flailing frantically to reach the handle next to the door.

Blaze gripped the railing with one hand to anchor himself to the tram doorway, then reached out with the other hand to grab Jake's wrist and yank him onto the doorstep. Both men threw themselves against the bi-fold door, slamming it in the face of the first CIP to reach the tram a second later.

In a moment, the tram was up to full speed, leaving the CIPs behind. A ragged cheer went up from Lorina and a few of the children.

"Way to go, Dr. Jake!"

Jake wiped sweat from his eyes and scanned the crowd of well-wishers. "Thank you, Tirza." He turned to Blaze with a sheepish expression.

"I know." Blaze didn't give Jake a chance to voice his thanks. "Long arms come in handy sometimes."

Jake nodded in agreement, breathing hard. Both men climbed the single step up to the passenger level of the tram and joined the throng of wall-to-wall children.

Blaze grabbed a vertical pole to steady himself and the children pressed against him in the crowded aisle as the shuttle turned a corner. He glanced around at the sea of short heads which seemed to fill every centimeter of the tram. The din of voices was incredible; the high-pitched chatter ran the gamut between excited laughter and nervous sobs. A few were looking around in stunned silence. Blaze resolved to get used to the clamor of children's voices. The smell of unwashed little bodies was also quite pungent, so he copied Jake's example and tried breathing through his mouth.

Blaze decided to make sure no one was standing on the kids who were asleep on the floor. He carefully made his way towards the back of the tram, taking in every detail from his higher vantage point.

He stooped down to pick up a boy sprawled beneath Lorina's seat. She was already sitting down again with a slumbering Niyati across her lap. "You can set him next to me, Blaze." Lorina glanced up at him with an expression filled with gratitude.

Blaze propped the unconscious youngster on the seat next to her. Lorina slipped her free arm around the boy's shoulders to keep him from slumping forward. Her fingers brushed Blaze's as she did this.

He was tempted to linger near Lorina, but Blaze knew there was work to be done. *And one more hurdle to get past: the CIPs at the airlock.*

He reached beneath another seat and extricated a tiny black boy from the small space. "What should I do with this one?"

"See if one of the bigger boys can carry him." Lorina tilted her head to indicate a potential helper across the aisle.

Blaze was able to hand over the limp child to a sturdy-looking preteen, who accepted his burden without a word of protest.

He noticed two Japanese brothers who were clinging to Jake. "Where we go, Doc?" the older one asked fearfully.

"Somewhere safe. Someplace where you won't have to beg for food or sleep on the street like a stray dog." Jake ruffled the boys' hair and gently extracted himself from their clutches, moving on to help another child.

"There's a little girl slumped down in the seat behind me, Blaze," said Lorina.

Blaze gave her a thumbs-up, reached for the child, and promptly put the little black girl he recognized from the park into the arms of a tow-headed preteen. "What's your name?" he asked his willing volunteer.

"Vladimir."

"Vladimir," Lorina's ears perked up. She turned her face towards him. "I need to thank you. You probably saved Niyati's life. If you hadn't warned Kirsten, we wouldn't have known she left the shelter – until it was too late."

"Does that mean I'll get some extra cookies on Sunday?" The boy grinned, turning pink from the praise.

"All the cookies you can eat." Lorina returned the grin. "And I'll bake them myself."

"Save a few of those cookies for me." Blaze winked at her, then scooped up another little boy from the floor. He handed him off to an older girl who was standing in the aisle. With Jake assisting, the two of them were able to get the sleeping kids off the floor and into the arms of older children who could bear their weight.

Lorina raised her voice to be heard above the din: "When we come to the lift, each of you will need to carry or help another child onto the ship. Understand?"

There were nervous nods all around. Blaze admired Lorina's authoritative tone; the children listened to her. *And they're probably too scared to offer any objections,* he thought.

As he maneuvered between children, inching his way towards the front of the tram, Blaze overheard a conversation between Captain Shepherd and Dr. Sorensen, who were standing together behind the driver's seat.

"If Acheron's already contacted his guards at the lift –" the Captain sounded uncharacteristically rattled. "Maybe I should go up first. It's me they want. If they arrest me, maybe it'll be enough of a distraction for the kids to board."

"Danae –" Blaze was startled to hear real fear in the doctor's voice. He paused for a moment to observe them out of the corner of his eye.

"I'll be fine, Erik." She didn't sound fine.

"Your crew needs you. These children need you. Once Acheron has you under lock and key, he won't let you walk out alive. You heard Lorina; the man's a monster. You can't be arrested."

Shepherd didn't reply.

"I want to see you again." Sorensen leaned closer – as close as he could get with the toddlers struggling in their arms.

Blaze concealed his astonishment. He had to listen closely to hear Shepherd's response: "The *Ishmael* won't be able to return to the station, not while Acheron's still breathing."

"That's not the answer I was hoping for."

The Captain's cheeks began to color. "I can't give you a different answer, not now."

Sorensen nodded, resigned. "I know."

Blaze realized he was staring and turned to face the back of the tram. He and Jake caught each other's eye and exchanged embarrassed grins.

Back to work, Blaze reminded himself. "Do you see anyone else on the seats or floor?" he called to Jake.

167

"That's everyone. I think we're ready." Jake didn't sound ready.

Captain Shepherd announced: "Coming to the lift! We can't fit more than 15 at a time on the elevator. I'll take the first group up –"

"No," Jake said, speaking over her. "Blaze needs to take the first group if we're going to lift on time."

The Captain narrowed her eyes at him. "I believe I'm in charge here, *doctor*. But," she gave Sorensen a meaningful glance, "I'll accede to your suggestion – this time."

"Yes, Captain," Jake responded, his tone apologetic.

There was a faint chime in Blaze's earcom, followed by Vipul's whisper: "I'm ready at the airlock. Let's just pray that this works."

"I haven't stopped praying since I left the ship," Blaze muttered in response. He felt relief at Vipul's report, but the feeling was followed by a fresh wave of fear. As the first crewmember at the airlock, Blaze would be the one to put the navigator's plan to the test.

Blaze picked up a sleeping child and moved to the door of the tram.

Jake informed him, "That's Adi you've got slung over your shoulder, and his sister Tirza is right behind you because she's not going to let him out of her sight."

Tirza seized Blaze's free hand. He glanced down at the girl with an indulgent smile.

"I'll keep the airlock open until everyone's on board, Captain." Blaze nodded to some of the children seated near the door. "Come with me."

The tram glided to a stop, and Blaze disembarked with the kids right on his heels. He offered another silent prayer as the lift ascended to the *Ishmael*'s airlock. He was surrounded by a group of children who were just as scared as he was.

"Hang on; it'll be okay." Blaze's mouth was dry with fear when the elevator doors opened to reveal a squad of eight CIPs barring the way to the airlock. He had to force his trembling legs to step into the access corridor and walk straight towards them, drawing Tirza after him as she continued to cling to his hand. The other children reluctantly followed, crowding so close to Blaze that he felt like a mother hen gathering her chicks under her wings.

The squadron leader stepped in front of Blaze, his hand resting on the butt of his pistol. "Stop! You do not have permission to board this vessel!"

"You might want to give us some space. These children have all been exposed to Zenithian Flu. I need to quarantine them aboard the *Ishmael*." Blaze hoped the tremor in his voice wouldn't betray the lie.

The CIP leader hesitated. "I'll have to clear this with Chief Acheron."

"You do that." Blaze managed a weak smile. "Be sure to let him know the longer you're exposed to us, the greater your chances of dying by the end of the week." He gestured to Adi and the other unconscious children. "These four probably won't last the night."

Tirza glanced sharply up at Blaze, her eyes wide with alarm, but he gave her hand a squeeze, hoping she wouldn't say anything.

To his amazement, the girl suddenly clutched her middle and gave a convincing moan. "Oh, my stomach!" She keeled over onto the concrete floor, her skinny limbs twitching convulsively.

Blaze struggled to hide his astonishment as the eight CIPs quickly backed away from the little group without a word, providing them with a clear pathway to the airlock. He stooped down and gathered up Tirza with his free arm. Her head and limbs hung limply by his side as he straightened up and faced the leader of the guards.

"You get them out of here," there was fear in the CIP's voice, "but I'm going to report this to Chief Acheron."

"Be my guest," Blaze said. "Vipul?"

The airlock cycled open in front of him. Vipul and Shima stepped swiftly out of the antechamber on either side of Blaze. Each was armed with a short metal tube, like a homemade harpoon gun. With a soft *wuff*, a length of glowing cable shot out of each make-shift gun, spanning the length of the narrow corridor and attaching itself to the wall on either side of the lift.

"What the --?" The CIP leader didn't have time to react before Vipul hit the keypad inside the antechamber. A sharp, crackling sound like static electricity emanated from each cable. The surprised officers pressed forward on either side of Blaze's group, but were unable to come within a decimeter of the invisible protective corridor Vipul had created between the ship and the lift.

"Magnetic field is up and running!" Vipul couldn't disguise a triumphant grin. "Welcome aboard, mate!"

Blaze said, "Let's go, kids!" He moved to the airlock, setting Tirza on her feet as he stepped into the antechamber.

The youngster turned and waved jauntily at the enraged CIPs as she followed Blaze into the entryway of the *Ishmael*.

"You're going to be a famous actress someday," Blaze told her.

"I know."

Despite the tenseness of the situation, Blaze couldn't help but laugh at the child's craftiness. "I don't know why you decided to play sick, but you probably saved everyone's life today, Tirza."

This time the imp just nodded, her expression thoughtful.

Idalis was waiting nervously in the entryway. Blaze handed Adi over to the Latina. Without a word, she herded the children to the starboard elevator.

Shima called back over her shoulder, "Blaze, take the tube from me so I can escort the next group upstairs."

"Yes, ma'am."

Blaze stepped over to the doorway and took the homemade harpoon gun from Shima, just as the lift opened to reveal a group of children escorted by Jake. The apprentice medic didn't exit the elevator, but went back down to help at the tram as soon as the kids were across the corridor.

Jake reappeared with the next group, and the next, and so on.

The CIPs fretted angrily and shouted orders into their earcoms as each group of children safely boarded the ship. Blaze wondered how long their luck would hold before CIP reinforcements came to block the lift at the street level.

Finally a group escorted by Lorina appeared at the lift. She was still holding Niyati. Blaze was relieved to see her. She brought the kids onto the *Ishmael.*

Blaze told her, "Idalis isn't back, so you'll need to take this group up."

Lorina flashed him a nervous smile, moving the children quickly to the starboard lift.

Idalis returned just as the next group came up from the tram, this time escorted by Dr. Sorensen. He handed off his toddler to a preteen in his group and went back down the lift when the children were safely through the airlock.

The ruse continued as the homeless children boarded the ship, 15 at a time. Once aboard the ship, they were taken up to cabins where, Shima assured Blaze, they were strapping-down for lift-off.

Blaze began to feel a nagging sense of uneasiness. *I'm just scared, – and who wouldn't be? Just stick to the plan,* he thought, mentally repeating the advice like a mantra.

Lorina didn't reappear to escort children upstairs, for which Blaze was grateful. He wanted her safe, and the situation at the airlock was precarious. He kept a nervous eye on the CIPs, particularly the leader who was carrying on a heated argument with someone on his earcom.

Blaze had a distinct impression that Vipul needed to go back inside the ship, but he ignored it because he was more concerned about the Captain. *Where is she?* She hadn't appeared on the lift with any of the groups.

"Twenty-eight more." Captain Shepherd's calm voice answered the question for him.

Blaze touched his earlobe. "Yes, ma'am." He felt a glimmer of relief until the lift opened on the next group, escorted by Jake. This time Lorina's cousin exited the elevator with the children.

"Stop!" The lead CIP started towards him, gun out and handcuffs ready, but stopped short of the magnetic field. "Jacob O'Brien, I've been instructed to arrest you."

"Well, unless you're planning to *shoot me*, officer -- which would be a really bad idea since I don't think any judge would approve of a CIP shooting an unarmed man -- I think I'll stay on this side of the cable. Excuse me." Jake tipped an imaginary hat and strolled over to the airlock, joining Blaze in the doorway of the antechamber. "The Captain's coming with the last group," he whispered.

"I don't like this," Blaze whispered back. "This is takin' too long."

"I'm just a nuisance; it's really the Captain they want," Jake whispered. "What'll we do if they arrest her?"

"What *can* we do? Get ourselves arrested – or shot? Then the kids'ill wind up on the *Elmina.*"

"I'm leaving the tram with the last group." Captain Shepherd's voice interrupted their debate.

"Yes, ma'am." Blaze repeated the announcement to Jake and looked over at Vipul waiting patiently on the other side of the airlock doorway. The impression became a shouted subliminal warning: *Get him aboard. Now.*

"Let Jake take your tube, Vipul." Blaze tried not to sound as nervous as he felt.

Vipul shot him a surprised look, but before he could respond, there was a commotion in the corridor. The CIPs standing behind the magnetic field on the left side of the airlock stepped aside for someone pressing in from behind them.

Blaze felt a fresh jolt of fear; he had forgotten that the access corridor wasn't isolated. Anyone could come up to Level 9 on another lift and approach the *Ishmael*'s airlock. He had also forgotten that Acheron wasn't their only enemy.

"Ganguli!" The deep voice was filled with contempt.

Vipul's eyes widened at the newcomer's approach. He shrank back against the round doorway with a look of horror on his face.

Blaze caught his breath as an imposing figure in a dark green spacer's uniform came into view. The man was holding a deadly-looking pistol twice the size of Shepherd's, and he was pointing it right at Vipul's chest.

"I told you what would happen if you betrayed me!"

Blaze had the sense to press a trembling finger to his earcom. "Captain, we have an emergency here."

"Ten seconds," Shepherd apologized. "I'll handle it."

"I'm sorry, sir, but you'll have to put your weapon away." The CIP who spoke wasn't the leader; the squadron commander was on the opposite side of the protected corridor. This officer seemed timid, unsure of herself.

The malevolent stranger paused, glaring at the speaker. "Your chief has been *shot*, and you're just standing here, allowing these criminals to leave the station?"

The CIP cowed, lowering her gun. "Sorry, Mr. Thanatos. You're right, sir, we'll arrest the crew."

Thanatos! Blaze felt paralyzed with fear. *How can I protect Vipul from a bullet? The magnetic field won't keep Thanatos from killing him!*

The lift doors opened. The CIPs glanced at the occupants and went into motion, all eight guns trained on the elevator.

"Captain!" Jake shouted.

"Stay back, Jake!" Blaze hissed the warning. "She can handle this."

Jake didn't move, but his face paled slightly.

"Run!" Shepherd shouted from the rear of the lift. She quickly passed her toddler over to a tall Asian girl. "Get on the ship!"

Sensing the peril, the terrified youngsters moved quickly to the airlock, where Shima was ready for them. Thanatos and the officers ignored the kids. The CIP guns were trained on the Captain, while Thanatos' weapon remained pointed at Vipul.

Danae Shepherd calmly stepped into the corridor with her pistol leveled at Thanatos. Now it was a standoff. "Lower your weapons, or I promise you Mr. Thanatos, who is the *real criminal* here, will get a bullet right between the eyes."

The CIPs hesitated; a few of them lowered their guns. Shepherd began to walk slowly towards the *Ishmael*'s airlock, carefully rotating her arm and then her entire body so the slave ship captain remained in point blank firing range. Her eyes never left Thanatos' as she took the tube from Vipul's shaking hand and took his place at the airlock doorway, positioning herself between the navigator and his ex-employer.

"Drop the gun!" The CIP leader ordered.

"You first." The Captain didn't take her eyes off Thanatos.

"Shoot them!" Thanatos shouted at the CIPs. "You're letting them get away!"

"We can't shoot them, sir. The men are unarmed and the woman might kill you," the CIP leader pointed out nervously.

"Then *I'll* shoot them!"

Blaze held his breath as Thanatos took aim, clearly intent on murdering the Captain and the navigator standing directly behind her.

Several CIP weapons shifted to point at Thanatos. "I'm sorry, sir, but we can't let you do that."

"Ganguli!" Thanatos roared, firing his weapon, but the Captain was a split-second faster on the trigger.

The slave ship captain went down.

But Thanatos' shot also made contact, the impact hurling the Captain and Vipul the last half-meter into the antechamber where they landed together in a heap on the floor.

Blaze felt the magnetic field collapsing the instant the shots rang out. He threw down his pipe and punched the 'emergency close' button for the outer door a heartbeat before the CIPs opened fire on them. The hail of bullets sounded like a swarm of angry bees bouncing off the airlock door.

Jake and Blaze moved forward as one, seized Captain Shepherd and Vipul under the arms, and dragged them into the entryway.

Blaze cycled the airlock shut and sealed the inner door. "Ting, taxi away from the dock!"

"Sure, as soon as the Captain gives me the signal," came the sarcastic reply.

"The Captain's been shot, you idiot!" Jake shouted. "Get us out of here!"

PART II:
EARTHBOUND

FOURTEEN
ROOKIE SURGEON

There was so much blood that Jake couldn't see the wound. "I'm not trained for this!" He knelt over the Captain on the entryway floor, took off the backpack and fumbled out his scanner. "I need Erik's help!"

"Don't tell Erik," Shepherd whispered, her eyes squeezed shut against the pain, her breath coming in ragged gasps.

Jake scanned her. It was bad. He turned his head and whispered to Blaze, who was bent over Vipul, "The bullet passed completely through her side."

"She kept her promise." This startling announcement came from Vipul.

Jake realized the navigator's eyes were open. "What?" He brought the scanner around, read the results. "The bullet's buried in your hip."

"She said she'd protect me from Thanatos," Vipul explained with an odd little smile. Jake wondered if he was already in shock.

"We've got to get them up to the infirmary!" Blaze's voice went up an octave. "Shima, do we have a gurney? We need two of them, quickly!"

"I am on my way," came the calm reply.

Jake dumped out the contents of the backpack and was relieved to find a can of Hemorrhage Freeze among the medical supplies. He quickly sprayed the left side of the Captain's torso from ribs to hip. "I've never lost a patient, ma'am. Please don't die on me."

"Ting didn't say *I* was going to die." She took a labored breath. "He said I was going to kill someone."

"It was a clear case of self-defense, Captain. If Thanatos is dead, I'd say you did the universe a big favor." Blaze watched Jake spray Vipul's left hip. "What can I do to help?"

"You can get down to the engine room," Shepherd whispered before losing consciousness.

Jake forced himself to stay calm and focused. "Shima, where are those gurneys?"

"We're on the lift," Idalis replied. "Ten seconds."

With Shima and Idalis' help, Jake and Blaze lifted Vipul and Captain Shepherd onto the gurneys.

"I'll help you bring them up to the infirmary," Blaze said.

"No, you'll do what the Captain ordered." Jake stabbed a finger towards the ladder. As much as he appreciated the engineer's offer to help, he didn't need a scanner to see that Blaze was close to needing a gurney himself. "Now take some deep breaths, and get moving. I can handle this."

The truth was that Jake didn't know if he could handle two gunshot wounds by himself. Shima and Idalis helped him maneuver the gurneys onto the lift and, once they were on the top level, into the *Ishmael*'s state-of-the-art infirmary. The women helped him transfer Captain Shepherd face-down onto the surgical table. There was sufficient space for Vipul's gurney, so they placed it against the wall and set the brakes.

"I don't suppose one of you could stay and assist me?" Jake glanced around the unfamiliar room and felt his stomach churn. He'd spent the afternoon assembling Molotov cocktails in the infirmary's lab, so he hadn't learned the layout of the surgery.

Idalis jerked a thumb towards Shima. "She's an excellent nurse."

Shima looked like she wanted to protest, but Idalis added a sincere, "she knows how to perform every job on the ship. I'd trust her with my life."

"I guess I volunteer." Shima shot the Latina a flustered look.

"Now, if you'll excuse me, Lorina and I need to make sure 148 children are properly strapped down."

Jake couldn't decide if Idalis' sarcasm was due to stress, but he promptly dismissed the thought because she was already gone. The door slid shut after her. Jake sniffed recognizing the scent of antiseptic air. The surgical room and its equipment would remain sanitized, even if its occupants were not.

"Preparing to leave Mars' atmosphere." Ting's voice over the com was nonchalant. "And, by the way, I can't make a jump without a navigator."

"The jump coordinates are already programmed," Vipul replied. "So shut up and fly."

"Got that," Marco said a few moments later. "Idalis just told me Vipul was shot, too. I guess that makes *me* the senior crewmember."

"Just shut up and fly!" Jake yelled.

"Well, I guess I won't need anyone's permission to ignore this 'return to port' warning, or this CIP 'wanted for murder' transmission. Good likeness of the Captain."

"Shut up, Ting!" shouted several voices over the com system.

The helmsman signed off with a distinct grumble.

"The sterile gloves are here." Shima calmly opened a drawer on the surgical table. She quickly strapped the patients down with padded cords, which secured them at the knees and shoulders. "The ride will get bumpy."

"When?" Jake asked.

"In about five minutes."

Jake turned to the monitor on the wall near him and asked it for the Captain's medical history. "No drug allergies. Where's the anesthesia?"

Shima pressed her thumb to the ID lock on one of the cabinets, opening it wide to reveal a refrigerated micro-pharmacy and synthblood supply.

Jake blinked, too surprised to comment. He hadn't finished looking over Shepherd's history, and Shima already had two IV bags in her gloved hands.

"There are two liters of the Captain's blood type in here. You will need to get Vipul's medical history," she hinted.

"Right, thanks." Jake turned back to Vipul's table.

"O positive, no allergies." The navigator's voice grew weaker. "I'm okay. Take care of the Captain first."

Jake checked his scanner. "No, you're not okay; you're going into shock. Shima, raise the room temperature, and hand me an IV."

There was no sarcasm in the housekeeper's tone. "Of course, doctor."

Both patients were quickly sedated. The monitors indicated that their systems were stable, but Jake didn't completely trust them. He hadn't been able to visually determine the full extent of the Captain's internal injuries.

When the turbulence hit, Jake was grateful he didn't have a scalpel in his hand. He gripped the edge of the Captain's table with one hand and worked at suctioning the blood away from the crater in her side with his other hand. He winced as he surveyed the exit wound and the missing pieces of flesh. *A few millimeters higher or closer to the spine and this would have been a fatal wound.*

"I'm going to need a lot of synthflesh to repair this," he muttered to himself.

"Do you need scissors?" Jake marveled that Shima could maneuver around the room without falling down, which is what he did – twice. She secured both patients' IVs and handed him a probe android for Vipul's hip.

"If you think you can handle the scissors, be my guest." Jake moved over to Vipul's gurney and was flabbergasted to discover the navigator's hip prepped for the procedure. The fabric of his uniform had been trimmed back just enough to expose the wound.

"Um, thanks." Jake threaded the probe into Vipul's left hip, trying to remember the way Erik had performed the procedure on Lucky.

"Is this your first gunshot wound?" Shima trimmed away the tough fabric of the Captain's uniform with a pair of blunt-nose scissors.

"No, but it's my first gunshot wound without Dr. Sorensen to guide me." Jake watched the probe android on the monitor and thought of a new concern. "Are we going to have to work in weightlessness?"

"No. This must be your first ride on a McConnell class starship."

"You got that right." Jake removed the bullet from the probe's clutches, and abruptly found himself on his backside when the *Ishmael* bucked to starboard.

"Almost through," Marco reported. "Hold on to your stomachs; we jump in 15."

Jake struggled to his feet.

"I think you need to scan the Captain again." Shima was watching Shepherd's monitor. "Her blood pressure is falling."

Jake moved as quickly as he could to the other table, already suspecting the problem before the scanner confirmed it. "The bullet must have damaged the renal artery. Her kidney's failing."

"Why did you not see this earlier?" Shima's calm exterior cracked. Her voice rose an octave. "Can you repair it?"

"It didn't show up until the IV began adding fluids to her system, overloading the damaged artery." Jake bit his lip, made a quick decision. "I'm not skilled enough to repair this; I'll have to remove the kidney."

"*What*? I thought you were a doctor, not a butcher!"

Jake flinched. "Sorry, I'm just a medical student, but I'm really good at removing organs, – trust me."

"I do not have a choice, do I?" Shima lapsed into stony silence and grudgingly helped Jake prep Shepherd for surgery.

Jake took a deep breath and selected a scalpel.

"Wait."

"Shima, I'm sorry, but I've got to do this quickly." He adjusted the mask over the bridge of nose. "I'm nervous enough as it is."

Shima gave a snort of disapproval. "No, I mean wait until the ship goes to Velocity. It has been 14 minutes."

"Oh." Jake resisted the urge to feel humiliated. He gripped the sides of the table with both hands.

"On my mark," Ting announced.

"Engines ready," replied Blaze.

"Three . . . two . . . one . . ."

Jake felt a sudden lurch, followed by an incredible amount of pressure that took his breath away for a moment. But the gravity quickly normalized and the ride became smooth. "That wasn't bad."

"Now you may operate." Shima handed him a laser clamp.

FIFTEEN
MESSAGES

Danae was swimming through a dark, peaceful fog. In the fog she saw faces drifting, smiling at her: Alex's, Shima's, Hugh's, Blaze's, Erik's, Acheron's. She did a double take at the police chief, but he was smiling like the others, as if he and Danae were old friends.

"Wake up, Danae," encouraged Alex's voice, although his lips didn't move as he spoke.

"Wake up." This time it was Erik's voice.

"Wake up." A different voice she couldn't place. Another face drifted into view. It was Thanatos. There was a hole in the middle of his forehead. Blood trickled from the bullet wound, running down his face like tears.

Danae gasped in horror and the fog faces were gone, replaced by a bright light that hurt her eyes. She blinked hard, trying to focus. She was lying on her stomach with her head turned to one side, facing a bedside lamp.

"You are awake." Shima's calm expression swam into view as she squatted at Danae's bedside. "Good morning, Captain."

Danae tried to lift her shoulders, but found she couldn't move. "Report, please," she managed to whisper, her mouth as dry as parchment.

"Marco made the jump 12 hours ago, Captain. You and Vipul are both here in the infirmary post-op. Vipul is doing well, and Jake put your kidney in the freezer."

"*What!* My kidney?"

"It was damaged during the shooting. He said a more experienced medic could replace it when we land on Earth."

Danae had so many questions she couldn't focus on vocalizing a single one. With great effort, she turned her head to the other side and found a drinking tube already in place. She took a long sip of water, then rested her chin on the mattress. "I guess it's safe to assume I survived. How are the passengers?"

"Sleeping, Captain." Shima sounded weary.

"That's what you should be doing. Help me up." Danae tried again to rise onto her elbows, but found her muscles completely unresponsive.

"I am sorry, Captain." Shima put a firm hand on her shoulder. "Jake said you are not to get up for at least 24 hours."

"Jake already tried to give me orders on the tram." Danae found herself getting annoyed again at the rookie medic. "I make the decisions around here, and I'm getting up." She made a valiant struggle to roll over, but succeeded only in stirring up a sharp pain in her left side.

"Lie still, Captain!" Shima urged. "Rest. Everything is under control."

There was a loud thump from out in the corridor, followed by peals of excited childish laughter.

"Sleeping, are they?" Danae eyed the housekeeper suspiciously. "Anything else you're not telling me?"

Shima's wise expression revealed nothing. "Everything is under control, Captain." But she quickly left the infirmary, leaving Danae alone with Vipul still asleep in another bed across the room.

The laughter in the corridor seemed to be moving away from the infirmary, but Danae was convinced the children were tearing the ship apart. "Lorina! I need a report!"

Lorina Murphy's voice over the com was hesitant. "Yes, Captain?"

"What's going on out there? I want to know what the children are doing to my ship."

"Everything's, um, under control, Captain."

Danae fumed. *They probably invented that excuse together.* "I'm not deaf. I can hear the circus in full swing. I want to know what you're doing to keep order."

"Well," the new steward sounded rattled, "Idalis and I managed to get everyone breakfast, and now I'm trying to organize some quiet games in the lounges." Danae could hear shrieks of laughter and running footsteps near Lorina's com. "They were either cooped up in the shelter all day yesterday or sleeping off sedatives, so they seem to prefer running up and down the corridors this morning."

Danae's temples throbbed. "Get them to settle down. Do you have a problem with that?"

"No, ma'am. I'm trying. It's just that there's so many of them and –"

"I don't want excuses." Danae knew she was being hard on the girl, but couldn't see an alternative until she and Vipul could get out of bed to help restore order. "There's four of you, one to supervise each lounge –"

"Excuse me, Captain, but there's only Idalis and myself." Lorina sounded like she was close to tears. "Jake was up all night taking care of you, and since he hasn't slept much the past two days, I sent him to bed. Shima was up all night, as well; she's so tired, I'm afraid she's going to collapse, but I don't think she'll go to sleep unless you order her to, Captain."

Danae softened her tone. "Just do the best you can."

"Yes, Captain."

"Shima?"

"Yes, Captain?" The housekeeper stuck her head in the doorway and regarded Danae with her large brown eyes.

"Go to bed."

"But –"

"I'm ordering you to get some sleep, Shima. Do you have a problem with that?"

"No, Captain." The door to the corridor slid shut after her.

Danae took a deep breath, summoning her strength for round two. "Jake!"

There was a muffled grunt from somewhere nearby. Danae realized the medic had been sleeping in one of the other post-op beds, out of her range of vision. "Are you awake?"

"Yes, ma'am." He didn't sound too awake.

She heard him stirring and then he was at her bedside, medical scanner purring near her ear. "Are you in pain?"

"Actually, I think you gave me too much pain medicine; I can't move."

"You just had surgery, Captain. You're not *supposed* to move."

Danae decided to ignore his sarcasm. "You can tell me the gory details later. Right now I want you to turn down the meds, and roll me onto my good side so I can at least see what's going on."

Jake hesitated. "Let me get some pillows." He was back in a minute. "Okay, I'm going to turn you onto your right side. Let me know immediately if you feel any pain and I'll stop."

Danae felt a firm hand on her left shoulder and another behind her left knee. She held her breath to keep from crying out as Jake rolled her onto her side. Now she had an unobstructed view of his glowering expression and unkempt hair. *Purple*

183

scrubs? It took her a moment to remember that Dr. Martschenko had kept the infirmary stocked with scrubs in her favorite color. *They looked a lot better on Natasha.*

"You were supposed to let me know if it hurt." Jake arranged pillows at her back and belly to keep her from rolling involuntarily. "How's that?"

"Terrific." She took some deep breaths. "Now I have some instructions for you. First, I want you to get me a datapad."

"I don't think you're well enough to work, Captain."

"I have a ship to run, medic. *My* ship. And let me remind you that you're *my* employee –"

"An employee who just saved your life," Jake interrupted.

"Who was just doing *his job*, the same way I did *my job* by protecting you from Acheron. So thank you and shut up, Jake."

Jake closed his mouth, his expression darkening mutinously.

Danae took a moment to compose her next instructions. "I want you to examine each child before we dock. I'm sure an orphanage, or whoever will take them, will require medical records for them."

"My first priority is your recovery, and Vipul's," Jake protested.

"I was expecting a response more along the lines of 'yes, Captain.' There's a datapad in my uniform that contains Kirsten Sorensen's information on the children from the shelter, – I'm assuming the uniform didn't wind up in the laundry or recycler. Now find that datapad and get to work, Jake."

"Yes, ma'am." He stalked away, stepped into the adjoining examination room, and returned a moment later with a datapad and stylus. He shoved these into her left hand and was gone.

Round three, Danae thought. "Ting?"

"Yes, Captain."

"Report."

"Smooth sailing, Captain. We'll make planet in 58 hours. No problems on the bridge. Can't say the same for the rest of the ship, but –"

"Thank you, Marco," she interrupted, "that will do."

"Yes, Captain. Ting out."

Danae asked Blaze for a status report, received a similar answer, and turned her attention to the datapad. She gripped the wafer-thin screen in her left hand, but found it nearly impossible to write with her right hand, since it was pressed against the mattress. With great effort, she switched hands. The left-handed scrawl was barely legible, but she had work to do.

She began to make a list of everyone she knew on Earth. First she wrote down the families of past and present employees, including those deceased. Then, she paused, thinking.

She reviewed her father's former girlfriends. One in particular had been determined to be the next Mrs. Ishmael Thompson, but Danae was grateful her father had come to realize the woman was just using him. *But she was a sharp attorney; she had connections,* Danae reasoned, jotting down the name *Rosamar Delacruz. And she likes kids. -- I think.*

Next she wracked her brain for business contacts who would be willing to take a risk to help her. The list was very short. She had not been to Earth in eight years. *People change a lot in eight years. Businesses go under in half that time.* She frowned and didn't add either contact to the list.

Danae looked over the names, evaluated, crossed out a few. She hesitated to add one more. *Someone who might be willing to go out on a limb to help me.* She wrote *Claire Thompson,* then set down the stylus.

The messages would need to be composed on a holo-vid for transmission, and Danae chafed at the idea of being stuck in bed for another 12 hours. She closed her eyes and began composing a message in her head. She would write it down when she had the strength. For now it seemed the rookie medic had been right about working: she was exhausted.

Danae cradled the datapad to her chest and fell asleep.

* * *

Mr. and Mrs. Edward Zimmerman

Transmission receiver #27-6493032

Hoboken, New Jersey

Mr. and Mrs. Zimmerman, I can't tell you

how much I miss your son, and I'm certain

Hugh's absence has been more painful for

you than I can imagine. Please forgive me

for the delay in returning his body to you.
This is why I am sending you this message:
to ask for your assistance, if possible.

Too timid, Danae thought, revising the last sentence.

I need a safe port to dock the ship. It needs
to be a private dock, if you know anyone
who would allow us dirtside. I regret not
being able to give you full details in this
message, but I only ask that you trust me,
as your son did.

Your son trusted me, and now he's dead. Okay, that's not going to be very convincing. Danae crossed out the last sentence. *How do I ask for assistance without disclosing all the murky details?*

Do you know anyone who would be willing
to adopt a shipload of orphan children?

Danae sighed, deleted the entire rough draft, and started over with a new recipient:

Keiko Costa
People Locators, Inc.
Transmission receiver #77-4847360
Santa Fe, New Mexico

Ms. Costa,
Eight years ago you helped me locate my
mother, Claire Brooks Thompson, for the

purpose of informing her of my father/her ex-husband's death. Although she chose not to attend his funeral in St. Paul, I was satisfied with your service in getting the message to her.

I now ask for your assistance in locating her again. This time I need to see her in person because I have some personal business to discuss with her. Enclosed you will find a copy of her pertinent information, including a DNA trace. Please send a reply to the Ishmael ASAP.

Sincerely,
Danae Thompson Shepherd
Ship transmission receiver #8493801

Dr. Qiu Ting, Chief Historian
Communist Party Memorial Library
Transmission receiver #101-0984736
Beijing, China

Honorable Sir,
I am writing to tell you that your son, Marco Polo Ting, is a fine helmsman, and I am grateful he has been a member of my crew for the past 10 years. The Ishmael is one of

> the most respected ships in the star lanes,
>
> thanks to the dedicated work of your son.

Danae was forced to stifle a laugh. *Let's not shovel it on too thick.*

> I humbly ask for your assistance in locating
>
> a private port for the Ishmael to dock. We
>
> are carrying very valuable cargo.

You have no idea how valuable. Danae continued to write, trying to get the wording right for each message. *As soon as I can get out of this bed, I'll go right to my office and start recording.*

She glanced down at herself and frowned. *First I'd better do something about the stench.* "Jake?"

The medic stuck his head out of the exam room with an impatient scowl on his face. "Anything I can do for you, Captain?"

"Yeah, you can help me to the head so I can take a shower."

"The synthflesh needs at least six more hours to adhere, Captain."

"Well, then you'll just have to give me a *sponge bath*."

Jake muttered something that sounded like, "I'd rather give myself an appendectomy."

"What was that?" Danae asked.

"Six more hours, Captain." The door to the exam room slid shut after him.

"Give it up, Captain," Vipul said with a chuckle. "That boy is more stubborn than you."

Danae glanced over at her fellow prisoner. "And what's that supposed to mean?"

"You're both determined to do the right thing, Captain, even if it puts you at cross purposes. Take it as a compliment." Vipul grinned and turned back to his book.

Danae sighed and turned back to her datapad.

SIXTEEN
FIRST DATE

With the *Ishmael* in Velocity, Blaze confined himself to the engine room. He didn't need to remain there 24/7 because he wore a sensor on his wrist, like a watch, alerting him to any problems with the system. But since this was his first jump, he used his novice status as an excuse to avoid the chaos of 148 children having the time of their lives on the upper decks.

Although grateful for the isolation, Blaze left the com open so he could hear what was going on. He intended to lend a hand if Lorina got into trouble, but most communications were routine:

"Shima, the android's got the next round of peanut butter and jelly sandwiches ready to go."

"Thank you, Idalis. I will send Vladimir up with Group B. First, I have to change a few diapers."

"Lorina, where's Group A?"

"I'm giving some of the boys haircuts in the third port lounge, Idalis. Are we attempting to wash all these kids this afternoon? What about clean clothes?"

"Togas," Shima replied.

"Excuse me?"

"We will make togas for them to wear while their clothes are being laundered," said Shima.

Lorina laughed.

Half an hour later, Blaze overheard a conversation that was anything but routine. He wondered if he should intervene.

"Lorina, what's all that noise?" Ting demanded. "It sounds like the galley walls are going to collapse."

"Just the happy sounds of children eating their lunches."

"Well, tell them to *shut up*! There's no excuse for that kind of --!"

"Perhaps you'd like to lend a hand if you don't like the noise level," Lorina interrupted, her tone arctic.

"If I could leave the bridge, I'd come in there and teach you something about keeping those kids under control. You're letting them run wild and —"

"If I were letting them run wild," Lorina interrupted again, "they'd probably break down the door to the bridge and teach you something about keeping your *big mouth shut!*"

"I'm the senior officer and you will not speak to me in that –!"

"Shut up, Ting, before I break down the door myself and swab the deck with your sorry --"

"Lorina!" Captain Shepherd's voice cut in. "Is there a problem?"

"No problem, Captain," she replied sweetly, not even breathing hard. "I was just suggesting to Mr. Ting that he keep his child-rearing advice to himself."

"I see. Marco?"

"Yes, Captain."

"Just for the record, Vipul and I are both awake, so you are no longer the senior officer."

"Yes, Captain." Ting signed off with his trademark grumble.

"How are you feeling, Captain?" Lorina asked. Blaze was amazed at how cool and composed she sounded after the shouting match.

"I'm fine." Shepherd replied. "I just want to get out of bed."

"I'm awake and I'm hungry," Vipul added.

"I hope you like peanut butter," Lorina said.

Blaze chuckled. "Com, lower volume."

The engine room contained a small alcove which served as the engineer's quarters when the ship was in space. There was a bed, small closet, head, and dumb waiter to the galley. An engineer could live quite comfortably for days in the basement. This would have been an ideal arrangement for Blaze, except for one crucial detail: he wanted to spend more time with Lorina.

As he pondered this dilemma, his lunch of two peanut butter and jelly sandwiches and an apple arrived in the dumb waiter. There was a paper note under the bottle of water, written in a distinctly feminine handwriting:

> Are you allowed to take breaks? Could you
>
> stop by my cabin tonight for a visit? ~LM

Blaze searched every nook and cranny of the engine room, but couldn't find anything to write with. He settled for an awkward message over the com. "Lorina?"

"Yes, Blaze?"

"Is 10:00 okay?"

"Okay," she replied.

"Ten of what?" Ting asked.

"Ten knuckles in your sandwich if you don't stop eavesdropping over the com!"

Blaze chuckled at Lorina's response. *Don't mess with her, Ting.*

* * *

Blaze left the engine room at 9:30 p.m. He wanted to stop by the infirmary before he went to see Lorina. He walked into the four by four meter infirmary post-op room, which consisted primarily of four beds welded to the floor, one in each corner. Two were occupied and a third looked as if it had been slept in. – *By Jake, no doubt*, Blaze thought. *I'll bet he had a long night.*

"How're you doin', Captain?" He nodded to her before moving over to the bedside of the other occupant. "Vipul?"

"Alive, thanks to you, mate." Vipul was lying flat on his back and smiling, though his dark features looked as pale as the sheets pulled up to his unshaven chin. "I heard your quick reflexes kept us from getting shot full of more holes." His smile turned down into a thoughtful frown. "I should have listened when you told me to go back inside the ship. How did you know?"

Blaze shrugged. "It's hard to explain; it's like the time I felt impressed to check on Shima in the lounge with Jackson."

"So you've got something in common with Ting?" Vipul asked. "You're psychic?"

Blaze snorted, laughing. "Far from it. I've just learned to listen to the little voice inside my head."

Vipul squinted at him. "What little voice?"

"My conscience." Blaze shrugged. It was hard for him to explain his spiritual impressions. "It was nothin'. I'm just glad you're okay." He turned to face the Captain. "You seem to be healin' well too, ma'am."

"I'd heal a lot faster if someone would help me out of this stupid bed." She didn't look up from a datapad. She was sitting slightly upright with an arrangement of pillows, though she didn't appear comfortable.

191

"First thing tomorrow morning, Captain." Jake stuck his head out of the examination room's open doorway, which was near the Captain's bedside.

"That will put me past your 24 hour sentence, warden." Shepherd stabbed at the screen with her stylus, clearly irritated.

"So sue me." Jake beckoned for Blaze to join him.

Blaze stepped into the smaller room where Jake was finishing up an exam on two Japanese brothers he recognized from the tram. They sat side-by-side on the stainless steel table, each clad in a beige bed sheet.

Jake adjusted the toga on the younger boy's shoulder. "I don't see anything red on your arm."

"Maybe he just imagine it," said the older boy, who was grinning broadly.

"Maybe you give me Indian burn too much," responded the younger, looking furious.

Jake folded his arms and regarded them with mock-sternness. "Do you mean to tell me you came in here to be treated for Indian burns?"

Both boys grinned up at him sheepishly.

"Go to your cabin; I don't want to see you back here unless you're coughing up a lung. Is that clear, Nagasaki?"

"Okay, doc."

Jake helped the snickering youngsters down from the table and sent them out of the room. The exam room door slid silently shut after them.

"You're great with kids," Blaze said, leaning against the exam table.

Jake shrugged and slumped into a nearby chair. "I'm not so good with adults." He nodded towards the door for emphasis. "Captain Shepherd is the most difficult patient I've ever treated. Plus, she wants me to examine every one of the kids before we land. I saw 36 today; that's got to be some kind of record for any doctor –, which I'm not."

"Not yet, but soon."

"Soon? Like after I get out of jail?"

Blaze laughed and shook his head. "I consider it an honor to be aiding and abetting two of the most selfless criminals in the galaxy: you and the Captain."

Jake looked embarrassed and changed the subject. "How's it going down in the engine room?"

"Actually, it's kind of quiet. I thought I'd visit the upper decks for some excitement."

"We've got plenty of that here. The Captain's gonna go ballistic when she sees what the galley and lounges look like. I promised Shima I'd keep her in the infirmary as long as possible."

Blaze cleared his throat, trying to measure his next words. "I thought I'd stop by and see Lorina."

"So what are you doing here?" Jake raised his eyebrows questioningly. "Go see her."

Blaze looked at the ceiling. "Well, I wanted to ask your advice first, . . . if that's okay?"

"Advice?" Jake chuckled. "About Lorina? Let's see: don't try to win any arguments with her, accept the fact that she can talk you into anything she wants, and don't take her out for sushi. She hates sushi."

"Maybe 'advice' wasn't the right word." Blaze shrugged, avoiding Jake's eyes. "I just wanted to make sure it was all right with you if I . . . um, see her . . . since you're her . . . family."

Jake howled with laughter. "Let me get this straight: you're asking my *permission* to date my cousin? What century are you from, Blaze?"

Blaze could feel his face turning red as Jake held his sides, laughing. "I just wanted to make sure it was . . . *okay* with you," he stammered, uncertain how to explain.

Jake nodded cheerfully as he opened an overhead cabinet and took out a precision needle. "Oh, I get it. You want to know if it's okay if you . . . sure, I understand. Lorina *is* an adult, if you haven't noticed. Everyone from Earth's infertile these days, but I can give you an injection of Sterilite --"

"No, no, no!" Blaze was flabbergasted at the implication. "That's *not* what I meant!"

Jake kept nodding and laughing as he checked a list of medications on the wall-mounted monitor. "It's okay, Blaze, really. One dose lasts for six months."

"No, you've got it all wrong! I have no intention of --," Blaze didn't know how to articulate his feelings. He couldn't understand how quickly Jake managed to jump to the wrong conclusion. "I like Lorina, but I wouldn't think of --" he shoved his hands into his pockets, unable to express it in words, "not unless she and I were, you know . . . married."

Now it was Jake's turn to be stunned. "Married? You're already thinking of marrying her, and you just met her yesterday? Are you crazy?"

"No!" Blaze shook his head in frustration. "I mean, maybe. Maybe yes . . . I know I'm crazy about her." He paused, trying to collect his thoughts as Jake stared suspiciously at him across the exam table.

"Let me start over." Blaze rubbed his forehead, trying to think. "I came here to ask you if it was okay for me to date your cousin. I don't know what I was thinkin'. I guess, in the absence of a father figure, that the courteous – and, yes, the hopelessly old-fashioned thing to do -- would be to ask the nearest relative – meanin' you -- for approval. I have no intention to do anythin' *beyond* datin' her, Jake. I just want to get to know her, that's all."

He pointed to the needle still in Jake's hand. "I won't be needin' that, not until the day I get married . . . to whomever that may be. I'm not sayin' it'll be Lorina. Like you said, I just met her yesterday."

Jake shook his head in disbelief. "You're waiting until marriage? What planet are you from, Blaze?"

Blaze shrugged. "I'm from Oklahoma."

Jake laughed. "Well, that explains it." He set the needle on the exam table and held up his hands in a gesture of surrender. "Okay, if it will make you feel better: you have my approval to date Lorina . . . not that I have any jurisdiction over her personal life! This is just an old-fashioned formality, right?"

"Right." Blaze nodded. "Thanks, Jake." He took a step towards the door, then paused. "Would it be okay if we didn't tell Lorina we had this conversation?"

Jake laughed again. "This wasn't a conversation, it was a huge misunderstanding. I wouldn't dream of mentioning it to her, unless I wanted two black eyes to match yours." He gave Blaze a shrewd look and picked up the needle again. "Speaking of which –"

"I thought we agreed I didn't need an injection." Blaze backed away.

"Don't be such a baby! This is just to clear up your bruises. I meant to give you some Arnica yesterday after I fixed your nose, but it's not too late to give it to you now."

"Oh." Blaze relaxed. He watched as Jake touched a selection on the monitor and filled the syringe from a small vial that appeared in the slot next to the screen.

"I'll need to inject this directly into your eye sockets," Jake said. "Have a seat."

The relaxed feeling evaporated. "That's okay; I think I'll just wait until the bruises go away on their own. You know, the old-fashioned way."

"Would you sit down?" Jake said, exasperated. "You didn't cry like a baby when I fixed your nose."

"That's because Lorina was there – distractin' me."

"Well, pretend she's standing right here and sit down."

Meekly, Blaze moved over and perched on the end of the exam table.

"Lean down, please."

Blaze shut his eyes and tried not to flinch as he felt a sting beneath one eye, then the other. He felt warmth spreading from his eyebrows to his cheekbones, reducing the swelling which had made it impossible for him to open his eyes wider than a half-slit. When he tested his eyes a few moments later, he could open them normally.

"That looks better already." Jake nodded. "Your shiners should be completely gone by tomorrow morning."

Blaze stood up and stepped over to the wall monitor. He blanked the screen and studied his reflection in the mirrored surface.

Jake noticed his dumbfounded expression. "Yeah, your nose is straight and there are faded shadows under your eyes instead of black and blue marks. Speaking of black and blue, weren't you planning to go see the woman who broke your nose?"

"Yeah, I was." Blaze shook Jake's hand. "Thank you." He walked to the door.

"Don't keep her out too late," Jake called after him as the door slid open.

"Yes, *Dad.*" Blaze didn't mind the teasing. He said goodbye to Vipul and the Captain as he left the infirmary and climbed down the ladder to the third level. The ship was quiet except for an occasional giggle behind a cabin door. He was impressed that Lorina, Shima, and Idalis had managed to get the kids to bed at a reasonable hour.

Blaze wished he had some flowers as he walked to Lorina's cabin. He felt awkward showing up empty-handed, and made a mental note to buy her roses when the *Ishmael* docked. He knocked quietly on the door, and felt a flutter of nervousness as he glanced down at his uniform to make sure it was clean.

When the door slid open, he immediately forgot about his appearance and focused on hers. "Hey, Lorina."

She was breathtaking in a pair of borrowed sweatpants and purple T-shirt, her strawberry blond hair unbound and flowing in loose curls around her shoulders. She put a finger to her lips and took his hand, drawing him inside her dimly-lit room. "Shh, Niyati's finally asleep."

Blaze glanced over at the tiny figure curled up on the right side of her double bed. "Oh." He hadn't realized the little girl would be sharing Lorina's cabin. "I haven't seen her awake."

"After the drug wore off this morning, she ran like a mouse on a treadmill all day," Lorina explained in a hushed tone. "I think she was afraid to go back to sleep; afraid she wouldn't wake up, or that she'd have nightmares about Acheron." She ushered him over to the only chair in the room, in a corner near the closet.

Blaze started to sit down on the floor next to the chair, but Lorina pushed him onto the seat and sat in his lap. Before he could blink, she had both arms around his neck, bringing his mouth to hers. He was completely out of breath before she released him from the kiss.

"I've been wanting to do that all day," she confessed. "I read somewhere that a girl can learn a lot from the first kiss." She gave him a disappointed look.

A wave of self-consciousness hit him again. "But -- I wasn't ready. Give me another chance."

"No, it's too late. There's only one first kiss." She snuggled against his chest and looked into his eyes with the grin of an experienced practical joker.

"So, – what did you learn?" Blaze was intoxicated by her closeness, but knew he wouldn't be able to relax until she leveled with him.

"Well, you seem inexperienced – not that I'm an expert," she said quickly, flashing him an embarrassed grin. "But your technique is good." Her grin warmed into a sultry smile. "Maybe you just need some more practice."

As she drew his face close to hers for another kiss, Blaze gently blocked her mouth with his hand. "Wait, don't I get to say what I learned from the first kiss?" He tried not to laugh at her astonished expression.

She sat up straight, both hands on her hips. "Okay, the joke's gone far enough."

"Lorina, are you afraid I'm going to say something you don't want to hear? I'm not a mind reader." Blaze wrapped his arms around her waist and drew her closer. For a fleeting moment he felt her tremble, but then it was gone. She smiled, but that one involuntary shiver opened up a world of understanding.

"You've never kissed anyone before, have you?" he whispered.

She shook her head and looked away, her cheeks turning pink. "I thought you said you weren't a mind reader."

Blaze grinned. "If I were, I wouldn't need to ask where you learned to kiss like that."

"Just from watching holo-vids," she mumbled, her face scarlet. She tried half-heartedly to squirm free of his embrace, but Blaze wouldn't let her go.

"Hey, it's okay; you don't have to be afraid of me. I really wanted to take things slow. I wasn't expectin' a kiss tonight."

He nodded at her skeptical expression. "I'm just as nervous as you are. I've never had a girlfriend; never had a second date, in fact. Never been head over heels –" he stopped himself, afraid he'd said too much.

Lorina relaxed in his arms. "I thought it was just me. I thought I was delusional to think a handsome college-educated man could be interested in an ignorant farm girl like me unless I was aggressive. I'm sorry I threw myself at you."

It took Blaze a moment to process the 'handsome' remark. "I always do the wrong thing when I feel insecure, but, believe me, I don't mind you bein' aggressive." He smiled. "Except when you're givin' out broken noses."

Lorina flashed him a 'who-me' pout which made him chuckle.

Blaze stroked her hair, entranced by the thick waves that felt like silk between his fingers. It took him a moment to focus on what he wanted to say. "I thought I was the delusional one. How could such a smart and gorgeous woman be interested in an awkward beanpole like me?"

"Very easily." Lorina brought her face close to his, but this time she paused, her lips a few tantalizing millimeters from his. "Shall we try that first kiss again?"

Blaze was happy to oblige. When they parted, he suggested, a bit breathlessly, "Maybe we could go up to the galley and get something to eat."

Lorina untangled herself from his arms and rose to her feet. "I shouldn't leave Niyati alone. What if she wakes up while I'm gone?"

Blaze felt a nudge of impatience, but tried not to show it. "Why don't we move her to a cabin with some other girls?"

Lorina moved to Niyati's bedside and leaned down to smooth the hair over her small forehead. "All the passenger cabins are crowded with kids. Most are three to a bed, and some of them are sleeping on the floor." She straightened up and turned to give Blaze a sheepish grin. "I know it's more comfortable than what they're used to, but I felt guilty occupying this large space by myself."

Again Blaze was reminded of how much the child meant to her. He decided to show some consideration. "Why don't we just sit in the corridor outside your door? That way we can talk without wakin' her."

Lorina flashed him a grateful smile. She took two bottles of lemonade out of her mini-bar and they sat on the hallway floor on either side of the closed door.

"Tell me about your family," Blaze said. "Are they still, um, alive?"

"Alive and well." Lorina smiled. "I can't wait to see them again, and I have you to thank for the ride home."

"You said you grew up on a farm?"

"Yes, a very large, remote farm near Wilmington. My grandfather was a visionary man. He knew hard times were coming and was determined that the O'Briens were going to be self-sufficient survivors. Our house is built underground like a giant bomb shelter. We raise everything we eat: grains, vegetables, fruit, cattle, chickens. Every piece of clothing I wore was sewn by my mother." She made a face. "I learned to knit socks when I was seven, and cut hair when I was 10."

"Sounds like an Amish lifestyle."

Lorina laughed. "Not quite. My uncle loves to collect solar tractors and state-of-the-art farm equipment, and he doesn't mind going into town for a pizza now and then."

"How many people live in your house?"

"Jake and me, of course, and Jake's parents, my mom, Jake's sister Deborah, her husband Sean, and their daughter Catherine."

Blaze sipped his lemonade thoughtfully. *Okay, try not to sound like the bull in the china shop.* "And your father?"

Lorina shrugged. "He left when I was three. Let's just say he didn't care much for farming . . . or being faithful to my mother."

Ouch. "Sorry to hear that."

She nodded, unperturbed. "Jake's dad has always been a like a father to me. The O'Briens are a close-knit family. It felt kind of cozy growing up, but after I graduated from high school, it felt isolating –, like a prison. All I wanted to do was go to college, but my options were non-existent. When Jake was at Syracuse, I tried to stay busy. I taught myself to play the guitar and," she hesitated, "I prayed -- a lot; prayed that I'd find a way out."

"I guess your prayers were answered." Blaze reached for her hand.

Lorina smiled. "The day Jake came home and said he needed to go to Mars College, I felt like I had a reason for living again. But the adventure was more than I bargained for." She shook her head. "It's ironic. Now I can't wait to get home."

Blaze felt a pang of sadness. *I wish I had a home -- and a family waiting for me.* He mentally shifted his focus back to Lorina. "Mars Station was a reality check for me, too. I'm curious: Where did you learn to forge documents?"

"I had a high school graphic arts teacher who was a retired Homeland Security officer. I learned how to produce official-looking seals and signatures from him, but the real challenge is in the paper itself."

Blaze was intrigued. "What do you mean?"

"There are special fibers and water marks that can only be seen when you hold a document up to the light. So I taught myself how to make the paper. It became a hobby, of sorts." She shrugged.

Blaze grinned. "So you're clever, as well as beautiful."

Lorina blushed and moved a little closer to him. "So, tell me about growing up in Tulsa. Did you get those great cheekbones from your father?"

199

"Actually, my mother was one-quarter Osage. I guess I got the cheekbones from her. I got the big nose from my dad."

"You don't have a big nose."

Blaze shrugged, embarrassed to have brought it up. "Well, it was crooked before I met you. I guess you did me a favor by breakin' it."

"You mean Jake did you a favor by fixing it."

Blaze grinned and reached over to trace the freckles on the tip of her small nose. "Somethin' like that."

Lorina playfully swatted his finger away. "You were going to tell me about Tulsa? You mentioned owning a horse named Blaze."

"Actually, Blaze was my grandfather's horse. I went to see him every weekend growin' up – my granddad, not the horse. We'd go ridin' and fishin' on the reservation, but my favorite thing to do was take a ride on his gasoline-powered motorcycle."

Lorina laughed. "I've only seen those in museums."

"I know. I still have no idea where he got the gas for it! Granddad was so much fun." Blaze felt a heavy weight settle in his chest. "I really miss him."

Lorina was quiet for a minute, stroking the back of his hand. "Tell me about your family."

He hesitated, nervous about sharing the tragedy of his family life. "What would you like to know?"

Blaze managed to answer Lorina's questions without getting choked up or tongue-tied. He was touched by how quickly her beautiful hazel eyes filled with tears when he spoke about losing his brothers and his mother's suicide, and again when he repeated the details of his father's losing battle with leukemia.

"You've been through so much, yet you found a way to keep your optimistic spirit alive." The sympathy in her expression was replaced with genuine admiration. "You're strong."

Blaze shook his head. "Is that why I get beat up so much?"

"You know I'm not talking about physical strength," she replied with a touch of exasperation. "I'm talking about inner strength, and courage. You're not afraid to stand up for what's right, even if it means getting your butt kicked once in awhile." She drew his arm around her shoulders. "I feel safe when I'm with you."

They sat up all night talking about life and how the war had changed so many things that were once familiar. They also laughed a lot, relating funny incidents from their lives to offset the somber discussions. Blaze didn't realize how much time had passed until he heard a muffled shout from inside Lorina's cabin. The door slid open and there stood Niyati, rubbing her big brown eyes.

"*Shundor amma!*" Niyati launched herself at Lorina, wrapping both skinny arms around her neck.

Blaze watched the reunion with a growing sense of uneasiness. "What did she say?"

Lorina smiled at him as she gathered the child into her arms and got up from the floor. "I don't know. She started calling me that yesterday. I guess it means 'red hair' or 'auntie.' Niyati, this is Blaze."

"Blez." Niyati acknowledged his presence with a suspicious frown and a tighter grip on Lorina.

"Nice to meet you, Niyati." Blaze forced a smile and got to his feet. He checked the time on his sensor and gasped in surprise. "It's almost 6:00 a.m.! The Captain'll have my head; I haven't checked the engines in nine hours! Sorry, Lorina, I've got to run." He leaned down for a quick kiss goodbye and dashed to the ladder.

"See you tonight!" Lorina called after him.

He gave her a thumbs-up as he descended out of sight.

* * *

"Blaze, report to the Captain's office."

Blaze pried his eyes open and managed to mutter a "yes, ma'am" as he sat up on the bed. Through the haze of half-awake, his first thought was that he'd done something stupid and put the ship in jeopardy. He pushed himself up and tried to work the stiffness out of his shoulders as he wandered over to the main control panel.

The engines were functioning normally, as they were supposed to, during a jump. There were no glitches in the navigation program, so Vipul had done his job correctly, as well. *I wonder if Ting messed up something.*

Blaze shook his head, knowing it was useless to speculate. He noted the stubble on his square jaw, realized a sprucing up was in order, and moved quickly to the head.

Ten minutes later, he was knocking on the door of Captain Shepherd's tiny office.

"Come in, Blaze." The Captain was at her desk wearing Chinese red silk pajamas. She appeared to be in pain.

"Captain, are you sure you should be out of the infirmary?" The words were out of his mouth before he could think of a more tactful greeting.

"You're starting to sound like Jake." She didn't look up from her monitor. "Have a seat."

Blaze sat. She continued to frown at her screen without speaking, so he counted to 10 in his mind before opening his mouth again. "Is there a problem, Captain?"

Shepherd met his gaze and gingerly touched her left side before speaking. "We need a place to land, Blaze, and for that I need to send some transmissions, asking for help. I don't have to tell you how complicated our situation is. We can't dock at a public spaceport while I'm wanted for murder, and we have to figure out where to take the children. I'm not keen on leaving them someplace where they'll become homeless again, but I don't think an orphanage can accommodate the entire lot. What's the answer?"

"I don't know, Captain."

"This is your assignment: I need you to break Velocity at 18:00 and resume again at 18:15. Do you have a problem with that?"

Several, Blaze thought. "I've only flown ships in simulators, Captain. I was never taught how to break out of a jump and return to it again without startin' over from scratch. At the very least, I'd need to do a complete systems check and install new navigation coordinates. That would take at least an hour. Why such a short time?"

"Because it takes a CIP station-to-station search probe only 16 minutes to locate a ship out of Velocity. Right now they don't know where we're headed because I never filed a flight plan with the Mars portmaster."

Blaze thought hard. "Theoretically, messages can be transmitted during Velocity."

"That's a theory I've never tested, and I don't plan to start now. I have to send 18 messages, Blaze. I can't risk having one of them scramble during transmission."

"What if we waited until we broke atmosphere to transmit them? No probes to worry about that way."

Shepherd frowned. "Are you suggesting we orbit Earth until we get a reply? We could be orbiting for days, maybe weeks."

"Is that a problem, Captain?"

"Food and patience are in short supply, engineer." She sat back in her chair, winced at the resulting pain, and leaned forward again. "But your plan makes sense. We'll stay in Velocity."

Blaze smiled. "Good. Now that that's settled, we should get you back to bed, Captain."

"I'm fine."

Blaze gave her an appraising look. "That's what you said when you tried to give me your husband's uniforms, Captain."

She looked like she was going to berate him, but her mouth twisted into a grimace instead. Her face began to glisten with sweat. "Well, don't just sit there; help me back to the infirmary. I'm going to tell the rookie medic to increase my pain meds."

"Yes, ma'am." Blaze stood and offered her his arm. "Let's take the elevator."

In the infirmary, they found Vipul hobbling around, trying not to put too much weight onto his left leg. "You forgot your anti-grav crutches, Captain."

"You also forgot your last dose of painkillers, Captain," Jake added, poking his head out of the exam room. "I told you not to overdo it. Your muscles need another day to re-grow before you can walk unassisted."

Blaze was supporting most of Shepherd's weight as he maneuvered her across the room to her bed. She was starting to tremble as she eased herself onto her right side.

"I'm –" she winced, "fine. "I don't have time to be incapacitated."

"You were shot, Captain." Jake moved quickly to her bedside and gave her an injection. "I had to reconstruct your side with synthflesh, and you're missing a kidney. Your body needs *time* to heal. If you keep pushing yourself, you'll be permanently incapacitated."

Shepherd stopped shaking. Her eyelids drooped. "Didn't I tell you not to give me any more sedatives, Jake?"

Jake set his jaw. "When you obey my instructions, Captain, I'll obey yours."

She started to argue, but faded out of consciousness. Blaze drew the covers up over her shoulder.

Jake sighed loudly and turned back to the exam room. "As soon as she's 100%, she's going to choke the life out of me, Blaze."

"I think you're right. Hope we've docked before then."

"Me, too. Now if you'll excuse me, I have another patient with a serious case of intestinal parasites." The door to the exam room slid shut after Jake.

"How about you?" Blaze turned to Vipul, who had been observing everything with a half-smile on his thin face. "Are you overdoin' it?"

"Actually, I'm underdoing it, mate. My hipbone and muscles have re-grown, and the soreness is tolerable. I'm just hanging around here because I love all the attention."

Blaze raised his eyebrows at the navigator and glanced around the empty room. "Whose attention are you referrin' to?"

"The kids, of course. Lorina brings in a few during mealtimes. I've been serenaded, entertained, fussed over." He indicated his bedside table, which was covered with an assortment of colorful get-well cards, apples, cookies, and other treats.

Blaze walked over and picked up one of the handmade cards. *Get wel soon, Mr. Vipel. Frum Kwame, age 5.* It had a brown stick person with a smiley face drawn on it. He glanced over at the Captain's bedside table and noticed it was bare.

Vipul noted his concerned expression. "The kids have been showering her with gifts, too, but it makes her uncomfortable. She's been escaping to her office at mealtimes."

Blaze glanced at the time. "I guess she's gonna sleep through the dinnertime entertainment. Mind if I stick around and watch the show?"

Vipul laughed and got back into his bed. "Be my guest."

Blaze sat down on the foot of Vipul's bed. He didn't have to wait long because the door slid open a minute later, and Lorina came into the infirmary with five children, each barefoot and toga-clad. One of the five was Niyati; she kept a tight grip on Lorina's hand.

Am I so insecure that I feel jealous of Niyati? Blaze didn't have time to analyze the thought before the little group burst into song. They sang *Happy Birthday to You* to Vipul in a language Blaze didn't recognize, though the tune was unmistakable.

When they finished, Vipul applauded enthusiastically, and Blaze joined in late, brought back to reality by a searching look from Lorina.

"Thank you, but it's not my birthday," said Vipul.

"We're just making up for the birthdays you might have missed." Lorina nodded to one of the older children who Blaze now recognized as Vladimir. The youngster brought the tray of chili and cornbread he had been holding over to Vipul.

"Thank you." The navigator accepted the tray with a big smile. "I feel better already."

The children beamed. As one, they glanced over at the sleeping Captain.

"I'm sure the Captain will be disappointed she missed your song," Vipul said.

Another child placed the Captain's dinner tray on her bedside table, and the little group departed. Lorina turned to give Blaze a wink before the door slid shut after her.

Blaze immediately felt ashamed of his jealousy. He stood up. "I guess I'll let you eat in peace; I need to get back to the engine room."

"Everything okay between you and Lorina?"

Blaze glanced over at the exam room: The door was still closed. He sat down again, grateful to have Vipul to confide in. "Everythin's great between me and Lorina, but I'm not sure how I feel about Niyati."

Vipul nodded. "They seem to be inseparable. Lorina's never come in here without her little shadow."

"Do you think this is just temporary?" Blaze knew he sounded desperate, but he couldn't help the way he felt. "I mean, I'm sure Lorina could find a nice family to adopt her. Do you think she's just lookin' after Niyati until that happens?"

"Why don't you just ask her about her plans for Niyati?"

Blaze shut his eyes, trying to imagine the outcome of that conversation. "Lorina would probably break my nose again if I even suggested it. I know she loves that little girl. She risked bein' left behind to try and find her." His shoulders slumped. "They're a package deal, aren't they, Vipul?"

"What do you think?"

Blaze wracked his brain, trying to isolate his real problem. "I think . . . maybe I'm just not ready to be a father."

"I think you nailed it, mate," Vipul sympathized. "Did you notice Niyati calls Lorina *shundor amma?*"

Blaze was startled. "Do you know what it means?"

"I remember a little Bengali; it was my mother's first language. *Shundor amma* means beautiful mother."

Blaze was flabbergasted. "Niyati's callin' her *mom?*" He covered his face with his hands. "What am I gonna do?"

"Well, it looks like you have two choices: learn to accept Niyati -- or stop seeing Lorina."

"You have a real knack for puttin' things into perspective, Vipul." Blaze grimaced, slowly got to his feet again. "Thanks for the reality check."

"It's easy -- when the problems aren't mine," Vipul explained. "Take your time and think about it. I'll see you later?"

"Yeah. Have a good evenin'." Blaze patted him on the shoulder and made his way back to the engine room. His own bowl of chili went untouched as he busied himself, tinkering with the solar engines.

Lorina's voice came over the com at 10:30 p.m. "Blaze, aren't you coming to see me?"

"Sorry, Lorina, I dozed off. I think I'm too tired tonight."

He felt guilty for lying, but he couldn't face her. Indecision weighed heavily on his mind. It seemed unfair he had to make a choice at all, yet he knew it wasn't Lorina's fault. *She has no idea I feel this way. I'm the newcomer to this relationship, not Niyati.*

"Okay, goodnight then." Her voice was filled with disappointment. "I'll see you tomorrow."

"Goodnight, Lorina." He deliberately made no promise about seeing her the next day, and that omission compounded his feelings of guilt.

Blaze knew he wouldn't be able to make this decision without some guidance. He knelt beside his cot and offered a heartfelt prayer.

SEVENTEEN
BLAZE'S CHOICE

Lorina hit the ground running at 5:30 a.m. It was Day 3 of chaos control, and she was mentally and physically exhausted. The *Ishmael* was scheduled to come out of Velocity in 10 hours, and she was looking forward to it. She thought about the transmission she had composed for her mother yesterday, at the Captain's request, asking for assistance in finding a safe place for the children. Lorina knew her family wouldn't be able to help, but they would certainly be elated to know that she and Jake were coming home.

Me, Jake, and Niyati. She glanced over at her tiny roommate who was still snoring softly. *I wonder what Mom will think of her. I know Catherine will be delighted to have a playmate. I just wish Blaze* – Lorina stopped that thought. She tried to focus instead on the simple task of combing the tangles out of her hair.

But no matter how hard Lorina tried to think about other things, she couldn't get Blaze off her mind. She couldn't help but notice the expression on his face whenever Niyati was with her. Lorina hoped he would come around and give Niyati a chance -- *or at least tolerate her, like Jake does* -- but last night's no-show had sent the message loud and clear: Blaze didn't want to be tied down with someone else's kid.

Lorina could sympathize with his feelings, but she couldn't change the way she felt about Niyati. She wasn't sure what would happen to the other children, but she had already made up her mind that Niyati would have a home and a parent who loved her.

So it's better to bail out now before I invest too much in a doomed relationship. I'll just end it quickly, she thought, stepping into the shower. *It won't hurt as much this way.*

Lorina hit the repeat button 10 times before she stopped crying. She put on a clean uniform, borrowed from Idalis, and went to wake Niyati.

"*Amma* cry?" Niyati sat up in bed, her dark eyes filled with concern.

"I'm okay." Lorina forced a smile. She helped Niyati into a blue dress, which was just a T-shirt borrowed from Shima, and combed her hair. "Are you hungry?"

Niyati took her hand as they started to the door. Already the shouts of early risers could be heard in the corridor. "*Amma* cry for Blez?"

Lorina winced. *Is it that obvious?* "It's okay, Niyati. I don't need Blaze to be happy." She picked up the child in a bear hug, blinking hard to hold back the tears. "Not when I have you. You make me happy."

Niyati seemed satisfied with the explanation, and Lorina couldn't spare any more time feeling sorry for herself. She stepped outside her cabin and assumed her drill sergeant role.

"Group A, time for breakfast!" Lorina cut through the din of children's voices with a shrill whistle. Eleven cabin doors slid open and more toga-clad children joined the ones already running around in the hallway. The 34 youngsters moved quickly to the ladder.

Out of necessity, Shima, Lorina, and Idalis had organized the children into four manageable groups. Each preteen had been assigned to watch over a child under the age of four, since the three women couldn't be everywhere at once. For the most part, the children looked out for each other. A few of the older kids were extremely helpful because they were used to caring for younger siblings. There were some troublemakers, but Shima kept them busy in the kitchen.

Lorina followed Group A up to the galley, shouting instructions the entire way, but the children knew the routine. They lined up at the counter for bowls of oatmeal, bananas, and cups of orange-flavored juice that the android had already prepared, sat down at the tables, and ate with enthusiasm. They then cleared their bowls and cups to the dishwasher's alcove and departed for the lounges or their cabins to entertain themselves until lunchtime.

Lorina finished spoon-feeding a toddler named Ahmed while Vladimir wiped down the tables for Group B. Shima was already herding the next 34 children into the galley.

"I have *Cinderella* playing in the second port lounge and *Pinocchio* in the starboard." The housekeeper took Ahmed from Lorina and handed her Monique, who was crying loudly.

Lorina began spooning oatmeal into Monique's tiny mouth. The toddler gobbled up her breakfast without a pause in her sobs.

"We need to distribute the clean clothing today," Shima called to Lorina from across the galley. She then calmly broke up a squabble between unruly 12-year-old Egyptian twin brothers and sent them to wash dishes as punishment.

Lorina glanced at Niyati, who was sitting cross-legged in the chair next to her, leisurely eating her banana. "How are we going to tell who owns which clothing?" she shouted back.

Shima shrugged and filled a cup with coffee. "The android can organize it by size, and we will just give each child whatever fits."

"Sounds like a good plan."

In record time, Group B moved out of the galley and Group C entered, herded by a sleepy-looking Idalis. Without a word, the cook took Monique from Lorina and handed her Pedro. Lorina parked the chubby 18-month-old in the chair on her other side and gave him a spoon.

"You're old enough to feed yourself, young man." She set a bowl of oatmeal in front of him.

Pedro abandoned the spoon and ate his breakfast with both hands.

"You get to clean him up," Idalis grumbled. The Latina didn't hide the fact that she resented the childcare duties on top of her demanding workload in the kitchen.

"I'll put it on my to-do list." Lorina was too tired to argue.

Shima herded in the 33 kids of Group D at 7:30 a.m. Lorina fed the last two toddlers, Dusit and William. Once Group D had eaten and departed, she checked that the dishwashing was under control, and then set out for the third starboard lounge where the older children liked to congregate.

Niyati cheerfully shadowed Lorina as she made the rounds from lounge to lounge, supervising children and trying to find things for them to do. The kids were quickly bored with holovids, so she spent the morning teaching a group of preteens how to play Rook, assembling an antique dollhouse for a mob of little girls, and supervising a make-shift game of soccer on the third level corridor.

"Just don't kick the doors, Vida!" Lorina shouted before hurrying to the lounge to break up two screaming girls who were pulling each other's hair.

Added to the general confusion were Jake's periodic requests. Every 15 minutes, Lorina had to find a child without a star drawn on his or her forehead, and send that child up to the infirmary for a check-up.

"The clothes," Shima reminded her as they passed each other in a corridor.

Lorina nodded. "I'll take one of the groups down to the basement after lunch."

Shima frowned. "The laundry area is very small. Perhaps we should take 10 at a time."

Great, that will take all afternoon. Lorina forced a smile of agreement.

Lorina fed the toddlers again at lunch as the four groups cycled through the galley to eat red beans and rice with tangerines for dessert. She selected 10 children from Group D and herded them down the ladder to the basement. Niyati happily followed her on the ladder, showing off like a monkey.

Lorina had never been to the basement and was uncertain which door led to the laundry. She was secretly relieved that all the doors were closed, including the one to the engine room; she didn't want to see Blaze. She paused, puzzling over an ID lock with *room sealed* glowing red in the display.

"Shima, which door?"

"Third one on the right."

"Thanks." Lorina touched the appropriate ID lock, and the door slid open. The children followed her inside the four by three meter compartment. Along one wall was a row of state-of-the-art steam washer-dryers. Another wall was filled with open cubbies, packed full of neatly-folded clothes. Lorina could see at a glance that the clothes had been organized according to size, with toddler clothes on the top left.

"Okay, who's first?" A black girl stepped forward with a shy smile. Lorina reached into a cubby on the second row, took a pair of girl's pink leggings off the top, and held them up to her for comparison.

Too long. She put the leggings back and selected another cubby. This time she found a dress that looked like a good fit. Lorina selected a pair of panties from the same cubby and sent the girl over to the makeshift dressing room, which was just a stack of empty food crates set up to block one corner from view. The child shed her toga and put on the newly washed dress.

Lorina moved on to the next child, searching for the right size clothing. It was a slow process, but by the ninth kid she was getting the hang of it, guessing the right cubby on the first attempt. She quickly finished dressing the group.

"Okay, you can all go upstairs now." As soon as the children departed, Lorina gathered up the pile of discarded togas and stuffed it into one of the washers. She was just about to ask Shima to send down another group when she realized Niyati wasn't in the room. *She must have gone up with the others.* This was unusual because the child never left Lorina's side.

Lorina stuck her head into the basement hallway and glanced around for Niyati. She heard familiar voices and realized they were coming from an open doorway across the corridor.

So this is the engine room. Lorina stood quietly in the doorway and looked around. Near the center of the mechanical labyrinth, Niyati and Blaze had their backs to her. Blaze was down on one knee and bent low, his ear level with Niyati's mouth. He seemed to be listening attentively, and Niyati seemed delighted to have his audience.

"What that?" Niyati demanded, pointing off to the right.

"I'll show you." He gathered her in his arms and stood, carrying her over to the console in question, which was lit up like a Christmas tree. "This is the Velocity control panel."

"Vewocity." Niyati giggled.

"Right. It makes the ship go fast."

Niyati studied the panel for a moment, then announced, "Blez make *shundor amma* cry."

Lorina gasped and quickly came forward. "Niyati." She snatched the girl away from Blaze. "I'm sorry if she's keeping you from your work."

Blaze seemed surprised at her abruptness. It took him a moment to formulate a response. "It's okay, Lorina, I don't mind showing her around."

Lorina shook her head; she was already on her way out. "I'm sure you have a lot to do, so we'll get out of your way."

"Lorina, wait. About last night –"

Lorina was grateful her back was to Blaze as she hurried into the corridor because she didn't want him to see her expression. "It's okay, I know how you really feel. You don't exactly hide your feelings."

"Could we talk about this, please?" Blaze followed her to the ladder.

"There's nothing to talk about." Lorina still had her back to him as she shooed a wide-eyed Niyati up the rungs.

Blaze grabbed her hand. "Lorina, I can see you're upset. We need to talk."

She was tempted to punch him with her free hand, but instead she faced him so he could feel the full impact of her words:

"There's nothing to talk about. You and I were just two lonely people coming together under stressful conditions. – I believe that's Webster's definition of a *fling*. It was just a fling. We don't seem to be compatible for a serious relationship." She glanced up the ladder at Niyati, for emphasis. "In a few hours, I'll be going home, so it's best if we go our separate ways now. I'm sure you understand."

The look of shock and disappointment on his face didn't help her feel vindicated. "Lorina, you're not a fling to me. I love you."

She drew in a sharp breath. "How can you love me when you've only known me for three days? "

Blaze's answer surprised her: "How long did it take you to realize you loved Niyati? It doesn't matter if it's been three years or three days or even three minutes! Love doesn't follow some logical timetable. It's hard for me to explain, but I've had this feelin' from the moment we first met; I *knew* you were the one."

Lorina could tell he was being completely honest. Blaze was the most sincere and caring person she'd ever met, and she was terrified to admit to herself that she felt the same way about him.

She tried to hide her vulnerability behind a mask of skepticism. "Are you sure it wasn't *pain* you were feeling when we met? You were bleeding, remember."

"It doesn't matter how we met; what matters is that we're together now." He was struggling with the words, his tone pleading. "I don't want to lose you, Lorina."

Lorina felt her bravado beginning to crumble. Tentatively, she reached out and took his other hand in hers. His palm was clammy with perspiration. She had never seen Blaze lose his composure before; he was actually trembling. She didn't know what to say.

"I know this is sudden, but what I really want –" he took a deep breath and blurted out, "what I really want to do is marry you."

Lorina was stunned speechless. She glanced up the ladder. Niyati was up to the entry level, looking down at her with concern. Lorina tried to compose her thoughts as she forced herself to look at Blaze again, only to discover tears glistening in his eyes.

This was not what she'd been expecting for a break-up speech!

She felt confused and scared; she struggled to put her fear into words: "Is this some kind of emotional game you're trying to play? You're trying to make me *choose* between you and Niyati, is that it?"

He placed his hands gently on her shoulders and looked into her eyes. "I'm not askin' you to choose."

Lorina felt a tremor in her knees. She tried to convince herself she was hearing right. "You're not?"

"I've spent a lot of time praying about what to do -- about us, Lorina. This mornin' I realized I'm just bein' selfish, that I'd regret it for the rest of my life if I let you go because I couldn't accept Niyati. I know I can't have you without her. I'll learn to love her, too, if you'll be patient with me. Like I said, love doesn't follow some logical timetable. With you, it was instant; with Niyati, I need some time to get to know her."

Lorina took some deep breaths and tried to get her own trembling under control. She shut her eyes and tried to think. *What's there to think about? This is insane! -- Isn't it? I've never met anyone like Blaze.* Then the thought came forcibly to her mind: *I'll never meet anyone like him again.*

It seemed like hours before she remembered that he was still waiting for her to say something. Lorina opened her eyes. "Can you ask me properly?"

Blaze instantly dropped to one knee and clasped her hands in his. They were now the same height, face to face. "Lorina Murphy, would you do me the honor of becoming my wife?"

Lorina couldn't resist teasing him. "You know, if 'taking it slow' was a class, you would have flunked."

"I know." He waited, not breathing.

Lorina smiled. "You don't mind if I keep my maiden name?"

Blaze threw his arms around her waist and kissed her. "Can't you just say yes like a normal girl?"

"You may have noticed that I'm not normal." Lorina nuzzled his ear. "Yes," she whispered.

"*Amma!*"

Startled, Blaze and Lorina looked up the ladder at their audience of one. Niyati was descending slowly, her expression scared and confused.

Blaze stood up and lifted Niyati off the rungs when she was level with his shoulders. "It's okay, Niyati."

"Blez make *amma* cry!" Niyati squirmed to get down. She reached for Lorina. "*Amma! Amma!*"

Lorina encircled Blaze's waist with her arms, trapping the girl gently between them. Niyati stopped struggling and watched, dumbfounded, as Lorina went up on tiptoes and Blaze leaned down, their lips meeting midway.

Blaze broke it off quickly. "Okay, let's agree no French kissin' in front of the girl."

Lorina laughed. "This is crazy. I can't believe I have an instant family."

"Blez make *amma* -- happy?" The child's perplexed expression made them both laugh.

"Very happy." Lorina thought for a moment. "I can't remember ever feeling this happy. I feel like I'm floating."

"Me, too. Maybe I should check the ship's gravity," Blaze joked.

Lorina sighed. "I hate to spoil this moment, but I have to get 138 more kids dressed."

Blaze set Niyati on her feet. "I'll help. I don't have to babysit the engines until it's time to break out of Velocity."

"Thank you, Blaze."

"Tenk you, *baba*." Niyati flashed him a sly grin.

Blaze's mouth fell open. "Did she just say what I think she said?"

Lorina's expression mirrored his surprise. "I think I know what *baba* means. It didn't take me long to figure out *amma.* You're too clever for us, young lady," she told Niyati with mock-sternness. "It looks like you wooed yourself into a family." She winked at Blaze. "Right, *baba*?"

"Who's your *baba*?" Blaze chuckled, shaking his head.

Lorina took one of Niyati's hands and Blaze took the other as they walked back to the laundry room. "Shima, send down another group."

"Okay."

Lorina's thoughts were light-years from her work as she and Blaze talked nonstop through the 14 rotations of children in and out of the laundry room.

"You don't mind waiting until we get to Wilmington? I want you to meet my Mom, and Jake's family."

"I wouldn't have it any other way." Blaze nodded, handing out underwear to the Egyptian twins.

"Are there any family members you'd like to invite?" Lorina found a blue dress in good condition at the bottom of a pile and sent Niyati to the changing area to try it on.

"No. I have an aunt in Colorado Springs, but we've never been close. It would be nice to have Vipul and Shima there, but I don't know what's gonna happen when we land. The Captain may only give us a few days dirtside."

Lorina was startled. She finished pulling a T-shirt over a three-year-old boy's curly black head. "You want to keep working for Captain Shepherd?"

"I guess I haven't thought about it until this moment." He grinned, embarrassed. "What did you have in mind for *our* future?"

Lorina returned the sheepish grin. "I don't know. I guess I was in the mindset of going home, but that wouldn't be practical for your career – or mine, come to think of it."

Blaze rummaged through a cubby, searching for boys' pants. "I guess I should ask: What career did you have in mind, sugar?"

Lorina was delighted to hear him use a term of endearment in his syrupy-sweet Oklahoman accent. "I can't envision myself being a steward forever, but I suppose we could stay on with the *Ishmael* until we decide where we'd like to live. I've always wanted to be a CEO, but it's hard to run a company when there's no way to earn a business degree."

"You can do anythin' you set your mind to. You don't need a business degree to start your own company." Blaze picked up several togas from the floor and put them into a washer.

"What a good idea, honey." Lorina started to laugh, shaking her head. "Jake's going to have a stroke when he hears me call you that."

Blaze looked worried. "I think he's gonna have more than a stroke since I told him two days ago that I just wanted to get to know you better."

"Ha!" Lorina startled the little boy she was buttoning into a faded green shirt. "He's going to call us crazy and try to talk us out of it. You'd think he'd figure out that arguing with me is wasted breath."

"He did mention that, when I asked him for some advice," Blaze admitted.

"Talking about me behind my back?" Lorina's challenge was softened by an exaggerated pout.

"Sorry. You can spank me later."

Lorina laughed until her sides ached.

"Blaze, report." Captain Shepherd's stern tone interrupted the festive mood. Blaze shot Lorina an apologetic grin and dashed across the hall to the engine room.

"Lorina," Jake's tired voice interrupted her attempts to fix the ancient zipper on Niyati's dress.

"Yeah?"

"According to my records, I've seen 147 children. Which one have I missed?"

Lorina glanced at Niyati. "I think I know. Hey, I'm impressed. I didn't think you'd be able to see every single one."

"It's amazing how much you can accomplish when you forgo sleep. Send Niyati up."

Lorina looked around at the last group of boys who were attempting to dress themselves from the tattered remains of the clothing collection. "Vipul?"

"Yes, Lorina."

"Could you donate a few T-shirts to this last group?"

"Send them up to my cabin."

"Thanks, Vipul." Lorina ushered the shirtless boys out to the ladder, pausing to poke her head into the engine room and blow a kiss to Blaze, who was busy at the main control board.

'I love you,' he mouthed.

'I love you, too,' she returned, exhilarated to say it for the first time. She realized it was exactly how she felt. *Somebody pinch me; I must be dreaming.* She reluctantly turned back towards the ladder. "I never thought I'd be swept off my feet by the first man I kissed."

Niyati raised her eyebrows at Lorina.

"Upstairs to see Jake."

"Okay, *amma.*"

Lorina wondered how to break the news to her temperamental cousin. She found the infirmary post-op room empty, with three beds still unmade. She and Niyati crossed to the exam room.

"How's it going, Jake?"

"I can't wait to get off this ship." He looked like he'd just rolled out of one of the beds.

Jake was all business as he helped Niyati onto the table and scanned her. "Make yourself useful." He tilted his head to the side, indicating the datapad on a side counter. "Take her hologram and write down any new information in her file –, if you know any. Most of the kids have only a first name or nickname, and an estimated birth date. Not exactly a detailed medical record."

Lorina twirled the stylus in her hand and watched as Jake gently probed Niyati's abdomen with his fingers.

"I guess you could put Murphy for her surname." Jake raised his eyebrows at Lorina. His tone was joking, but his expression was serious. "You are planning to adopt her, aren't you?"

"Actually, I wrote Smith for her surname." Lorina held her breath, waiting to see if Jake would take the bait.

Jake frowned distractedly as he stared at the scanner screen. "So you're saying *Blaze* wants to adopt her?"

"No, I'm saying Blaze and I will both be adopting her, right after we get married."

Now she had his undivided attention. "What are you talking about?" He set down his scanner and faced her, arms folded across his chest.

"Blaze and I are getting married."

Jake rolled his eyes. "Yeah. *Maybe.* Someday. Aren't your grandiose plans a bit premature? You just met the guy on Wednesday."

"And he just proposed to me this afternoon."

Jake's mouth fell open; he seemed incapable of speech for a full 30 seconds. Finally he burst out with, "That's *insane*! You can't make that kind of decision without weeks – months – to think about it! We're all close to cracking under the stress, Lorina, but it doesn't mean you should go do something *crazy* like marry a guy you barely know!"

Lorina kept a check on her temper, letting him vent. "So I'm just crazy from all the pressure?"

"Sure, once we get off the ship, you and Blaze will both realize that all you needed was some *time alone* to relieve the stress – not a lifetime commitment."

"*Time alone*?" Lorina stole a glance at Niyati's curious expression and realized the ridiculous term was meant to obscure the topic for her ears. "Blaze wants to spend his life with me. *Time alone* never came into the conversation, Jake."

"Sure, we'll see how he feels about the whole commitment thing after he gets some time alone tonight."

Lorina suppressed the urge to punch him. "For your information, Blaze and I won't be spending time alone together until *after* the nuptials."

Jake gave her an appraising look, his expression running the gamut between total disbelief and grudging astonishment. He struggled mentally for a few moments, then shrugged in defeat. "I think you're crazy to rush into this, but Blaze seems like a decent guy. He did tell me he would wait until he got married."

Now Lorina gave him an appraising look. "When did he tell you that?"

"Right after I offered him a shot of Sterilite." Jake sighed and turned back to Niyati, who was watching them both with a puzzled grin on her face. "Are you *sure* about this?"

"I've never been so sure about anything in my life." Lorina was relieved to feel the tension fading between them. "I don't feel rushed. Sometimes you just know if something feels right, Jake." She put her hand over her heart. "You can feel it right here."

Jake smirked. "In my line of work, we call that acid reflux."

Lorina returned the smirk. "Well, how about giving me a shot of Sterilite for my acid reflux?"

"Okay," Jake laughed, reaching into an overhead cabinet. "Drop your pants, cousin."

"*What*?"

Jake filled a syringe and handed it to her. "Okay, fine. Give yourself the injection. It goes right in the fanny, Mrs. Smith."

Lorina grinned as she took the needle from him. "It's Murphy. I'm keeping my maiden name."

"Whatever." Jake laughed. He slipped off his father's wedding band and handed it to her. "I guess you'll be needing this."

"Thanks, Jake." Lorina came around the exam table and hugged him.

Jake shrugged, his expression unhappy. "At least this trip to Mars was beneficial for one of us; I'm back to square one."

"Captain Shepherd might want to keep you on as med-tech."

Jake laughed derisively. "I think she'll be looking for a new medic as soon as she reloads her gun. And uses it on me."

Lorina helped Niyati down from the table. "She may still need you until she can hire a licensed medic."

Jake opened his mouth to respond, but was interrupted by an announcement from Marco Ting: "Coming out of Velocity in 15. Strap down for re-entry."

Lorina pocketed the syringe and left the exam room with Niyati in tow.

EIGHTEEN
INHERITANCE

It's worse than I thought. Danae leaned against the wall, resting her weight on her right leg. As tempting as it was to start shouting, she kept her mouth shut as a pack of children dashed by, heading to their cabins to strap down. At least, some of them were moving quickly; many were laughing and strolling leisurely along the corridor. *There'll be broken bones when we hit the stratosphere.*

"Group B, get moving!" Lorina's piercing whistle got the stragglers' attention. She corralled a knot of giggling preteens, steering them away from the third starboard lounge. "Where's Pedro, Amina? He's your responsibility. Find him quickly."

Danae watched, impressed, as the children followed Lorina's instructions. In a minute, the corridor was clear, and cabin doors closed. Lorina sprinted for the port lounge, not even pausing to acknowledge Danae's presence.

Danae limped to the elevator and rode up to the top level. She thumbed the ID lock on the door to the bridge, entering it for the first time since leaving Mars Station. "Report, Ting."

"Everything's fine," was his cryptic response. The helmsman was always nervous right before a Velocity break. Danae noted his white knuckles on the controls.

"Breathe, Marco, you've done this 1,000 times. This is routine."

"I've never flown the ship with a rookie engineer, Captain."

Danae sat down at the com board behind Ting and summoned the recorded transmissions from her office. "I trust Blaze. As I recall, my father had complete confidence in a rookie helmsman, just out of flight school. He let you dock at Titan without supervision."

"And you'll recall that I took out three airlocks in the attempt." Ting's beady eyes were fixed on the screen in front of him. "I took a pay cut for two years to finance the repairs."

Danae chuckled. "All stop as soon as we break the stratosphere."

"Yes, Captain."

"Breathe, Ting."

"Yes, Captain."

Danae slipped on her shoulder straps and fastened the seatbelt over her thighs, well below her injury. "Blaze, how does the hull look?"

"Heat shield is functioning at 100%, Captain," came the prompt reply.

Danae touched the button for ship-wide com. "All passengers and crew strap down for Velocity break – no exceptions. Five minutes and counting. I want passenger status reports. Idalis?"

"Group C is strapped down, Captain. I'm going cabin to cabin to verify."

"Lorina?"

"Group A is strapped down, Captain. Shima and I are working on Group D."

"Shima, what about Group B?"

"All strapped. I checked every one of them myself, Captain."

Danae switched back to ship-wide com. "I want it understood that *no one* is to unstrap until I give the word. If you're not secured, you *will* be seriously injured. Four minutes. Captain out."

At one minute, Danae began the standard countdown. It was a mundane task, but necessary for Blaze and Marco to coordinate shut down simultaneously. "Three . . . two . . . one."

Velocity engines cut out smoothly. Danae got a brief glimpse of Earth on her screen just before the *Ishmael* began re-entry.

Of all the planets she frequented, Earth was Danae's least favorite. Its gravity offered the most uncomfortable descent imaginable for any size ship. Only an experienced spacer could come through the ride without developing a migraine. The *Ishmael* shook violently as it attempted to penetrate the stratosphere.

Danae gripped the arms of her seat, but the constant jarring sent shock waves of pain through her left side. She remembered Jake's suggestion about taking a double dose of painkillers for re-entry, but she had insisted that she wouldn't need it. His recommendation that she strap down in a post-op bed had also gone unheeded. Subconsciously, she knew she was just being stubborn, but she resented being ordered around by a boy.

Even if the boy's right.

It took every bit of Danae's self-control not to cry out. Tears seeped from the corners of her eyes, but she blinked them away, determined to hang tough. "Marco?"

"Almost through," he gasped, his teeth rattling uncontrollably when he opened his mouth to speak. Despite the bucking helm, she knew Ting had control of the ship. "Five minutes."

I'm not going to make it five minutes, Danae thought. She felt a patch of synthflesh tear away from her still-tender wound. She glanced at her side and saw a thumbnail-size dark stain spread until it was the size of her fist. "Jake?"

"Wha-wha-what, Cap-tain?" he gasped.

"Gurney." It was too much effort to utter more than a single word.

"'kay." Jake dispensed with the multi-syllabic courtesies, as well.

The pain increased dramatically until it was all Danae could do to hang on to the fringes of consciousness. When Ting announced, "We're clear," and the jarring stopped, the pain was still like a serrated knife in her side.

Danae unstrapped herself from the seat and rose shakily to her feet, holding onto the chair for support. "Full stop, Ting."

"I'll give you 60 seconds of full stop, Captain."

Danae leaned over the com board to send the transmissions. The effort of pushing a few buttons was overwhelming. Her head was spinning and she felt nauseous.

"Captain, you're bleeding."

Danae hadn't heard Jake come up beside her with the gurney. She couldn't think of a snappy retort, so she settled for a curt nod. Jake took her arm to help her onto the gurney, but the moment the com board was no longer beneath her for support, she collapsed into his waiting arms.

Jake lifted her onto the gurney, careful not to jostle her left side. "It's a good thing you don't weigh much, Captain."

"It's a good thing you didn't say 'I told you so'."

Jake almost smiled. He drew a needle out of his breast pocket. "Painkiller, ma'am?"

"Make it a double." Danae welcomed the sting in her arm and the immediate relief it brought. "Ting, maintain a leisurely orbit at 2,500 kilometers an hour. And have Shima wake me the moment *Ishmael* receives a transmission."

"Yes, Captain." Danae noted the helmsman's frown at Jake. "Are you sure it's wise to let *him* operate on you again?"

Danae's patience evaporated. "Jake saved my life once already! I'm confident he can handle a minor repair! If you are *incapable* of offering any useful advice or predicting any positive outcomes, then you should – *Just* – *Shut* – *Up!*" She turned her face towards the ceiling.

"I just . . . see things," Ting muttered, defiant. "I can't help it, Captain."

"Yes, you can!" She was shaking now, furious. She noted the alarm in Jake's expression but seized his wrist to prevent him from giving her another injection. "Just keep your predictions to yourself!"

"But –" Ting protested.

"No matter what you see, I don't want to know! Even if you see me drop dead in my oatmeal tomorrow morning, I don't want to know about it! You will keep it to yourself! Do you have a problem with that?"

"No, Captain."

"Get me out of here, Jake." She realized she was bruising the medic and released his wrist. "Vipul, do you feel well enough to take the helm for a few hours? I think our pilot could use a break."

"Can do, Captain," came the prompt reply over the com.

"I'm fine, Captain," Ting protested.

"Get some sleep, Ting! That's an order! Jake?"

O'Brien's face was an unreadable mask as he rolled her gurney back to the infirmary. He carefully transferred her onto the surgical table, face down. "I'm going to patch your wound now, Captain."

"Fine. Put me out." She was grateful he couldn't see her expression.

"Yes, ma'am."

* * *

"Captain, we have two transmissions." Shima sounded weary.

"Please put the screen where I can see it." Danae tried to rouse herself from her post-op fog, but found it too much effort to bother. "How long have we been in orbit?"

"Nine hours, Captain." The housekeeper's hand on her shoulder was comforting. "We are somewhere over China." Shima propped a monitor in front of Danae's eyes.

The first message was from Ting's father. It was in Mandarin with no translation. Dr. Ting scowled through the entire 30-second spiel. "Doesn't look encouraging," Danae muttered. "I was hoping time would ease the rift between Marco and his old man. Next."

Shima skipped to the second holo-vid. This one was from Jake's father, who looked exactly like Jake except for the dark tan and salt-and-pepper crew cut. Danae listened with detachment as Jacob O'Brien explained why he and his family had been unable to find a port for the *Ishmael*.

"Please believe me, -- we would do something if we could. We want to help the children, and we commend you for making this courageous move to save them. We're grateful to you, Captain Shepherd, for bringing Jake and Lorina home to us. We'll be waiting to hear where you dock. God bless you."

"There is an addendum transmission attached," Shima said. "It is for Jake and Lorina."

"Naturally." Danae sighed, resting her chin on the mattress. "Tell them they can view it in my office."

"Yes, Captain."

As soon as Shima left the post-op, Danae began her com inquiries. "Blaze?"

"Yes, Captain?"

"How are we doing on fuel?"

"We've got 36 hours, Captain." His voice was filled with concern. "That includes dockin' time."

"What about solar --?"

"That includes solar engine time, as well."

Danae frowned. "Thank you, Blaze. Idalis?"

"Yes, Captain?" Danae noted her disgruntled tone.

"How are we doing on food?"

"I've got four more meals planned. Then I'll have to get creative."

"What do you mean by 'creative'?"

"I mean figuring out what to make with five kilos of rice and a liter of salsa."

"Can you make soup?"

There was a pause. "I might have a few cans of beans and corn to make a thin soup."

"So you can manage five meals, Idalis?"

"Yes, Captain."

"Let the kids help themselves to the snack bars. That should get us through until docking."

"If you say so, Captain." Idalis signed off.

"Jake?"

"Standing right here, Captain." His tone was missing the sarcasm for a change.

"When can I get up?"

Jake checked the bandage on her side. "You're good to go if you promise to use the anti-grav crutches."

Danae turned carefully onto her right side and sat up. "Thank you, Jake."

He nodded. "If you'll excuse me, Captain, Lorina wants to view our transmission."

Danae returned the nod. "I'm sure it'll be good to see your family again." As Jake left the infirmary, she thought of Alex and her father. *I wish I could see their faces again. You are one lucky young man, Jake.*

* * *

"Captain, I have a transmission from Mr. and Mrs. Zimmerman." Shima sounded like she was having a difficult time getting the words out.

Danae lifted her head from her desk where she'd been dozing. "Send it to my office. How many have we heard from so far?"

"Sixteen, Captain."

"Who hasn't responded yet?"

There was a pause as Shima checked the list. "Rosamar Delacruz and Keiko Costa."

"Delacruz may not be on Earth, but we should definitely hear from Costa."

"Yes, Captain." Shima signed off.

"Captain, I'm switching to solar engines," Blaze announced.

"How much time?"

"Four hours," was the grim reply.

"I'll be making a decision shortly," Danae promised, although she had no idea what that decision would be.

"Yes, Captain. Smith out."

Danae played the transmission from the Zimmermans. It was short and succinct. They were sympathetic to her situation, but unable to assist. "And we'd appreciate it if you'd return Hugh's body to us as soon as possible," Mr. Zimmerman added, signing off.

The transmissions had all been the same. No one had the motivation or financial means to help the *Ishmael* find a safe port. Danae was coming to the uncomfortable conclusion that she would have to find a public dock and take her chances with the local law enforcement.

She massaged her temples for a minute before making a ship-wide announcement: "All crewmembers will meet on the bridge in five minutes." She left her office and waded through a soccer game in the corridor to reach the lift.

On the bridge, Marco didn't look up from his position at the helm. She knew it would be a long time before he looked her in the eye again, but she was too preoccupied with the present crisis to soothe his bruised ego. She stepped over to the navigator's control board and leaned against the chair, putting her weight on her right leg.

Jake nodded to her as he walked onto the bridge. He took a spot near the doorway. Lorina showed up without Niyati, for a change. Danae had begun to wonder if the child was surgically attached to her.

Blaze walked in right behind Lorina. Danae noted the cozy way they stood off to the side together, – not exactly touching, but conspicuously close. They couldn't keep their eyes off each other, and, despite the seriousness of the *Ishmael*'s present situation, they couldn't stop smiling dreamily at each other.

Since the *Ishmael* had a long history of shipboard romances, including her own, Danae had no objection to what went on behind closed doors – as long as it didn't interfere with the operation of the ship. But this relationship posed a new problem: Danae hadn't planned on hiring Lorina after this jump to Earth. In her mind, the steward/head babysitter was a temporary solution to a unique situation.

But if I let her go, I might lose a good engineer. Danae mulled over the dilemma for a moment. *Well, I guess I could keep her on; it would be worth it to keep Blaze happy. But there's no way I can hire Jake, not until he has a real medical license.*

Danae shook her head, impatient with herself for getting sidetracked. *Focus. There's serious work to be done.*

When all seven crewmembers were crowded into the small room, Danae began without preamble: "We need to land --

somewhere, anywhere. We're almost out of fuel, and we don't have any offers for a safe port. Suggestions?"

"Can't we just stop orbiting and reserve what fuel we have left?" Jake asked.

Blaze shook his head. "It only works in space. If *Ishmael* stops moving, gravity will pull us down."

Jake shrugged, embarrassed. "Sorry, basic physics is way over my head."

"Can we set down in an open field somewhere?" Idalis spoke up. "There's lots of wide-open space in, say, Mongolia."

"Too cold for the children," Lorina said. "We don't have coats. Some of them don't even have shoes."

"A warmer place, then," Vipul suggested. "The Australian Outback?"

"Nice in theory," Blaze said, "but we need somewhere to refuel. The ship can't set down in the middle of nowhere."

"It looks like we don't have a choice," Idalis argued. "With the Captain wanted for murder, we're all accomplices. Any port would have us arrested on sight."

A protest was poised on Danae's lips, but a loud *ping* from the com board distracted her.

Shima leaned over the controls, studied the monitor. "Transmission coming in, Captain. It is from Keiko Costa."

"Play it." Danae lowered herself into the chair at the navigator's controls.

"It may be too personal for us to hear." Shima gave Danae a concerned glance.

"We don't have time for niceties, Shima. Play the transmission, audio only."

"Yes, Captain." Shima touched a button and a Japanese-accented female voice filled the small room.

"Captain Shepherd, good to hear from you. I'll get right to the point. I have some bad news and some more bad news for you. First, you're not going to be able to meet with your mother because she died two years ago."

Danae felt a chill as all eyes turned towards her, but she kept her face a mask of indifference. *So she's finally gone. I'm surprised her liver lasted this long.*

"Second, I did some digging and learned that her estate has been sitting in probate, waiting for you to claim it as her only heir. Here's the deal: your mother was quite the socialite after she returned to Earth. She married and divorced five times. She may have been an alcoholic, but she was awfully shrewd about prenuptial agreements. She walked away with quite a chunk of money from each ex-husband.

"But here's the other bad news: For some reason, your mom was fascinated with real estate. Your entire inheritance is property. There's no money; not even a dime to pay off the property taxes you're going to owe. Shortly before Claire died, she invested every penny in a huge sugar cane plantation near Lahaina, Maui."

"Jackpot," Jake whispered. Danae pretended not to hear.

"Since no one was left in charge to farm the land since she died, the property is worthless in its present condition. It would be difficult to sell, and it would probably cost you 10 million to start it up again as a working plantation, so right now it's just four square kilometers of volcanic soil with a run-down sugar processing plant and some outbuildings. There's also a large house on the property, although I don't know what condition it's in."

By this time, there was some wide-eyed interest among the members of the crew, but no one said a word as Danae turned to stare out the helm window.

Costa continued: "Attached you will find a survey of your sugar cane plantation and the necessary documents for your DNA impression. Please return them to me at your earliest convenience, and I'll forward them to the probate lawyers. I'm sorry not to have any good news for you. Take care. Costa out."

There was a long, awkward silence as the crew waited for the Danae to speak. Finally, Shima couldn't seem to stand it any longer and blurted out, "I am sorry about your mother, Captain."

Danae turned away from the window and gave her a blank look. "Well, don't be, because I'm not." She ignored the startled expressions. "It seems we have a place to land. Ting," she glanced over her shoulder at the helm, "How close are we to Hawaii?"

"We're just passing over Cairo, Captain." The Chinese pilot's expression was etched with concern. "We need six hours, minimum, to make Maui, and we've only got four hours of fuel left."

"So what can we do?" Jake asked.

"We can limp along on the solar engines indefinitely," Blaze said. "As long as we stay on the sun-side of Earth so the panels can absorb energy. But we need full engine power to land."

"Assuming we stay in the sunlight, how long does it take to bring the engines up to full power?" Jake asked.

Blaze glanced at Danae for help. "Twenty-four hours," she replied.

"We don't have 24 hours!" Idalis protested. "The soup we served for lunch was the last of the food!"

"You're right. We don't have 24 hours." Danae spoke over the hysterical cook. "But we have another option: a glided landing."

"What!" Ting rose from his seat. "That's not an option, that's suicide!"

Blaze grimaced but remained silent, his eyes fixed on Danae's.

Jake seemed afraid to ask. "What's a glided landing?"

"Just what it sounds like." Danae folded her arms. "We fly as close as we can and cut power, glide in for a landing."

"You mean *crash land*?" Lorina turned to look imploringly at Blaze.

"No, we won't crash." Blaze put a hand on Lorina's shoulder. The engineer spoke soothingly to the group: "*Ishmael* is shaped like a bird; a classic glider design. Theoretically, it can be done."

"*Theoretically*?" Jake looked like he was going to be sick.

Shima's calm exterior showed signs of cracking as she put her hand over her mouth. Idalis began muttering nervously to herself in Spanish. Only Vipul remained silent, his expression resigned.

"I've never done it in simulation," Blaze admitted.

"Neither have I!" Ting's face was paler than usual as he scowled at Danae. "It's crazy! It will never work!"

"Which is why *I* will be piloting the ship," Danae faced him squarely, her mouth set in a grim line. "I won't have a nervous Kamikaze at my helm."

"What is a Kamikaze?" Shima asked from behind her hand.

Ting made a disgusted noise. "Check a history book, Shima, because that's what this ship's going to be – history!"

"That's enough!" Danae shouted at him. "Shut your mouth!"

Ting gave her a furious look and stalked past her towards the doorway. "If anyone decides to come to their senses, I'll be in my cabin."

"And you can stay there!" Danae bellowed after him. She stepped over to the seat he'd just abandoned and took her place at the helm. She paused, getting her voice under control before speaking to the others. "Blaze, I'll need you baby the solar engines as much as you can. Everyone, return to your duties."

"Yes, Captain." The chorus of responses was definitely lacking enthusiasm.

"Jake," Danae called after him before he exited the bridge. "Give everyone, and I mean everyone, a space-sickness pill or patch."

The medic looked at her with a face that seemed to have aged five years in the past five minutes. "Yes, Captain." He hesitated. "Captain?"

"What?"

"Have you ever performed a glided landing?"

"No." Danae noted his expression and decided to offer him a morsel of hope. "But I watched my father do it once when we ran out of fuel before we secured dock on Venus Station."

Jake took a deep breath. "What happened?"

"We made it with some minor damage to the hull." Danae shrugged.

Jake hesitated again. "I don't suppose Venus Station is surrounded by hundreds of kilometers of ocean, Captain?"

"We'll make it, Jake. Trust me."

Jake looked unconvinced. "Yes, ma'am."

NINETEEN
DEADLY DESCENT

Jake tried not to keep glancing at the time as he searched the infirmary lab for space-sickness meds. He found a box of 50 patches stored in a cabinet with other non-prescription meds, but knew it wouldn't be enough. He turned to the wall monitor and requested the hypodermic formula for the same drug "suitable for children."

He winced when the recipe came on-screen. It would be time-consuming to make 100 injections, and time was something he didn't have. "Vipul, if you're not busy, I could use a hand."

"I've got two hands," the navigator replied. "I'll be there in five."

Jake leaned against the workbench and noticed his trembling hands for the first time. *I've got to calm down. Think about something else.* He turned back to the monitor. "Transfer O'Brien transmission from Captain Shepherd's office and replay it."

Marilyn O'Brien's cheerful face immediately came on-screen. Jake felt the familiar pang of homesickness begin to overshadow his nervousness as he focused on his mother's soothing voice. Each family member had recorded a brief 'welcome home' message for him and Lorina. Jake felt himself beginning to relax as he studied their faces.

He couldn't recall his father looking so old, or his brother-in-law so tired. *We haven't been gone that long -- have we? Seven months?* He glanced down at his hands and was relieved to see that they were still. He would need steady hands to play pharmacist. *Okay, I can do this.*

Jake blew out a long breath and faced the screen again. Catherine was saying goodbye and blowing kisses. He smiled at his niece. "See you soon, angel."

Last onscreen was Deborah, but she wasn't smiling. "Hello, Jake and Lorina," she took a deep breath and blurted out: "Sean and I have discussed it, and we want you to select one of the children for us to adopt."

Jake frowned. Hearing it a second time did nothing to diminish the element of surprise. He would never have imagined this type of request from his baby-hungry sister.

231

"Sean would like a son, of course, but I'm willing to accept any child you feel would do well in our family." Deborah paused for a moment, listening off-camera. "Sean says a sibling group would be okay if at least one is a boy. Race and age don't matter, although it would be nice to have one younger than Catherine. She's always wanted to be a big sister." She smiled for the first time. "Thank you, in advance, for giving us the opportunity to bring another child or children into our family. We'll see you soon. Deborah out."

Mentally, Jake had already made a decision about which children would do well in the Baker family, but he still had to ask the little girl and boy if they wanted to be adopted. His experience with street kids had taught him that they weren't always willing to give up their independence.

As soon as the transmission was over, Vipul came into the lab. He was walking without a limp, but still favoring his left leg. "What can I do to help?"

Jake brought the recipe back up on the screen and turned to face his former patient. "I know you can make bombs, but how would you rate your pharmacy skills?"

Vipul shrugged. "I made rice wine once, in my dorm room at Oxford."

Jake handed him a pair of sterile gloves. "How did it turn out?"

"Imagine the flavor of old tires mixed with sauerkraut."

"Well, I need you to help me make Banspace, and it doesn't matter what it tastes like because it will be for injections."

Vipul nodded. "Let's do it."

* * *

Jake knew they would be cutting it close. He went from room to room with Vipul, Shima, and Lorina, giving Banspace injections and strapping the children down.

"Vladimir, you can have a patch." He pressed one behind the left ear of the nervous-looking youth. "Your roommates –"

"Mikhail and Bao," Lorina supplied.

"-- will need the shot." Jake eyed the two smaller boys, estimating their weights. "Two cc's for each," he told Vipul, who quickly filled two syringes from the large vial of red liquid tucked into the crook of his arm.

Bao flinched as the needle went into his skinny forearm and started to cry.

"Good job," Lorina told him as she began strapping him down on the bed between Vladimir and Mikhail.

Jake assisted with the padded straps over the boys' shoulders and knees. He was beginning to get the hang of it, but wondered aloud if it was a good idea to leave their hands free.

"They're not prisoners, Jake, they're passengers," Lorina reminded him. "They'll be less likely to panic if they can move their hands."

"They can remove the straps," Jake argued, dropping the soiled needles into the portable sterilization unit Shima held out to him. He quickly removed two fresh syringes from the base of the unit.

"They won't."

"Now remember: don't get up until the Captain gives the all-clear," Jake told Vladimir.

The boy nodded fervently from his pillow. "I'll make sure they don't get up, Dr. Jake."

The adults quickly moved to the next cabin and repeated the process.

"Okay, Group A is finished." Lorina wiped her sweaty brow as the door to the last cabin on the second level slid shut behind them. "Let's go up to third and finish with Group D."

"Thirty minutes," Captain Shepherd said over the com. "Vipul, I need you on navigation."

"On my way, Captain."

"We need to hurry." Jake handed five patches to Vipul. "Give these to the other members of the crew, – and take one yourself. Thanks for your help."

The navigator nodded somberly and stuck a patch behind his left ear. He handed the vial of Banspace to Shima and ascended the ladder first. The other three quickly followed.

Jake, Shima, and Lorina moved through more cabins, inoculating the children and strapping them down.

In the last cabin on the port side, Jake found the two he had been hoping to locate, Tirza and Adi. He turned to Lorina. "I'll strap down with them; I need to talk to them anyway."

Her eyes widened, comprehending. "Okay, give me my patch. Niyati's waiting in my cabin." She sprinted for the corridor on the starboard wing of the ship.

"Thanks for your help, Shima." Jake pressed a patch into the housekeeper's slender brown hand.

Her fingers closed around his for a moment. "You have done a good job caring for everyone on the ship, Jake. I am sorry I misjudged you earlier."

Jake was too surprised to think of a response. He settled for a feeble nod.

Shima filled two fresh syringes for Tirza and Adi, handed them to Jake, then moved quickly to her cabin across the corridor.

"We're beginning the descent into Maui," the Captain announced. "I strongly recommend that everyone strap down *now.*"

Jake shut the door to the cabin and approached Tirza and Adi, who were sitting on the bed, clinging to each other. "I need to give you two a shot."

"No way!" Tirza darted out of his reach.

"Please, it's really, really important."

Little Adi held out his arm willingly, and Jake pressed the needle to his skin.

Adi yelped, but then told Tirza, "Didn't hurt!"

Tirza shook her head. "You can't make me."

Jake didn't have the time or the inclination to struggle with her. "That's fine." He climbed onto the middle of their bed and lay back with his hands behind his head. "You'll just get sick and throw up all over the place when the ride starts to get bumpy."

Adi climbed over Jake and stretched out next to him. "You strap down with us, Dr. Jake?"

"Yeah. I need two brave kids to protect me."

Tirza flopped down on the other side of Jake. "I'm not going to throw up!"

"We'll see." Jake sat up and drew the knee strap across the bed. He saw a problem with this arrangement. "Okay, if I put this across your knees, it will hit me right here. I'll start singing soprano, so I need to raise it a bit. Okay, Adi?"

"Okay." Adi giggled.

The shoulder strap took a little more maneuvering; if it secured his own shoulders, it would be at neck-level for the children. Jake moved the strap down until it was even with their shoulders. "It's not too late to have the shot, Tirza."

"Please, Tirza," Adi said, "I don't want you to throw up on us!"

"No."

Jake resigned himself to the fact that he was going to have a sick, hysterical child next to him during the landing. *God, please just help us* land *in one piece.* He secured the strap and stretched an arm out over each child. "You two hang onto me. It's going to be a rough ride."

As soon as the words were out of his mouth, the turbulence began in earnest. Adi moaned nervously, so Jake decided to distract them with good news.

"How would you and Tirza like to have a mom and dad?"

"Why'd we want a mom and dad?" Tirza sneered. "They'd just beat us."

"No, they wouldn't! This new mom and dad would be very nice to you. I know them because the mom is my sister. She really loves children."

"You mean we could live at your house?" Adi asked.

"Yes, at my house. I lived there growing up. It's very comfortable. You could have your own room with a bed and new clothes and lots of toys. You could go to school and never have to worry about getting enough to eat because your new mom and dad would take care of you."

Tirza made an impatient noise. "Nobody has a house like that. That's just something you saw on a holo-vid."

"No, it's not. It's real." Jake tried to think of how to explain it to the skeptical child. "Do you know what adoption is, Tirza?"

"No."

"Adoption is when loving grownups bring children who need parents into their home and take care of them."

"We don't need anyone."

"Really? You mean you *like* living on the street and being hungry all the time? You wouldn't want to live in a house with some nice people who would take care of you?"

"Why would someone want us?" Tirza asked softly, her face scrunched into a puzzled frown.

"Believe it or not, they just want to be your parents." Jake found her hand and gave it a squeeze. "You could be a little girl again, Tirza. And I could be your Uncle Jake."

"And you can be my uncle, too?" Adi asked, his dark eyes wide. "What's a uncle?"

Jake laughed. "Someone who's in your family. Did I mention you'd have a sister named Catherine? You'd also have a grandma and grandpa, and a great aunt . . . and a dog."

"A dog! I want to have a dog and a mom and dad, Tirza," said Adi. "Let's go live with Dr. Jake."

"But what if they don't like me?" Tirza's lower lip began to quiver. "What if they want to keep Adi 'cause he's cute, but they think I'm ugly?"

Jake was relieved to see her defenses breaking down. "They'll think you're beautiful. They want both of you. I promise."

Tirza shut her eyes and seemed to be pondering the possibility. Jake knew how hard it would be for a little girl who had only known life on the streets to imagine a home and a family. He decided to let the subject rest for now. There would be plenty of time to bring it up again before they went to Delaware.

"Blaze, cut the power now," Captain Shepherd ordered over the com.

"Engines are off," Blaze replied.

Adi's small hands gripped Jake's elbow. The *Ishmael* shuddered and Tirza seized Jake's other arm in a death-grip.

Jake shut his eyes as the ship descended into the maelstrom. It was much worse than re-entry. He was grateful for the pillow under his head, which cushioned his brain enough for him to remain conscious. He couldn't imagine the Captain and Vipul *sitting* on the bridge and guiding the ship under these conditions – and both of them still recovering from the shooting. He tried reciting the Lord's Prayer in his mind, or at least what he could remember of it.

Adi whimpered, but Tirza started to scream. Jake's temples throbbed from her piercing shrieks. He couldn't move either hand to cover his ears because both children were clinging desperately to him. He prayed for temporary hearing loss as he endured her screams of terror.

A violent bounce silenced the screams as the air pressure suddenly dropped. Jake found himself gasping for breath. The little hands clinging to his arms went slack, and he realized both children had passed out. His own consciousness was beginning to elude him when he heard a sharp groaning, grinding noise from somewhere below decks. Another violent bounce tested the strength of the straps, and suddenly everything came to a shuddering halt.

"That's it, we're down!" Vipul's voice over the com was triumphant. "Jake, we need you on the bridge!"

Confused, Jake struggled to release the shoulder strap and sit up. "I'm on my way," he managed, breathing hard. He could feel the air pressure adjusting to a tolerable level. He dug his scanner out of his hip pocket and quickly checked Adi and Tirza. They were okay. He released the knee strap and turned Tirza onto her side, facing the edge of the bed.

That's for when you wake up and puke, stubborn miss. Jake climbed off the foot of the bed and found himself on his hands and knees; it still felt like the ship was caught in the throes of a minor earthquake. He tried to regain his equilibrium for a moment before getting to his feet and stumbling out to the corridor.

Jake could hear a few groans coming from behind closed doors, but figured most of the kids had been knocked out in the dizzying descent. He hoped there would be nothing more serious than frazzled nerves to deal with later.

Shima appeared at her doorway, looking a bit shaken, but she silently joined him at the ladder. They climbed to the top level.

On the bridge, they found Captain Shepherd slumped down in her chair with a bloody gash on her forehead. Vipul was sitting at the navigation board, looking a bit dazed but unhurt.

Jake quickly scanned the Captain. "She's got a concussion, but she'll be okay. Shima?"

"I will get a gurney." Shima headed for the infirmary.

"What happened?" Jake asked. He glanced at Vipul as he stuffed the scanner into his pocket and carefully examined Shepherd's head. She groaned and opened her eyes, but still seemed dazed.

Vipul shrugged. "I think she took off a shoulder strap to reach the backup decelerator. I heard her gasp when we hit that last bump. When I looked over, she was out cold."

Jake squatted down so he could lean the Captain's head against his chest with one hand. With the other hand, he released her remaining shoulder strap and seat belt. He noted the blood on one of the levers on the control board. "Yeah, looks like she hit it hard."

"I think the *Ishmael* cracked the hull on the tail section, but we're lucky to be all in one piece. Thanks to her."

Jake glanced at Vipul again. The navigator met his gaze, then his dark eyes suddenly went wide. "No!"

"What is it? What's wrong?"

Vipul gestured frantically at the helm control panel just behind Jake. "Fire! There's a fire in the engine room!"

237

Jake felt his stomach drop as he craned his neck to see the red light blinking near his elbow. "Blaze? Blaze, report!"

There was no response.

Jake hoped the com was malfunctioning. "Vipul, take her!" He fumed with impatience as the navigator unbelted himself from his seat and took Jake's place in supporting the woozy Captain.

"Blaze!" Jake sprinted past an astonished Shima who was coming in with a gurney. He took the ladder three rungs at a time.

There was a smoke-like vapor curling through the basement corridor. Jake wondered why the fire alarm hadn't sounded. He noticed that the doors at the end of the hall were open or hanging askew in their frames.

"Shima, which one is the engine room?"

"Second one on the left."

So the com is *working.* Jake pounded on the door and pressed his thumb to the ID lock, but it remained shut. "Blaze!" He shouted at the ceiling in frustration. "Shima!"

"The engine room door emergency override can only be performed by the Captain or the medic," Shima explained apologetically.

"*I'm* the medic!"

"We forgot to change it after Dr. Martschenko died. I am sorry!"

Jake felt like howling, although he knew this wasn't her fault. "Suggestions?" he managed through clenched teeth. "Quickly?"

"I – I do not know!"

As Jake dropped his head in despair, he noticed the spot of fresh blood on the pocket of his scrubs shirt.

Captain Shepherd's blood.

"Problem solved!" Jake pressed the bloody fabric against the ID lock. The door slid open and he stumbled into the smoke-filled engine room. In here, the fire alarm was howling loud enough to hurt his ears. "Blaze!"

The acrid smoke made his eyes burn; it was impossible to see anything through the gray haze which completely shrouded the room. "Fire extinguisher!" he shouted at the ceiling.

There was a loud *whoosh* and the smoke was sucked straight up into the ceiling vents. A purple liquid saturated the room in a brief five-second shower and the fire was out.

Why don't they do that automatically? Jake thought in frustration as he raced to Blaze's side. The engineer was sprawled face-up on the floor, lying unconscious in a pool of blood. Jake didn't bother with the scanner; he grasped Blaze's wrist.

His pulse was slow and weak. Jake found Blaze's sternum with his other hand and checked for breathing. He inhaled once, but the exhale never came.

Jake gripped his friend's wrist, checked again for a pulse. It was gone.

TWENTY
SAFE PORT

"Come on, Blaze. Come on! -- Shima!" The voice was familiar, but he couldn't place it.

"Here is the laser clamp. You must stop the bleeding."

"I'm trying."

There was pain everywhere, but especially in his right leg. The pain was sharp and throbbing as if a knife had pierced his thigh. He felt a sudden blast of cold, which he recognized as Hemorrhage Freeze.

"I've got a pulse, but it's weak. Keep the synthblood IV wide open. Let's get the artery closed."

He heard fabric tearing. The pain increased, but he couldn't make a sound to let them know.

"There is so much blood, I cannot see. We should be doing this up in surgery –"

"There's no time!" There was no anger in the words, only frustration.

"I know." Her response was calm. "Here, try this clamp while I hold the bone."

He was cold, very cold. There was something hard and tight over his mouth, forcing air into his lungs.

"That's got it, but his femur looks like a jigsaw puzzle. I'm going to need another liter of synthblood before we can move him up to surgery."

"I will be right back."

He tried to focus; he wanted to say something. He took a breath, and suddenly the pain was unbearable.

"Easy, Blaze. You don't want to wake up now."

He felt a gentle sting, like an insect, in his forearm. The pain, the voices, everything, was gone.

* * *

Blaze became aware of voices again, but this time he felt no pain.

"He fractured his leg."

"People don't die from broken legs, Jake!" A lovely voice, familiar, and very excited about something.

"The force of the landing must have knocked him across the room. I'm guessing he crashed into one of the steel chairs bolted in front of the control boards. The bone splintered and tore through his femoral artery. If he hadn't landed on his back -- lying on the artery, which slowed the bleeding, -- there's no way he would have survived. I found him right when his heart stopped."

"I can't believe . . . I almost lost him."

"Calm down, Lorina. Breathe. I put three liters of synthblood in him and put his femur back together. He'll be as good as new in a few days."

"Why wasn't he strapped down?"

"Good question. I'll be sure to ask him when he regains consciousness."

"Deceleration," Blaze tried to join in the conversation with something intelligible.

"Did he say something?" Lorina's voice was excited again.

"The sedative's wearing off." Jake's voice. "Blaze, can you hear me?"

It took real effort to open his eyes. He squinted at the bright light, trying hard to focus on the lovely face swimming in front of his. "The ship was descendin' too fast and I needed to manually raise the flaps and create some drag," he explained. "That's why I wasn't strapped down."

"I understood maybe half of what you said." Lorina's palm against his cheek was warm and soothing.

"I heard something about deceleration," said Jake. "I'm amazed he has the strength to say anything."

"How is Blaze?"

Blaze squinted, trying to focus on the newcomer. It was Shima.

"He's going to be okay," Lorina answered. She gripped his hand tightly and blinked hard. "Thanks to Jake."

Shima smiled. "Yes, Jake is a fine doctor. We are lucky to have him aboard."

"I'll remember you said that when I'm doing 10 to 15 for good behavior," Jake said.

"I'm sure the prison on Maui has a nice view." Lorina smirked.

Shima ignored their banter. "Did either of you inform the Captain the cold storage was damaged?"

"Cold storage?" Lorina asked. "Is that where all the vapor was coming from?"

"There are four bodies in storage," Jake explained. "That's why the Captain was so eager to hire us. One of them was my predecessor, Dr. Martschenko."

Shima nodded. "One of them was the Captain's husband."

Lorina looked horrified. "I didn't know. What are we supposed to do with four dead bodies?"

"Buy refrigerated coffins," Blaze suggested.

Lorina covered his mouth gently with her fingertips. "Hush. You don't need to worry about any of this."

There was some commotion behind Shima. Niyati burst into the room and flew straight at Lorina, hugging her left leg.

Idalis came in behind the girl. "Sorry. She insisted on seeing *amma* and *baba*." She nodded to Blaze with a half-smile. "I see *baba* is awake."

Blaze tried to chuckle, but it hurt to exhale. He took a shallow breath and managed a weak "Hey."

Lorina said, "Thanks for looking after her, Idalis."

The cook nodded. "It's getting late, so the Captain wants to wait until morning before venturing outside the ship."

"How are the children?" Blaze asked.

"No serious injuries, unless you count hunger pains." Idalis paused. "I guess this would be a good time to say I will miss all of you – except Ting."

"What do you mean?" Shima asked.

"I'm resigning, *amiga*. I just signed on to cook meals, not risk my life or babysit hundreds of children. If I leave now, I can catch a flight to Phoenix while I still have a few dollars left on my credit flash."

"But this is just a temporary –" Lorina protested.

"I'm not going to be arrested as an accomplice to murder!" Idalis cut her off. "I have my whole life ahead of me, and I'm not going to spend it in prison!"

"I am sorry you feel that way," Shima murmured, looking troubled.

Blaze saw that Niyati was clinging to Lorina, frightened by Idalis' raised voice. "When do you leave?"

"Tonight, while it's still dark. Vipul's waiting to open the airlock for me. I think it's only five kilometers to Lahaina from here."

"Be careful." Lorina shook her hand. "Goodbye, Idalis."

"*Adios,* Lorina. Help yourself to the uniforms in my cabin." Idalis hugged Shima, nodded to Jake and Blaze, and quickly left the infirmary.

Jake sighed loudly and lifted his datapad. "Add another new problem to the list."

Lorina frowned. "We don't need a cook if there's no food."

"Yeah, that's problem number one," Jake agreed.

"How bad is the damage to the ship?" Blaze asked.

"I thought I told you not to worry." Lorina leaned down and kissed him. "Get some sleep."

"Sleep," Niyati echoed, yawning in agreement. Lorina took her by the hand and left the infirmary.

"I must check to see if the Captain is keeping ice on her head. Goodnight, Blaze, Jake." Shima slipped away.

"So how bad is it?" Blaze asked Jake, who was busy writing on his datapad.

"Bad." Jake frowned. "Let's just say the fire was extensive. You almost earned your nickname the hard way."

"Very funny."

"Seriously, you were lucky to leave the engine room alive."

"Thanks to you."

"Everybody keeps saying that, but I was just doing my job."

Blaze recognized the embarrassment in Jake's tone and changed the subject. "So, we're stranded?"

Jake shrugged. "I don't feel bad about being marooned on a Hawaiian island. I happen to like pineapple, coconut, and fish."

Blaze tried to laugh again, but it turned into a grimace. "Chest hurts."

"Twenty minutes of CPR will do that." Jake injected something into Blaze's IV. "Your leg is in a splint because the artery and muscles need time to re-grow, so don't even *think* about trying to get up. You need to be a more cooperative patient than the Captain."

"So I'm just supposed to lie here and feel sorry for myself?"

"Yes, you are. Though I'm sure Lorina will be glad to distract you occasionally. We'll take care of the ship and the kids. You can just lie here and think of a clever way to introduce yourself to your future mother-in-law. She'll be here in a week."

Blaze's jaw dropped. "She's comin' here?"

"The whole family's coming. It took them only 15 minutes to respond to Lorina's transmission. I think my dad sold a tractor or something to pay for the flight." Jake grinned. "I hope you like bangers and mash at the reception."

Blaze shut his eyes. "Exactly how long was I unconscious?"

"Long enough." Jake laughed. "I'm going to sleep over here if you need anything. Captain Shepherd told me I have a cabin, but I haven't seen it yet."

Blaze began to feel drowsy. "Goodnight, Jake."

* * *

"Blaze, this is Hope Nguyen."

Blaze grinned up at the chubby Asian woman in the purple muumuu who came into the post-op with Vipul. "Hello."

Vipul handed Blaze a plate overflowing with scrambled eggs, buttered toast, and slices of fresh pineapple. "Hope owns a little restaurant a few kilometers down the road. She's been kind enough to provide breakfast for us."

"All of us?" Blaze asked, impressed. He accepted a fork from Vipul and forgot about manners as he inhaled a bite of eggs. "Oh, excuse me. This is delicious, thank you!"

Hope flashed a gap-toothed smile. "Go ahead and eat. You look like you've missed a few meals."

"The locals have turned out *en masse* to see what all the commotion was last night," Vipul explained.

"It sounded like thunder," Hope said. "But when I walked down Lahainaluna Road this morning and saw all the children running around the ship, I figured you folks could use some help."

"Does the local population include CIPs?" Blaze tried to sound nonchalant.

"No, they rarely come out this way." Hope gave him a curious look. "Why? Do you need to file a crash report with the land owner?"

"The Captain *is* the land owner," Vipul explained. "And we actually meant to land here. – It wasn't a crash."

Hope laughed. "If you say so. Nice meeting you, Blaze."

Vipul turned to give Blaze a helpless glance as he escorted Hope out of the room.

Blaze quickly polished off his breakfast and took a long swig from his drinking tube. He had just set the plate on the bedside table when Lorina came in with Niyati.

"Good morning." She leaned down and gave him a kiss.

"Good morning," Niyati echoed with perfect inflection. She puckered her lips and made kissing noises at him.

Blaze laughed and immediately regretted it as a fresh band of pain wrapped around his chest. "What's goin' on outside?"

"We're attracting a lot of attention from the locals. The Captain's getting nervous because two people already asked her if they could adopt children."

Blaze raised his eyebrows. "Seems like she'd be pleased to abdicate some of the responsibility."

"She is, but she wants to be sure these people are legit. Remember why we left Mars."

Blaze nodded. "It sounds like she could use a social worker."

Lorina grinned. "It sounds like we're getting into the adoption business."

"It would be a logical solution, although I'm sure Captain Shepherd didn't plan on runnin' an orphanage."

"I don't think she planned anything except getting the kids off the station. She limited her options when she killed Thanatos."

"It was self-defense, Lorina. I'm a witness, and I'll stand by her if it ever comes to trial. Acheron should be the one facin' prison time, not the Captain."

Lorina was unfazed by his defensiveness. "I'm on your side. And Captain Shepherd's. But we've got more immediate problems to deal with." She began ticking off points on her fingers. "First, we can live aboard the ship indefinitely, but we need to be able to feed everyone. For that, we need money. Second, the ship needs major repairs and new solar engines. For that, we need a lot more money."

"And I can't do a thing to help just lyin' here," Blaze grumbled.

"Sorry, *baba*." Niyati patted his arm. Blaze smiled indulgently at her.

"Third, we have to ship three bodies to their homes: one to New Jersey, one to Kiev, and one to Milan. That will be expensive."

"What about the fourth body?"

Lorina frowned. "The Captain wants to bury her husband here as soon as possible. She's already chosen a spot near the house."

Blaze winced. "I forgot what she's goin' through. What are our options for the first two problems?"

245

"Shima has taken it upon herself to solicit donations from the crowd. So far Hope Nguyen has offered to feed us today and tomorrow, and a grocer named George Osaka dropped off a solar truck-load of bananas, pineapples, and fresh vegetables."

"Well, that's a good start."

"Yes, but we need a long-term solution if we're going to be here awhile. Vipul thinks repairs to the ship will take a month unless we can move to the nearest repair dock, which is on Oahu."

"That'll cost a fortune."

"That'll never happen with the Captain on the CIP's Most Wanted list," Lorina agreed. "So as soon as you're well enough to get up, we can hitch a ride into town with Mr. Osaka and start buying parts for the *Ishmael*."

"We?" Blaze echoed, raising his eyebrows.

Lorina looked embarrassed. "Jake convinced the Captain I could persuade any merchant to give us the parts we need – on credit."

Blaze smiled. "I'd have to agree with him. So when can I get out of bed?"

"In 48 hours."

Blaze's smile morphed into a scowl. "That's a long time."

"Not long enough, in my opinion," Captain Shepherd spoke from the doorway. She strode into the room with only the slightest of limps and came to Blaze's bedside.

Blaze glanced at the new bandage on her forehead.

The Captain noticed his glance and nodded. "Yes, it was a rough landing. But your deceleration maneuvers are the only thing that kept us from becoming a smoking crater in the middle of the field. I want my engineer to make a full recovery, no matter how long it takes."

She nodded to Lorina. "So now let's talk about the two of you."

Blaze and Lorina exchanged a cautious glance.

"Me, too," said Niyati.

The Captain glanced down at the girl with a half-grin. "Yes, I forgot you were part of the plan."

"What plan would that be?" Blaze asked, feigning ignorance.

Shepherd waved a dismissive hand. "I already know about the wedding."

"We were going to tell you, Captain," Lorina said, "when the time was right."

"It's okay. Timing is one thing we all struggle with, -- especially me. But I'm going to remedy that right now."

Shepherd folded her arms. "Blaze, I want to keep you on permanently as my engineer." She didn't wait for a response from him before facing Lorina. "I want your blushing bride to stay on as well, although we'll have to rethink the title of steward to more accurately reflect her position."

"Which would be --?" Lorina asked.

"Chief babysitter. Or perhaps 'child development coordinator' would sound more professional?" Shepherd shrugged. "You get the idea. There's a family suite on each wing, so take your pick and I'll convert your cabins back into guest quarters. Do you want the positions?"

Blaze and Lorina exchanged another glance. He noted the happy gleam in her eyes.

"We accept your offer, Captain," said Blaze.

"Yes, Captain, thank you," Lorina said. "What about Jake?"

Shepherd reached into the cargo pocket of her uniform and took out a datapad, which she handed to Lorina. "I approached him first. I thought about letting him go since he doesn't have his medical license, but after he brought you back to life, Blaze –," she shook her head, "I'd be a fool not to keep him. He's resourceful and courageous." She appraised both of them with a serious expression. "You all are. I asked the impossible of you, and you came through with flying colors."

Lorina quickly read her contract and nodded, pressing her thumb to the screen.

The Captain accepted the datapad from her and verified that she was, "Lorina Murphy of Wilmington, Delaware – welcome aboard, officially."

Shepherd glanced at Niyati. "I'm not sure if the *Ishmael* will continue to ferry paying passengers between stations, but it may continue to be a passenger ship – of sorts." She paused, frowning thoughtfully. "Now that I know what we're up against, I feel a renewed responsibility to help Shima. I want to find her niece Zuri." She nodded at Blaze's awestruck expression. "We've got our work cut out for us."

Blaze glanced at Lorina's determined face and decided to speak for both of them. "You can count on us, Captain."

"It would be an honor to continue working for you," Lorina added, squeezing Blaze's hand. "Even if it means we don't get paid very often."

"It's good to have most of my crew on the same page. Now all we have to do is figure out where to get some financing, and start finding homes for these kids."

"Excuse me, Captain, but couldn't you just ask for a donation from each person who wants to adopt a child?" Lorina asked.

"It makes sense because I have to have money to feed everyone." The Captain frowned. "But asking for money would be too much like selling them. Can you imagine how quickly an innocent attempt to solicit funds turns into plain old bribery?"

Lorina nodded. "Sorry, I didn't think of that."

"There's a lot of problems we have to work out, Lorina, so please keep thinking. I need all the suggestions I can get." Shepherd started towards the door. "Oh, and I'd like you and Marco to check out the house this morning."

Lorina made a face at Shepherd's back. "Why Ting, Captain? Why not Jake or Vipul?"

"Jake and Vipul are already on their way into Lahaina to buy coffins." Shepherd turned to give her a knowing grin. "I need you to persuade Ting to do as he's told and stay out of trouble. He's useless when we're dirtside, and I need to find something constructive for him to do. Do you have a problem with that?"

Lorina shot Blaze a get-me-out-of-this look. "No, Captain."

Blaze gave her a sympathetic smile. "Niyati can stay here with me. Have fun."

"That's two spankings I owe you." Lorina shook a finger at him as she followed the Captain out of the infirmary.

"Lookin' forward to it!" Blaze called after her.

TWENTY ONE
PREMONITION

The gorgeous Maui weather lifted Lorina's spirits as she followed Captain Shepherd through the open airlock and descended the portable staircase to the black soil. The sun warmed her face. The breeze smelled of ocean and grass and palm trees. The sounds of children laughing and playing soccer and tag were music to her ears. *I know they're happy to be off the ship. I wish Blaze could come outside, too.*

Lorina glanced around at the scenery for the second time that morning. The *Ishmael* had set down in a rolling field of wild tropical grasses, dotted with an occasional coconut palm. There were green hills in the distance, just beyond the sugar cane processing plant, which stood about 100 meters away from the ship. The mammoth white building had vines growing up the sides and rows of boarded-up windows. There were several dirt roads bisecting the field and running alongside the plant, but these were overgrown with weeds. One paved road led from the plant to the nearby Lahainaluna Road. Lorina had noticed few solar cars on the main road. Most of the locals who had come by to gawk at the children had come on foot.

The plantation was beautiful; it reminded her of the O'Brien farm because it felt safe. At least, she hoped it was safe. Lorina kept a sharp eye out for anyone in a CIP uniform, but so far the only adults she'd seen were dressed in shorts or muumuus. They came in groups of twos or threes to watch the children for a few minutes, make inquiries if the Captain or anyone else was within earshot, and then, curiosity satisfied, went away. Lorina could make out a few modest houses farther down the main road, but it seemed like the Captain's new plantation was safely out in the sticks.

Her mood began to darken as they approached Marco Ting, who was leaning against a coconut tree, watching the children play. Lorina could sense his dark mood from 50 meters.

"How am I supposed to convince him to do anything useful? He's like a human thorn bush, Captain."

"Thorn bushes don't talk," Shepherd said. "Yes, he's a bit abrasive, but –"

"A bit?" Lorina lagged behind, trying to put off the task as long as possible.

"Okay, he's sandpaper, but Jake assured me you can work miracles with the most stubborn souls."

Wait'll I get my hands on that crater mouth, Lorina thought.

Shepherd reached Ting's side. "I have an assignment for you."

The Chinese pilot eyed Lorina suspiciously as she reluctantly joined the Captain. "What's she doing here?"

Captain Shepherd continued as if she hadn't heard. "I want you and Lorina to check out the house together. Decide if it's inhabitable, and note what work needs to be done. You should inventory the contents, note what can be sold, and report back to me."

"What about Shima –" Ting began in a complaining tone.

"You'd rather take over Shima's job of looking after the children?" Shepherd glared at him.

Ting shut his mouth and jammed his hands into his pockets.

"Okay, then." Shepherd turned on her heel and started towards the large white Victorian-style farmhouse, which was past the processing plant and faced the main road.

Despite the creeping vines and the overgrown hedges, Lorina felt impressed that someone had taken exceptional care of the house. As they got closer, she could see the paint was in good shape. The windows weren't too dirty and none of the panes were broken, which would be the norm for an abandoned house.

Captain Shepherd led them up the steps to the wide front porch, which was littered with dead palm fronds. She dragged open the screen door, which was off one of the hinges, and pressed her thumb to the unusual red ID lock on the paneled front door. The lock hummed for a moment before they heard the latch click open.

Lorina was impressed. "How did they program the lock to accept your DNA if you've never been here before?"

"It's an heir-lock," Shepherd explained. "It can compare my DNA to my mother's, – which is why it took so long to open. She had to press her weight against the front door to get it to swing open on its squeaky hinges. Then she pulled a datapad out of her pocket and handed it to Ting. She took a handlight out of another pocket and gave it to Lorina.

"Have fun."

"Captain," Lorina decided to try one more time, "is it really necessary for two people to search the house?"

Shepherd didn't even bat an eye. "If you fall through a hole in the floor or get bitten by a black widow spider, you might want someone else along to help." She fixed Lorina with a stern look. "Do you have a problem with this assignment?"

"No, ma'am." Lorina didn't look at Ting as she switched on the handlight and trudged into the dimly-lit house. The first thing she noticed was the smell. She gasped at the dank odor of mildew and stagnant air. "First thing we should do is open some windows."

Ting said nothing as he walked in behind her. They stood in the two-story foyer for a moment, listening to the Captain's retreating footsteps on the wooden porch. Lorina played the light over the huge cobwebs on chandelier above.

"Let's get this over with," Ting muttered.

Lorina bit back a retort and led the way into the first room off the foyer. It was a huge dining room. "Start making a list."

Ting sneered. "I don't take orders from you."

"The Captain told us to take inventory. Write down 'maple dining room table with 16 ladder-back chairs, maple side table."

Ting slapped the datapad against his thigh. "This is a waste of time."

"Why don't you quit if you don't like it?" Lorina marched into the central hall off the dining room.

"What?" Ting was right on her heels. "What did you say?" He grabbed her shoulder and spun her to face him, his eyes smoldering like two live coals.

"You heard me!" Lorina slapped his hand away. "Don't you ever touch me again! If you're so unhappy with the new working conditions, why don't you follow Idalis' example and leave?"

"It's none of your business why I choose to stay!"

"It is if I have to listen to you complain all the time!"

Ting took some deep breaths, hands clenched at his sides. He responded coldly: "I'm not the one who needs to quit. You have no idea what it's really like to work on a starship. Three days from Mars to Earth is nothing. Wait until we make a three-week jump from Venus to Ganymede, then you'll see. I'm a helmsman because I like the solitude. A naïve dirtsider like you would lose your mind after a week in space."

Lorina started to argue, "No, I won't –" but Ting spoke over her.

"Think about it: no fresh air and sunshine for weeks or months at a time. Nowhere to go when you want a change of scenery. It's a grim business working in space, but everything was just fine until we all came down with Zenithian." He spun away from her, glaring at the wall. "Then Vanni died."

"Who's Vanni?" Lorina was confused.

"Giovanni Medici, the engineer. The one your gangly Prince Charming replaced."

Lorina struggled to keep her own hands at her sides so she wouldn't strangle him. "Don't you dare insult my fiancé!"

Ting ignored the threat. "Then the Captain went completely out of her mind and decided to rescue all these filthy kids!"

"They're not filthy!" Lorina couldn't listen to his raving any longer. "Just because they lived on the streets, you think you're better than they are? You think they don't deserve families and a place to call home? You think their lives are worth less than yours?" She could feel the blood rushing to her face as she began to scream at him. "You're the one who's filthy! You think they deserve to be slaves, just like that animal Acheron!"

"Shut up!" Ting rounded on her so they were standing nose to nose. "Shut up! Don't compare me to Acheron! I'm nothing like him!"

"You're exactly like him -- because you only care about yourself! Oh, poor Ting, nobody loves me! Well, how can you expect anyone to care about you when you hate everyone and everything -- including your job!"

"I don't --!" Ting began heatedly, but Lorina shouted him down.

"Idalis told me how you spend your time dirtside – in bars and brothels, getting drunk and picking fights with men twice your size! Captain Shepherd must be crazy to put up with you for as long as she has!"

Ting looked like he wanted to hit her, but Lorina wasn't through. "You hate the children because you're incapable of loving anyone! You don't even love yourself!"

She spun away from him and stormed down the dark hallway. Her temples were throbbing from all the shouting, and she desperately needed some fresh air.

Her little toe made contact with the corner of a bookcase. Lorina howled, hopping on her uninjured foot. She cursed under her breath, angry, frustrated, and in pain.

"Are you . . . okay?" Ting's tone was bordering on civility.

Lorina was surprised. Perhaps something she said *did* get through to him. She bit back a sarcastic remark, and tried to dredge up some self-control. "Fine. We're not getting much work done."

Ting seemed subdued as he joined her in the hallway. He started writing: "Dining room table with 16 chairs, side table."

Lorina made no comment about his softened attitude. She decided to take advantage of it while it lasted. She turned the handlight back on and examined the bookcase that had caused her so much pain. "Large faux-mahogany bookcase, filled with paperback romance novels." She took one out and examined the yellowed pages under the light. "*Hearts on Fire,* published August, 2066."

"Old, but some books don't improve with age."

"They might be worth something." Lorina put the book back on the shelf with the others and grimaced as several silverfish scattered over the rotten bindings. "The furniture is worth selling. If we look carefully, we might find something of value."

"Wishful thinking," Ting said.

Lorina decided to ignore the remark. She didn't feel like arguing anymore. "Let's get to work." She shone the light around as they finished walking the hallway. "That looks like an original oil painting. That leather chair is in good condition."

They walked through a swinging door into a spacious kitchen. Lorina hoped no food had been left lying around to attract mice and other vermin. She took a deep breath and opened an overhead cabinet.

No mice; only dishes lying under a thick layer of dust. She took a plate off the top of a stack and read the label painted on the back. "Lenox, fine china." She turned the plate over and looked at the pattern under the light. "This is at least 100 years old."

"Might be worth something," Ting agreed, writing on the datapad.

After this, Lorina found the search much more interesting, despite the presence of Ting. She went through the kitchen carefully, noting the place settings of silverware, tarnished black.

"Liquor cabinet." She took a bottle from the shelf and blew the dust off it. After a few sneezes, she read the label. "Irish whiskey, and its 50 years old. The seal is still on the cap; it's unopened."

"That's probably worth 50,000 credits, although you couldn't pay me to drink it."

Lorina counted the bottles. "Twenty-three."

Ting dutifully noted it on the datapad. "Maybe we should look for more obvious valuables since I don't think there's much demand for ancient liquor."

Lorina put the bottle back in the cabinet. "The Captain wants us to inventory everything."

Ting looked like he wanted to argue, but managed to keep his mouth shut for a change. He pried open a window, admitting some fresh air into the dusty gloom. "Next room?"

There was a living room with a grand piano, four leather armchairs, a curio cabinet full of Lenox figurines, and a reproduction Tiffany lamp. The huge downstairs bedroom included a maple four-poster bed and a large jewelry box on the dresser.

Ting whistled at the contents of the box. "I can't believe no one boosted this when Shepherd's old lady died."

"Not everyone's a thief. The locals I've met seem honest." Lorina ignored Ting's derisive snort and found a leather purse in a dresser drawer. She transferred the jewelry into the purse, one piece at a time. "Two pairs of diamond earrings, a string of black pearls, a gold ring – looks like it's set with an emerald --, a diamond tennis bracelet with sapphires, and two thick gold chains."

Lorina ran her fingers over the velvet in the bottom of the jewelry box, checking to make sure she hadn't missed anything. When she realized it was loose, she set down the handlight, worked her fingernails around the edges of the fabric, and lifted it out.

There was a paper envelope in the bottom of the box with *Danae* written on it in faded handwriting.

Lorina pursed her lips, thinking. "It's been two years; I'm sure the Captain won't mind waiting another half hour before we give this to her. Let's check the upstairs." She put the envelope in the purse and slipped the strap over her shoulder. They walked down the main hall, back to the foyer.

The gracious curved staircase led upstairs to another central hallway. Lorina counted six large bedrooms and four bathrooms, each furnished as nicely as the downstairs rooms. "We should get to work cleaning up this place. I think it would make a wonderful orphanage."

Ting twisted open the squeaky latch on a window and struggled to raise the sash. "And who's going to live here and run this little utopia?"

"How about you, since you like children so much?"

Ting snorted and opened another window. "Captain Shepherd means well, but she shouldn't have gotten involved. Now we're stuck with all these kids."

Lorina felt her anger refuel. "Maybe she realizes there's more important things in life than money!"

"Are we through here?" Ting pocketed the datapad and headed back to the staircase.

"Maybe you could find a reason to be happy if you focused on something besides yourself!" Lorina shouted after him.

She heard him start down the steps, but then he stopped. Lorina walked to the top of the stairs and looked down at the helmsman.

Ting turned around and looked up at her, his eyes smoldering again. "Do you know what I see for this place, smart girl?"

Lorina frowned, suspicious. "Am I supposed to be impressed by another one of your gloomy predictions?"

"Yes, you are." Ting sneered. "I see years of struggle and poverty and pain as hundreds of children pass through this house. I see Captain Shepherd overworked, depressed, and disillusioned." He got a far-away look in his eyes. "I see death here."

"Whose death?" Lorina felt a knot in her stomach.

"I don't know; I only know that it will be someone close to you."

Lorina felt like all the air had been sucked out of her lungs. "You're . . . you're lying! You're just trying to scare me!" She gripped the banister to steady herself.

"I never lie about my premonitions."

"So you have one good vice to make up for all your bad ones?"

Ting spun around and started back down the stairs without another word.

"You're wrong!" Lorina felt like hurling the handlight at his head. "Good things will happen here! It might take a lot of work, but it will be worth it! Every child we help will make a difference! You can't see anything good because your heart's made of stone, you miserable excuse for a human being!

"Selfish coward!" she screamed at him as he headed out the front door.

The helmsman paused, but didn't turn around. Then he was gone.

Lorina was sobbing as she pulled the front door shut and made her way back to the ship. Ting's words seemed to reverberate through her head: *It will be someone close to you.* She was nearly sick from fear as she wondered who would die. *Dear God, not Blaze -- or Niyati -- or Jake! I can't lose any of them! He's wrong! Ting has to be! He's lying, the foul . . . amoral . . . !* She couldn't think of a word bad enough to describe him. *He's trying to scare me. And he's succeeding.*

Lorina tried to pull herself together as she climbed the ladder to the infirmary. She didn't want Blaze to see her this upset after what he'd been through.

She paused in the doorway and looked into the quiet post-op room. The first thing she noticed was the pile of dog-eared Dr. Seuss books on Blaze's bedside table, along with a plastic tea set and a half-naked black baby doll that was missing an eye. Her gaze shifted to the two sleeping occupants, and she felt a sense of peace push aside her fear.

Blaze was flat on his back on his narrow bed, with Niyati curled up under his left arm. The girl was snoring softly, her dark head nestled against his neck, her thin arm draped across his chest.

"They're so bonded, it's almost nauseating," Jake whispered, startling her.

Lorina glanced back over her shoulder at her cousin. "When did you get back?"

"Just now. I'm supposed to be looking for a place to store the coffins, but I thought I'd check on my patient first."

Lorina tilted her head, indicating her sleeping family. "Do you still have any doubts about Blaze? I don't."

Jake shrugged noncommittally as he leaned against the doorway and studied her face. "Those don't look like tears of joy. What's wrong?"

"Ting, -- and his premonitions." Lorina wiped her eyes on the back of her hand.

Jake frowned. "I'll bet Ting didn't predict the local med-tech cutting his tongue out with a dull scalpel."

Lorina shook her head. "You can't force him to change. He's just a slimy little maggot."

"I wish the Captain would fire him."

"She won't. I think he'd have to leave on his own, although I'm not sure why he stays where he's not wanted." Lorina looked over at Blaze and Niyati again. "Maybe something will get through Ting's tough exterior someday."

"Like my fist?"

Lorina laughed softly and turned back towards the ladder. She patted the purse on her hip. "I don't want to talk about Ting right now. I have something the Captain needs to see."

"Don't let Ting make you start doubting yourself, Lorina."

"I won't -- as long as I have great bodyguards like you and Blaze around."

"If we're not around, feel free to kick him where the sun doesn't –"

"Jake!" Lorina laughed. "Believe me, I've thought about it." For a moment she was tempted to tell him about the premonition, but decided to spare him the anxiety.

Jake walked into the infirmary, and Lorina went down to the Captain's office to deliver the envelope.

TWENTY TWO
TRANSMISSION

Danae was starting to get a headache. She was tired of feeling overwhelmed; there was too much to think about, too much to do. She fidgeted with the cargo pocket of her uniform, which held the unopened letter from her mother. She couldn't decide whether she wanted to read it.

You know what it is. It's just an apology for all those years of neglect. 'Please forgive me for being a bad mother' and all that kind of garbage.

Danae left her pocket alone. The letter could wait; there were more urgent matters to attend to. She left her office and descended to the entryway, just in time to greet Jake, who was coming in through the open airlock.

"Captain, we've come to the conclusion that it would be easier to move the bodies outside on the gurneys, rather than try to get the coffins inside through the basement airlock."

"Shima can herd the children over to the field on the far side of the house – I don't want any of them to see." Danae nodded. "I'll give you a hand with the bodies."

Jake frowned. "Vipul and I can handle it, ma'am."

Danae shook her head and turned back to the ladder. "It will take at least three people to lift Alex Shepherd onto a gurney." She felt a lump in her throat, but tried to ignore it. "He is – I mean, he was, -- a big man."

"Then I'll get Ting to help us."

Danae was getting used to Jake's stubborn streak, but she was determined to see this task through. *I owe it to my crew . . . and my husband.* "I can handle it, Jake. Let's get moving before they thaw." She turned back to the ladder. "I'll bring the gurneys down."

"Let us do this, Captain. You don't have to keep up the act."

Danae's anger sparked quickly; she rounded on him. "You think this is an act?"

Jake seemed to have an argument prepared as he folded his arms across his chest and faced her. "You don't think I know how difficult this is for you? It's normal to grieve, Captain. It's not healthy to keep a lid on your emotions."

"How I feel is no one's concern, Jake. Do you think the crew is going to respect a Captain who weeps at every little setback?"

"I don't consider four deaths a little setback. The crew would respect you more if you showed some emotion, Captain."

"That's your opinion. I'd lose my ability to discipline if I appear weak. That's something my father, the former captain of this ship, drilled into my head. The former medic and I had an understanding, Jake." She scrutinized his expression to see if he understood the implication. "Dr. Martschenko helped me keep my emotions under control, and I want you to do the same. Do you have a problem with that?"

Jake set his jaw. "I have a huge problem with that. This is more than a control issue for you, Captain. It's a medical issue. I'm not going to give you meds so you can keep suppressing your grief."

"Then maybe I need to rethink my decision to keep you on the crew!"

Jake seized her shoulders before she could make a move to stop him. Furious, Danae began to pull away, but the intense expression on his face made her pause.

Jake took advantage of her hesitation to deliver a stern reprimand: "You can fire me if you want, but I thought we'd established a working relationship based on trust. I need you to trust me with your health, Captain, – your mental health as well as your physical health."

Danae felt her anger slowly cooling. "Let me go."

He released her immediately, but didn't back off. "I'm not trying to undermine your authority, Captain. I'm trying to get you to let down your guard for a moment. I can't imagine how much energy you expend wearing this brave face 24/7. No one will think less of you for grieving."

"Captains don't cry, Jake."

"Maybe not, but widows do."

Danae glared at him. "Are you finished?"

Jake took a deep breath. "I strongly recommend that you let Vipul and me take care of the bodies. Please."

"Are you always this stubborn?" Danae asked, frustrated the argument had come full circle.

"Are you?"

Danae glared at him for a moment before turning back to the ladder. "I'll be in my office."

* * *

Danae slit open the envelope with her thumbnail. She glanced up to make certain the door was closed before she took out the letter and unfolded it.

She didn't recognize the handwriting. *But it's been 20 years – I don't even remember the sound of her voice.* She smoothed the single sheet of paper flat on her desk and read:

Dear Danae,

I know this letter is going to come as a complete surprise to you after so many years of silence, but I couldn't leave this life without a word of farewell to my only child. I know I was a poor excuse for a mother, but I want you to know how proud I am of you. You turned out well, despite my efforts to make your childhood miserable. There's so much I want to share with you, but I have a feeling you wouldn't be interested in reading my sordid life history, so I'll get to the point:

I hope you like the sugar cane plantation. I bought it specifically with you in mind. I thought if you ever got bored with space, you might like to have a beautiful place to come home to. I did the research and chose Maui because it was untouched by chemical weapons. The land is still pure, and the people are still friendly. Please consider this my pitiful way of saying 'I'm sorry.' I can never make up for all the years we lost, but I hope someday you'll find it in your heart to forgive me.

I love you always,

Mom

Danae crumpled the letter and stuffed it into a desk drawer. *Forgive you someday, Mom? You were right about one thing: you were a poor excuse for a mother.*

Danae wiped at her uncooperative eyes and leaned back in her chair, her hands moving unconsciously to her flat belly. She spent a few minutes lost in thought, wondering what a little boy named A.J. would have looked like if she hadn't miscarried.

I wonder if he would have helped me learn to forgive her. Maybe if I become a mother someday, she shuddered at the thought, *I'll have to find a way to do that.*

* * *

Danae helped Shima distribute the last of the sandwiches and boxes of juice. The children wandered out into the field, sat cross-legged on the ground, and ate their lunches in cheerful groups of three or more. She watched approvingly as some of the preteens fed their assigned toddlers.

"Ms. Nguyen has been very kind to us." Shima began filling a trash-bag with sandwich wrappers. "I think Lorina and I can prepare some of the food Mr. Osaka gave us for dinner tonight. She says she has a good vegetable soup recipe."

Danae couldn't seem to focus on what Shima was saying. "The kids are getting dirty again."

"They enjoy playing outside. I do not think they played much on Mars Station because they were always searching for food."

"Do you think Blaze will be well enough to start on the engine repairs tomorrow?"

Shima smiled in her infinitely patient way. "I think so, Captain. He seems eager to get back to work."

Danae nodded distractedly. "I should probably advertise the jewelry in the local newspaper."

"I am sure it will bring a good price. Hopefully it will be enough to pay for new solar engines." If the housekeeper was puzzled by the Captain's scattered comments, she gave no indication.

"I'd like to start cleaning up the house tomorrow; make it livable for guests. The O'Briens will be here in a few days."

Shima nodded. "Once the solar panels on the roof are clean, the house should have enough electricity to run the lights and the well."

Danae nodded and brought out her datapad with a to-do list. She bit her lip as she read the first item: *Send bodies into town to be shipped home*. This was checked off. Second on the list was even more painful to read: *Bury Alex*.

She looked towards the house where Vipul and Marco were digging the grave in a corner of the backyard, near a row of hibiscus bushes. Danae could see that Marco was only up to his waist in the black soil, so there was still a lot more work to be done. "I should be helping them."

Shima slipped an arm around Danae's shoulders. "They can do it, Captain."

Danae started to protest, but it was impossible to argue with Shima. The girl's serene demeanor was like a soothing tonic for her nerves. Danae leaned her head against Shima's slim shoulder. "Sorry I've been so focused on myself. I should be asking you, 'How are you feeling?'"

Shima sighed, very softly. "I will be fine. I have lost everyone I have ever loved, except you, Captain. You are my only family."

Danae found herself blinking back tears. "You should call me Danae. I miss hearing the sound of my own name."

"I will call you Danae when the others cannot hear us. Otherwise, I must call you Captain."

"Captain seems so formal, so . . . unapproachable."

"It is a title of respect." Shima glanced towards the road. "Someone is coming."

Danae straightened up and followed her gaze. Two women in bright African-print dresses and matching head-ties were approaching them. Shima waved them over.

"Are you Captain Shepherd?" asked the first one, breathless with excitement, as soon as they drew close. She was a slim, middle-aged black woman with silver-framed glasses and a quick smile.

"Yes," Danae began, offering her hand.

The woman seized it in both of her bony hands and pressed it reverently to her cheek. "We're so happy you've come! You're an answer to our prayers!"

Danae was too startled to think of a response.

"Don't scare her, Zina," said the second woman, stepping forward. She pried Danae's hand out of the first woman's grip and shook it firmly. "I'm Yvette Lindsey and this is my younger sister, Zina Stedman."

Danae nodded, glancing back and forth between them. They did appear to be related. "How do you know my name?"

"Our neighbors told us you were here," Zina's eyes danced with excitement, "that you brought orphan children from Mars Station."

Both women turned to look at the children, their eyes darting everywhere as they tried to get a glimpse of each one.

"They're so beautiful!" Yvette was unable to disguise her own longing. "I've never seen so many."

"All my life I've wanted to be a mother." Zina's voice was quavering. She turned to give Danae a pleading look. "My husband fought in the war. He was right there in New York City after it was destroyed. There are so many toxins in his body that we were unable to have any children of our own. You understand, Captain?"

Danae nodded slowly as she took out her datapad again. She had heard many tales like Zina's since yesterday. "Let me take down your names and com numbers."

There were 17 other names on the datapad; *Ishmael*'s popularity was rapidly expanding. Danae worried that word would reach the CIPs in Lahaina, and that she'd be in prison before any of the kids found a home.

"Please, ma'am," Zina grasped Danae's sleeve. "Could I take a closer look," she pointed, excitedly, "at that darling little boy right over there?"

"I'm sorry, but I don't know anything about you." Danae gently removed Zina's hand.

Zina and Yvette's mouths dropped open simultaneously as they turned to give Danae a searching look. Zina's eyes filled with tears. "Are you saying we can't adopt any of the children?"

"I'm saying that I need to see your homes and get more information about you before I let you adopt one, or however many you want," Danae added, trying to get them to lighten up.

"Well, come on, we can show you right now!" Yvette grabbed Shima's arm. "My house is just down the road."

Danae quickly took charge of the situation. She gently extricated Shima's arm from Yvette's clutches. "Ladies, I understand your impatience, but it will take time to sort this out. Right now I don't have a social worker to coordinate adoptions. I need to be sure these children go to safe and loving homes, you understand?"

"A social worker? That's a good idea," Yvette said.

Danae nodded, relieved to see they were calming down. "You'll just have to wait until I hire someone."

"In the meantime, the Captain is accepting donations of food and clothing for the children," Shima said.

The two sisters exchanged a nod of agreement. "We'll do anything we can to help," Zina said. "I'll go to the thrift store and clean the place out of children's clothes."

"I think my friend Lucia knows a social worker in Kaanapali," Yvette said. "I'll have her give him a call."

"Thank you for understanding." Danae shook both of their hands and gestured for them to go. "We'll be in touch."

"Thank you, Captain Shepherd." Yvette wiped her eyes, tugged firmly on Zina's arm.

"God bless you!" Zina was wiping her eyes, too, as she reluctantly turned to leave.

Danae watched them walk to the road before releasing a big sigh. "I can't keep this up. Shima, can I put you in charge of public relations for now?"

Shima smiled. "If you wish, Danae, but I am also uncomfortable with all the attention. Perhaps Lorina?"

Danae nodded thoughtfully. "I'll talk to her."

"Captain!" Jake's shout came from the airlock.

Danae and Shima turned around to see the medic waving frantically.

"Keep an eye on the children, Shima. I'll send Lorina out to help." With that parting advice, Danae sprinted the 50 meters to the *Ishmael*. "What is it?" she shouted.

"Transmission!" As soon as Danae was ascending the stairs, Jake called down to her: "It's from Erik."

Danae felt a pang of fear, followed by a crushing wave of guilt. *How did he find us? But he's probably in jail!*

"Come with me," she told Jake as soon as she was standing beside him in the round doorway. "I have a feeling you should view it too."

Jake nodded, looking worried. He followed her up the ladder.

Danae thought of a new concern as she climbed. "Blaze?"

"Yes, ma'am."

"I'm sorry to disturb your rest, but we've received a transmission from Mars Station. Do you think it's safe to view?"

Blaze hesitated only a moment. "Are you wonderin' if it's rigged to send our location back to the sender?"

"Yes, exactly."

"Let me take a look at it first. I'll meet you on the bridge."

"Cancel that!" Jake said. "You stay off that leg!"

"Then bring me a wheelchair, cousin."

Danae stepped off at the top level and paused a moment to glance back at Jake. "You heard the man, doctor. Let's get him to the bridge."

Jake frowned at her but kept his mouth shut.

Danae marched into the post-op. "Lorina, Shima needs you outside."

"Okay, okay, I'm going." Lorina was on her feet and moving to the door. She blew a kiss in Blaze's direction and departed with Niyati in tow.

"Keep your weight off the leg." Jake brought the wheelchair to Blaze's bedside.

"I can do it." Blaze shifted his legs over the side of the bed and eased himself into the chair with minimal assistance from Jake.

Two minutes later, the engineer was studying the schematics of the mysterious transmission on the com control board. "This is a general broad-band transmission, Captain. Dr. Sorensen didn't know where to send it –, except Earth. There doesn't seem to be enough memory to suggest a boomerang rig."

"If you think it's safe, that's good enough for me." Danae spoke to the com: "Play Sorensen transmission." She held her breath and watched the screen over Blaze's shoulder, with Jake looking on over his other shoulder.

When Erik's holographic features came into view, Danae gasped.

The doctor had a dark bruise under his swollen right eye and a butterfly bandage near his left temple. There were several bruises along his jaw, which couldn't be disguised beneath his week-old growth of white-blond beard.

"Acheron!" Jake hissed under his breath.

Danae gestured for him to be quiet as Erik began to speak.

"This transmission is intended for Captain Danae Shepherd of the passenger ship *Ishmael,* bound for Earth, October 23rd." Erik's tone was strangely formal, his face impassive. "Captain Shepherd, I hope you arrived safely. I was informed that you had been shot trying to leave the station. Please let me know of your condition, and advise me on your present location. I was questioned by the CIPs – as you can see -- but they released me without further incident."

Jake swore and then hastily apologized for his language.

This time Blaze gestured for him to be quiet.

Erik continued: "I'm sending you this message to ask for your assistance. Kirsten and I have been ordered to suspend our work here. The CIPs have already shut down the Outreach Clinic." Erik looked off-camera for a split second. "The shelter is scheduled to be closed next month. Kirsten and I are prepared to leave the station with you, along with approximately 85 more children."

Erik hesitated. Again Danae noted his split-second glance off-camera, but he continued in the same matter-of-fact tone: "Please send a reply as soon as you receive this transmission, Captain Shepherd. Thank you. Sorensen out."

"It's a trap." The words were out of Jake's mouth before the screen blanked.

"I know." Danae gripped the back of Blaze's wheelchair to steady herself.

"Are you sure?" Blaze glanced over his shoulder at Danae.

"Positive. He wouldn't have addressed me as Captain Shepherd."

"He looked off-camera twice," Jake added. "He was forced to record this message. I know Erik; I worked with him for months. He wouldn't let anyone shut down his clinic; not while he's still breathing."

Danae nodded. She hid her shaking hands in her pockets. "He told me he would never leave the station while there were still homeless children who needed him."

"What can we do?" Blaze turned his wheelchair to face Jake and Danae. "We can't send a response, obviously. But we can't just leave him in Acheron's clutches."

Danae bit her thumbnail, trying to think. "We're stuck here for at least a month, unless we can hire a work crew. And we still have to organize this orphanage. I can't bear the thought of ignoring this message, but I don't see another option." She looked away from their concerned expressions. "I'm sure Erik would understand our dilemma."

"What if we sent him a message from another location?" Blaze asked.

Danae leaned closer. "What do you mean? What location?"

"We record a transmission, but have someone else send it to Mars."

"Who did you have in mind?" Danae asked. "Who would be crazy enough to risk bringing a garrison of CIPs down on them?"

Jake spoke up. "My family."

Blaze frowned and shook his head. "I thought your family preferred to keep outsiders away from their farm. You can't jeopardize their security."

Jake shrugged. "Dad could always send the transmission from Wilmington."

Now Danae began to have her doubts. "Acheron knows you're from Delaware. The manhunt would begin in earnest once he has a location."

"What choice do we have? We've got to get some kind of message to Erik." Jake set his jaw in an expression that was becoming familiar to Danae. "We owe him that, Captain."

"I'm not arguing with you, Jake. I like the idea of sending it from a different location, but let's consider all the angles."

Jake opened his mouth to argue, but Shima's voice over the com distracted them:

"Captain, the grave is finished. I do not wish to rush you, but the sky is growing dark and it looks like a thunderstorm is headed our way."

Danae felt a chill as she realized the time had finally come to say goodbye. She couldn't put it off any longer. She found it ironic that she was with Jake and Blaze, the only two crewmembers who knew she was struggling to contain her grief. It was tempting to let down her guard, as Jake suggested earlier.

Danae didn't look at either of them as she took a deep breath and made a decision. "Bring the children aboard and we'll leave the new crew to supervise them while we bury Alex."

"Yes, Captain," Shima replied, softly.

Danae turned on her heel to leave, but was startled to find Jake in lockstep with her. "You'll need a fourth pallbearer, Captain."

Danae didn't argue, for once. She was already waging a losing battle with her emotions.

TWENTY THREE
THE LOST SHEEP

The distant rumble of thunder was the background music for the first funeral Jake had ever attended. He thought it ironic, considering how many corpses he'd examined during his brief medical education. He helped Marco secure the extra-long unfinished wood coffin to the anti-grav unit. Jake let Marco take the unfamiliar remote control. The helmsman put the anti-grav into motion; it moved slowly across the uneven ground towards the house. The unit was so tiny that the casket appeared to be floating in midair.

Shima and Captain Shepherd walked quietly behind the men. Jake stole a glance back once and saw the Captain crying. Shima kept a supportive arm around Shepherd's shoulders. Jake noticed there were tears streaming down the housekeeper's face, too. He faced forward again and made it a point not to glance at Marco. He was grateful the helmsman had enough courtesy to keep his mouth shut.

"Do you want to say a few words, Captain?" Jake asked when they arrived at the grave.

Shepherd didn't reply. They watched as Marco worked the controls, and the anti-grav lowered the coffin into the dark hole. As soon as the casket touched bottom, the anti-grav wriggled out from beneath the casket and climbed the side of the grave up to Marco's outstretched hand. The helmsman placed both the unit and its remote into the cargo pocket of his uniform.

Jake grabbed a shovel and began filling in the grave. Shima and Marco joined in. Jake kept an eye on Shepherd as he worked, but she seemed to be lost in a world of her own as she wept, rocking back and forth on her heels, her arms crossed tightly over her chest. Her eulogy – or whatever she was speaking through her tears -- was drowned out by the breaking storm. Jake wished he knew a scripture or hymn appropriate for the occasion, but, since he didn't, he just kept shoveling.

The rain began before the burial was finished, but Jake kept at it. In five minutes, they were soaked to the skin, and Shepherd began gesturing for them to quit. Marco and Shima set their shovels aside, but Jake continued to pitch dirt for a few more minutes, even though it was almost too dark to see. When a bolt of lightning lit up the sky, he threw down his shovel and they ran to the *Ishmael* in the driving rain.

Jake was the last to ascend to the airlock. He stood dripping in the entryway with Captain Shepherd and Shima for a few moments; Ting had already gone up to his cabin. Jake was relieved to see his new employer finally grieving in earnest. She sobbed in Shima's arms, her face buried in the housekeeper's shoulder.

Jake caught Shima's eye and mouthed, 'Are you okay? Can you manage?'

Shima gave a barely perceptible nod and continued to pat Shepherd on the back. Jake moved quietly to the ladder.

* * *

The next day, the work began in earnest. Blaze was out of bed on anti-grav crutches and tearing out the charred solar engines with Vipul's assistance. Shima and Lorina took care of the meals and the children. Marco, Jake, and Captain Shepherd tackled the house.

Jake, who would grade himself an 'F' in domestic skills, was assigned to clean the five bathrooms. He had plenty of time to think as he scrubbed two years' worth of grime off the marble tiled showers and floors, and stainless steel toilets and sinks. He took down the light fixtures and cleaned out the dead insects.

While he worked, he went over the past week in his mind. *How did I get here? How did I go from a promising medical career to this volunteer-fugitive lifestyle?*

Erik, of course, Jake realized with a guilty flinch. *I should be thanking him for taking a chance on me. I learned so much under his tutelage,-- and I won't let him rot in Acheron's jail.*

As he wiped dead insects off the window ledge, Jake glimpsed a sweaty Marco hacking at the vines in the backyard with a machete. Ting looked irritated at the task he'd been given, but he kept at it. Jake wasn't happy with the prospect of working long-term with the helmsman, but he assumed they wouldn't see each other much on the ship since their jobs were so different. He felt sorry for the crewmembers who would have to work closely with Ting. *But Vipul and Blaze have a lot more patience than I do. They'll manage.*

Captain Shepherd stuck her head in the doorway, startling Jake out of his reverie. "The solar panels are clean. Are you getting any water?"

Jake turned a tap, and a brown trickle sputtered into the sink.

"It should clear up; just let it run for a few minutes. I'd help, but I have to interview a social worker named Gordon Grey."

"I hope he doesn't mind working for free." Jake grinned.

"That's probably more than a social worker normally earns." Shepherd returned the grin. Her large blue eyes were clear, with no sign of redness from last night's funeral. She swept a bandana off her dark curls and wiped her hands on the legs of her dirty jeans. "Do I look okay to do an interview?"

Jake realized for the first time that Danae Shepherd's cheerful personality must have been buried underneath all the pain, stress, and grief of the past week. *Not to mention all the confrontations with me,* he thought, feeling a twinge of guilt for adding to her burdens. "I think you look beautiful."

Jake froze; horrified he'd spoken the thought aloud.

Shepherd raised her eyebrows. She looked more amused than shocked.

"I meant to say you look well, Captain! You seem strong enough to handle any new challenges. From a medical point of view, you look healthy and well-rested, and one could interpret that as beauty, but I meant it in a non-flirtatious, respectful kind of way --"

The Captain burst out laughing. "Okay, calm down, Jake. You always say exactly what's on your mind, -- no matter how embarrassing it is!"

Jake could feel his face flaming scarlet. "I'm sorry, Captain."

"Well, I'm not."

He blinked at her, confused.

"A woman always likes to hear she's attractive, but we'll keep this little *faux pas* a secret, along with our shouting matches." She winked at him as she turned to leave. "You're not such a bad-looking guy yourself – and I mean that in a non-flirtatious, respectful kind of way."

Captain Shepherd vanished down the hall before Jake could think of a response. He sprayed cleaner onto the sink counter and went back to work, his mind in a whirl.

* * *

"I have a new assignment for you."

Jake set aside the datapad with the list of supplies needed to restock the infirmary. "Yes, ma'am." He felt some trepidation as he turned to face Shepherd, but she was casually leaning against the doorway of the lab, her mind clearly a million kilometers away from his earlier foot-in-mouth blunder.

"I need you and Blaze to go into town and meet the buyer for the black pearls. Then I want you to use that money to buy a solar van –"

"A van, Captain?"

"Yes, a 15 passenger van. If we're going to run an orphanage, we'll need some ground transportation. Ruth Nguyen told me there's a used solar car lot on Front Street." She went on without missing a beat, "After you have the solar van, you can purchase the solar engines."

"We'll have enough money for everything?" Jake was dumbfounded. "How much are black pearls worth?"

The Captain smiled. "The Tahitian black-lipped oysters have been extinct for a decade. Black pearls are priceless. You'd better take my gun because you're going to be carrying a lot of cash."

Jake shuddered at the thought of carrying a weapon. "Couldn't we put the cash on a credit flash?"

Shepherd shook her head. "Sorry, but you and I can't use our flashes anymore, not unless we want Acheron to find us."

"What about Blaze's flash?" Jake persisted.

"Maybe," she replied, thoughtful. "I guess he and Shima would be the only untraceable crewmembers. No, scratch that -- Shima's name is known to Acheron, as well. If Idalis were here, we could use her flash without any worries, but she's probably in Phoenix by now."

Jake couldn't tell by the Captain's matter-of-fact tone if she was upset by Idalis' departure. "I guess we'll use Blaze's flash. You should change into something less conspicuous. Blaze is waiting for you at the airlock."

"Scrubs are all I have, Captain. I wore these into town to buy the coffins."

"And that worked fine because you looked like a coroner. But you need to look sharp to haggle with the solar car salesmen, and purple's definitely not your color."

Jake flushed self-consciously. "What do you suggest?"

"Visit a men's clothing store first. Use Blaze's flash, but don't go crazy; you don't need much for off-duty wear. Oh, and you should get a haircut."

Jake squirmed like a chastened child. "Yes, ma'am."

The short ride into town in Mr. George Osaka's rattletrap solar truck was uneventful. Jake watched with amusement as Blaze gawked at the scenery; it was the engineer's first glimpse of Lahaina. The historic whaling village was comprised mostly of a few quiet streets filled with stores, restaurants, and weather-beaten houses. Since the village was on the ocean, there were lots of piers, but not many boats.

Mr. Osaka let them out on Front Street, at a used book store called Island Secrets, where they were scheduled to meet the owner.

Blaze was wearing jeans, a T-shirt, and tennis shoes. He walked with only a slight limp. Jake felt like an idiot in his scrubs; he eyed the clothing store across the street as they stepped through the screen door of the shop. Blaze nudged him, bringing his attention back to the bookstore and the attractive Polynesian woman who was coming towards them with a large duffel bag tucked under one arm.

"Do you have it?" Her smile was disarmingly beautiful.

Jake fumbled with the cloth-wrapped bundle which held the valuable necklace, and hesitantly handed it over to her. She, in turn, pressed the duffel bag into Blaze's hands. Both parties examined the contents of the exchanged bundles and were satisfied.

"Thank you." She dazzled Jake with the smile again and walked away, disappearing into the back room of the store.

Jake found himself back out on the sidewalk as Blaze escorted him quickly to the nearest bank, across the street.

"Let's hope Maui is up-to-date on interstellar currency," the engineer muttered as they waited in a short line for a teller.

"How can a bookstore owner make this kind of money?" Jake asked.

Blaze cautioned him to keep his voice down. "Books are extremely valuable. Captain Shepherd was able to raise enough cash to leave Mars Station just by selling some of the books she had on the ship."

Jake thought of his room back in Delaware, which was packed floor-to-ceiling with textbooks. *I'm rich, and I didn't even know it.*

When it was their turn to approach a teller, Blaze set the duffel bag on the counter and held out his left thumb. "Can I make a deposit to this?"

The gray-haired teller blinked at him behind her thick glasses. "That's one of those new debit cards, right?"

Jake tried not to grimace.

"Can I make a deposit?" Blaze repeated patiently.

"I'll have to check with the manager." She stood up. "Wait here."

Jake felt himself beginning to perspire. *If we can't use the credit flash, what are we going to do with all this money?*

The teller returned from a back office carrying a datapad with a credit flash slot.

Jake started to breathe a sigh of relief, but a sharp nudge in the ribs from Blaze's elbow cautioned him to stifle it.

The teller waited for Blaze to slide his thumbnail through the slot. "Now, how much do you want to deposit, dear?" Her eyes bulged as Blaze started piling stacks of cash in front of her. She bit her lip and went to work counting it. Jake tried not to fidget as she tapped numbers into the oldest calculator he'd ever seen.

"$2,750,000." The teller's hands were shaking as she finally looked up from the mountain of bills. "Where did you get so much money?" She glanced suspiciously at Blaze.

"We're starting a business," Jake tried to explain.

Now the teller's eyes focused on Jake. He could feel his face beginning to turn red as she scrutinized his wrinkled scrubs. "Really?"

Great, we're going to jail! She probably thinks we stole this cash!

"It's for an orphanage," Blaze was beginning to sound flustered himself, "just outside of town."

"An orphanage?"

Jake saw her reach beneath the counter; he assumed she was activating the silent alarm. He knew they would never be able to gather up all the money and get out of the bank before the police came. *I hope Blaze can run with that leg,* he thought, preparing to abandon the cash and flee.

The teller's hand emerged, clutching an old datapad which was probably her personal property. "Is this the orphanage you're referring to?" She showed them the front page of the *Lahaina Times* on the screen.

Jake felt his heart start beating again. Beside him, Blaze visibly relaxed. The teller gave them a puzzled look as they leaned forward to study the article.

Ship Is a Dream Come True for Maui's Childless Families

Beneath the caption was a hologram of the *Ishmael* with a group of children playing in the foreground. Jake read the article:

> The passenger ship Ishmael landed at the abandoned Luna sugar cane plantation, near the end of Lahainaluna Road, on the evening of October 28th. There were 148 homeless children from Mars Station aboard. Ship's captain Danae Thompson Shepherd is reported to be the heir to the Luna property. According to local sources, Shepherd plans to turn the place into an orphanage, and is eager to place the children into adoptive homes just as soon as she can hire a social worker.

> Most of the children are Mars-born, and all are between the ages of 14 months and 13 years. They are reported to be in good health. When asked if he came willingly

with Captain Shepherd, one Vladimir (no last name given), age 12, said, "Absolutely! On Mars I lived on the streets and people, especially the CIPs, treated me like a dog! I was always hungry. Captain Shepherd brought us to this beautiful place called Maui. I hope she can find a family for me."

Shepherd refused to answer questions for reporters, but did promise to advertise in the Lahaina Times when the orphanage was up and running. Crewmember Heshima Oryang stated that no fees would be required for the adoptions, but that Shepherd would gladly accept donations of food and clothing for the children.

"Yeah, that's us." Jake gave the teller a cautious smile.

A smile lit up her wrinkled face. "That's wonderful! My daughter in Wailea has been desperate to adopt a child."

"Well, send her to Captain Shepherd in a week or two," Blaze said.

The teller beamed at them both and turned back to the datapad. "This should do it." She held it out to Blaze so he could swipe his thumbnail flash again. "Be sure to let me know if you have any trouble using it around town, dear."

"Thank you."

Back out on the sidewalk, Blaze whispered to Jake: "If Acheron put out a warrant for Captain Shepherd, it's only a matter of time before the local CIPs show up to arrest her. I wish we could have kept her name out of the paper."

Jake nodded, sobered by the thought. "Let's get moving. Clothes first, then a solar van, then two solar engines."

"Then I'm hiring a team of subcontractors to help install the engines."

"Can we afford that?"

"We can't afford not to, Jake." Blaze looked determined. "The Captain's not safe here, and we've got to help Dr. Sorensen."

"I won't argue with that."

* * *

"Everyone, this is Gordon Grey, our new social worker."

Jake looked up from his cutting board and found a dishtowel for his pineapple-juice-dripping hands. Shima set aside the rice she was measuring into the cauldron-size steamer and scooted around the counter ahead of him, joining the Captain, Vipul, Lorina, and Niyati in the galley.

"Call me Grey." The portly, bald Aussie shook Jake's sticky hand. He had a firm grip and a genuine smile that never left his tanned, weather-beaten face. Even when the man was speaking, the smile lines remained etched around his twinkling blue eyes.

Jake had never met such a cheerful person. He found himself returning the smile; Grey's sunny disposition was contagious. When he stooped down to give Niyati a handshake and a smile, Jake could tell he genuinely liked children.

"Grey understands our time constraints," Captain Shepherd caught Jake's eye and nodded, her expression grave, "and is going to start placing the children immediately."

"Is there a lot of paperwork involved in an adoption?" Lorina asked, her hands on Niyati's bony shoulders.

"Nah." Grey grinned. "There's no standard format anymore. I can file a single report for each child at city hall. I'll do one pre-placement and one post-placement home visit for each applicant and that'll do it."

Lorina looked relieved. "Then this will be your first pre-placement visit. You're standing in Niyati's home."

Grey laughed and drew a datapad out of the cargo pocket of his shorts. "Spell her name for me."

Jake thought of a concern. "Captain, what'll you do with the children who don't get placed right away?"

"They'll live in the house, of course. Grey will be part of the live-in staff, and his wife Olivia signed on as the childcare supervisor." Shepherd grinned. "I was serious about starting an orphanage, Jake. If I can come up with the cash or find a sponsor, I'll convert the processing plant into a school."

"If we're returning to Mars as soon as the ship's repaired, who's going to run the orphanage?" Lorina glanced expectantly at Grey, but Shepherd's answer surprised them all.

"Shima will be the orphanage director."

Shima's mouth fell open and she sank slowly into the nearest chair. "But . . . but I have no experience, Captain. I want to stay with you," she added fervently.

"I trust you, Shima," Shepherd explained. "I'm sorry to spring this on you, but I need to place this enormous responsibility on the right shoulders. No one here has experience running an orphanage, but you are the most capable person I've ever known. I have no doubt you can do this." Her voice dropped to a whisper. "I need you to do this."

Shima looked like she was going to burst into tears. "Yes, Captain, I will do it, --for you."

Jake cleared his throat and hastened to change the subject. "What else needs to be done, Captain?"

"Plenty." Shepherd showed him a datapad. "I've tried to break down the work into manageable tasks. Do you think your family would be willing to help us?"

Lorina nodded. "My mother doesn't know how to take a vacation."

"My dad's good with machinery," Jake said. "I'm sure he'd be able to help Blaze install the solar engines."

"I'm hoping they'll be installed before they get here," Shepherd admitted. "For what I'm paying the mechanical subcontractors, it should have been done yesterday." She began reading off her list of assignments to the crew:

"Shima, plan menus for the next two weeks and organize the kitchens in both the ship and the house. You'll be responsible for preparing the lunches, and Lorina will cook the dinners."

"Lorina, organize the donations and make sure each child has at least two changes of clothing and one pair of shoes. We've received quite a few toys, so those will need to be distributed as fairly as possible. Purchase anything else they need. Olivia is prepared to help you."

"Vipul, I want you to find bunk beds, as many as you can get your hands on. See if you can exchange some of the king-size beds in the house with the locals. I want the house ready to accommodate 48 children; eight in each of the upstairs rooms.

We've got to move the kids off the ship if we want to lift in a week."

A week? Jake was stunned by how quickly things were progressing. *A few days ago, Vipul was predicting a month.* "What's my assignment, Captain?"

"I want you and Marco to sell everything on this list." Shepherd handed the datapad to him. "After that, I want you to landscape the backyard so it looks good enough for a wedding reception."

Jake groaned. "I have to do all this with Ting? Why don't you just ask for a miracle?"

The Captain raised her eyebrows as she turned to leave the galley. "I just did."

* * *

Jake heard a car door slam and threw down the hedge clippers. He raced around to the front of the house, nearly colliding with Lorina as she leaped down from the front porch. Blaze and Niyati followed her from the house at a more sedate pace. Jake caught a glimpse of Vipul's sheepish grin from the driver's seat just before the doors to the mint-green solar van were flung open.

"Jake!" Marilyn O'Brien reached him first, enfolding him in a spine-crushing hug. She was laughing and crying at the same time. "I didn't think I'd ever see you again!"

Jake finally had to extricate himself from her smothering embrace. "I can't breathe, Mom."

Marilyn relinquished him to his father's enthusiastic hug, but continued with the commentary: "You're so thin! What have they been feeding you? And you look so much older now with that crew cut. Doesn't he look older, Jacob?"

"He's a man now." Jacob soberly passed his son to his sister, who was finally releasing Lorina from a smothering embrace of her own.

"Jake!"

"Hi, Aunt Beth!"

She whispered into his ear as she hugged him: "I'm so proud of you. What a wonderful thing you've done for these children."

"Thanks." Jake didn't have time to respond before Catherine was squeezing herself between his legs and Beth's.

"Jake!"

Jake took a step back and picked up his niece. He hugged her for a long time, content to listen to her excited chatter about plane rides and starships and "the really tall man Lorina's gonna marry!"

Jake glanced over at his cousin-to-be, who was weathering the O'Brien storm of attention with an uncertain smile on his face.

"Look how tall he is," said Marilyn, as if Blaze was deaf. "Lorina, you didn't tell us he was a skyscraper!"

"Mother!" Deborah plucked Catherine out of Jake's arms and gave him a hug. "Don't embarrass him." To Jake she said, "Good to see you! Which one? Which one?" She turned her face eagerly towards the field of children.

"In a minute." Jake greeted Sean with a handshake. "There's one more introduction to make before I take you to meet Catherine's new siblings."

"Siblings? There's more than one?" Deborah was like a kid on Christmas morning, her eyes shining with excitement.

"We've already met Blaze," said Sean, looking uncharacteristically impatient as he scanned the crowd himself.

"I wanna meet my brother!" Catherine pouted.

"You will," Jake said, "just as soon as you meet Niyati."

"Who's Niyati?" Catherine asked.

Jake spotted the child hanging back from the cluster of strange adults with a nervous thumb in her mouth and tears welling in her eyes. Fortunately, Lorina noticed her at the same time and rushed to pick her up.

"I'm so sorry, sweetheart. I almost forgot you in all the excitement." She turned to face the O'Briens. "I want everyone to meet my daughter, Niyati."

Blaze cleared his throat. "Our daughter."

There was slack-jawed silence for about 15 seconds, then Beth threw her arms around Lorina and Niyati. "I'm a grandmother!" She started to wipe her eyes on her sleeve. "Why didn't you tell us? I've barely had time to get used to the idea of having a son-in-law!"

"I didn't want to overwhelm you with too many surprises." Lorina was blinking back tears herself. She went on to explain how she found Niyati in the alley, gained her trust, took her to Mother Teresa's, looked after her for months, and then risked being left behind to find her before the ship left Mars Station.

"She's being modest," Blaze spoke up, "she faced down Acheron with a gun to get Niyati away from him. Lorina has nerves of steel."

"And a heart of gold." Beth took Niyati from Lorina and gave her a gentle squeeze. "Welcome to the family, Niyati. You can call me Grandma."

"Granma," Niyati agreed, giving her a big hug.

Jake was beginning to feel a bit queasy from all the family togetherness. He drew Deborah, Sean, and Catherine aside as his parents and Beth fawned over Niyati and Blaze.

"Tirza and Adi are right over here." He led them across the field towards the ship, where a group of younger children was playing tag in the shade of three large coconut trees.

"Tirza and Adi? Unusual names," said Sean.

"They're Hebrew names, I think," Jake explained.

"Hebrew!" Deborah laughed, but it was a good-natured laugh. "The perfect additions to an Irish Catholic family."

"Tirza is seven and Adi is three." Jake pointed them out as they drew near and gave his sister and brother-in-law a minute to observe the dark-haired children. "Tirza is very protective of Adi, and she's more stubborn than I am, so it will take her some time to get used to not being the boss anymore."

"I didn't think it was possible for someone to be more stubborn than you, little brother."

Jake was relieved to see a teasing smile on Deb's face. "I hope you like them as much as I do."

"I know we will." Sean got down on one knee as Adi spotted them and shyly came over. Tirza, ever vigilant, was right on Adi's heels.

"You must be our new mom and dad." Tirza walked up to Deborah and inspected her.

Deborah squatted down so she was eye to eye with the girl. She shook hands solemnly with her. "It's nice to meet you, Tirza."

Jake glanced over at Adi and saw that he had already climbed up onto Sean's knee and was allowing Catherine to trace his face with her fingertips.

"That tickles," Adi laughed.

"Do me next," said Tirza, seizing Deborah's hand and leading her over to Catherine. "Are you my sister?"

Jake held his breath, expecting to hear a complaint from Tirza about Catherine's blindness or missing forearm, but he was pleasantly surprised to hear, "Hey, you're pretty! You've got curly hair like me!"

Catherine beamed. Deborah glanced over at Jake to give him an approving smile, and he quietly slipped away to give the new family time to get acquainted.

* * *

Jake fidgeted with the kelly-green necktie. It had been a long time since he'd worn a suit, and he wasn't used to having his neck confined. He stopped squirming when he noticed his mother's stern look.

Marilyn O'Brien was standing near him. She was officially in the front row of the 'chapel,' which was actually an open space in the sugar cane field. She was standing because there were no chairs, but this promised to be a short ceremony. Beth stood next to her, already dabbing her eyes with a tissue. Deborah, Sean, and their kids were standing on the other side of the front row. They'd left an aisle for the bride.

Jake was standing beneath the latticework archway he'd discovered in the potting shed a few days ago. His mother had decorated it with palm fronds and fresh flowers. It was attractive, but it looked like it would blow over at the first sign of a breeze. Jake nonchalantly reached behind his back with one hand and gripped one edge of the archway to give it some stability.

Standing to his right was Blaze, who was also sweating in a suit, this one borrowed from Alex Shepherd's wardrobe. The groom looked very happy. Jake had a difficult time imaging what was going through Blaze's mind.

He's marrying a girl he met two weeks ago. How can he be absolutely sure Lorina's the right one for him? How can she be sure? Blaze went from 'hello' to 'I want to spend the rest of my life with you' in three days! Is there really such a thing as love at first sight?

"Jake?" Blaze whispered out of the corner of his mouth.

Jake glanced at his friend's nervous expression and wondered if he was having an attack of cold feet. "Yeah?"

Blaze's request was so quiet, Jake barely heard him. "Do you think I could get a shot of Sterilite after the ceremony?"

Jake struggled to contain a laugh. "Relax," he whispered back, "Lorina beat you to it."

Blaze nodded, looking relieved.

Jake snickered quietly, ignoring his mother's scathing glance.

He glanced over at Shima, who was standing on the other side of Blaze in the maid of honor's position. She looked gorgeous in a form-fitting blue and yellow muumuu, her black hair unbraided and reaching halfway down her back in shiny ringlets. Shima caught him staring and flashed a dimpled smile.

Jake glanced down at Niyati, who was standing in front of Shima. The little girl was wearing a pretty purple muumuu and holding a basket of hibiscus blossoms. She looked nervous and close to tears. As Jake watched, she edged over to Blaze until she was close enough to touch his leg.

Blaze reached down and gripped her tiny hand. Niyati visibly relaxed.

Jake was astonished at how quickly the engineer had settled into the role of Niyati's father. *If I ever become a dad,* he shuddered at the thought, *I hope I can handle it as calmly as Blaze.*

Gordon Grey was standing behind Blaze in the minister's spot. The cheerful social worker looked official in his black suit and tie, although he had confessed to Jake earlier that he hadn't attended a wedding ceremony in over 15 years, and had never performed one. As a notary, Grey was the only one in the entourage who could legally endorse the marriage license, so Lorina convinced him to do the honor of officiating. Jake thought the Aussie seemed to be taking it all in stride. He'd even found an old Bible somewhere.

To complete the small gathering was the rest of *Ishmael*'s crew -- including a scowling Marco -- in the second row, and a number of new local friends and orphanage supporters in the third and fourth rows. A group of eight volunteers, supervised by enthusiastic adoptive mothers Yvette Lindsey and Zina Stedman, had offered to keep an eye on the children during the ceremony and reception by keeping them entertained aboard the *Ishmael.*

Jake smiled to himself as he thought about how quickly the homeless kids were being placed into good homes -- 31 in the past four days, including Tirza, Adi, and Niyati. The toddlers were claimed quickly, along with several sets of siblings. Marilyn and Beth had worked feverishly alongside Grey, helping him process applications and make home visits all over the island. They informed Jake that at least 30 more children would be placed in Maui homes before the *Ishmael* headed back to Mars Station.

Beth was seriously thinking of signing on as a live-in childcare worker. Jake suspected she was using the job as an excuse to stay close to Lorina and her new family. *She's really taking this 'Grandma' role seriously.*

Jake was awakened from his reverie by Shima's lovely alto voice. She began to sing "Here Comes the Bride," *a cappella*, in Swahili. He didn't understand the words, but the melody was unmistakable. It gave him goose bumps to listen.

Lorina walked down the short aisle on her uncle's arm. She was dressed in a long Irish lace wedding gown which had been in the O'Brien family for generations. The once snowy white lace had faded to a creamy yellow over time, but it was still beautiful. Jake's mother, aunt, and sister had each been married in the antique frock. Lorina wore her hair up in a braided bun and held a bouquet of purple hibiscus blossoms in her left hand. She looked radiant, and Jake felt a sudden pang of sadness as he realized he was losing his best friend.

Lorina's smile was focused on Blaze, but she glanced at Jake for a split second and winked at him. Jake winked back. *I'm happy for her.* He was comforted by the thought of working with Lorina and Blaze aboard the *Ishmael.*

Jake's father kissed Lorina on the cheek and placed her hand in Blaze's. Niyati reluctantly let go of Blaze and allowed 'Granma' Beth to hold her. The bride and groom turned to face Grey.

"We are gathered here today to witness the union of these two wonderful young people," Grey began. He'd found a traditional wedding service somewhere, and was performing it enthusiastically.

Jake barely heard a word as he sweated in his suit and watched his cousin and cousin-to-be exchange vows. In five minutes, they were slipping on the rings; the same troublesome rings that brought Jake and Lorina to Mars in the first place. Two minutes after that, they were kissing.

Then Grey said, "I would like to present Mr. and Mrs. Robert Jon Smith."

Lorina and Blaze were all smiles as they turned to face the applauding group. However, instead of walking down the aisle together, Lorina held up her hand to request quiet.

"Today, we also want to publicly introduce our daughter." She and Blaze each took one of Niyati's hands. "Please welcome Niyati Elizabeth Smith."

Jake joined in the applause as the wedding party and guests retired to the festively decorated house for a luau-style reception, catered by Hope Nguyen. There was a heaping platter of bangers and mash right next to the grilled mahi-mahi on the dining room table. An Irish-Polynesian band played an unusual assortment of songs on the deck, overlooking the freshly-mowed and landscaped backyard.

For an hour, Jake danced on the lawn with his mother, his aunt, his sister, Lorina, and Shima. He twirled Niyati, Catherine, and Tirza around for a few minutes before filling a plate from the buffet and retreating to a rocking chair on the front porch, where it was quiet.

He peeled shrimp and admired the freshly-painted sign hanging in front of the house: *The Lost Sheep.* It was Lorina's idea to give the orphanage this name, and he thought it was very appropriate. It reminded him of a scripture of a shepherd leaving the 99 and going in search of the one sheep that was lost.

"Isn't it customary for the best man to offer a toast?" Captain Shepherd sank into the rocker next to his.

"Blaze doesn't drink," Jake explained, "and he requested that we skip the toast. Which was fine with me; I hate giving speeches."

Shepherd nodded. "We lift in three days."

"That soon?" Jake dipped his shrimp in cocktail sauce and chewed appreciatively; he hadn't eaten shellfish in over a decade. He glanced over at his employer.

Shepherd looked out of character in a close-fitting pink and green muumuu that showed off her curves nicely. Her dark curls were tousled attractively, and Jake was surprised to note that she was wearing make-up; her lipstick left pink imprints on the rim of her glass. He really wanted to offer her a compliment, but decided it would be safer to keep his mouth shut. *Another 'you're beautiful' comment, and she'll definitely think I'm flirting.*

"We've managed to get a lot accomplished with five extra adults working full time on the ship and the orphanage. I'm grateful to your family for coming all this way to help us."

Jake nodded. "My folks have always been generous people."

"You know," the Captain set her glass on the floor next to her chair, "there's a good chance we'll all end up in prison on Mars Station. I could use a medic here at the orphanage. Are you sure you want to lift with the *Ishmael*?"

"Just try to keep me dirtside, Captain."

Shepherd laughed. "It's taken me awhile, but I think I finally understand your stubborn streak. It seems to run in the family."

"We're going to find Erik." Jake was serious. "He's going to be your orphanage medic."

Shepherd nodded slowly. "I hope you're right. And when he and Kirsten are safe, we're going to find Zuri."

"You don't believe in taking on small projects, do you, Captain?"

"Not anymore, Jake. It feels good to have purpose in my life. The children, the orphanage, my crew – these are the things that really matter."

And family, Jake thought, careful not to remind her of what she'd lost. He set his empty plate on the floor. "Would you care to dance, Captain?"

Shepherd grinned as they got to their feet. "I don't know. Shima told me you stepped all over her toes."

"Did she?" Jake laughed. "I didn't think I was that bad."

They walked around to the backyard just in time to see Lorina throw the bouquet. It flew over the heads of the single women and went right to Marco Ting. He caught it, scowled at the resulting laughter, and flung it hastily over his shoulder.

This time the bundle of hibiscus sailed straight into Danae Shepherd's hands.

Author's Note

This story takes place in the future, but the reality of homeless, exploited, and abandoned children exists today on a global scale. For every orphan like Niyati who finds an adoptive home, there are 1,000 children left behind, living on the streets, in crowded orphanages, and in filthy refugee camps all over the world. Child slavery is also a present-day reality; no country is exempt from this atrocity. I felt prompted to write *The Orphan Ship* to shed some light on the forgotten children of our world.

There are hundreds of worthwhile charities for children. Please consider opening your heart to help or adopt a homeless child.

SterlingRWalker.blogspot.com

Acknowledgements

The Orphan Ship was a long time in the making – many years, in fact. First, I need to thank my family for being so patient with me whenever I was absorbed in my writing. I owe a lot to the wonderful people who patiently endured my 'hobby' without complaint. Thanks, Walkers, I'm grateful for your love and support.

Second, I need to thank my writing groups who suffered through the early drafts, and gave me lots of good advice. Thank you, Sara Garland, Nick Olson, and Joe Kovacs, my Washington, D.C. writing group. Thanks to my friend David Bailey, who recommended some much-needed changes to Part I. Thank you, Mickela Sonola and Laura Bridgewater, my Holly Springs writing group, for giving me the confidence I needed to look for publisher. And double thanks goes to Laura for editing the final draft for publication. One more huge thank you to author Tamara Ward, who helped me format the manuscript for Amazon Kindle and Createspace.

Third, I need to thank my cover artists: my talented son Nathaniel Walker, who painted the background, and my friend Michelle Ishihara, who painted the Ishmael for the foreground. Thanks also to Tami Huntsman, who was kind enough to take my photo for publicity and helped me create my blog, and to Cindy Harrison for helping me format the cover art for the book. I appreciate everyone who helped spread the word and get my name out there as a new author. I owe much of my success to you, my friends.